THE MELANCHOLY OF WINTER

THE BRIEF LIFE OF EDMUND OF RUTLAND

By J.P. REEDMAN

Copyright December 2024, J.P. Reedman/Herne's cave
Cover by J.P. Reedman

TABLE OF CONTENTS:

CHAPTER ONE

CHAPTER TWO

CHAPTER THREE

CHAPTER FOUR

CHAPTER FIVE

CHAPTER SIX

CHAPTER SEVEN

CHAPTER EIGHT

CHAPTER NINE

CHAPTER TEN

CHAPTER ELEVEN

CHAPTER TWELVE

CHAPTER THIRTEEN

CHAPTER FOURTEEN

CHAPTER FIFTEEN

CHAPTER SIXTEEN

CHAPTER SEVENTEEN

CHAPTER EIGHTEEN

UK AMAZON LINK TO AUTHOR PAGE:

https://www.amazon.co.uk/J-P-Reedman/e/B009UTHBUE

USA AMAZON LINK TO AUTHOR PAGE:

https://www.amazon.com/stores/J.P.Reedman/author/B009UTHBUE

CHAPTER ONE

The wind was fair from the south and the gulls were crying. Blinking into the sunlight, I stared upwards, watching as the seabirds wheeled through the ship's riggings. Sails flapped and boomed as the breeze caught them, and in the distance, I could hear a strange, unsettling sound, a dull roar mingled with the thump of waves against the prow and the grind of shallower water over pebbles.

People, crying out—but I had no idea why they were shouting, and it made my heart grow troubled. Unknown territory lay ahead.

"Little Ned!" A familiar voice sounded next to my ear, blocking the wind's whine and that distant human cacophony.

Turning quickly, I almost collided with my older brother, Edward, who was running down the deck towards me. We bore similar names, Edward and Edmund, our parents calling us after the two of England's most famous saints. However, the nickname for both names was 'Ned,' which did not help to differentiate between us when one was to receive praise and the other got a lashing for some misdeed. So, as I was younger by a year, I was christened 'Little Ned' or 'Ned Parva' in Latin, while my brother was 'Big Ned', 'Ned Magna', amongst other sillier pairings like Mickle and Muckle or Great and Small.

Unfortunately, the little/big nicknames fit in other ways besides the difference in our ages. Although Big Ned was eight, and I, seven, he towered over me in height, his shoulders broad, his legs long and sturdy. On the other hand, I was short, perhaps even slightly shorter than the average lad my age, and much more delicate in appearance. Our height was not the only difference, either—I had dark blue eyes and hair that had darkened from yellow to brown as I grew out of nursery age, while Ned had twinkling hazel eyes and dark chestnut locks. I had the look of my sire printed all over my face while Edward was the reverse—he was tall, a true Plantagenet like our ancestor Lionel of Clarence, but with mother's graceful, curving nose and shapely mouth.

"Come on!" He pushed past me, waving frantically as I hesitated. "You'll miss our landing at Howth if you linger here on the far side of the ship!"

"But—but can't you hear that noise? A mob, yelling…What if they are angry and want to hurt us?"

We were crossing the perilous, rough seas to Ireland, where my father would govern as Lord Lieutenant on behalf of our sovereign Lord, Henry VI, King of England. The appointment was a great honour, I supposed, but I was not entirely convinced. Gossips back at our castle of Fotheringhay claimed the Irish were barbarians with outlandish clothes and an impossible language—and that assuredly would hate us dwelling in their country. I understood these claims were likely no more than idle talk by men who had never travelled beyond their own shire, but it was true that Father, at first, seemed in no haste to assume his position in Ireland, despite having ancestral claims from Elizabeth de Burgh, daughter of the earl of Ulster, wife of our princely ancestor, Lionel. Elizabeth and Lionel's Irish lands, and the Lordship of Trim and Leix, had passed to our family through our grandmother, Anne Mortimer, whom us children had never met, for she had died birthing our father.

Edward grasped my shoulder and shook it, rolling his eyes in frustration. "Don't be a goose, Edmund! The people aren't angry. We've done nought to warrant their anger. Come and see! Hurry, or you'll miss it."

He yanked me over to the ship's railing on the starboard side of the cog. The vessel was gliding serenely into a shallow harbour. I let out a shout of delight at the sight of seals cavorting in the water but quickly bit my tongue, embarrassed by my own excited display. I must behave like a dignified Duke's son, not a street urchin.

Looking toward the quayside, I saw houses and smelt smoke that bore a fresh, peaty fragrance quite different from the smoke of the fires that burnt in our family castles of Fotheringhay and Ludlow. Groups of people clustered on the waterfront, singing, dancing, and playing on instruments unfamiliar to me. And yes, they *were* dressed differently from Englishmen, even the peasants who tilled the fields. The men wore short woollen coats covered by a mantle, while the women wore similar clothes decorated with ribbons that fluttered as they twirled in time to the shrill, piping music. Despite their humble stature, the colours they wore were bright and variegated—the cloaks were fashioned of cloth patches, each one dyed a different vivid hue.

"Are—are they friendly, d'you think?" I nudged big Ned with my elbow, not knowing what to make of the kicking, twirling, and beating of painted drums. The folk on the quayside almost reminded me of Christmas mummers.

"Yes, silly." Edward made another eye roll. "They cheer for us. For the House of York!"

Lithe as a cat, he hauled himself up on the ship's rail, which made our nursemaid, standing a few feet behind us, grow pale and quivery. Furiously he waved his arm, his hair a burnished cloud on the stiff wind, and the folk on the shore began waving back even as their raucous music grew louder.

Anticipation began to grow in my belly, and I darted over to Big Ned and began to pull myself up on the rail next to him. The wind buffeted me, nearly making me lose my grip—Ned grabbed the back of my doublet, holding me safely in place.

"Edmund, Edward, get down from there at once!"

We clambered back down from our precarious perch upon hearing the whip-sharp voice of our mother, Duchess Cecily. Slowly, she processed across the deck in our direction, stately as ever, although suffering some discomfort; she was great with child, her rounded belly barely concealed by her sumptuous cloth-of-gold gown. At her side were our younger sisters, Bessie, crimson-cheeked from the wind, her dark gold curls mussed, and little baby Meg with her solemn grey eyes and hair soft as a rabbit's pelt. The only member of our family not present was our older sister, Anne, ten summers old and already wed to Henry Holland, Duke of Exeter. She was living in his mother's household until old enough to dwell with him as his 'true wife'—whatever that meant. She often sent tear-stained letters to Mother saying she hated her 'beastly' husband and his kin, but Mother had admonished her in a sternly-worded missive detailing the duty of daughters. I felt slight sorrow for Anne, who seemed genuinely appalled by Henry, but not that much, because all the York children would be contracted to strangers in the end, whether we liked their looks and manners or not. Already rumours had run rife about Father seeking a marriage for Edward with one of the French King's daughters, either Jeanne or Madeleine, but nothing had ever come of these whispers. Luckily, no such match had been proposed for me. Girls were too annoying with their dresses and dolls.

Mother's shadow now stretched over Ned and me, the tall cone on her head, awash with a peacock-hued swirl of veils, making her appear a fearsome giantess. "Come to my side," she ordered. "Soon we shall dock and you must behave in princely fashion. The House of York must not be shamed. Your sire wants to build a good reputation in Ireland."

Obediently we scurried to Mother, standing one on each side, like a pair of guards. Demoted from her place, Bessie stuck her tongue out at us, narrow-eyed with pique. I dearly wanted to pull an equally gruesome face at her, but Mother's keen eyes missed nought, even when she appeared otherwise occupied, and I did not want the beginning of our new life to be marred by a punishment.

The cog had drawn up alongside the quay. A crusted old anchor flew over the side and splashed noisily into the harbour waters. A hefty thud made the ship's timbers shudder as the barnacle-encrusted hull bumped against stone and wood, and sailors began running here and there, hurling ropes and shouting instructions to their fellows. Small rowing boats and wherries began circling around our vessel like a shiver of sharks, preparing to carry our possessions to the shore. A barge covered by a cloth canopy bobbed in the swell, waiting for us to disembark.

Father left his place in the prow where he had been standing with the ship's Master and hurried to the rail. A ladder was thrown up against the cog's flank; he climbed down it onto the barge, where he sat on a throne-like chair beneath the canopy. One of Father's squires sidled over, eyeing me and Big Ned. "His Grace says you are next!" he informed us, not entirely respectfully, considering that our sire was his master. "Hurry! Her Grace your Lady Mother cannot be kept waiting long—not only is she heavy with child, the wind might whip off her hat and make her the subject of unseemly merriment! You young rogues wouldn't want that, surely?"

Ned cast the impertinent squire a withering look and proceeded down the ladder, clambering rung to rung with the agility of a Barbary monkey. Less sure of myself, I scrambled after him, the stiff breeze battering my skinny frame and tossing coils of my hair into my eyes. I grasped the ladder desperately with both hands; it was made of heavy woven cord and whipped around wildly, even though two footmen on the barge weighted down the bottom. Oh Jesu, what if the wind blew me off and I landed in the water? I might drown or die of shock—or shame—before anyone could rescue me.

A hand reached up to steady me; my father had risen from his seat and come over. I tried to take another step down but the accursed rope ladder wound around my leg. In frustration and despair, I uttered a forbidden oath-word but Father had a tight hold on my midriff.

"I won't let you fall, my little Ned," he whispered in my ear, breath warm against my wind-frozen cheek, and he disentangled me, lifted me down, and placed me under the canopy beside my brother. I cast Big Ned a glance, fearful that he might regard me with contempt for having shorter, clumsier legs than his.

But he was paying me no heed. Edward was watching the activity on the cog's deck. Catching my elbow, he nodded towards the ship, its riggings black against the bright sky. "The girls should be coming down next. I don't know how they'll fare on that ladder. They cannot climb."

"I'll wager Bessie can," I said. "I've seen her shimmy up an apple tree in the orchard at Fotheringhay."

Big Ned pursed his lips and gave me a little shove. "Edmund! You forget. They are *girls*. They have to be proper when on public display. They are wearing fine gowns and shoes, not old smocks and pattens."

I cleared my throat and pointed upwards. Clattering noises came from the cog's deck as sailors ran about, tying ropes to what appeared to be a swing and then testing the security of their knots. "Hah! They may have found a safe way to get our sisters and mother onto this barge."

A wooden seat draped in gold cloth was suspended over the ship's rail. Reluctantly, her lower lip quivering with fear, Bessie climbed onto it, holding onto her skirts as the wind made them bell outwards. She sat to one side, clutching the armrest so tightly her knuckles went white. A nursemaid lifted Meg in after Bessie, and told her in no uncertain terms that she must hold on tightly—"Else you'll fall in the sea and be gobbled up by a great toothy whale, just like Jonah!"

Round-eyed with fear, Meg nodded obediently and clutched the seat with both hands. An order was shouted from the cog and slowly the chair was lowered to the barge's deck. My sisters scampered off in all haste and ran to join Ned and me under the canopy.

"I thought you might fly off and float down using your skirts to break your fall!" Big Ned leaned in Bessie's direction, smirking. "They were billowing out like a pennant!"

Bessie reddened, clutching at her skirts as if she feared they would fly up again and embarrass her before all. "Stop it, Edward! You always tease me! I shall tell!"

I ignored their silly spat as the seat was hoisted back up to the ship's deck. Ned and Bessie fell silent, and all the York children stared as our mother, impossibly regal despite her size, climbed into the lift. Primly, she sat down, gown tucked around her heavy body, her veil blowing out like her own personal banner.

Even more carefully, inch by inch, the chair was lowered to the barge. Mother stepped off without assistance. "Well, here we all are." She glanced at Father. "This strange new land."

Big Ned and I had long suspected our mother was displeased about leaving England, but she seldom stayed behind when her husband fared abroad, unlike many other noble wives. She journeyed with Father almost everywhere, even when he was engaged in warfare. That is how it came to pass that Ned and I were born in France.

"All will be well, Cecily," Father said in a low voice. "It is only for a short time, I am sure."

Her mouth quirked. "You may be right, Richard. It will be a short stay if we run out of money, and since you have not received a penny of your rightful pay…."

"Wife!" He cast her a pained look. "We have spoken of this before. It is not fitting…"

Mother heaved a sigh. "So far from home, I think his Grace the King might forget about his cousin York. Jesu, Richard, he has not even paid what you are owed from your time in France. You kept the peace there, you rid Normandy of the *faulx visages,* the masked raiders who ravaged the land—and what happened after that? Your position was handed on a platter to that pompous Edmund Beaufort!"

Father flushed red to his collar. "Enough, Cecily. Let us not start this appointment with clouds of doubt hanging above us. Look—the local villagers have turned out to greet our family. I must show them that I will give them security and good lordship and that I have their interests at heart through the legacy of my mother, Anne Mortimer."

The barge swished through the choppy waters and veered towards a wharf decorated with flowers and banners. As expected, soldiers in colourful livery were waiting to escort us to the castle of Christopher St Lawrence, Lord Howth. Taking great care, we processed over a sturdy plank leading from the barge onto the wharf. Exuberant townsfolk rushed towards us, striving to get a closer look—our guards panicked and held them back with some difficulty.

Suddenly silence fell, eerie after so much noise, and the crowds parted like the Red Sea Out onto the harborside rode a nobleman on a caparisoned destrier, accompanied by a party of several dozen armoured knights under a banner I did not recognise.

"It must be Lord Howth," whispered Big Ned.

Approaching our party, Howth dismounted and bowed to Father and Mother, enquiring about the sea journey and offering any assistance they might need in the following days.

We children stood aside, bored with all the formalities. The sun had gone and a light drizzle fell from a grey sky. Bessie scowled as her rich gown grew soggy and lost its shape. Meg began grizzling, patting at her damp hair.

After several more minutes of talk, Lord Christopher gestured to servants waiting at the rear of his small entourage. Three covered chariots rolled up, wheels clacking noisily as they bounced over the cobbles. Our parents climbed into the first, while we were ushered to the second, along with our nursemaids, who were all of a flutter in this strange new country. Some had never journeyed further from Fotheringhay than the town of Oundle. I am sure the giddier ones believed they would be cooked and eaten should the wild Irish singing and stamping beyond our guard of honour get hold of them.

Lord Howth himself came over to see us safely into our transportation, a broad, pleasant-faced man wearing a scarlet chaperon and rich velvet robes. "Welcome to Ireland, children." He ran a strong blue gaze over us. "Soon you will reach my castle, where you may rest or play, as you will, with permission from your noble parents, of course. My own children are of an age with you—they will be happy to show you their home and see that you are entertained."

We thanked him as courtesy dictated, and he smiled and drew the curtain across the window of the chariot with a gloved hand. Hoofs began to clop, and cheers rose from the onlookers, then we were off on our journey to Howth Castle, the carriage rocking unsteadily from side to side on a deeply rutted road that we couldn't see but definitely felt. Bessie almost tumbled out of her seat, save that a nurse grabbed her.

"Do you think they'll let me look out?" Ned eyed the curtain speculatively and then the prim nurses who pretended they had not heard a word.

"No, I don't want them to!" frowned Bessie. "You'll let the rain and wind in. And we…we don't want anyone peering in at us, do we, Meg?"

She nudged little Margaret, bundled in a warm cloak brought out for the journey. She gave a slight shake of her head from inside her warm cocoon.

"This displeases me," said Ned. "If we are to live here, I want to see the place and learn all about it. Surely, you do too, Mistress Em?"

"I certainly *do not*, Master Edward!" exclaimed Em, the eldest of our nursemaids, save Anne Caux, the mistress of the nursery. Her visage filled with horror. "It's not safe. Did you not see those savage men leaping about on the quay in their coloured rags? That straggling hair, those long beards—shuddersome oafs!"

Edward grinned mischievously at Em. "Fear not, I won't let them besmirch your honour, Em. If they should cause gross insult to you, I shall behave exactly as my ancestor King John when he met Irishmen for the first time!"

Em's brow furrowed. "Oh? What did he do?"

"He pulled the long beards of their kings and made them bawl like bulls!"

Our other companion, Anne Caux, pursed her lips. She, born in Normandy, was the eldest and by far the most educated of our nurses, and she brooked no foolishness. "The Irish nobles complained that King John was a very unpleasant fellow indeed. They called him 'an ill-mannered child, from whom no good could be hoped.' You surely do not wish to be tarred by the same brush, do you, Master Edward?"

"No," said Big Ned thoughtfully. "If I were a king, I'd try to make men love me, not despise me." I glanced at him, only a single year my elder, but already seeming princely and wise. I would never tell him I thought so, but I looked up to him and tried to emulate him—although it was useless. I was ever in his shadow.

The journey to Howth Castle took only a little while longer. We realised we were no longer on the open road when we heard gates clang open and the rumble of our carriage's wheels over paving stones. Delicious smells wafted to our nostrils—courtyard odours of poultry and pigs, of the brewhouse and bakehouse.

My belly growled. I had a huge appetite, as did Ned, but while he grew somewhat stout in winter when forays into the countryside for exercise were impossible, I always remained whipcord-thin. Ned's seasonal plumpness was the only feature of my brother that I did not envy. I had heard tales that Father's uncle, Edward, first Duke of York, was so fat he ended up suffocating in his armour during the Battle of Agincourt, one of the few English casualties on that miraculous day. It was a lie; he was large and stocky, but not so corpulent he could not fight, and the truth was that he stood by his standard and took every blow till his bascinet helm was crushed into his brain. Nevertheless, I was glad to be perennially lean so that no one could ever create such fantastical tales about me…

Edward was leaning over, shoving back the curtain that shielded us from the outside world, despite the shrieks from Bessie and Em and the pursed, disapproving lips of Mistress Caux. Ned and I scrambled to the window, staring out into a busy castle bailey full of vegetable stalls, women carrying baskets of bread and herbs, clucking chickens that pecked at grains scattered on the ground, and a stray pink-skinned pig chased by a puffing boy with a long switch. The castle itself was stately and handsome, if small and still under construction. The courtyard was filled with busy stone masons, master builders, ropemakers, and blacksmiths. The clang of hammers rang loud on the air.

A steward emerged from the keep to greet our chariot; he spoke English, but his accent sounded odd to our ears and his speech was so quick we only understood one word in three. Nevertheless, by his hand gestures, we deduced that he wanted the York children to follow him into the castle. We tumbled from the confines of our carriage with gladness, our sisters following with the nursemaids, who examined their new surroundings with a jaundiced eye as they sought for any signs of the wild Irish warriors they feared.

The nurses almost looked slightly disappointed to see that in Lord Christopher's household all the servants were orderly and kempt, and wearing versions of English dress.

As the steward led us to our lodging, we saw our Lord Father and Lady Mother being greeted by Lord Christopher and his wife, Lady Anne Plunkett, a tall, thin woman wearing a beaded headdress that Mother was eyeing speculatively.

Once ensconced in the castle's nursery chamber, trays began to arrive from the castle kitchens. We wondered if there might be some exotic treats or strange morsels such as roasted squirrels, but dinner turned out to be similar to our usual fare—barley bread, duck eggs, beef—although our server, a sprightly lad with flame-red curling hair, told us, when pressed, that hedgehogs were sometimes consumed at Lord Christopher's feasts. We made faces. *That* did not sound appealing at all.

Later that evening, we were summoned to the Great Hall to be formally introduced to Lady Anne and the St Lawrence children. Just us boys—our sisters were sleepy after the arduous sea journey and had been put to bed as befitting young children. The girls' absence made Big Ned and I feel even more grown-up and important. Sons of a great magnate, we strutted proudly through the corridors to our meeting while the servants gawked.

Howth Castle's Great Hall was dimmer and smokier than that at Fotheringhay, the stonework slate-grey between the banners and tapestries. A large fire burned in a central hearth, casting out sparks and thick, pungent smoke.

I coughed, my eyes watering. Big Ned started rubbing his eyes too. "The smoke is so…strong…" he choked.

"You will soon grow used to the scent," the steward said, leading us across the chamber. "Peat is what we burn in Ireland, and that is what you smell."

Mother and Father were seated upon the dais beside Lord Christopher and Lady Anne. Near our hosts stood a veritable army of young boys. Christopher welcomed us and then introduced his sons one by one. Eldest was Robert, maybe thirteen years old, his scowling face making it obvious he wished to be doing anything but greeting English interlopers. Next was William, burly and bucolic, then skinny, non-descript Thomas, and Almeric, stocky like William but with cheeks freckled rather than rubicund. Last was a chubby baby named Lionel, gurgling in its nurse's arms.

"I am sure on the morrow the sons of York and the sons of St Lawrence can make merry together while I speak with his Lordship, the Lieutenant," said Lord Christopher, smiling benignly at us all, even as Robert's scowl deepened. "You won't be bored here, my young lords. Rob, Thom and Almeric will show you the forests and other sights that lie within my lands. Mayhap you will see some deer or hawks. Does that please you, my fine young guests?"

Edward and I nodded emphatically. Strange new terrain was always of interest and castles could be claustrophobic and unbearably noisy at times—especially one only half-built. On the dais, Robert's scowl had become a grimace. Ned elbowed me when he thought Father could not see. "Look at that brat's face. A gargoyle!" he whispered, and it was all I could do to control my mirth.

Tomorrow was going to be an adventure indeed.

The sun decided to shine with golden radiance the next morn, which was even more unusual, we heard, than in England. Scrambling about like eager pups, Edward and I leapt from our shared bed, throwing scented water onto our faces and running fingers through our hair. A nursemaid usually dressed us, but we were reaching an age where we found such attention embarrassing, so we helped each other into outdoor raiment from our clothes chests and scampered out to meet the little party gathering in the courtyard.

Expression sour, Robert was waiting, his eyes heavy-lidded as if he was still half asleep. William, Thomas, and Almeric were more lively and cheerful, chatting merrily with each other as they mounted up on solid ponies.

A tall man wearing a feathered cap approached me and Edward. "I am Sir John, Lord Christopher's Marshal. I shall accompany you today, along with other members of his lordship's household. I will ensure your comfort and safety. I assume you are accustomed to the saddle?"

"We've been riding since we learnt to walk!" said Ned enthusiastically. "I only ever fell off once!"

"Excellent," said Sir John, "for I have already chosen a pair of mounts for you. I trust you will find them to your satisfaction."

He gestured to two grooms who scurried to the nearby stable block, returning with a couple of sleek, dappled-grey ponies. Ned and I swung into the saddles, slipping our feet into the stirrups—although my brother needed to call for a groom to make adjustments as his legs were so long.

Robert St Lawrence was now the only one unmounted. His arms were crossed and his eyes flashed furiously. "Marshal, you did not order *my* steed brought," he snapped, his tone imperious.

Sir John's mouth twitched. "Master Robert, 'twas not two days ago that you shouted at the stableboys that no one but you must ever touch your horse, Midnight. I merely obeyed your command."

William gave a little snicker, then covered his mouth, pretending to cough. Robert said nought but stalked huffily towards the stable. Bawling drifted from the doorway and shortly thereafter, he reappeared riding on a small raven-black horse with a white star on its forehead. A pretty beast—certainly much prettier than its glaring rider.

With Robert finally mounted, our exploration party trotted out the castle's sallyport onto the hillside behind. The sky was robin's egg blue, and the trees on the hillsides a vivid shade of green. Sir John took us on a path behind the castle, which led to a heavily forested hunting ground. Here, pine, yew and ash wove together, their twisted roots moss-furred, and giant stones thrust up like giant's bones from sprays of dew-jewelled ferns.

Robert sat astride his mount in brooding silence, but William was friendly enough, riding alongside Ned and me. "Don't mind Rob." He peered over his shoulder at his kinsman. "Ever since he hit thirteen summers and got a spotty face, his mood has been worse than an angry bear. I heard tell a maiden laughed at him when he tried to kiss her and told him his face had craters like the moon."

Edward and I snorted with laughter. Neither of us could imagine being so offended for such a reason. Robert glared but fortunately was out of earshot.

"I don't have to worry," said William, tapping his broad chest, "about girls and their fickle opinions, that is. Father has picked me for the priesthood. I'll soon be sent from Howth to a monastic school."

"And you are happy with that?" asked Edward. "I cannot imagine such a life, although it is a worthy one."

William shrugged. "Happy enough. It's a good position for a second son...and look at me, it's not as if I'd make a good fighter! No, I'll serve God and live a quiet and—hopefully—comfortable life."

William then launched into a history of the area, showing off his intellectual prowess, and we soon agreed that he would be far better with books than broadswords. "This place was not always called Howth," he told us. "It's not an Irish name but one given by invading Norsemen. Its true name is Benn Edar."

Big Ned scratched his head. "The names here are unpronounceable! What does Benn Edar mean?"

"Benn is hill or mountain," said William. "Edar is more uncertain. Some say the name comes from 'Etar', an ancient chieftain ruling a tribe called the Firbolg, Men of the Bags. Many myths linger about this hill."

"Babe's tales!" spat Robert, butting in. "It's embarrassing that you feed our sire's guests such infantile pap!"

William was clearly used to his brother's temperament as he ignored his rude outburst. "You will soon see a monument from the ancient time of the Firbolg. It is older than the Romans or the Greeks, many claim."

Our company passed into a shadier section of the wood. Pines leaned close and ferns flapped at our ponies' fetlocks like the pale green hands of woodland sprites. Ahead, slouched amidst the greenery, stood a primitive stone structure. Stumpy pillars of gargantuan width supported a sloped capstone of even more immense proportions. Quartz strands ran through the top stone, glittering as shafts of sunlight pierced the heavy foliage.

An air of antiquity hung over the place, and a strange stillness—no birds sang, the winds were hushed.

"What...what is it?" Edward looked puzzled.

"A grave," replied William. "Aideen's Grave. She was the wife of the Irish hero, Oscar. He was slain at the Battle of Gabhra and Aideen died of a broken heart. Oscar's father, Oisin, buried her here, or so the legend goes."

Ned dismounted and walked to the cairn, peering into the inner chamber. I scrambled off my pony and followed, not wishing to be left out. Inside was only a haze of grass, yet I fancied a tang of decaying leaves mixed with Jesu knew what else lingered. Despite my efforts to feign boldness, the hairs bristled on the back of my neck.

The other boys dismounted and gathered at our backs, save for Robert who trudged over to a servant and demanded a mazer of watered-down ale 'while the children played.'

"I found something here once," said Almeric, rather shyly. "Something special."

"What is it?" I asked. "Can you show us?"

The boy reached into a pouch secured to his belt and brought out an object, holding it up to the light. A little leaf-shaped arrow-head, made from some kind of translucent stone.

"Elf shot," I said slowly. "Such arrowheads turn up in England too, although I have never seen one myself." The day had taken on a dangerous feel—countryfolk claimed that elves shot these missiles at travellers, causing them death or disablement from the deadly 'elf-stroke'.

Glancing over, Robert gave a derisive snort. "More tales fit for the nursery. I assure you, Edward and Edmund of York, nought in these woods can harm you, unless you happen to devour a poisonous toadstool or two."

William made a face as we listened, irritated, to Robert's mockery—and then all hell broke loose. A flurry, a flutter came from the shadowy end of the burial chamber, and a brown bird, its wings whirring with the wind of its speed, flew out as if fired from one of the new-fangled *handgones* that Father talked about. The bird whistled past me, its wingtip skimming my cheek, and I fell back, gasping, for it seemed to me an evil omen.

But that was not all. The bird sped straight as an arrow towards the gloomy pines, skimming the forelock of Robert's steed before it vanished. The horse let out a shrill whinny and reared on its hinds. Robert, who had looped the reins tightly around his wrist, was thrown partway out of his saddle. He roared in rage and fear as his mazer flew up into the air, showering Robert and all members of our party with watery ale.

The Marshal made a grab for the reins, but Robert's horse reared once more and then bolted, taking a yelling, half-unseated Robert with it.

"No! Robert!" William ran helplessly after his brother. The two younger De Lawrences were screaming, unsure what to do.

Sir John flung himself onto his own steed, cursing—but it was Edward who was quickest to attempt a rescue.

Dashing through the ferns, he sprang in front of Robert's mount and milled his arms, shouting in an authoritative voice. The beast slid to a halt mere inches from him, its eyes wild with terror. He lunged for the bridle, but the horse flung its head about wildly—and came pounding back towards Thomas, Almeric, and me as we stood, transfixed with shock, before the monoliths of the Grave of Aideen.

Again, Edward moved with speed and decision, flinging himself onto Robert who, completely out of the saddle now, was being dragged by one arm along the bumpy ground, still howling. "Stay still, stay still!" Ned shouted as Robert kicked and writhed. Taking his little eating knife from his belt, he slashed through the reins wrapped around Robert's wrist. Robert collapsed into a heap, and free of its screeching burden, the spooked horse began to slow its pace. One of the grooms caught it before it reached Aideen's Grave and calmed the beast without further incident.

Robert rolled onto his back, groaning and clutching his wrist. Sir John rushed to his side. "Master Robert, are you hurt?"

Fiercely, Robert shook his head. "No, no...don't touch me. Don't look at me!"

He was more hurt than he let on, for his lips were bloodless and his cheeks white. Welts where the reins had gouged his flesh stood out on his forearm.

Edward climbed to his feet and offered his hand. "Let me help you up."

"I don't need..." began Robert, scrambling onto his knees, his fine raiment smeared with mud, He put his hand down to push himself up and yelped in pain. Teeth gritted, he whispered, "If that offer is still there, I will take it, Edward York. And Sir John, I might need you too."

Ned and the Marshal each took hold one of Robert's arms, hauling him onto unsteady feet. As they escorted him toward his now-placid mount, he glanced aside at Edward, a quizzical expression on his face. "I-I have been churlish to you this day. Why did you bother to help me?"

Edward smiled. "Better to make friends than enemies, and there was never any real reason for us to be enemies. Your father and mine seem to see eye to eye, and I hope we will be able to do so, too."

Pride towards my brother swelled in my heart as he mounted his pony and rode down the hillside, conversing with Robert, who had grown more personable, despite the pain of his injured wrist. Ned had a certain quality about him, a way of soothing tensions and putting others at ease. A brief thought flashed through my mind, about how our father had a claim to the English throne that some said was superior to the present King Henry's. If Fate had been kind and Bolingbroke had not usurped the throne of Richard II, Father might have been King and Ned his heir.

Edward would have made an excellent King someday...

"What are you thinking about?" William trotted his pony up to me as the party began to descend the hill toward the misty turrets of Howth castle.

I shrugged. "Nought. Just what might have been—but cannot be."

We stayed for several more days at Howth Castle. All the great Irish Earls began arriving with their retinues to meet with Father and renew oaths of allegiance to King Henry. Lord Christopher had a harpist come in to play, which delighted Mother, Bessie and Meg, and there was a bagpiper too, enthusiastically playing his wheezing instrument of torture (for so it sounded to my ears—pure torment, as if a dozen cats had their tails trodden upon.)

Robert came swaggering up to Ned and me, no longer our enemy if not exactly a friend. He owed much to Edward; his arm, maybe his life, and he was clever enough to realise it. Men had been dragged to death behind a bolting steed on many occasions. "I am to go hunting later in the week," he said, stiffly formal. "I would like to invite you, Lord Edward, Lord Edmund, if it pleases you."

"It does," said Ned, "but are you able with your arm?"

"I will do what I can," he replied with a tight-lipped smile. "Mayhap you can be my right arm for me, Edward. After all, your quick thinking saved it."

"I will," said Ned. "An honour."

Robert blushed and strolled away, clearly embarrassed by his own honest admission.

Later, aware of the incident at Aideen's Grave, Father wisely told us that Robert's unpleasant demeanour was merely because he was uncertain of his place in the world. He feared that his sire's importance, and his own in the future, might be eclipsed by having an official representative of King Henry in Ireland. "His father was of similar nature when he was younger, I am told," he said. "He made sure the rights of the St Lawrence family were never overridden by anyone, even royalty. One day, a grampus was caught in the bay."

"What's a grampus?" I asked. It sounded like a monster in a Bestiary.

"A sea-creature, a type of dolphin. Twice as long as a man is high. Such a beast is normally considered a 'royal fish' and a possession of the Crown. The King swiftly laid claim to it. Lord Christopher argued that the grampus was *his* because from time immemorial every such sea-beast found on his shores was considered his property. The arguments dragged on for a while—until Henry waved the matter aside."

"The King was generous."

"Not really," Father laughed. "Lord Christopher had already eaten the beast at a banquet! If he'd waited any longer, it would have been spoilt and useless to either king or churl!"

Ned and I guffawed with laughter.

"The lesson is, my sons, tread carefully in this country," said Father, growing serious. "They are proud people in Ireland, not just the native Irish chieftains, but those whose ancestors came from England to settle over three hundred years ago. So consider what you say and do. They will not appreciate arrogance—and if they find any, they may well beat it out of you and would not be wrong in doing so."

At last, the Irish nobles and knights had departed, their oath sworn to King Henry through Father as his minister. It was time for us to go too, to secure our own castle at Trim. Robert and his brothers came into the bailey to say farewell. "Maybe…maybe we could meet again someday, Lord Edward," Robert stammered. "Go hawking perhaps. Up on the hill."

"Perhaps," said Ned politely, although by the tone of his voice, I doubted it would ever come to pass. He did not want Robert St Lawrence as an enemy, but he had no desire for him as a close friend either.

Our entourage left our host's castle and travelled inland. Rain bucketed from a stormy sky, pounding on the armoured backs of the soldiers and making flags and pennants droop like sodden leaves. For once, I was glad Big Ned and I were still too young to journey long distances on horseback. We were cosily confined in a chariot, wrapped in mantles lined with squirrel fur and picking from tasty sweetmeats while playing a game of dice. Our sisters were in a separate chariot this time, so we were quite undisturbed, except for the occasional snores from our Em, who had fallen asleep to the rocking of the carriage.

After a while, the thrum of the rain ceased on the wagon's covering, and a crack of wan yellow sunlight entered through the curtained window. Ned and I forgot our dice game and peered out cautiously. A wide, fast river, the Boyne, ran alongside the trackway, shining silver in the burgeoning light. The threatening clouds swept away over the plain beyond the river, and a rainbow arced across the firmament in all its wondrous colours.

The road forked, and in the distance stout grey walls announced that we were nearing a town. A tall, martial castle keep, cruciform-shaped and with pennants flying from the parapets, loomed above the town defences. It appeared exceedingly large, much bigger than Howth and maybe even larger than Fotheringhay, our primary home.

Our entourage headed for one of the town gates, pausing to allow shepherds to drive in a fleet of unruly, baaing sheep before processing up the town's main street as trumpeters played a fanfare and heralds proclaimed our arrival. People had emerged from houses and shops to watch, and bells rang from church towers, abbeys, and priories. Ned and I waved and smiled, eager to make a good impression.

Soon the houses thinned, and a low bridge came into view, crossing the castle moat. It was fed from the river, which also formed a natural defence on one side. Beyond was a titanic gatehouse, its entrance fanged with iron like a dragon's maw. The portcullis lifted, and the family of York entered the bailey while the trumpets blared so loudly, they sent birds shrieking from the turrets and out across the plain.

Ned and I alighted from our carriage and scampered over to our parents, who stood with the steward, evident by his richly furred mantle and chain of office.

"A fine castle, is it not?" Father shaded his eyes against the glare of the sky as he stared upwards at the bulk of the imposing stone keep. "I have never seen a keep quite like it—I have counted twenty corners!"

"It is wonderful, Lord Father!" Edward and I shouted in excitement, eager to explore. There were other impressive buildings too—a three-towered forework to defend the keep in an attack, an attached stable for our horses, a huge Great Hall, a separate solar housed in an earlier tower, a mint, and various buildings housing kilns, a bakery, and a brewery. The scent from the bakery made my stomach growl with hunger—although I'd already eaten many a sweetmeat on the journey here.

"I am pleased you like it." Father stood with his hands on his hips, still admiring the strong walls and towers. It was probably the happiest I had seen him look since we left England. "Trim, along with Dublin Castle, will be our main homes for the foreseeable future."

CHAPTER TWO

The family had not long settled into Trim Castle when Father took a trip to Ulster in the North. Ulster was part of his inheritance through Elizabeth de Burgh. Instead of using his regular banner of the Falcon and Fetterlock, he raised a standard embossed with the Black Dragon, which both Ned and I thought wonderfully ferocious in appearance, perhaps even better than a gryphon or lion. Eyes pleading, we expressed our deepest wishes to travel in his company, but Father said 'no' in no uncertain terms.

"You are far too young," he said sternly, while we whined around his chair like hungry little hounds seeking scraps. "You are not yet wise enough in the ways of the Irish people. Stay at Trim with the tutor I have hired, Master Terrance. The greatest thing you can do for me is to learn your lessons, and honour your Lady Mother, The Holy Virgin, Christ and God—not necessarily in that order."

After Father departed for Ulster, his Black Dragon snapping at the tumbling clouds, Ned and I were introduced to the newly hired tutor our sire had mentioned. Terrance was his birth name, but although his father was an Englishman, he had an Irish mother and so he went by the outlandish nickname of 'Tadgh'. Rangy and tall, he had curling brown hair and eyes that held a mischievous twinkle. He glanced from Ned to me, me to Ned, making faces, before hooking his thumbs into his belt and drawling, "So you're the two young miscreants I've been given to teach. Edward and Edmund. This should prove an interesting task by the look of you two rapscallions."

For a second, we gaped in petrified horror, fearing that our schoolmaster was a tyrant and would bring the switch to our tender backsides for the slightest misdeed (as Father always said would happen, if needed, noble-blooded or not) but then we noticed Tadgh's lips curving in a sly grin.

"Your faces!" he crowed. "Come, lads, I'm just joshing with you. You needn't fear me—as long as you learn all that I teach you and don't play the fool."

"We won't!" Ned crossed his arms, a little defensive. "I'm no fool. Neither is my brother, Edmund."

"Good to hear, Master Edward." Tadgh waggled a finger. "Because fools aren't tolerated lightly here in Ireland. You might think you've got away with it, but you'll soon find out when the locals run rings about you, that the jest is on you." He gestured to a worn wooden bench propped against the wall, its surface carved with the names and curse words of generations of bored schoolboys "So, sit down, my dear new scholars, and we'll begin without further ado."

Tadhg soon taught us the basics of what we needed to know in our new life—what to say, what not to say, how to act, and how not to. He also taught us Irish history, as well as the customary Latin and theological study—he told us that in his youth he had been destined for the church, so had grown quite learned in those subjects. "But then my sire died, so a church life was not to be. I followed a different path. Probably the better one—I am not holy enough to become a priest." He flashed his lopsided, rascally smile.

"Now, with your good father the Duke in charge here at Trim, you'll be wanting to know all about the place," he continued. "The name of Trim, in Irish, is *Baile Átha Troim*." The strange language of the Irish, even more unintelligible than Welsh, rolled musically off his tongue. "It means 'Town at the Ford of Elderflower Trees.'" He grinned, running a hand through his shaggy curls. "A pretty name…and the elderflowers make good wine."

"Do you know who built this castle?" he went on, gesturing to the walls around us, stained with ash from torches, hung with faded tapestries in deep reds and blues.

Big Ned and I glanced at each other and shrugged. "An ancestor?" Edward hazarded a guess.

"Aye, but what was his name? Have you viewed any old genealogy scrolls?"

We shook our heads in tandem.

"Then listen close. 'Twas Hugh de Lacy, who was given many lands in Meath in the days of old Henry II. A fine castle builder but a rash fellow, he married as his second wife an Irish princess called Róis Ní Chonchobair."

"Why was he rash in taking a new wife?" queried Edward. "Men do it all the time."

"Ah, he was a very naughty fellow and 'forgot' to ask permission from the King. Henry began to suspect that Hugh desired to become King of Ireland. Henry recalled him to England, and Hugh had his knuckles rapped…' He smirked, hand falling to a switch on his desk he claimed he used 'frequently' on incorrigible pupils—but which he'd never used on us thus far. "However, old Henry relented in the end and returned Hugh's Irish post. He didn't get to enjoy it for long, alas. While building another strong castle, he was ambushed and killed by Gilla-Gan-Mathiar O'Maidhaigh. Isn't that a wondrous name, lads? I should teach you how to spell it! Anyway, Hugh's oldest son Walter inherited Trim, but his other son by the fair and fragrant Princess Róis was made a bastard by order of King Henry. A petty revenge for that unlicenced, hasty marriage."

"How do these de Lacey's tie to our family?" I asked. Most of the noble families of Britain and the Pale in Ireland were related to some degree, making marriages a nightmare of unexpected consanguinity and multiple papal dispensations. However, the most distant, far-flung ancestors were hard to ascertain for all but the most dedicated priest or scholar.

"Your family—the House of York—has not one but two lines of descent from Hugh de Lacy," Tadgh said, holding up two ink-stained fingers. "One from Walter's daughter, Egidia, who wed Richard De Burgh, and one from another daughter called Maude, whose granddaughter, Joan de Geneville, married Roger Mortimer, Earl of March."

"Our grandmother on Father's side was Anne Mortimer," I said.

"Indeed, she was," said Taidgh. "Born at Westmeath, daughter to the 4th Earl of March. God rest her soul."

"Father's claim to the throne comes through her," I blurted thoughtlessly—and was rewarded by Edward's sharp elbow in my belly, making me gasp like a fish. Mother had insisted we not talk about our royal ancestry outside the immediate family, for fear of it reaching the ears of King Henry or Queen Margaret. They already knew of it—everyone did—but to hear it spoken might bring about accusations of desire for the crown.

Tadgh stared at me, doubled over and clutching my gut, and then at Ned, who wore an angry, resentful look. Our tutor, instantly deducing why Ned had reacted with such fury, smiled his crafty little smile and put a finger to his lips. "Do not fear, young lords. Your words are safe with me; I am not one for tittle-tattle. But have a care. Not all men are as loyal as your friend and teacher, Tadgh."

Time spent with Tadgh was not all learning dates, names, and history. Soon he took us on foot into the town of Trim to familiarise ourselves with our new surroundings. A corn market selling grain led to a fishmongers' pitch that smelt so strong of scales and guts we had to pinch our nostrils shut, and that progressed into a butchers' area where the fleshers hung haunches of beef and whole pigs on iron hooks. Beyond the busy marketplace were goldsmith's shops filled with jewellery fashioned from fine Irish gold, a tannery and a dyers' where the red-smeared workers looked like battle victims, and even a goodly sized wine shop selling imports ferried down the river—which Tadgh made sure he visited to make some purchases, while Ned and I stood outside munching on meat-filled hot pasties he had purchased from a pieman's stall.

Another journey took us to St Mary's Abbey, a House of the Augustinians. Fronted by a slender, austere tower, the whole monastery was crafted from a handsome yellow stone that glowed gold in the dawn and fire-red at sunset. We could see it shining at sunrise and at dusk from the tiny slit windows of our bedchamber in the castle.

"The Abbey is a very holy place," said Tadgh. "A site of pilgrimage for all Ireland. It holds a carved statue of the Blessed Virgin, and miracles have occurred among the pilgrims who come to revere her. Cripples walking, the blind seeing, the flatulent finding due relief—the usual sort of miraculous thing." He gave us his trademark grin and winked, sending us into gales of mirth.

Despite Tadgh's joking impiety, Ned and I were now desirous of seeing this holy statue. Tadgh leading us on, we joined a line of pilgrims clamouring for admission into the abbey, some leaning on crutches, one supine on a bier, one missing a hand, another with both eyes covered by rags and a little child with a grimy face guiding him. The child's feet were bare and black with dirt. A monk was dealing with the crowd, tutting and saying that soon it would be Matins and admissions to the shrine would cease until Mass was over.

However, the monk's beady eye fell upon us as we hovered behind the footsore travellers, and he recognised Tadgh and bustled over, his cassock swinging around his bony ankles. "Tadgh! I hadn't expected to see you at St Mary's. I heard you were engaged at the castle."

Tadgh gestured to Ned and I. "I am, Brother Fergal. My new pupils—the Lord Lieutenant's sons, Edward and Edmund, young but earls both, newly come from England."

Brother Fergal looked us up and down as we pretended to be studious and pious, rather than two curious schoolboys out on a jaunt. "Come with me, he said, guiding us away from the waiting supplicants and into the abbey's interior through a private door. Behind us, the waiting pilgrims muttered darkly.

The abbey church's interior was as grand as I expected. Pointed arches, aisles full of lacy tomb embrasures and carved effigies, chantries aglow with cresset lights, colourful saints' statues in niches on tree-like pillars, a vast ceiling of stars and angels. Brother Fergal guided us toward the choir, his sandals making a steady slapping on the floor tiles with their patterns of birds, sun, flowers, and vines.

The last contingent of pilgrims was being ushered out and the brothers readying for the next deluge. Fergal took us on another route through the church, weaving between pillars decked with biblical scenes of the Annunciation, the Visitation, and the Nativity. Passing the Rood Screen's row of gilded saints, Fergal veered into a side chapel. "Wait here," he ordered.

Entering the chapel, he spoke in low tones to the brethren within. When he returned, Fergal said, "You may enter now. My fellow monks have agreed to keep the shrine clear of outsiders until you are done, your lordships."

It was a shock to realise that this honour was granted because of our parentage, and I thought, guiltily, of the dirty, shoeless child waiting at the door with his blind grandfather as I slipped into the chapel, head bowed.

Upon a stone altar stood the miraculous statue of the Virgin, surrounded by gold, silver and gemstones left by supplicants. She was large and appeared to be ancient, the wood she was carved from was smooth and shiny, warm nutbrown on the unpainted surface of her face and hands. Her robe was coloured the customary blue, but the coloration had sunk into the porous wood to create a deeper hue—the sky of afternoon turning dusky. A metal nimbus surrounded her head, its spokes long and shimmering in the gloom.

Tadgh knelt to pray, and Edward and I did likewise, although I was not quite sure what to pray for. Safety for my family? Father's success in Ireland? A return to England with no Beauforts to confound us? I found myself thinking mostly of my mother, and how she would want to visit the Virgin's shrine, especially as she was big with child.

As I thought of her upcoming travail, my mood darkened, for she was no longer young, and many women did not survive the birth of a baby. So I earnestly pressed my hands together and prayed to the Blessed Virgin that Mother would come through childbirth unscathed again.

We had not long in our devotions, for the pilgrims, scattered away by the monks, were pounding upon the church door, each one eager to kneel at the shrine, offer up a few coins or gewgaws, and hope for healing or some other kind of easement in their lives.

"Come on now, lads." Tadgh placed a hand on each of our shoulders, pushing us back towards the nave of the abbey church. "We've had our time, thanks to my friend Fergal. To be sure, you'll visit again with your noble parents. The folk outside have waited long, and for many it will be their one and only visit."

Returning to the outside world, we wandered beyond the abbey's boundary walls. Clouds had rolled back in while we were at the shrine and the river water had turned dark, boiling in its bed like a cauldron.

In the distance, a trumpet call rang out, the shrill, brazen sound echoing back off the walls of the castle keep. Tadgh stopped in his tracks, head cocked, listening. "Did you hear that, lads?"

Edward and I nodded. "What do you think it is?" asked Ned, trying to restrain a growing excitement.

"I am thinking, lads," said our tutor, "that your good Lord Father might well be on his way home from Ulster."

CHAPTER THREE

"It went well. Better than I could have hoped for."

Father sat in the smoky Great Hall, face reddened by the wind, black rings from tiredness around his eyes, but exuding an air of triumph. He had never looked more at ease, despite his exhaustion. At home, a cloud of doubt followed him as he wrangled with his opponents in the government—I'd once heard one of the servants mutter to his fellow, unaware that a small boy played with toy soldiers behind a screen in the solar, "It is as if Duke Richard waits for the axe to fall and smite his head from his shoulders—just like his own sire—whether deserved or not."

Mother joined our father upon the dais, queenly and reserved as ever, but her eyes told of her delight at his return. "Tell me of it, Richard; I am eager to hear your news. And our sons..." She nodded in our direction. "You can see they chafe at the bit to learn of their sire's deeds."

Father took a deep breath and glanced around, his gaze taking in not only his family but all those massed in the Hall—knights, local lordlings, squires, stewards, chaplains, ladies' maids, our nursemaids, the serving staff. "On my journey, the Irish nobility treated me with the greatest courtesy. Not as an unwelcome invader but as the heir to the lands of the de Burghs. You will shortly see what I have brought back in the baggage train—gifts heaped high, presented by local lords and chieftains. Gemstones, Irish gold crosses and tablets, fine furs for winter warmth, and heaps of dyed woollens. Men flocked from afar to gaze upon my person, and I swore to aid true Irishmen in any way possible, as long as they were willing to pay homage to King Henry as their overlord. Once, not so long ago, I admit I was reluctant to come to Ireland, believing I might be at a loss here, outside the sphere of political life in England—but now, with Ulster receiving me with grace and a clearer idea of what tasks lie ahead, perhaps I was mistaken. This move might be the making of the House of York, not the ending of it."

Mother continued to smile and nod as he spoke, but her eyes showed a lack of enthusiasm. She missed the comforts of our English castles and the great ladies she considered friends, including, at one time, even Queen Margaret herself. She often complained to her tiring-maids that Irish fashions were almost forty years out of date: "And I refuse to show my face in public dressed in a gown more suited to the time of my mother, Joan!"

Father rose from his chair on the dais, torchlight glinting on his jewelled chain of office. "Further to my recent trip, I have decided to show my mettle and prove that I am an active and well-disposed lord to *all* the people of this land. Once I have given thanks for my success in Ulster, I plan to depart, for a time, to Dublin Castle. Trim shall remain my main seat, but Dublin is Ireland's most important city and closer to what shall be my next…conquest."

Mother's head jerked around rapidly at his final word, her smile melting away. "Richard…"

"Not now, Lady wife." Father firmly but in a kindly tone bound her to silence. "We will talk after I have rested from my long ride. When you come to me, after supper, have the children brought too."

Some hours later, after Father had bathed and supped, the chamberlain collected Edward and me and escorted us to our sire's quarters. Mother, Bessie, and Meg were already there, the girls looking sleepy for the hour was late; full-dark with the moon long risen. The chamber was warm, with a peat fire, the aroma now familiar, burning in a large brazier. A carafe of wine stood on the table and a jug containing watered-down ale for us youngsters. There was also a tray of honey cakes and breads that Big Ned was eyeing hungrily.

Ned and I settled on a bench. My sisters sat on little footstools, while Mother reclined in a chair massed with satin pillows. Father sat next to her, hands in his lap, his legs outstretched to get the fire's warmth.

"I could see today, my dearest," Father looked towards Mother, his eyes intent, "that you were concerned by the idea of a move to Dublin. Speak freely here of your concerns."

Mother laid a hand on the mound of her belly, draped in tawny satin. "Oh, surely you can see, Richard, that it is late for me to travel...unsafe, and I dare say it, uncomfortable."

Father sighed. "I ask much of you, but, as ever, I want you nearby, Cecily. Not just to give comfort as my wife, but because you give good counsel on many subjects. Listen, I must strike while the iron is hot to assert my position in Ireland and win the minds, if not the hearts, of its inhabitants. Right now, trouble brews in Wicklow, a mountainous area beyond Dublin—the clan of the O'Byrnes raid their neighbours' livestock and indulge in much lawlessness. Those knights and lords who recently paid homage to the King through me are eager to prove their loyalty by bearing arms against the O'Byrnes. I must lead them into Wicklow ere their enthusiasm wanes, for I have learned already that men's hearts may be quickly set aflame here, but just as quickly that flame can be snuffed out."

"I have enjoyed Trim," sniffed Mother. "I am comfortable here."

"And we will return, I promise, when all is done. You may not be able to ride on campaign like a man, Cecily, but you could be an ambassador to the ordinary folk of Dublin—the women and children—all of whom I am certain will be curious about an English Duchess."

"So I am to be a curiosity." Mother raised her smooth white brows. "How delightful. But fear not, Richard, I trust your knowledge, and if you say it is important we fare to Dublin, either for war or to build bridges, I am sure you are correct. My duty as a wife is to follow you, and I will. I just pray Dublin Castle is clean and well-lit upon my arrival, and that a decent wetnurse can be found for the coming babe. I made enquiries here but..."

"You will not be disappointed, Cecily. I am assured Dublin Castle is in good repair, and have already sent men on to prepare for our coming. As for Dublin town, it is far bigger than Trim and..." He grinned and reached out to pat her hand. "You might well be able to find the hats and stylish dresses I understand you've been missing. I, too, do not want you to go about dressed like your mother!"

Our family attended a Mass of thanksgiving for Father's safe return at the invitation of the Abbot of St Mary's. When the service ended, Mother went to pray at the Virgin's shrine, taking Bessie and Meg with her. Father spoke with the Abbot for a long while and presented him an offering in a small leather bag. The bag jingled noisily as it thudded into the Abbot's hand.

The holy man's whiskery visage flushed with pleasure at this unexpected gift. "Thank you, thank you, my Lord Duke!" He ferreted the bag away in his voluminous robes as if he feared Father might snatch it back. "You are most kind, most generous. All the Brethren will pray for the success of your forthcoming enterprise and look forward to your victorious return to Trim."

Father inclined his head, then gestured for Ned and I to attend him. Mother and the girls appeared through the heavy candle smoke and joined us. Leaving the abbey church, my sire glanced up at the needle-like tower of the abbey church, the clouds and birds dipping around its pinnacle. "I promised the Abbot repairs and assurance that all pilgrims have safe passage to St Mary's as long as Lord Lieutenant on this isle. But I am eager to show all the folk of Trim that I will not forget them while in Dublin. Today I will also make a journey to St Patrick's Church." He glanced at Mother, who was about to get into a litter for the return journey to the castle. "Dearest wife, will you accompany me?"

"I fear the babe lies heavy and uncomfortably today." Mother rubbed her belly. "This one has made me thoroughly dyspeptic. I only hope that my ailments do not engender a sour and aggrieved temperament in the child."

"You must go and rest, Cecily." Concern was etched on Father's visage. "Ask for some ginger wine; it will ease your digestion. Take our daughters with you—but Edward, Edmund, I would appreciate your company."

I was enthusiastic. Big Ned and I were too young to join Father in military matters, but we could make our presence felt in an event like today's. St Patrick's, another ancient church within the town, was somewhere Tadgh had not yet taken us. He was joining us today, waiting in the marketplace at Father's summons.

"I am here to educate you, my lads," he said as we spotted him and ran in his direction. "You can't get rid of me, I'm afraid, even outside the schoolroom."

"But we *like* to be with you, Tadgh!" I insisted. "You're better than our old Tutors at Fotheringhay who were all so dull! You tell us about gory battles, like when the Norseman Sigurd chopped off Máel Brigte's head and tied it to his saddle by the hair, but the head's teeth cut his leg as he rode and Sigurd died of an infection! So he was killed by a dead man!"

Father glanced from me to Tadgh and smothered a laugh. "Is that what I pay you for, Master Terrance?"

"Ah, well, if it gets them interested in history, surely 'tis a good thing."

"Indeed…go ahead. I would hear what you teach my sons today. Maybe I too can learn. It is good to know of the place where one governs."

"I've already mentioned Saint Patrick to you," said Tadgh, as we traipsed across the town, Father with his guard, Ned and I alongside our tutor. "A Welshman, brought to Ireland as a slave. When he was freed, no one here ever expected to see him again, but he crossed that miserable, rough sea again to perform his heart's desire—converting the Irish to the true Faith. He's held in high esteem throughout the country for his courage and holiness, and it is believed he built Trim's first church with permission from High King, who had recently abandoned his pagan ways. So, this is a special place of great holiness we visit today, my young lords."

The church soon came into view, not as grand or eye-catching as some of the newer religious houses, but square and squat, built of slatey stone that seemed to suck the brightness from the sky. It had a stern, almost forbidding air, or perhaps its austerity and lack of decoration only made it appear so. However, as we approached the door, humble and low, with no carvings of Norman beaked monsters or grand tympanums, a sensation of calmness swept over me. The wind died, as did the birdsong from the nearby bushes. A sliver of sunlight struck the tower, transforming it from gloomy to incandescent. The birds began to sing again, like an Avarian angelic choir, and from within the church nave, I heard the voices of human choristers rising in a song of praise.

If there was a place of true, ancient sanctity, it was here at St Patrick's church.

Father was greeted by the resident priest, Father Norreys, an old man as grizzled as a blackthorn root but with a shrewd look about him. He invited him inside, and Tadgh, Ned and me followed, while the rest of the company remained outside in the churchyard. Along the walls of the nave stood the tombs of founders and dignitaries, differently cast than in England. An alien flavour touched the stonemason's art, making images that were holy and yet somehow primitive and profane—such as the bodiless and faceless woman and man, he heavily bearded, she wearing an old-fashioned headdress that appeared on one tomb. Christ nailed to the cross was carved between them, while stone angels bearing censers soared over His wounded body. The Blessed Virgin and St John stood on a lower level, and on the level lower still, a fell beast with two tails coiled upwards to bite at the foot of the cross…

Further on was a frieze showing the martyrdom of Thomas A Becket, venerated in Ireland as well as at home, and an unusual plaque depicting three fishes with a crown above them. "What do you think they mean?" I whispered to Ned.

"Maybe the fishing was good in the Boyne that year?" answered Ned, face serious but eyes laughing.

Tadgh's hot breath touched my ears; he had overheard us. "Why, the fishes represent the Holy Eucharist, of course, Master Edmund, and the miraculous multiplication of the loaves and fishes."

We proceeded further down the gloomy nave. Father was explaining to Father Norreys how Sir William Oldhall, his chamberlain, would assume administrative duties in his absence, with the blessing of his brother Edmund Oldhall, Bishop of Meath and Lord Chancellor of Ireland. The priest's smile faded and he appeared uncomfortable; Father had told us trust in English rule had been eroded under one of the previous Lord Lieutenants, John Talbot, who proved a harsh, quarrelsome governor.

Not wishing to appear like eavesdroppers while Father attempted to put the priest's mind at rest, Ned and I moved off to examine a free-standing carving bathed in light from the triple window set high in the wall. A line of saints stood in ornamental niches, each holding up the instrument of his martyrdom—Thomas with a raised spear, Matthias an axe, Andrew the saltire on which he was crucified, James Minor a Fuller's club, and Bartholomew a curved flaying knife...

"Do you think dying hurt them?" I whispered to Ned. "Or did God take the pain away?"

"It hurt," said Ned, gazed fixed on the saltire.

"My sons." Father returned with Norreys, flushed but slightly smiling. "It is time to go. My business here is concluded."

I glanced at Father Norreys, whose expression had grown benign again. Father whisked us away, a stout hand on each of our arms. "The priest seems happier now," ventured Ned.

"Aye, he has not only my assurances about Oldhall's conduct but the one thing all priests desire for their churches—money."

"I thought we didn't have much money..." I blurted like an idiot.

Father's fingers bit into my skinny shoulder. "Hush, Edmund; hold your tongue. I do not have great riches, like some, it is true—his Grace the King, alas, keeps forgetting what he has long owed me, but as a Duke of the blood, I must be seen to give to worthy causes. I must make a mark here in Ireland...*our* mark, the mark of the House of York, that is bound to the esteemed de Burghs. In the future, this church of St Patrick, of greatest antiquity and veneration, will bear a tribute to our family. I have given a donation to rebuild the chancel and for a large window to admit more light, the latter of which shall bear a carving, as is customary, of its patron."

"Of you!" I cried, then, remembering he had told me to be quiet, pressed my palm over my over-eager mouth.

"Yes, I shall appear in stone wearing my ducal crown—although only Christ knows what the Irish masons will make me look like! But that matters not. However, it is not just that." He pointed across the room to an elaborate piscina, almost resembling a baptismal font in size and shape. It had armorial shields upon it, but in the gloom, I could not make them out. They appeared dull and worn; the once-bright paintwork flaked away.

"See that piscina? I will have my coat of arms tooled into its surface and the work repainted in a fitting manner. So all men here shall remember York, friend to Ireland, heir to Ulster through his mother, Anne, who was born on Irish soil, and through Elizabeth de Burgh, his ancestor. Once we are done in Dublin, mayhap we can return to St Patrick's Church and see the work when it is complete."

Father ruffled my hair, not something he often did in public. "I have a great vision for you in Ireland, Edmund. Not yet, but in the future, I hope you will stand before this piscina and remember me well…"

My sire then returned to Father Norreys, telling us to wait outside. "What did he mean about having hopes for me here?" I whispered to Edward as we strode down the aisle.

He shrugged. "I'm not privy to his thoughts, brother. You'll have to wait and see. I am sure it will be worth waiting for, whatever it may be. Father has a special softness in his heart towards you, of all his children…"

"No," I blustered, cheeks hot with embarrassment "That's not true, Ned. You are his heir…"

"That does not mean you aren't his favourite."

I wanted to argue, not wanting there to be any truth in his words. Oh, I had heard it before—skulking servants sniggering in dark corners, idle tongues wagging: 'There goes little Lord Edmund; you'd almost think he was the eldest son the way his sire dotes upon him. I heard that he was given a splendid Christening in Rouen cathedral, while the one held for Master Edward was a subdued affair. One can only make one assumption from that…'

"You're wrong, Ned," I managed to sputter. "So wrong."

Edward folded his arms and walked swiftly the aisle, outpacing me and Tadgh. A dagger of sorrow pierced my heart. I did not want my brother to turn from me, nor did I want to see a shadow of pain mar his normally merry face.

Tadgh stopped me from going after him, his hand clamping on my elbow. "No, Edmund; let him go. I heard what he said; it is not a subject worth pursuing. If you do, you will still be brothers, to be sure, but you may not be friends. I would hate for that to happen—wouldn't you?"

CHAPTER FOUR

Dublin was a large, sprawling town set alongside the slow, brown waters of the River Liffey, although it was the Poddle, a tributary of the great river, that formed the moat surrounding the town walls. Dublin Castle was neither as large nor as imposing as Trim, but its walls were solid and well-maintained. King John had ordered it built over two hundred years ago, and Meiler Fitz Henry had completed the work, which stood proudly till this day—with some repairs, of course.

Mother went about the castle apartments ordering finery to improve their comfort, paying particular attention to the lying-in chamber, where she would soon retire to give birth. She was pleased with the quality of the woven rugs and colourful tapestries she received from the Weaver's Guild, although the latter products still could not compete with the fine work from Flanders.

She was less pleased, though, when she realised Dublin town was, well, *odiferous*, to say the least. I vaguely remembered Rouen, and had of late visited Coventry with Father, and there was always an aroma of animal dung, flesher's shops, and sweat from the crowds, but Dublin had a decided odour problem even more unpleasant than that. The Liffey and the Poddle were both slow and turgid, especially the latter, which formed a wide, dim pool behind the castle walls, sucking the light from the sky under its waters until it appeared a huge ebony mirror.

The smell was indescribable, rotting vegetation, stagnant water, with the scent of dead animals, emptied privies, and household rubbish thrown into the mix.

Big Ned and I ran about the shore holding our noses, while Tadgh lingered behind us, watching with amusement. "That lake gave Dublin its name—Black Pool." He nodded towards the noisome waters. "The Norsemen used to come here. An old monastery stood on the shores once, but the Vikings burnt it down—and probably burnt the monks with it."

I stared out over that flat water, gloomy even in the brightest sunlight. Unspeakable things bobbed to the surface. "There are ships out there now."

Tadgh nodded. "Ships for trade and war still come in and out, although the silt often makes it difficult for unskilled captains. The Dubliners trade with Chester in England—they send furs and fish, and Chester sends salt in return. Salt for the rich man's table." Looking suddenly melancholy, he gazed out over the pool.

"Do you think Father will allow us to go into Dublin town?" asked Ned, tugging at Tadgh's sleeve. "I'd love to go. So would Edmund. You could be our guide."

"I do not know if he would agree," said Tadgh. "He might consider it too...*unfamiliar* for such young lads." He smiled. "But there is no harm in asking. If you never ask, you never get—remember that, my lads."

It turned out that Mother, despite her condition, was more than eager to go into town to replenish what she considered an insufficient wardrobe for a lady of her status. Since she would have her entourage for protection, Father permitted us to go too.

Mother journeyed out of the castle in a chariot painted with white roses while Ned and I rode in a second, plainer carriage with Tadgh. We breathed in the scents of the bakeries on Cook Street (mercifully masking the scent of the river and pool) and trawled the length of Fishamble Street, where the fishmongers shouted and yelled as they sold the shining silver catch on trestle tables. Birds dived in, often sniping up a fish head, and the alleyways were full of hungry, expectant cats.

While Mother and her ladies visited the tailors, hatterers, and cordwainers, the rest of us, with a few armed stalwarts deployed for our safety, journeyed on to visit the Cathedral of the Holy Trinity, where a famous knight called Strongbow (another ancestor of ours, I was told) lay beneath a fine tomb, his effigy mailed and displaying his shield, prepared to give battle unto eternity. Near him lay another effigy, or rather half an effigy, of a small lad. Broken in two, it clung pitifully to the wall, features smoothed away by the touch of passing visitors over the centuries.

"They say that is Strongbow's son." Tadgh nodded towards the pitiful little tomb. "His father cut him in twain because he proved cowardly in battle."

Horrified, Ned and I stared at our tutor. He shrugged. "I didn't say it was true—but that's what the storytellers blurt into eager ears round the fire. So it is, lads, never forget—tales often grow in the telling and veer away from the truth of events."

"You mean become lies," said Ned flatly, crossing his arms.

"You could say that, although sometimes these lies are breathed through silver and become marvellous legends. More often, though, they are dragged through muck and become distorted, where a hero is made the villain and a villain the hero of the piece."

Assuming our visit was over, I strolled toward the church door with Ned on my heels, but Tadgh coughed and put his hands on his hips. "And where do you think you are going, my young lords? I am feeling a bit footsore—and thirsty."

He led us across the cathedral's polished tiles, past memorials and chapels ablaze with hundreds of candles, to reach a wooden door behind the frontage of a chantry. Shoving the door open, he revealed a lightless staircase burrowing into the underbelly of the church. A great deal of noise emerged from below; not churchly sounds like monks or choirs singing, but bellows of laughter, the buzz of conversation, even the faint wheeze of a pipe.

"What—what is down there?" Ned peered cautiously into the gloom below, as if fearing he might be viewing the entrance to hell itself.

"The crypt!" answered Tadgh, setting one booted foot upon the top step of the steps leading into the tumultuous darkness.

"A crypt!" It was my turn to feel alarmed. I imagined underground vaults full of mouldering revenants dicing, dancing, and drinking as if they were still living men.

Tadgh cast me a despairing look. "You do not think it's full of ghosts, do you?"

"Of course not!" I retorted, although I was lying. I feared very much that it was.

"Good! Then off we go, my young scholars. A new lesson for you!" exclaimed our tutor, and he began to hop merrily down the old, worn stone steps into the cathedral crypt.

I glanced nervously at Edward, uneasy and intrigued at the same time. "Should we, Ned?"

"I want to see," he replied. "Tadgh wouldn't bring us to harm. Besides, Father's soldiers are outside the cathedral, waiting. We could shout for help."

"Then it should be fine," I murmured, although I was still a little nervous.

Ned took my hand in his in a reassuring, brotherly way, and together we hared down the decrepit stairs after Master Tadgh. Behind us, the heavy door slammed shut.

We emerged into a scene of friendly chaos, blinking timidly in the light of numerous flambeaux. It seemed we were in a tavern, rather than a crypt—but yes, there were age-worn memorials there too, cobwebby effigies peeking out from behind long tables. Men filled benches, drinking from pottery beakers and roaring with mirth. Many wore the saffron yellow cloth favoured by the Irish peasantry, while others wore garb more familiar to our English eyes: long wool tunics and cloaks dyed with un-fast dyes, which gave them a patchy effect, a blur of varying colours.

Tadgh sat down on the end of a bench, and a fat man in a stained white apron waddled over, and they spoke together in the Irish tongue, incomprehensible to us, save for a few rude terms such as *póg mo thóin,* which meant to kiss bare buttocks... A few moments later, a foaming mug was thrust into Tadhg's reaching hand and rising towards his waiting lips. We were not forgotten, though—as we joined our tutor, the barkeep returned with two half-sized mugs of watery ale and a pair of hot pies, savoury sauce bubbling through vents in the golden crust. Drink and food kept us occupied while Tadgh spoke with other patrons of the tavern and imbibed a second mug of spiced ale.

"Why do you look so surprised?" Tadgh asked, as he finished his drink and wiped the foam from his moustache on his dangling sleeve. "Don't you use the churches in England as meeting places for the folk of your towns? Are they all silent, severe tombs where the sound of a footfall or a cough will bring out an angry priest to chase you away?"

"Of course not!" said Ned, startled. Churches were used for gatherings and gossiping—we'd heard that in St Paul's men even played ball and occasionally damaged the stained-glass windows, much to the chagrin of the clergy. "But we didn't expect a full-sized tavern—not with all these graves about!" He gestured to the plaques and effigies strewn about the crypt. Not far away, a drunkard was singing to himself as he dribbled liquor from his mazer onto the stony lips of a marble knight.

Tadgh tipped his bristly chin in the direction of the besotted fellow. "A tad disrespectful, but I don't think your man in the tomb is going to be complaining!"

Ned and I had to agree.

Finishing the final crumbs of our meal, we exited the underground tavern and met our small company outside. It was later than I thought, and we had to hurry to the clothiers' section to meet with Mother's entourage. I feared we might feel the full force of her wrath for our tardiness, but her maids were escorting her to her rose-painted chariot just as we rounded the corner of the street. Several servants followed her carrying chests, so I surmised her day's shopping in Dublin had gone well. Her glowing cheeks and smile confirmed my suspicion.

As she ascended the portable wooden stairs set down so that she could enter the carriage with ease, she halted, one delicate gold-buckled shoe resting on the rung, and glanced at us boys. "You have learnt much from your tutor, my sons? I spied you coming from the church. I am most pleased and hope you remembered to pray for your sire who must soon depart upon his campaign."

"Yes, Mother," answered Ned in a bold, firm tone. "We have learnt *much* about the church…"

I hid my face behind my brother's shoulder to hide my ale-induced smirk. Mother would never have approved of our activities that afternoon, and I did not want Tadgh to face censure or dismissal if she found out.

Tadgh was, by far, the best tutor we'd ever had.

Mother settled in her chariot; we ran to climb into ours. Clouds had gathered, and the first raindrops were splashing down, dappling the canopies of our carriages.

As the rain's intensity increased from shower to torrent, the horses drawing the wagons pulled out of the square and plodded up the road to the castle. Lightning crackled and the air was filled with sulphurous odours that almost overwhelmed the reek of the Liffey and the Black Pool. Urchins in rags raced before us, shrieking, covering their hair with their hands as their mothers scooped them up and bore them out of the storm. On a street corner, a group of men and women were gathering despite the weather; one played on a little drum painted with a spiral and another on a long, thin pipe. Some of the younger girls leapt and danced in wild ways that even the saltatrixes at Father's banquets could not emulate, their uncovered tresses flying in the damp. A statue appeared amongst them, carried aloft by a woman whose face was as withered as a winter apple, sinking in over her toothless mouth. Ancient was she, yet her eyes were blue and gold and alight with religious fervour. As the statue bobbed closer, we saw that it was of a female saint dressed in nunly raiment, with a gilded halo bright around her head.

The folk in the saint's procession danced closer, drawing together. Some began to sing, voices raised above the tumult in the skies:

Felix Hyberniam
Beat Lagenia
De clara Brigidam
Gignans prosapia.

De qua leticiam
Sumat ecclesia.

Presignant Brigidam
Multa prodigia
Futuram placidam
Celesti gracia.

De qua leticiam

Sumat ecclesia.

Tadgh crossed himself. "That is our St Brigid of Kildare, beloved amongst the Irish people. A holy abbess, she tended an eternal fire that still burns to this very day, attended by nineteen sisters of her order. She brought about many miracles."

"Like healing the sick?" I asked.

"Oh, yes, *that*...don't they all," said Tadgh. "But our Brigid had other skills. She once turned a wooden pillar into a living tree and hung her cloak on a sunbeam to dry. One night she held a feast for some high and mighty churchmen, but realised she didn't have enough food to feed them all. So she prayed to God and turned nettles into butter, water into beer, and tree bark into tasty bacon." He smacked his lips. "A great saint is Ireland's Brigid of Kildare. Bacon—makes my mouth water just to think of it."

The saint's procession swirled by, the drums and the pipe and the singing and chanting gradually fading into the distance.

The rain stopped once more, and a sweeping rainbow, the sky behind it black as pitch, arched over Dublin town, while the west brightened and burning light splashed over the walls and towers of monasteries and churches, wiping the stains of dirt and dung from streaming cobbles and dancing off the crenels of the castle.

Dublin was indeed a strange and wondrous place, I decided, as our carriage, several paces behind Mother's, rolled stolidly through the hazy storm-light to the castle gate, open wide and welcoming beneath the banner of the Falcon and Fetterlock. I had been sorry to leave Trim, but it seemed adventures could be found anywhere...

Father had mustered enough troops to subdue O'Byrne and his rebels. The nobles who had sworn oaths to him and King Henry at Howth and Trim swarmed into Dublin, filling its streets, hostels, and taverns with soldiers. Wains bristling with arms crowded the castle bailey while clan leaders gathered in the Great Hall to reaffirm their loyalty.

"The time has come to tame the O' Byrnes." Father had summoned me and Ned to his closet. "They have unlawfully stolen lands around Wicklow and their chief lives as a petty king. I will bring him to heel."

"Will you bring back his head?" Ned said, hopefully.

"I hope it will not come to that, my son." Father smiled wryly. "If needs be, I will use such force, but I would rather steal O'Byrne's livelihood than his life." He beckoned my brother closer to his desk, holding his gaze, his look serious. "Justice must always be tempered by mercy, if possible. Remember that, Edward." Then he glanced over at me, his countenance still earnest. "I pray you, too, take heed of my words, Edmund."

"When will you return?" I asked mournfully.

"I cannot say. I will try to get back to Dublin before Michaelmas. But I can promise nothing. Now come, kiss your Lord Father farewell."

Behind the walls of Dublin Castle, Ned and I waited with bated breath to hear news of Father's expedition into Wicklow. I spoke to all of his enterprise with pride and assurance, but in my secret hearts of hearts lingered a gnawing fear that Father would be killed fighting and our family taken hostage or worse.

"Do not worry so much, Little Ned," said Edward as we practised archery in the castle bailey. His arrow thunked into the black, a decent shot. "If such a dreadful thing happened, the King would save us, either by paying ransom or by force."

"Would he?" My arrow, caught by a stray gust of wind, went wide and clattered against the wall behind. "Maybe Edmund Beaufort would whisper in his ear that he should leave troublesome Yorks in enemy hands. Maybe Henry would agree. The Queen definitely would."

A muscle jumped in Edward's jaw. "Then it would fall to me, as Father's heir, to break free of captivity—and head to England to teach Beaufort a lesson and claim what is mine! That's after I avenged our sire, of course. Would you follow me, brother?"

"Yes!" I put another arrow to the bowstring.

"Then you must learn to shoot better!" he said with a knavish grin, as he loosed his own arrow and struck the butt straight in the black yet again.

With a yell of pretended outrage, I flung down my bow and dived on him. We fell to the ground, engaged in a mock wrestling match, smearing our fine velvet doublets with mud as we flailed and kicked…and laughed like loons.

Suddenly we heard a bell toll above the gatehouse and saw the portcullis lift. Father's herald rode in, his hair a dark banner in the wind. We both sat up, watching. "Do you think this looks right?" I whispered. "I cannot tell from his expression if he brings good news or evil!"

"Difficult to tell from here," admitted Edward, jumping to his feet and picking up his discarded bow. "There is only one way to find out! Up you get, Edmund—let's go!"

Our sire returned to Dublin as a conquering hero, just as he had when he overcame his foes in Ulster. He had harried the O'Byrnes into surrender and finally submission. In the Great Hall, full of earthy peat smoke and the warm glow of the candelabras, amid the sounds of Irish harps, psalterium, and timpan, he sat on the dais with Mother telling us of his adventures while we attended upon him like pages, refilling his cup and bringing him delicacies prepared in the kitchens—*crustades* and mushroom tarts, bread with honey butter, and Hirchones or Urchins, little pork meatballs made to look like hedgehogs, with shards of almonds for their prickles. (Ned and I had already gorged on these tasty fancies between servings.)

"I rode through Wicklow like the Devil himself," Father told our Lady Mother, as Ned and I settled onto stools at his feet, waiting for our next call. "I burnt byres, drove off cattle, and fired a wooden fort or two. I was afraid such harsh policy might rouse other clans besides the O'Byrnes, but I took the risk and it paid off. It seems the O'Byrnes' neighbours care little for their antics—they were much despised for cattle raiding and general thievery. Their lord, Oenghus the old O'Byrne, soon realised he was beaten and sued for peace. He came to my tent, doffing his cap, his eyes woeful, and swore to pay his taxes as promised. I told him that was not enough. He needed to agree to cease harrying his neighbours, and as an added punishment, I wanted his clan to wear English-style garments and learn to speak our language fluently."

"Do you truly believe these wildmen will hold to their promises?" Mother's expression betrayed her scepticism.

"I am sure they intend to, for the moment, but I imagine many of their good intentions will vanish like smoke once my troops withdraw from their lands. I will keep an eye on the O'Byrnes, though, Cecily—if they break their oath, I will come down on them like a hammer on the anvil."

Mother sipped her wine thoughtfully. "After you saw to the O'Byrnes, you sent a letter saying that you had other 'business' outside of Wicklow ere you returned home. What on earth was that about, Richard? The change of plan concerned me, and your lack of detail was ominous."

He fiddled with the rings on his slender fingers. "It was a matter that could not wait. I rode to Drogheda to receive Henry, the son and heir of Eoghan O'Neill, another important Irish leader. He swore to be my vassal years ago but stole portions of my hereditary lands instead. He never bothered to return them, despite vowing that he would. In those days, I was out of sight and out of mind in England, so he did as he pleased."

"And the meeting with this Henry O'Neill was satisfactory?"

"Satisfactory enough. Eoghan could not come himself, being infirm and aged, but Henry went to his knees and confirmed the family's allegiance to me as Earl of Ulster."

Mother's lips lifted. "What about the pilfered lands? Did they forget about them yet again?"

"I made sure they did not. The O'Neill has promised to return them, and Henry said he would provide us with a thousand men if ever needed as a token of his good will, but…you know how it is, dear wife. Talk is cheap, and men here are very good at talk—lots of it, often convoluted, no doubt to fool us plain-spoken English folk. They may seem your closest and dearest companions by the words that spill from their lips—but in truth, they are mocking you so cleverly you'll never know. But we shall see what the future holds. Once the clans realise I am unlike old Talbot and will reward them well for loyalty, relations should improve."

"I pray it is so." Mother fingered a large red stone dangling on a chain of gold around her slender throat. "Especially if we are going to live here long."

A frown touched Father's brow. He was aware Mother still longed for England. But duty was paramount and if he succeeded as Lord Lieutenant of Ireland, he would rise in esteem in the eyes of King Henry. His rising star might even eclipse the shooting one of Edmund Beaufort, who had the King's ear in all matters, or so men claimed.

"I plan to open Parliament soon," Father continued. "I will stamp hard upon the lawlessness gripping parts of this land. I will show men the mettle I am made of, both here and in England."

"You will show them exactly what it takes to rule a country." Mother's voice was soft. Her eyes were downcast, the shadow of her lashes dark on her cheeks, but I noticed her keenly watching for his response below those shadows.

He coughed and spluttered on his wine a little. Ned handed him a linen napkin to wipe the corner of his mouth. He shoved it back at Edward when finished with it; the crumpled cloth was smeared red, as if by blood, and I almost heaved. I clutched my belly, bloated from gorging on those 'hedgehogs'.

"Well, yes, Cecily," Father murmured, gaze troubled, "but we have spoken on this matter before, and agreed…"

"Yes, I know." She reached out to clasp his wrist. "Silence is safest. So I will say no more and return to playing the part of an insipid wife without a thought on any political matter in her pretty head."

"No…no, that will *never* be you, my dear wife."

Her plucked brows lifted, her eyes dancing with gentle mockery. "I won't ever be *what*, Richard? Pretty?"

He spluttered again. "Confound it, woman. You know damn well I have never so much as looked at another in all the years we've been wed. You are more than merely 'pretty'; you were not called 'The Rose' for nought."

"Ah, Richard…always so serious." Reaching out, she touched his cheek, though she almost immediately withdrew her hand—over-affection in public was considered inappropriate for such highborn figures. "I jest with you, but only in part. You have not mentioned my new Escoffion, purchased yesterday in Dublin. I was most pleased to find a haberdasher of skill, and think the piece suits me well."

She gestured upwards to her extraordinary hat, newly collected from the haberdashers. Two spreading padded horns covered by violet-hued silk and adorned with seed pearls towered on her head, giving her two hands of added height.

"It…it is certainly….*imposing*!" stammered Father, at a loss for words. "Was it expensive?"

Mother's nostrils flared slightly. "All valuable creations have cost."

Father uttered a low laugh. "As do you, my dearest—but I would have it no other way. You look every inch a Queen. Just do not let any of the Bishops see you in that hat!"

"Whyever not?" asked Mother.

"They believe such raiment is prideful, even wicked. One even wrote a rhyme about it—*God that bears the crown of thorns, Destroy the pride of women's horns.*'"

"How ridiculous," sniffed Mother. "There is piety—and I consider myself a pious woman—and then there is *stupidity*. And some of these bishops are the very worst, seeing sin where there is none and ignoring actual sins taking place beneath their long noses."

"I am glad you will not sit in the council chamber before that Bishop," said Father. "He is coming hither for Parliament, and I fear you would tell him your true opinion of his ditty!"

"I wish I *could* tell him but most likely I will be engaged in women's work at that time. The deadliest toil. Labouring."

He grew solemn. "I wish I could assist you with it and ease your pain, Cecily."

"Pain and strife for women is as God willed because of Eve's sin." Mother waved a dismissive hand. "Let us not talk of it. Edmund? Edward? I know you are both wafting around the back of my seat like flies. Make yourselves useful. Bring your sire and me some sweetmeats, will you?"

Ned and I jumped to attention, bowed to hide our blushes, and rushed off to do her bidding. Mother was imperious as a Queen—she who must be obeyed!

CHAPTER FIVE

Mother entered confinement with her ladies and Father began preparations for the opening of Parliament. Ned and I continued our studies with Tadgh and sloped around Dublin Town in our free time, eyeing the wares in the market, eating pastries purchased from the bakers, listening to the hum of the streets and the tolling of the bells of the monastic houses crammed inside the town's towered walls, St Mary's, home to the Cistercians; St Mary le Hogge, a nunnery; St Saviour's, abode of the Dominicans; St Thomas's House of the Austin Canons. There were other lesser houses, too; the Friars Minor, the Carmelites, and the Friars of the Sack.

Not having spent much time in large towns, everything seemed both overwhelming and terribly exciting. Sometimes Tadgh took us to the port at Merchant's Quay, where we could watch the ships come in. A huge crane stood there, manned by muscular porters who changed positions like guards to keep the hoisting rope moving and lift the incoming and outgoing cargo. If they failed in their duties, Tadgh told us, they would be fined and cast from their positions.

So that we would not fail in *our* duties to be good Christian sons, Tadgh also took us to St Mary's Abbey to pray for our mother's safe delivery. The imposing abbey held a life-sized wooden statue of the Virgin holding the Christ child in her arms. Ned and I prayed heartily, kneeling at her candle-ringed feet, before Tadgh spirited us away to partake of stew in the kindly monks' refectory. We were permitted to speak, but the Brethren were not—they motioned to each other with their hands instead of using words. One of Tadgh's kin was a monk here, and he escorted us to the Abbot, who agreed (as the head of the Order, he alone was permitted to use his tongue) that we could view a certain book in the library, one of the abbey's great treasures.

"Come with me, young masters," said the Abbot, his voice rusty and hoarse from using it only when receiving visitors. "I shall take you myself."

The abbey library was small and close, the air dusty and filled with the 'old book' scent. A young brother sat within, his brow furrowed in concentration as he copied an ancient manuscript with a steady hand. The Abbot brought us to a little desk and told us to wait while he found the book he wanted to show us.

"I hope you lads are lovers of books." Tadgh stood behind us, arms folded. "For that's what the treasure is, not plate, a chalice, or a crozier."

The Abbot puffed up to the desk, carrying a jewelled case in his arms so tenderly one would have thought it contained a holy relic. Lovingly, he placed it on the desk. "This is known as a 'book shrine'. It holds a great and holy manuscript over seven hundred years old."

Ned and I drew near to take a closer look. The case was made of bronze and gilded silver and studded with deep blue cabochons. On one side knotted serpents writhed; on the other were lions rampant within quatrefoils. The front bore an engraving of the Crucifixion, and around the rim was engraved: *My King had me gilded, my Lord Domnall restored me, Tomas the Craftsman fashioned this shrine.*

"Books…" Tadgh cleared his throat. "Books are a treasure beyond gold and jewels, lads. The words within can cut like swords; a man's deeds, good or ill, can be recorded, and thus he might still live a thousand years after he was placed in the tomb. A man may take a book and learn of ancient Romans and Greeks and the arts of war; he may also learn the history and lore of his own people. With books, the past may leap into the present. Are they not magnificent creations?"

Both of our parents were well-read but Mother particularly so. In her personal library she had *Les Quatre Fils Aimon*; Bokenham's *Legends of Holy Women*, *The Book of Ghostly Grace*, and many others, including numerous breviaries and collections of tales and legends. She permitted us to read some of the latter, but only sparingly.

I reached out to touch the book's case, then snatched back my hand. It felt almost sacrilegious to touch it, as if I sacrilegiously pawed a saint's shrine.

Edward's expression was thoughtful. "One day, I wager books will freely be available for all men to read, not just for those in holy orders or men of means. They won't be in jewelled cases—those will remain for the most precious book—but may be bound in cloth or leather. These lesser books could cover many subjects, not only religious or historical matters. Maybe chess, or dance…or…or dogs."

I stifled a peal of laughter. "Dogs?"

"Or maybe homunculi," countered Ned, deliberately trying to make me roar. "Or how about Blemmyas with their faces in their chests?"

The Abbot gazed indulgently at us and whisked the book shrine back to its usual place as if he feared we might start picking off the jewels. "My young charges are getting rather tired." Tadgh ushered us from the monastic library with a few quick shoves between the shoulderblades. "My thanks, Abbot. If you ever do get any books on homunculi, make sure to let Master Edward here know…"

We fared back towards Dublin Castle, stopping briefly at the tavern in the crypt of Christ Church and feeling rather wicked knowing that our parents would never approve. But we would never tell on Tadgh; he had become our friend as well as our tutor. Loyalty was everything.

The castle was very busy with great lords from all over Ireland riding in for Parliament, alongside those of mixed Irish and English descent, the former long-bearded and garishly clad, laden with gaudy gold adornments, and the latter silk and velvet-clad, mimicking the English court in their fashions, although, as Mother had noted, their styles were some years out of date. Ned and I watched them with glee, laughing at the wilder beards or haircuts, or the rusty armour that seemed near as old as Rome to our young eyes.

Two days we spent spying and prying, hunkering down in the stables to admire the Irish horses—and they were sleek beauties—or playing with the giant, shaggy wolfhounds that ranged around the bailey, scarcely controlled by sweating, red-faced squires. In the eventime, we sat outside the banquet hall, listening to the music, both English tunes, courtly and staid, and some wild Irish tunes, which filled us with a fierce madness—probably, we decided, because we had distant Irish blood ourselves, from Brian Boru himself, a mighty king who fought the Norsemen. Sometimes the passing servants would give us titbits, tutting, "Young masters have already had their supper—why, you'll both turn into piglets!" We didn't care, if God willed it, piglets we would be, and we ate greedily, our fingers greasy with sauce, sugared fancies leaving white smears around our mouths.

On the night of the second day, when the raucousness had died down and we were lying in our shared chamber, twined together like two contented pups, we were woken by a distant cry, a woman's wordless pain-filled moaning.

Breathing heavily, Ned sat bolt upright in bed. I wakened at the same time, clutching his arm. Mother's labour pains must have begun. For the last two births, we had been kept far from the birthing-chamber too young to realise all its dangers. Excitement over a new sibling became heartbreak when no babe lay in the cradle after Mother's travail was done. Our little brothers William and John had died within minutes of their birth.

Would this new babe, born in this distant Irish castle, meet the same fate? And what of Mother's own health? The day she had announced that she was with child, her ladies had grown sorrowful, murmuring, "Too many babes…Her Grace grows too old."

"What should we do, Edward?" I whispered. My brother's face was a pale moon floating in the darkness.

"Nothing we can do, little Ned." He caught my hand; his fingers were cold but oddly comforting. "We can only wait. This is…*women's business*. Even *Father* is not allowed to see what is happening."

"I do not like it." I pushed off the rumpled coverlet and stared at my scabbed knees. "Why?"

"It's the curse of Eve," he said solemnly. "That's what priests teach. Mother said it herself."

"It doesn't seem fair, Ned. Mother is pious and good. Why should she be hurt, maybe even…"

"Hush, don't say such things; it's bad luck. But, yes, it seems unfair. Here, put the cover back; it's cold."

He dragged the quilt over us, forming a tent. "I won't be able to get to sleep," I warned. "Not now."

"I understand. I won't sleep either. How about if I tell stories…."

"What stories?" I asked.

"Good ones," he laughed. "What about King Horn?"

"Who is Horn?" I frowned. "I know of King Arthur."

"Tadhg who told me the tale of Horn. It's an English story set partly in Ireland. Do you want to hear? Horn's not as famous as Arthur, but…"

"Go on, Ned." Anything that distracted me from my fearful thoughts was welcome.

"Horn was the son of King Murry, ruler of the land of Suddene. Marauding Saracens attacked Suddene and Murry was slain in battle. Young Horn, only fifteen, was captured and condemned to death but the Emir, the lord of the paynims, took pity on Horn and his companions, Athulf and Fikenhild, and set them adrift in a small boat. After being tossed about on the seas in their tiny craft, they came at last, almost despairing of life, to the shores of a fair green land called Westernesse, whose King, Ailmar, welcomed Horn and his friends and placed them under his protection. Now, the King had a beautiful daughter, Rymenhold, and she and Horn soon become betrothed."

I made a face. "I pray this story will not have *kissing*."

"I'll leave it out."

I lay in the dark listening to Big Ned's soft whisper as he recounted Horn's adventures and how Horn became King. I could no longer hear cries from below, the sound blotted out by the quilt, my brother's soothing voice, and the howl of the wind rising around the castle towers. Despite my earlier avowal to stay awake, my eyelids grew heavy.

I nestled into Ned's side, felt his arm slip sleepily over my back. I slipped into a shallow slumber and by the intermittent breaths I heard beside me, I guessed Ned, too, was asleep...

The bells for Prime had not long rung when hurried feet sounded in the corridor outside our chamber door. We woke with a start, remembering what had transpired the night before. Springing from the bed, we flung on robes against the cold of the room. Outside, it was still as dark as midnight.

The chamber door banged open, without a knock. Tadgh stood outside, hair standing up like a cockerel's plume, as if he, too, had just rolled from the comfort of his bed. "My young friends, Duke Richard wants to see you. Get some shoes on your feet ere they become solid blocks of ice and come!"

Hastily we slid on calfskin slippers and followed our tutor to Father's apartments. At the door, Tadgh set a hand on my shoulder and then Ned's, gently squeezing, attempting to reassure us. "Go on, lads," he whispered. "His Grace is waiting."

Father stood by a carved fireplace, the flames making shadows dance across his weary face. Clearly, he had spent the entire night awake. Despite that, he wore his finest clothes, a blue velvet houppelande with gold patterns of leaves and falcons, and a pair of expensive Krakow shoes.

"Edward, Edmund..." He glanced up as we entered and bowed. "I have news this morn. "Not long ago, your Lady Mother was delivered of a son. You know how your brothers Henry and John died shortly after birth..."

A gasp broke from my lips. The new child must have perished like the others! My heart sank.

"Well...this time I bring you good tidings. The babe is good-sized, whole of limb, and suckling well. My sons, you have a brother who shall be named George, after the blessed St George, patron of England."

George was a chubby baby with an angry red face and a tuft of curling hair who bawled furiously at the slightest provocation. Shortly after his birth, his Christening was held in the chapel, attended by many Irish nobles who had been summoned to Parliament. Two of them had been chosen as godfathers—James Butler, Earl of Ormond, and James FitzGerald, the Earl of Desmond. Butler was a high-coloured fellow with a son, also named James, whom the castle maid servants all made eyes at. They thought he was extremely handsome. I could not see the attraction myself—toothy, grinning and primping were the words I would have chosen—but there you have it. Girls see things differently.

My sister, Bessie, became insufferable after George's birth, kissing and cuddling him whenever she was permitted, even when he screamed with what sounded like pure rage. She would not let Ned and me come close, insisting that we would drop him on his pate like clumsy oafs. In reality, she was far more likely to cause such a tragic accident because she was younger and weaker, but the nursemaids indulged her whims while hovering like mother hens in case she should drop our new brother to his doom. Scowling, we were ushered from the baby's nursery and told to go and play with our 'toys'—an insult, for we were both surely out of childhood and well on our way to becoming men. Grumbling, we found the courtyard and bashed seven bells out of each other with wooden practice swords to show our prowess to any passers-by. No one did pass, so eventually we sought the kitchens and begged cook for some sweet tarts—and so was the rest of our day spent, eating and complaining about our sister and girls in general.

Once Parliament was over and the Irish nobles departed, marching from Dublin Castle in an array of gaudy banners, Father informed us that we too would leave once Mother was churched. We would winter in Trim, where Father thought the air was less contaminated, which would prove healthier for us all, especially baby George. So there was hasty packing and wains sent forth, and all the chaos that such a move entailed. I hated it, for we had to continue our lessons and the castle was in such an uproar it was difficult to concentrate.

Finally, the churching was done and the wagons were all packed, groaning under the weight of beds, tapestries, drapes, and household members. We set off across a wintry landscape, cloaked by freezing fog and pungent peat-smoke. First, there was a diversion, a trip to a holy well at Mulhuddart, where Mother desired to give thanks for George's safe delivery. Tadgh told us the village's name meant 'Mound of the Milking,' and that it had been a sacred place even in heathen times. Now the Ladyswell was a pilgrimage site under the protection of King Henry, who founded the Guild of the Blessed Virgin Mary to guard the well and see to its upkeep.

When we arrived, we found the well a popular place as well as a holy one. Cloak-shrouded figures huddled in the fog, praying, some rocking back and forth, arms in the air as if entranced.

Tadgh nodded towards several toothless old women on the path, leaning on each other for support, their grey hair hanging in long damp tangles. "They come for the rheumy pain in their bones. The waters are said to ease the pain."

Mother climbed carefully from her curtained litter, attended by her ladies, who helped her out and held her arms. Her face was drawn; she was still suffering pain after George's birth. On tottering but regal feet, she approached the holy well. The Guild members who tended Ladyswell had received advance warning of her visit and stood in a respectful semi-circle with bowed heads.

Ladyswell was surrounded by a dark grove, shielding it from the eyes of outsiders. This gave it an eerie, haunted look—since I had come to Ireland, I had learnt that almost every tree, hill, river or lake held some kind of spirit or elf. Father told me I was foolish to mull on such creatures, for not only were they unwholesome, they did not exist—but still I wondered.

Mother entered the shadowy trees, their crowns capped with mist. A nurse followed behind, holding George who was bawling as usual. The rest of us remained outside while Mother prayed to the Virgin, and her ladies placed compresses dipped in the sacred water on her skin.

By the time her ablutions were over, Big Ned and I were both shivering, the coldness of the ground reaching up our legs through the soles of our shoes and making our knees ache.

At least George had fallen silent. I offered my own little prayer to the Virgin for that small comfort.

It was a season of shadow, storms, and snow. Ned and I raced around Trim castle, play-fighting in our warm woollen cloaks, or venturing into the town market with Tadgh. With envious eyes, we watched boys skate on the frozen river; we were not permitted, of course. Edward begged Tadgh to let us try skating just once, that we'd come to no harm, that Father would never know—but this time our tutor put down his foot and refused.

"I've let you two get away with more than I should have," he said, his usual grin absent. "If it became known I'd let you risk injury or worse…" He glanced over his shoulder at the massive corner turrets of the castle keep. Birds sailed above them, screeching. "Your sire would have my head off in a trice and up there on a spike for those gulls to eat!"

"No, he would not," I insisted, but flushed, for I had spoken a lie. If under Tadgh's watch Ned and I were injured or worse, I had no doubt a harsh punishment would be forthcoming.

So, with sorrow, skating was thrust to the back of our minds, and instead we engaged in the indoor pastimes—marbles and Hoodman's Blind, draughts and chess. Ned usually won at chess as he was an excellent strategist, but I improved daily if I concentrated hard. When not amused by games, we pored over the pages of a huge bestiary, filled with illustrations of exotic beasts, including the hairy, four-footed Behemoth, an Elephant with a tower filled with archers on its back, a single-horned Monocerus, and a Sea-Monk, a fish that resembled a tonsured monk. We hoped that, in kinder times, we might one day see *real* beasts at the Tower of London, where the King kept a number of animals given as gifts by foreign rulers. Sadly, the menagerie was somewhat depleted at present. The lions, most noble of the Tower's bestial occupants, had died off and their keeper, one William Kerby, relieved of his position. Still, monkeys, baboons and a striped horse from afar were still worth a visit.

Close confined during the inclement weather—it snowed or rained every day, and once we woke to find trees, walls, fields, coated with ice—Ned and I noticed that Father seemed less content than when he had his first victory in Ulster.

"I wonder what's wrong." I whispered as we watched Father stride through the smoky Great Hall, not even noticing his two eldest sons were present. His brow was furrowed beneath his velvet chaperon.

"You won't tell anyone?"

"Of course not—I am not a tittle-tattle!" I was indignant.

"Money worries, Little Ned. Father has still received no wages from King Henry. He needs to raise levies but the law forbids it. Yet there's no other way to keep the peace; Father fears some of the clans thirst for war despite fair words lauding peace in parliament."

"How did you find all this out?"

He shrugged, his cheeks pinking a little.

"Earwigger!" I elbowed him in the ribs. "You were listening at his chamber door!"

"Someone had to do it," Ned argued. "I'm not some little child from whom secrets must be kept."

"Yes, you are, Edward," I said with unaccustomed viciousness, for it seemed to me that he implied *I* was but a child while he was not. "At least in our sire's eyes. Do you sit in Parliament with him? Ride out to war? No, you're only a boy, even as I."

Edward looked furious, and I was instantly sorry and even a little afraid, for at times Ned had an awful temper, as did many who bore Plantagenet blood. I was less inclined to wrath than my brother, who bubbled over like a simmering cauldron and quickly cooled when heat was no longer applied. Instead, I held my anger behind a forced smile until at last I could not endure and answered my tormentors with my fists.

Ned stepped back, sheepish. "You're right; I was being foolish. I am still deemed a child in men's eyes. Sometimes I forget, because I am so tall, that I am not the age I appear. Forgive me, Edmund, if I offended you. You are not only my brother; you are my dearest friend." He clapped me on the arm. "In any case, I fear all is not well. Who knows, we may end up returning to England."

I gasped. I had grown to enjoy Ireland. Yet I understood that the House of York was becoming sidelined in our native country. We weren't in Ireland as a merchant family seeking its fortunes, nor were we merely wealthy landowners eager to make a mark upon the land. Our blood was royal, and the King had sent us abroad to get us out of the way. I hated to admit it, but it almost felt as if Father had been exiled, although that word was never spoken.

Winter dragged on, and Father's frowns grew darker and Mother distant and perturbed. Edward and I threw ourselves into games of war suitable for lads our age—just in case we should be needed in some kind of intrigue. Tadgh was nervous and out-of-sorts too, unlike the happy-go-lucky fellow we'd first met; he sat about, preoccupied, and had the habit of chewing on his nails.

And then it happened.

No, not war with the Irish, but something far, far worse.

Our brother George was stolen.

CHAPTER SIX

The day started ordinarily enough. Mass, Latin, history lessons, mathematics lessons, a quick respite with the hawks out in the mews under Tadgh's watchful eye. We had been on our way to our bedchamber to get heavier cloaks since the northerly wind was raking under our doublets with claws sharper than the birds of prey—and that's when we heard screams from the direction of the nursery. A woman's scream, followed by a gaggle of mixed voices male and the sound of howling and sobbing.

Filled with trepidation, I glanced at Ned. What if our healthy, angry, red-cheeked baby brother had taken ill, as babes often did, and…

"Let's see what's happened!" Edward gave me a shove toward the nearest door. "Hurry!"

We raced through the castle corridors, ignoring Tadgh, who appeared in an archway and shouted for us to stop. Today, our family's safety was more important than obedience. Reaching the nursery, we piled in, almost tripping each other in our haste, and beheld a scene of chaos.

George's wetnurse was screeching and tearing her hair. Another maid was trying to comfort her. Mother and her ladies were there too—Mother looked angry rather than upset, which gave me hope that George was unharmed. Relief rushed through me.

But then I glanced towards the cradle.

George was not in it.

Once again, fear gripped me.

"Mother, where is the baby?" Ned pushed his way past the wetnurse, pointing to the empty cradle.

Mother folded her arms. "It seems that he has been taken."

"Taken?"

"Yes, this silly goose of a wetnurse…" She glared venomously at the wailing woman, who was rocking back and forth as if she'd lost her wits. "She befriended one of the scullery maids and foolishly invited her up here—a new girl, a simpleton who talks more than she works. She left the babe alone with this chit to use the privy—and when she returned, George was gone. I cannot imagine the kitchen wench means him harm, for she is stupid, not malicious, but he must be found—and returned—as soon as possible."

I thought Mother exceptionally calm under the circumstances, but she was an exceptional woman—as my father and others often said.

Ned tugged on my sleeve. "Edmund, we must begin a search! Let us go before...before Mother realises and forbids it!"

Running out of the nursery, we thundered down the stairs into the bailey. Search parties were being mustered; armed men filled the courtyard, some mounted, most on foot. Dog-handlers streamed from the kennels, their charges baying and dragging against their leashes in excitement.

Hidden amidst all the commotion, Ned and I slipped through the milling crowd and out the main gate, where an alarum bell clanged a stony warning. The streets beyond were unusually bare of townsfolk, and those we did see stared towards the castle with fear or suspicion. They hurried away as we passed, casting us looks dark and unfriendly, as if, suddenly, we were not the sons of a great lord whose heritage made him closer to them than any English prince before him—but sons of an enemy oppressor who even now sought to assail them...

Ignoring the growing fear and anger in the town, we ran down the main street towards the river. Ice mud splashed our calves and ruined our newly-laundered hose. A growling dog sprang at us from an alleyway—we yelled at the beast in unison and it slinked away.

"Where are we going?" I panted, trying to keep up with Edward's longer, swifter strides.

"The new servant Mother mentioned—I saw her in the kitchen with Cook," he flung over his shoulder. "She gave me a fritter. Her name sounds something like New-la and she said she lives with her mother near the Leper Hospital. So not far! Hurry!"

We rushed onwards and soon the solemn, grey Hospital of Mary Magdalen loomed into view, its leprous inmates mercifully hidden behind stout walls.

We darted past, fearful of noseless men and women with faces covered in wrappings, and continued towards a row of ramshackle huts nearby; this was Trim's poorest area because of its closeness to God's afflicted. The cottages here were low-roofed and flimsy, with old, greening reed rooves. Their gardens were laid bare, full of churned mud, without any winter vegetables. At the end of the row stood the saddest hovel of all, and from its ramshackle door wafted the familiar howls of an angry baby.

Edward and I cautiously approached the hut. It was a mean place, no doubt about it, with holes in the thatch and the walls buckling in the damp. A single huge sow came grunting out of a pen and rooted amidst shite in the yard.

I was revolted but also felt a guilty pang, for none of my kin had ever dwelt in such poverty. The priests said it was as God decreed: the rich men in their castles and the poor tilling the fields, waiting for the day when 'the meek shall inherit the earth'. It might be how the Almighty ordained it, but it hardly seemed *fair*...

Nevertheless, I hardened my heart and put on a scowling, ferocious face—these people, whatever their intentions, had stolen my *brother*. The gate was roped shut, so I clambered over the fence, Ned following, and together we stormed the door, flinging it open with a crash.

As we burst into the cramped hovel, several women began to shriek and flap around like chickens who had lost their heads to the poulterer's knife. They looked much the same, bony and dirt-smudged, wearing clothes more like sacking than dresses. I recognised the kitchen wench, a small girl with a flat face and tangled reddish-yellow hair. She possessed few teeth and what remained jutted from her mouth. In her arms she held George, howling, his face crimson. His screams were joined by those of another babe rolling in a crude cradle.

The oldest woman in the house, who could have been any age from thirty to one hundred, cried out when she saw our fine clothes and sank to her knees on the floor. "You've come from the castle, haven't ye? The Lordship's lads, lookin' for the youngest babby. God have mercy, I swear we meant the wee creature no ill. Nuala—my daughter—" She glared ferociously at our kitchen maid who began to weep. "She's never been right since she was small. Fell on her head as a babe she did, and has given us nought but grief ever since! When she was taken on at the castle, we thought she'd be under the cook's eye and smarten up, but…but she's ruined it, ruined it all!"

"I didn't mean to, mam!" gasped the simple girl, Nuala. "I only wanted to show you his Lordship's babby. Thought he might bring us good luck, I did…"

"Oh, you stupid, stupid *amadan*," cried Nuala's mother, and clambering to her feet, she grabbed Nuala's ear and twisted it viciously. "Good luck, indeed. We'll be lucky if we don't all end up with nooses round our necks, dangling from gibbets in the market square while the crows peck out our eyes."

Niamh began to wail like that fabled creature from Irish legend, the *Bean-Sidhe*, whose keening betokened death. Even so, her noise could not outstrip that made by George, whose roaring grew ever louder, if such a thing was possible from such a small infant.

"Just give us the baby," said Edward, exasperated. "We don't want to see you hurt, no matter how stupid you've been. Just give us our brother."

The older woman delayed no longer, ripping George from her daughter's spindly arms and thrusting him at me as if he were a sack of cabbages. I clutched him awkwardly as he wriggled and bawled, terrified I might drop him on his head and make him addle-pated like the befuddled Nuala.

"You'll be telling your father, won't you?" Nuala's mother slouched in despair, making her look even more aged. "You lads won't hurt us, but he will…"

Edward glanced at me; I shrugged almost imperceptibly. I had no idea of Father's reaction to Nuala's folly, even though George seemed perfectly well, if somewhat grubby, and his disappearance had no sinister motives.

"I will speak with the Duke," Ned said slowly. "I'll tell him that you realise that you committed a great wrong and there was no malice in your actions."

"I suppose that is the best that can be done," said the older woman, her rheumy eyes watering. She grabbed Nuala, shaking her. "Look what you've caused, my girl. Trouble, pure trouble…"

Edward and I fled the hovel, and I wrapped George in my cloak against the icy wind, uncaring that I was chilled myself. He needed protection far more than I. Mercifully, he began to quieten, his screams becoming a dull grizzling, as we trudged back along the muddy street to Trim Castle.

As we neared the castle walls, we spotted one of the search parties with Father leading it on horseback, his face taut with worry. We charged towards him, and it made my heart leap to see him go from despairing to joyous as he realised we had George.

Flinging himself from his mount, almost tripping in haste, he snatched the baby from us, eliciting another furious screech from George's gummy mouth. "He...he's alive!" he said to no one in particular, his voice heavy with relief—and wonder.

Father summoned his Master of the Wardrobe, who had ridden out of the castle with him. "You have six children, don't you, Ralph? Well, here, have one of mine." He shoved George into the surprised man's arms. "The Marshal will escort you to the Duchess without delay."

"Yes, my Lord Duke," the man mumbled, and he hurried off with the Marshal in the direction of the gatehouse.

"Now..." Father still looked pale and strained, his assuaged fear for his youngest son transforming into anger, "you two will lead me to the miscreant who dared abduct a son of York."

Ned took a deep breath. "Lord Father, I must say something..."

Father frowned, impatient. "What, Ned? Spit it out. We haven't all day. I want this serious matter dealt with."

"It was a foolish prank, no more," said Edward. "The girl from the kitchen, Nuala; she meant no harm. She was proud of working at the castle. She only wanted to show George to her family."

"So she *stole* him. Stole the child of a Duke of the blood royal." Incredulous, Father gaped at Edward. "You defend her, Edward? You wish for her to be pardoned for this heinous act?"

"She does not know right from wrong, Father. Her mind is a child's. She was terrified when she realised what repercussions could come."

"Yes," I butted in. "She is poor, Father. I think the punishment of her life is great enough."

"Oh, do you?" Father fixed me with a stern stare—but hints of a smile flickered at the corners of his mouth. "Quite the little statesman, are you not Edmund, despite your size. But I fear you do not realise the seriousness of this crime."

"Did Christ not say, 'Blessed are the merciful, for they shall receive mercy'?" Ned interjected.

Father swung toward my brother, which gladdened me for his scrutiny made me uncomfortable. "So, one son is a statesman and judge already, and the other a theologian," he said dryly. "At least I know your tutor has been teaching you well—and not just dragging you into the tavern in the crypt of Christchurch. Yes, I know all about that…"

Ned cast me a nervous glance, and my throat tightened with fear at what might come next.

Father placed his hands on his hips, steely-eyed and very threatening, the epitome of an arrogant and angry prince. "Lord Father," Ned's words tumbled out in a rush, "do not punish Tadgh—one could say our journey to the tavern showed us the evils and temptations all men face and was…*educational*!"

Our sire's eyes widened in surprise, and a moment later he burst into laughter. "Yes, I am sure it was. Very educational indeed. Oh, fear not, I will not be overly harsh on Tadgh. He has made you feel at home, and his heart is good even if his methods of teaching are…unusual. But tell me—what punishment do you think fitting for the ones who stole and hid your baby brother?"

"Y-you would make us pass judgment on those poor folk?" Ned gulped.

Father folded his arms. "That might be appropriate. After all, you met them and I have not. You seem to have sympathy for them and believe they are not malevolent. The girl's a simpleton, I can vouch for that, for I met the poor creature during her employment. There is only one thing I say to you—*some* kind of punishment must be given. Abduction is a hideous crime. It cannot be ignored."

Ned looked uncomfortable, staring anywhere but our sire's face. I danced nervously around like a skittish colt, despite my best efforts to stay still. What was Father expecting? Flogging, a cut-off hand as for a poacher? The family driven out of Trim to fend for themselves in the wilds? Long imprisonment in a dungeon?

It was Ned who finally spoke, his words rushing out in a tumble. "Since there was no true ill-intent, the punishment should be light for the reasons Edmund mentioned. These folk are already bowed with suffering. But, malicious or not, they cannot be trusted after what happened, although it appears the girl Nuala acted alone. Her mother was wrathful and will punish her harshly, I am sure. I suggest she faces no imprisonment—but that she loses her position in the castle."

"But Ned, her family will starve!" I swung around, clutching his arm.

Ned yanked out of my grip. "I am not saying she should be banished from Trim…just from access to our family. Put her to work in the herb gardens, weeding and planting. She may fare better with her hands in the good earth where there will be no distractions or temptations. She can still earn money to support her family, but some of her wages can be docked as a fine for…for a set time. A year and a day."

Father was nodding and rubbing his chin thoughtfully. His red-hot anger had died; come and gone, like lightning from a clear sky.

"Edmund—do you agree with Edward's judgement?"

"I do, my lord Father!" I piped. "Maybe Nuala could have some tutoring to…to keep her on the straight and narrow. I'd offer to teach her letters myself and guide her…"

"Tutoring? It's supposed to be a punishment, Edmund, not a reward."

"I suspect she might see it as a punishment, though," I said.

Father roared with mirth then, his whole demeanour changing. "You have won, my boys," he said, pulling us both into a quick hug—an affectionate gesture that was rare in public. It struck home how afraid he must have been for George, and that unnerved me, for I always thought of him as fearless.

"You accept my terms for Nuala's punishment?" Ned asked, surprised.

"I do. Now let us go back to the castle as swift as we may. I must attend to your Lady Mother's wellbeing—and I also need a good-sized goblet of wine! Or maybe two!"

Neither Ned nor I saw Nuala again, but not because of George's brief abduction. Governing grew increasingly difficult for Father; he continued to receive no payments from the King, and his coffers were barer than ever. Trouble in Ireland was also brewing as he had foreseen.

He told Mother that he wanted to write to her brother, Richard, Earl of Salisbury, asking him to witness that he had received no payments from King Henry and that his enemy, MacGeoghegan, had burnt a town, killing women and children alike.

Ned and I, lurking in the hall after our lessons, overheard this conversation and eyed each other in concern. "There's going to be fighting again," Ned whispered. "Just as suspected. I can feel the tension in the air—can't you? Why is King Henry letting this happen? Why does he not pay Father and send supplies? Fie on him, the useless old loon."

"Edward!" Our mother's steeple-hatted shadow loomed over us as the door to Father's solar opened. "Hold your tongue! I will not countenance such talk in this household."

"You heard?" Edward gasped awkwardly.

Her lips pursed. "We women know all about listening at doors, for sometimes it is the only way the curious can obtain the gossip of the day. But it is unseemly for a Duke's sons to hover in the shadows like snoops, and wilfully spew evil about our sovereign lord. Come into the light—your sire has bidden you come forth."

Shamefaced, we trundled into the solar under her steely gaze. Father was seated at a table with a quill in his grip, his usual scribe nowhere in sight. The quill surprised us as it meant he was writing to our uncle in his own hand, impressing upon him the seriousness of his plight.

"Good eventide, boys," he said calmly, as if Ned and I had done nothing wrong. It made us both squirm more than shouting would have done. We stood upright, manfully waiting for some kind of discipline, whether it was with a rod or the deprivation of games and merry pursuits.

But punishment did not come. Father laid down his quill and approached us, clapping us on the shoulders as if we were fellow comrades in arms, not two boys still too young to wield a real sword.

Mother stood arms folded over her green and gold brocade. "They were caught in the hallway, snooping—and speaking disrespectfully too."

"Disrespect? For whom?"

"The King!" Mother answered, voice sharp.

"Eavesdropping does not become a duke's sons." Father's tone was still, mercifully, mild. "And having a loose, foolish tongue is worse. You've been warned before. Swear you won't behave so again."

"We swear!" we cried, almost in unison.

"If you are troubled, come speak to me. You are old enough now that I might talk to you on serious matters. You are no longer small children fit only for the nursery—you are growing into young men and will soon be treated as such."

We struggled to stand up straight as possible, endeavouring to look knightly and mature. Princes not poltroons...

"Therefore, I will tell you of events. You already are aware my finances are in dire shape, since the King has not paid what is owed, despite many reminders." The corner of his mouth lifted in a bitter half-smile. "But do not get me wrong, my sons; the King is *not* to blame. He suffers from bad guidance given by evil men, and I fear the Queen advises him poorly too, for she is much smitten with Edmund Beaufort..." Another bitter, knowing smile. "Despite the chaos and losses Beaufort caused in France, Henry loves him well."

"I heard Edmund Beaufort was her paramour!" I exclaimed.

"Edmund!" Mother reddened. "What did your sire just tell you? It is dangerous to mouth scurrilous gossip of *that* nature. Dangerous for your entire family."

I flushed to the roots of my hair. Edward side-eyed me and mouthed *I bet it is true*.

Father sighed and returned to his desk, scattered with papers. "Can we leave off with slanders fit only for fishwives? Let me tell you of things of greater importance." He sat, his stance weary. "I am going to war. My old 'friend', MacGeoghegan, is causing trouble in Meath—as I am sure you have already heard. So, my purse being empty, I am informing your Uncle Salisbury of my troubles—I want him to know I would sooner lie in my grave than have any man think Ireland was lost by my negligence."

Ned and I both erupted into fearful outcries at hearing our father speaking of death in such an impassioned way.

He shushed us with a motion of his hand. "Our time here in Ireland may be coming to a close. Your uncle will, I have no doubt, Uncle speak for me at court, and vouch for my fidelity. But it may still come that we are to return to England soon, but, by God, I will not let Ireland pass easily from my hands."

Ned and I were silent. We had grown used to Trim and even had some freedoms there not permitted at home in England. Heads bowed, we both stared at our feet, at a loss for words—and worried too, for even though we realised Father had not been paid for his duties, we had been too naïve to understand how money-poor our family truly was, despite our high status.

"Has your inquisitiveness been sated?" Mother ushered us from the chamber as Father returned to his writing.

Ned and I nodded, feeling. Worry gnawed at my heart too as I thought of other possible realities, none of them good. What if Father's soldiers deserted because of late pay? What if he was overwhelmed by the wild men who served this MacGeoghegan; what if he were…

I could not bear the thought of any of it. Mumbling an excuse to Ned, I fled to the castle chapel, where I lit a candle with shaking hands and sat in silent prayer for at least an hour, while outside I heard the tromp of men and beasts in the bailey and the lonesome shrill of an Irish flute.

Change was coming. I felt it in every fibre of my being.

Father rode out to meet his opponent, the fractious MacGeoghegan, with the King's royal standard raised, its Leopards and Lilies snapping in the breeze.

I watched from the walls of Trim Castle. Confused, I called to Edward, "Ned, when Father went to war before, he marched under his banner of the Black Dragon. Why is he flying King Henry's now? The King is not coming to Ireland, is he?"

Ned leaned between two sturdy crenels, watching the soldiers vanish into the far distance. "I doubt that—but I think I understand why Father is doing it. When we first came here, he rode out as an Irish lord, a descendant of the de Burghs and the O'Briens. Now he is impressing upon MacGeoghegan that it is the King of England he will have to deal with if he does not cease hostilities."

"Do you think Henry would come to fight if we needed his help?"

Edward stepped back from the crenelations, the pallid sunlight picking up red-gold strands in his thick brown hair. His countenance suddenly looked older, troubled… and filled with an adult's woes.

"No," he said. "I do not."

Father returned to Trim haggard and downcast. MacGeoghegan's army had vastly outnumbered his, and fearing a bloodbath, he had sued for peace at once. MacGeoghegan's son, leading the enemy soldiers, had agreed to parlay but pressed a hard bargain. He wrung a promise out of Father that he would pardon any man who had rebelled against him in return for an end to MacGeoghegan's raiding.

Edward and I were eager to ask Father what had transpired. After all, he had recently told us he would consider taking us into his confidence. However, we were not permitted to see him at all.

Mother stepped into our path as we pleaded with Father's unrelenting chamberlain outside the solar door. "No," she said firmly, "your sire is holding important meetings in the wake of these unfortunate events. He will see you when he has time. Off to chapel with you both, to pray that God will grant wisdom to your Lord Father and guide his hand in whatever happens next. And when you are done—off to your chambers. Your supper shall be sent to you; no one will eat in the hall tonight."

Ned and I skulked off, frowning and irritated. After we had finished our prayers and eaten our supper of pottage and broth, we stayed up late, playing chess in the window embrasure. It was a fine, calm night—no rain, for once!—and a round, ruddy moon hung in the sky, its light shimmering off the river below the castle walls.

Edward beat me soundly in our game, but he seemed moody and morose. He stared out the window, hands clenched in frustration.

"What is it, Ned?" I retreated to the bed, leaping on it and hauling the covers over my legs. "You're bothered about something."

"No, I'm not." He moved the green and white marble chessboard aside and stacked up the chess pieces carefully; they were a gift from Father and carved from jet and polished to a sheen.

"Yes, you are."

"No, I'm *not*." A little tic twitched under his right eye.

Was he angry with me?

"Edward?" I gulped in dismay. "If I have offended you in some way, I am sorry! I don't know what I've done!"

He flung himself on the bed' putting his hands over his face for a second. "I'm not myself tonight. Edmund. You know how a messenger from England arrived a day before Father returned from meeting MacGeoghegan's forces? Well, I have a feeling, a *very* strong feeling, that soon we will be going home. Father even said it was a possibility a few weeks back, remember?"

"Yes, I remember. Why are you upset? It was never expected we should cut off all ties with England. There was no guarantee we would stay here forever. Father is a great magnate. It makes sense that he travels on both sides of the Irish Sea."

Edward sighed and flopped onto his belly, laying his head on his arms. "If what I believe is true, little Ned, I fear we will leave Ireland under a cloud. And our homecoming in England may not be a pleasant one."

CHAPTER SEVEN

As late August heat parched the ground and the Boyne ran low, leaving exposed mudflats, the York family left Trim Castle for the last time. Disturbances in England were now of such concern Father could not avoid them by dwelling over the sea. In fact, now he was champing at the bit to get home, for he found out his reputation was being sorely besmirched in his absence, in a way far worse than anything previous. A Kentishman called Jack Cade, angered by high taxation and English losses in France, had brought an army to Blackheath. Defensive ditches were dug and wooden stakes thrown up. When King Henry failed to treat, Cade led his rebels across London Bridge, firing shops and pillaging. Uprisings were common in every king's reign, and normally this would have been just one more. But Cade did more than protest against Henry's policies. He called himself a 'Mortimer' and wore Father's insignia of the Falcon and Fetterlock on his badge.

Father was furious to hear this, but also deeply concerned, for it put suspicion on his motives. He wrote to the King, but with the kind of counsel Old Harry was keeping, all wondered if the King would even read his letter. The gate had been thrown open; seeds of doubt had been sown.

Two days after leaving Trim, we reached Dublin with our baggage train. Tadgh rode with us, his mood low and sorrowful. Down on the quay, Edward and I said our last farewells to our Irish tutor. We started our goodbyes with the formality of princes, wishing to show decorum and little emotion, as would be expected of us as adults, but ended up hugging Tadgh and blinking back tears, while he mussed our hair and made comforting sounds.

"You be dutiful to your Lord Father," he said, "and may the devil fly off with all your worries. *Slán agus beannacht,* my young friends." And then, before we could say more, he walked briskly away and vanished into the crowds thronging the quay.

Crossing by barge to a waiting cog, our family set sail for England shortly before sunset. The sky was red and gold, striped with a long, low clouds that flew out like the burning banners of war. Behind us Dublin Town grew empurpled with shadows, and then, as the light diminished, it turned black, its spires and towers in stark silhouette against the plum-hued glow lingering in the western sky. Seabirds shrilled, flapping around the riggings, and the air was over-rich with the scent of salt, fish, and the wafting fragrance of the city.

The prow turned as the ship's Master and the Boatswain shouted orders to the crew, and before we knew it, we were speeding into the descending night. A mist bank rose like a spectral wall at the end of the harbour, reminding me of Tadgh's tales of the entrance to the Irish otherworld, unexpectedly reached by hapless mortals. The vapours rolled over the cog, smelling even more strongly of the sea, and then the ship breached it and we sailed on a starless sea, ploughing foam-capped waves that slapped the sides of the boat with huge booms.

Bessie, still standing on the main deck, began to look sick. "It is time to go into the cabin," said Nursemaid Em sternly, taking our sister's hand.

"Must we go too?" groaned Edward.

"Yes, Master Edward," frowned Em. "The Duchess has expressly ordered that *all* of you are safely tucked up in your sleeping quarters. You don't want me to summon Mistress Caux, do you, and tell her of your stubbornness? No more arguments. Come with me before you get blown over the rail."

Glumly we followed Em to our cabin. Mother and Father were already there, hidden behind a painted screen. We children had pallets and a lantern to give us light if we needed to use the piss-pot. George was grizzling in the arms of his wetnurse. I hoped I would not get sick from the rocking of the boat and disgrace myself. Like Bessie, I had begun to get a little queasy; the pie I'd eaten earlier lay heavy in my belly.

I looked to my saviour—Ned. He leaned back against a scatter of cushions, stretching out his legs. He glanced from Bessie and Meg to me. "So...who would like to hear the tale of 'Jonah and the Whale'?'

The trip across the Celtic Sea was uneventful until we came within sight of land. "Ship ahoy!" one of the sailors shouted, pointing toward the coastline.

A small cog was sailing towards us at rapid speed. From its mast fluttered the insignia of Beaumaris town, a castle resting on a ship, with a shield bearing the Three Lions on the left.

Watching the vessel approach from on deck, Father looked grim, his arms folded defensively over his chest. "Are they here to arrest us?" Ned asked, his voice a dry croak.

"I know not their intent." Father raised a hand to shield his eyes against the brightness of the afternoon sky as the ship turned, rolling on the shallow waves. "I have no doubt that their presence means trouble—but at least it is poorly manned and I see no bows or other weapons."

"Why would they arrest us?" I glanced plaintively at Father, my heart thumping.

"Do not worry, Edmund. You will not be harmed. It is me they wish to…speak to. I am sure some *agreement* can be reached."

Our ship slowed, faltering in its course; the other cog had drawn close now, close enough to see a stout man in a huge chaperon that resembled a crushed strawberry standing in the prow. A golden chain glinted around his neck.

"It's Thomas Norris from Beaumaris Castle," I said, recognising him.

I was confused; the captain of Beaumaris had seemed a congenial fellow when my family had stayed at the castle for a night before proceeding on to Ireland.

Today, Norris looked anything but friendly, and was accompanied by several other officials, their Lancastrian S collars gleaming in the wan sunlight. Close, I could see there *were* armed men on board, but only a handful and their swords were sheathed.

Drawing close to our ship, Thomas Norris shouted to the ship's Master, "I seek to board this vessel in the name of his Grace, King Henry. I bear a message of great import for Richard, Duke of York."

The Master glanced uneasily at Father, who gave a slight nod. "Let them board. I will hear what they have to say."

A rowboat was sent out, and Norris and his companions were ferried to our cog. As they climbed on board, their stony expressions were obvious, their mannerisms abrupt. Norris had changed utterly from our first meeting, his demeanour now vaguely threatening.

Standing with legs apart in a belligerent stance, he began to speak. "My Lord of York, I am here to inform you that permission for you to put ashore at Beaumaris has been rescinded."

Father took a step in Norris' direction, only halting when he saw his follower's hands drop to their sword hilts. "Thomas! What madness is this? You treated me and my family with kindness when last we met. Jesu, man, we broke bread together."

Thomas Norris's fleshy visage began to grow pink. "Much has changed since your departure, your Grace."

"So it would seem." Father's tone grew cool. "But such change was not of my making. Surely you know that, Thomas?"

Norris's countenance was now almost as red as his chaperon. "I have my orders, my Lord Duke."

"From whom?"

Thomas Norris tilted up his fleshy chin, defiant. "From none other than William Say, usher of the King's chamber."

Father's eyes grew grey and cold as the surrounding sea. "William Say. And for what reason has this preposterous order been given? Did he tell you?"

Norris cleared his throat, a guttural rasp that set his chins wobbling. "He believes that you have returned from Ireland without permission, perhaps with mischief on your mind."

"Mischief? Do not play with words, man. What do you mean by 'mischief'?"

"This man Cade, who has recently caused much trouble in London. He called himself Mortimer."

"You think this miscreant is my creature because of the name he assumed?" Father slashed the air with his hand in frustration. "Madness! Madness...and slander. Sirrah, it seems to me that in a roundabout way, you are calling me a traitor."

"I call you nought, York. I am only obeying orders," mumbled Norris. He reached to his belt, yanked out a rolled parchment. "Here...this is from Lord Say as you will see by the seal."

Father snatched the parchment, examining the seal for a brief second before breaking it open. His eyes slid down what was written inside. "So...not only am I forbidden to land at Beaumaris, I cannot take aboard food or drink to refresh any of my company. Not even the horses are spared from this restriction."

"Correct, my Lord Duke," said Norris. "Now, since you have seen and accepted that this order from William Say is genuine, I trust you will abide by its terms."

Father stared stonily at the short, hefty man as an uncomfortable silence fell. Then he sighed and shrugged. "This is foolishness; before God, I am loyal to King Henry. But I will not argue, not here, like this. I will depart to a friendlier port."

"May you find one, your Grace," said Thomas Norris through gritted teeth, and he gestured for his men to return to the rowboats and make for their own vessel.

Father watched him leave, his face impassive. Once Thomas Norris's boat was almost at the shoreline, he approached the ship's Master. "Down the coast, if you would. There are other places friendly to me. I plan to head for my castle of Denbigh."

Ned and I had never visited Denbigh before. Despite the gravity of our situation, we were excited to see the castle's robust stone towers louring on an outcrop that gave views across the Vale of Clwyd. The fortress had a stormy history, belonging long ago to the Welsh King Dafydd Ap Gruffudd before it was granted to Hugh de Lacey, Earl of Lincoln, who rebuilt it in English fashion. Like Trim, it was Father's fortress through his Mortimer inheritance.

The castle was of unusual design, its gatehouse guarded by three huge, octagonal towers that Father told us were unique. Eight more towers bristled from the thick walls, and defensive ditches and terraces ran around the exterior. I was cheered to see its strength, ideal for defence, although I did not want to speculate what would happen if there was a siege, with Father's coffers barren.

"I do not understand, Ned." I trawled around the bailey with my brother, checking out the guardhouse and drawbridge, and the sallyport where our family could make a hasty escape if needed. "Why is the King so angry? Father did his best in Ireland! Did old Henry expect more of him? How could he do more when the King never paid him?"

Expression gloomy, Ned shrugged. "The King can be fickle, Edmund. You know what they say about him…" He tapped his head with a finger.

I bit back a laugh; it was wicked to speak so about our sovereign and we'd already had warnings about our impertinence in that regard—but yes, even children were aware that Henry's wits seemed to wander, and he acted more monk than monarch.

"He's easily led," said Edward. "That's what I've heard. And for whatever reason, he favours Edmund Beaufort."

I climbed up on the wall walk and sat on the sun-warmed masonry, banging my heels listlessly against the stonework. "Why is Beaufort so special? Father said he was useless in France. Even the French King disliked him. He caused King Charles to declare war, and then failed to hold onto any lands. He lost Caen, which was Father's own property…"

"Stop, Edmund." Ned squatted beside me on the wall. "There may be listeners, even here. Our Lord Father and Lady Mother have already warned us about being *indiscreet*."

"I only want to know!" I wailed. "The King used to be on friendly terms with Father. What had changed?"

Big Ned flicked away a stray ant that had crawled from the stonework onto my knee. "It's Cade's Rebellion that has made the King so disagreeable. The fact he called himself Mortimer. But I dare say, wicked though he was, Jack Cade was a bold fellow!"

"You defend him?"

"No. He is dead anyway, killed by the Sheriff of Kent. But I was amused to hear that his followers invaded our Uncle Buckingham's pleasure gardens. They danced around with ash-smeared faces, wearing long beards of horse-hair and claiming the Queen of the Fairies had sent them!"

"I had not heard." I chuckled at the image in my head of these hairy woodwoses waggling their false beards at a horrified and raging Uncle Buckingham. Humphrey Stafford, husband of Mother's sister, Anne, was decent enough but rather high-and-mighty and highly particular—a steward once farted at a banquet he held and he sent the man packing, never to return. I am sure he would have been apoplectic to see hirsute men trampling his flowerbeds.

"You can hear plenty of stories from the castle garrison if your ears are keen," said Ned. "But it's not only Cade and Beaufort who have caused issues with the King. There's also the Duke of Suffolk…" A shadow crossed Edward's face.

I knew little of Suffolk, save that he was close to the Queen and no friend to Father. He was strongly disliked and had the unflattering nickname of Jackanapes, implying he was a chained monkey. "What's he done?"

"It is not what he's done; it's about what was done to him. Not long ago, he was murdered, Edmund. Henry had sent him into exile, but he was apprehended by a ship that followed him—they hacked off his head with a rusty blade and threw his body onto the beach at Dover."

I crinkled my nose in disgust. "An unhappy end. Are you saying Henry believes Father…"

"There was bad blood between Father and Suffolk over Somerset's appointment to Normandy. Men remember that. It is foolishness, of course. But dangerous foolishness, especially if it is laid out as truth to the King."

"What is to become of us, Ned?" I said, angry at myself for the sadness that filled my voice, unbidden. Why could I not sound brave and defiant? "We cannot stay hidden at Denbigh forever."

Ned reached out to ruffle my already unruly hair in the way Father did on rare occasions. At that moment, he seemed much older, the difference in our ages more than a year. Once, that might have bothered me; today, sitting on the walls of Denbigh Castle and learning that the world seemed to have turned on your family, it did not.

"Father will find a way to make this better," Edward said. "Have faith, brother. He will do it."

Father decided to move from Denbigh Castle a few days later. The fortress was deep inside Wales and he was afraid he might get trapped there without access to the majority of his supporters. Our entourage headed slowly, cautiously, across country towards Ludlow, his main holding in the Marches, which was some twenty-five leagues distant. All the way along, he stopped frequently and sent scouts ahead to check for hidden attackers, and after a nerve-wracking start, our moods lightened, although no merriment showed on Father's unhappy visage.

Glad were we when our company reached Ludlow, standing in the debatable lands that straddled Wales and England, and of yore scenes of many bloody skirmishes and raids. The castle was a favourite of our sire's, and as the family processed past the church of St Lawrence and the Buttercross with its well-worn steps, I stared with pride at its vast walls, dull red in the muggy autumnal sunlight, and the lofty donjon tower keeping watch over the town. The Falcon and Fetterlock fluttered proudly from the topmost turret.

Before long, the company had entered the bailey, riding past the round Norman chapel that was perhaps the oldest part of the castle. Released from our stuffy carriage, Ned and I careered about the castle like moonstruck loons, our moods soaring. Father watched but sent no one to stop our play as we veered from stables to kennels to mews, choosing favourite horses and hawks and playing with a litter of puppies.

Later, we attended chapel, and tubs were brought to our chamber where we were scrubbed of all the sweat and grime of our long ride through Wales. Delicacies were laid out on boards—dates and cheeses, pasties and sweetmeats. Candles and lanterns burned; a merry fire crackled in the fireplace; the air smelt of dried herbs. The bed's cover was neatly turned back, the hangings shielding it embroidered with Yorkist symbols. Almost instantly I felt at home.

After our parents had dined, we were called to their chamber. Our Norman nurse, Anne Caux, was with them; so too were a pair of weedy men in scholarly black robes. Both wore sour expressions and one had a drooping moustache he could have strained his wine through.

I glanced at Ned, wondering if we were due for some kind of telling off. Had we been too noisy in our exploration of the castle? Had we laughed too hard? Run too fast? Had they discovered that we had pilfered two hot pies from the kitchen when the cook had stepped out for a moment?

"As you know," Father began, "most sons of noble houses leave home to receive knightly training at about the age of seven. You both have passed that age."

Ned and I froze. In private, we had spoken many times of the day when we'd be sent to another nobleman's house for knightly training. The day we would be separated, the bond between us sundered. Yes, we had sworn that we would ever remain best friends as well as brothers, but we had seen, even in our short lives, how families grew apart as circumstances changed.

"Do not look so woebegone!" laughed Father. Mother smiled a little, trying to hide it behind a kerchief, for this was clearly a serious, defining moment in our lives.

Father alighted from his chair. "After much consideration, I have made a decision regarding your future. Rather than send you to the households of other men, you will remain at Ludlow to receive your education. We live in tumultuous times; I would prefer to keep you here, under my eye. Mistress Caux will stay, so you'd best mind your manners and show yourself as dutiful and hard-working—or I shall surely hear about it."

"Or I," interjected Mother. Next to her, Anne Caux suppressed a smirk; we both adored Anne but knew she'd tolerate neither insolence nor rambunctious behaviour and would not fail to dutifully report it.

"Thank you, my Lord," Edward began.

Father waved a hand. "Enough, Ned. Let me finish what I was saying. I intend to leave for London to clarify what I have been accused of and reveal the truth of the matter to the King. Your Lady Mother shall take the other children to Fotheringhay, a more homely place than Ludlow. While I am away, your tutoring will be overseen by these two fine gentlemen standing behind me. Master Browne will teach you the trivium—your Latin, along with logic and rhetoric. Master Cadnum will take on the quadrivium—geometry, mathematics, astronomy...and music. You shall also begin your arms training in under the care of the Marshal."

Ned and I glanced at each other excitedly at the latter announcement. Learning the arts of war was what all noble youths desired unless they were to join the priesthood or the monks. Even then, some monks were war-like and handy with the quarterstaff and blade.

"You may go." Father dismissed us from his presence. "It is your time for slumber and I must plan my journey to London."

We filed into the well-lit corridor, our excitement palpable. Laughing, Ned gripped my arm. "Can you believe it, little Ned! We're to remain here together, training for our knighthood. I did not foresee that!"

"Neither did I. I thought we were done for because we scoffed those pies!"

A huge grin split my brother's face. "What do you say, Little Ned? Should we go and see what else we can lift from the kitchen? We are growing lads and need our sustenance, after all!"

CHAPTER EIGHT

Father left for London with a strong band of followers nearly the size of an army. The thought unnerved me, for if others believed this gathering was indeed an army, they might go on the offence in the belief he was heading to London to cause trouble. Nonetheless, Edward and I cheered him on as he rode from the castle, his trumpeters sounding a fierce tantara that echoed from the castle to the tower of St Lawrence's amidst the jutting black-and-white houses of Ludlow.

In the days that followed, Ned and I threw ourselves into lessons and training. Luckily, our tutors, though strict and sour, agreed that noble boys should have some freedom. After our schooling was done, we spent hours riding in the nearby forest, fishing in the Teme, visiting the town and the church, where the choir stalls were carved with fabulous creatures and figures of fun—an ugly scold in cow's horn headdress, a bat-winged harpy, a mermaid flanked by dolphins, tricksy Reynard the Fox, a cheating ale-wife dragged off to Hell while the demon Tutivillus read out her sins. Amidst these were King Henry's Antelope badge, the Bohun Swan, the Hart at Rest of Richard II—and of course, Father's Falcon and Fetterlock.

While on our daily perambulations, Ned and I heard scraps about events in the world beyond the town gates. Before he arrived in London, Father had managed to communicate with the King by letter, and Henry had all but apologised to him for the unfriendly greeting he'd received at Beaumaris. What happened then was more dramatic. Gossips said Father had insisted on seeing the King in person but was denied when he reached Westminster—so he forced his way into Henry's chambers...

Tales of these events flew from all the various factions, and men in the streets sang jaunty political rhymes about the lords of England and their grievances—

The Root is dead, the swan is gone,
The fiery cresset has lost its light—

And England makes moan to God Almight
The bear is bound that was so wild,
For he's lost his ragged staff,
The Cartwheel is spokeless,
For the counsel that he gave.
And the Falcon flees and has no rest,
Till he knows where to build his nest...

The Falcon referred to Father and his lack of standing at Henry's King's court. Edmund Beaufort had returned to England after his shameful losses in France and yet still been granted the position of Constable of England and Captain of Calais; more than he deserved after his disastrous policies. This appointment would rankle, and fester like an infected sore in its unfairness—Ned and I knew this even though we were but children.

Father returned to Ludlow late in October. I fretted for what seemed an eternity while he conducted immediate business concerning the castle and town, then rested after his long ride.

"What shall we ask him?" I asked Ned breathlessly, striding back and forth on the vivid patterns of our imported Turkey carpet. "There's so much I desire to know!"

"We must find out whether he truly broke into the King's own chamber to confront him." Big Ned sat cross-legged in the window embrasure paring an apple. "If it's true, God must have smiled on him that day! The risk, the audacity—all those guards about, eager to make an arrest, particularly if Edmund Beaufort or the Queen had been whispering in their ears."

I nodded, imagining Father sweeping into Westminster like some present-day Achilles, flinging sentries aside and insisting that the King listen to his assertions of loyalty. Henry would see the error of his ways, embrace Father and call him 'dearest Cousin York', and all the world would be set to rights.

The bedchamber door creaked open. Master Browne stood in his mussed ebon robes, his imported Italian spectacles glinting on the bridge of his craggy nose. "His Grace will see you now. Up, quickly, so he does not think you slothful."

Edward and I hastened to the solar, hesitating outside the thick oak door as we straightened our creased doublets and scraped off dirty pawprints and dog hairs from the kennels. Satisfied, we knocked and entered to Father's call, bowing low.

Father was seated in a low chair; his barber had been in, so he was shaven and the longer length of his hair shorn—shorter, it was curling, rather like our sister Anne's and also, by the look of it, baby George's.

"My dear sons!" he said. "Come and tell me how things have been at Ludlow."

He gestured for his squires to leave and we leapt upon him, gabbling about a hawk that nipped Ned's thumb, a pony ride where I fell into a stream, a hound that ate an entire haunch of beef set out for that night's supper. He listened to our tales with amusement before asking if we had been dutiful and written to our Lady Mother at Fotheringhay. We proudly told him we had.

With our own exploits recounted, Edward shyly asked him what had *really* happened in London with the King.

Sighing, Father leaned back in his chair. "So you've heard the rumours. Some of them, at least, are partly true."

"So you *did* burst into the King's throne room!" I squealed.

He inclined his head. "I needed to move swiftly. I feared Henry's guards would drag me away before I could present my case."

"And…the *other* thing…" Ned's voice dropped to a conspiratorial whisper. "There was talk that you…that you *struck* the King because he seemed too addled to understand what you were telling him."

Father choked back a nervous laugh. "Jesu, is *that* what the tittle-tattles say? No, that part is a lie. I may have *felt* like it when Henry rambled and failed to see what evil his favourites wreaked, but I would not dare touch an anointed king. If I had smitten him, I would not be sitting with you here in Ludlow. My head would be on a spike on London Bridge!"

Seeing my horrified face, he said quickly, "Henry is not a monster, Edmund, nor is he rash; he would only do such a thing if he truly felt threatened. And I would never touch him, because even in anger I am not a fool."

"Are you going to stay here long?" Ned asked hopefully. "Will you be here for Christmas?"

Father shook his head. "No, Parliament opens in November, and I am obligated to go. I came to Ludlow to see you boys ere duty called me elsewhere, and one never knows…"

His words trailed off, and once again doubts and despair enfolded me. The King may have shown no malice towards Father, but he was changeable and the slightest sign of friendship could be withdrawn at any time. Father said Henry was no monster, but he was a weak man swayed easily by those who *were* monsters.

It seemed monsters lurked around every throne…

Father stayed at Ludlow for the next few weeks, and Ned and I did not voice our fears but behaved as if we dwelt in a peaceful land, our castle cut off from the perils of the world outside. We rode out to visit other nearby castles, such as Wigmore with its priory where many of our ancestors lay buried. We went hawking on clear days and once hunted for deer in the neighbouring woods. I shot at one but missed—and though I pretended that I was sorry for my poor aim, I was secretly glad it had escaped my arrow. My target was only a young buck not yet fully grown. Let it run a few more summers in the sun before it met its final fate!

Not long after All Soul's, Father departed, intending to visit Fotheringhay before continuing on to London. Ned and I watched from atop the castle walls, making a show of boldness and high excitement, but as the sound of his trumpets diminished in the far distance, we stood in silence, side by side, our breath blowing white in the cold air. The sun seemed to have fallen from the sky, its setting all too early these days, leaving smudges of blood across the sky.

The year marched towards cruel winter as our Father the Duke of York once again marched toward London Town.

The following year was full of rumour, brought to us in brief, untrustworthy, and truncated forms. Some claimed an MP called Thomas Young had tried to see Father designated as King Henry's heir presumptive, since Henry was, after many years of marriage, still without offspring. Thomas was arrested for his presumption. Bloody, brutal punishment was meted out to those who spoke ill of the King's reign and expressed support for Father. Those charged with sedition were hanged, drawn, and quartered, their heads tarred and arranged on London Bridge. Unrest spread, and further afield in Kent, even more men were executed—so many that chroniclers called it 'a harvest of heads.'

So much for Henry not being a monster. He had no taste for death, but he allowed his favourites to wreak destruction while they knelt at his feet and claimed they had done it for love of him.

Father returned to Ludlow, alternating between melancholy and nervous anticipation. Edward and I dared not speak to him most of this time, and immersed ourselves in our scholarly pursuits. Briefly, our sire journeyed west quell a feud between the Courtenays and Lord Bonville which had set parts of Devon aflame...but he was not gone long. The combating families pacified, he returned to Ludlow in time to greet Mother who had travelled hence from Fotheringhay.

As her maids assisted her from her carriage, I was shocked to see how frail she appeared. She had birthed another baby boy since we saw her, but he had come too soon and died within hours of birth. Greeting us, she seemed distant and distracted, and eager to access her chambers. We received no embraces, no tears of joy. Though Mother was never given to ostentatious displays of emotion, her behaviour was different, subdued and marked by a weariness that reached the bone. She looked almost shrunken beneath the white wings of her butterfly headdress.

As she vanished into her apartments, I caught Ned and drew him into a window embrasure where we could talk privately. "Do you think Mother is ill? She looks so...different."

He leaned his face against the window pane, filled with new leaded glass. "Mother is *old* now, Edmund. She is no doubt sad about the baby dying—at her age, great ladies often cease to have more children. I would imagine she needs much rest—and she is consumed by worry about the state of England nearly as much as Father."

"I hope there are no more babies," I muttered, "if it harms her and the babies all die…"

"Oh, little Ned, such an innocent." Reaching over, Ned chucked me under the chin as if I were an infant. "It's her duty to bear children, and up to God how many. After all, that's what humans are here for, to multiply and have dominion over the earth."

I gritted my teeth, staring moodily out the window. I hated when he spoke to me as if I were a gormless infant when we were so close in age.

He put his hand on my shoulder; I resisted the urge to shrug it off. "Oh, stop sulking, Edmund. We will make her smile again once she has rested. Her arrival is good news! I believe she is going to stay for Christmas. What a splendid feast we shall have with her and Father together."

"I wish Bessie and Meg were coming—and what about George? We might not even recognise him when we see him next. And Anne, what about her? We haven't seen her for *years*, ever since she went to Exeter's household."

"You can't expect the children of York to traipse around England like travelling mummers seeking fairs!" laughed Edward.

I began to laugh myself, imagining myself dressed in a fool's motley and banging on castle doors with a pig's bladder. I'd bang on Edmund Beaufort's door and let fly with a fist instead of the bladder.

"I've made you mirthful—laughter is good in hard times," said Ned. "Come on, brother. Let us finish our duties and prepare ourselves to break bread with our Lord Father and Lady Mother."

I soon grew glad of our family reunion, even though the other children were at Fotheringhay. Mother's health improved and she began to smile again, as Ned had wisely predicted. Father had grown increasingly talkative, though he ranged between anger at the slights he had endured from the King's advisers, and an unnerving haughty confidence where he spoke as if *he* were King. I felt as if a fire had kindled within him; a torch that burned too hot, too bright, sparking and burning all around it, before dying into melancholic darkness. In all honesty, the heat of that fire troubled me more than his subdued, despairing lows, for it was apparent that thoughtful, measured Father had grown scarlet inside as the Plantagenet temper burst into flame.

Christmas neared and snow fell, furling the undulating countryside in a glittering mantle. The Teme froze solid, and finally Edward and I were permitted to skate, watched carefully by Anne Caux and several quick-footed male servants, who were ordered to fish us out if disaster struck and we plunged through the ice.

Ludlow's Great Hall was decorated with boughs of greenery cut from the nearby woods—holly wreaths full of blood-hued berries; swathes of green ivy, bunches of mistletoe cut from the highest branches of oak trees where they grew in abundance. The fragrance of these cuttings added a pleasant woody freshness to the hall, overwhelming the scent of fires, dogs, and stale food.

When Christmas Day dawned, Edward and I attended Mass in the castle chapel with our parents. As we left, the bells in St Lawrence's and other churches and priories tolled, clangour sharp on the crisp wintry air. We wore our best long gowns of rich velvet trimmed with warm fur, and we buzzed with excitement, for soon Advent's deprivations would be over and we could gorge ourselves until our bellies rebelled...

We were permitted to sit at a table this year; a great honour for lads our age, even noble ones. "You are no longer little children," Father said with a twinkle in his eyes. "Therefore, you may dine with your Lady Mother and me at the Christmas Feast and hold yourselves like Christian princes."

Time crawled slowly by as we waited for the summons to join the banquet. Ned lit a notched candle so that we could have an idea when we might eat; wax formed twisted serpent shapes in the candleholder but still no one came to fetch us.

"I am going to faint from hunger!" I cried dramatically, falling backwards on the bed.

"Here!" Edward flung a slab of stale bread he had secreted in his garments. We both gnawed this crust like a pair of rats to keep the hunger pains at bay. Finally, a squire bustled up to collect us, and at the Great Hall's entrance the Chamberlain, holding his wand of office aloft, announced us using our titles of Earl of March and Earl of Rutland.

A server guided us to our allotted bench; we would share one Mess between us. All eyes were upon the sons of York, especially Ned, since he was the heir and already as tall as a boy of fourteen summers.

A type of trumpet called a *buisine* sounded, and the first course of the Christmas Feast was brought in. First, a drink was poured so the feasters could open their bellies before proceeding: red wine mixed with creamy milk and sprinkled with spices. I was given a full goblet, though it contained more milk than wine. After that, platters of salted stag, veal loin, a stuffed chicken decorated with gold leaf were borne in from the kitchens to the accompaniment of a jongleur. Next were pigeons baked into gilded pies, sturgeon stewed in parsley and vinegar, and lastly the traditional boar's head on a golden platter, its bristles brushed with silver and its tusks glinting wickedly in the candlelight. An enthused cry went up as the head was placed on the high table, and the Carver, dressed in festive green, strode forward bearing a carving knife nearly as long as a sword, and began to cut the meat.

As slices of pie, fish and deer were served, a trio of musicians sidled into the hall, playing on tabor, lyre, and shawm. In strong, cheerful voices, they sang the 'Boar's Head Carol', the sound lifting to ring amongst the carved angels in the rafters:

The boar's head in hand bear I,
Bedecked with bay and rosemary.
And I pray you, my masters, be merry
Quot estis in convivio !

The boar's head, as I understand,
Is the finest dish in all England,
Which thus bedecked with a gay garland
Let us servire cantico!

This Boar's Head I bear
Caput apri defero ,
Singing praised to Our Lord,

Reddens laudes Domino

The carol finished with performances by a troupe of tumblers, acrobats, and stilt-walkers. Platters of *Entremet*s were brought forth—frumenty dyed shocking saffron yellow and cherry-red, and a capon fashioned into a knight who carried a little wooden lance and wore a feathered helmet, and sat astride a roast piglet with dried fruit bursting from its mouth. Edward and I laughed and clapped at that one. For those whose taste ran to sweet rather than savoury, there was also a tower crafted from marchpane, sprinkled with expensive sugar and caraway seeds. A little princess poppet peered from a window.

Lastly a wondrous pie arrived, the Shredded Pie, made from scraps of various meats and fruits doused in sticky suet and layered within a pastry shell. An oval lid covered the innards, and a tiny marchpane figure of the Christ Child in the manger lay on top. He was edible like the Tower, but was deemed too holy for anyone to eat.

The musicians appeared again, and dancers swarmed onto the floor. A farandole was followed by a circular Carole and a Basse Dance. To my surprise, my parents alighted from the high table and joined in this final courtly dance. The weariness and sorrow that had afflicted Mother had lifted, and she looked most comely in a flowing blue gown with fur trim and silver tissue falling like mist from the peak of her hennin. Her maids had painted her lips, cheeks, and eyes in a subtle way, and even her young sons could see why she had once borne the name 'the Rose of Raby.'

As our parents performed the steps of the stately dance, they gazed long into each other's eyes, unaware of any others in the hall. They smiled, cast private glances, twined their hands like young lovers. I noticed a new ring gracing Mother's finger, flashing purple in the fluttering candlelight. Set in gold and heart-shaped, I assumed it was her Christmas gift.

Having drunk more wine than we were used to, Edward and I found this rare open show of affection between Father and Mother quite hilarious and muffled our laughter with our napkins, horrid little oafs that we were.

After the dance finished, Father returned to the dais and called for an end to the Feast. Mother departed to her apartments, surrounded by a flock of her ladies, and the banquet finished in a fanfare of trumpets. Servants rushed in, shovelling scraps of food into voiders, to be hauled to the gates and distributed to Ludlow's poor.

Tipsy, Ned and I made to leave, but in the corridor we were confronted by one of our tutors, Master Browne, saturnine and sinister in the guttering light of the cressets. "Well," he said, his freakish moustache quivering. "I have been keeping my eye upon you from afar."

"You were spying on us?" gawped Edward. "How…how *dare* you!"

"I am entrusted with your education, and education is far more than academic studies. You are of royal blood, a Duke's sons, not halfwits born in a stable."

Ned folded his arms, mimicking Browne. His eyes were big and glassy from too much drink. "And what did we do that was so terrible…you old snitch!"

Dumbfounded, I stared at my brother. So did Tutor Browne, for one stunned moment. Then out came his bony hand with a switch, and he struck Ned on the elbow, making him yelp and drop his arms.

Edward turned puce. "You b…"

"Not another word!" hissed Browne, his voice menacing. "You know I have permission to chastise you if necessary. As for your misdeeds—the two of you were sniggering like ill-bred churls when your noble progenitors danced upon the floor. Shameful! Get you hence to bed and reflect on what you have done. Tomorrow, you shall report to me in the schoolroom immediately after Mass and I will hear your Latin. And stop glaring at me, Master Edward, ere you get another smack. After all, it is said in Proverbs -*Do not hold back discipline from the child. Although you strike him with the rod, he will not die.*"

Ned tensed beside me and I grabbed his wrist. "Ned, no. Be still."

Praise God, he came to his senses, the hot light draining from his eyes. He made a small bow to Tutor Browne. "My apologies, sir. You are correct. I have not acted respectfully towards my Lord Father and Lady Mother, and failed my duty to them as their faithful son. I have also acted disrespectfully to you. I apologise."

Brown glared down at me. "And you, Edmund? You were complicit. What do you have to say for yourself in this matter?"

"Like Edward, I was thoughtless," I whispered. "And rude. I ask forgiveness too."

Our apologies mollified him a little. He lowered his switch. "Go, then. I expect to see you early tomorrow morn. I may tell your sire of your misbehaviours...or I may not. That will depend on your proficiency in Latin lessons on the morrow."

We fled for our chamber, dismissing our servants. Mistress Anne Caux was in bed with an ague so she was not there, thankfully, so no more questions. Crawling under the coverlet, only one candle burning on the nearby wooden chest, I whispered, "Ned, do you think Browne will tell?"

Edward shrugged. "I doubt it. Can you see Mother's face if he told her what we were laughing about? He would not dare!" He grinned devilishly. "It *was* amusing. The way they danced...for such an *old* couple! Hah, I would not be surprised if we had another brother or sister soon, one to replace poor little Thomas..."

I scowled. We were not ignorant; we had seen cows, horses, dogs mate, and even once or twice stableboys and dairymaids flopping around in a tangle of discarded clothes. But the thought of our parents embroiled in such acts? Improper, and a little unsavoury. It was easier to imagine, foolish though it was, that our siblings had been deposited in the castle cradle by cranes or pelicans, as babies often were in the myths of the Greeks and other ancient peoples.

"Do you really think so?" I said.

Ned buried his face against the bolster. "Who knows... God's will and...all. Ugh, I feel sick now, little Ned; all that drink has curdled in my gut. And to think we must get up before dawn for Mass, and then head to lessons."

"Master Browne won't be keeping us in the schoolroom for long," I said. "Tomorrow is Saint Stephen's Day. A saint's day. He wouldn't dare." I sighed, rolling on my side and propping myself up on my elbow. "I wish we were back in Ireland—remember St Stephen's day there, when the Wren Boys danced around Trim in straw hats while holding dead Wrens?"

"Yes," said Edward. "An odd custom, but not any stranger than mummers, I suppose." He grimaced, holding his gut. "But you are right. Browne cannot imprison us in the schoolroom. We will be expected to go with Father to distribute coins to the poor. Browne wouldn't dare keep us from our filial duties. Silly pompous old grizzleguts! I mean did you hear him—'our noble progenitors'? Who even speaks like that these days?"

I giggled. "It sounded ridiculous."

"Like that hairy spider descending from his lip!"

I convulsed with mirth, my sides shaking.

Ned groaned and clutched his head. "Not so loud! My head is pounding and I feel…strange. I might be sick—damn that wine! Maybe if I lie still all will settle."

I slipped from under the covers, blew out the candle, and crawled back into the warmth of the bed. Soon Ned began to snore, punctuated by a few rank and noisy farts.

Sleepless, I lay on my back, staring at the ceiling, deep in my own thoughts. Of fears. Of family. Of the duty of princes.

Once 12th Night was over and all our visitors had departed, the castle returned to winter's gloom. The weather was inclement, snow and sleet driven over the turrets on a harsh northern wind, and so Mother remained at Ludlow. She and Father were closeted together often, but as the days dragged on, their glances were no longer longing but concerned. Father called on Ned and I to serve them supper in the solar, to 'show what we had learnt of manners,' and soon the reason for their displeasure became apparent.

Father sat behind his desk of polished oak wood, writing a letter. No scribe had been summoned—he wrote in his own hand as he had done in his letter to Uncle Salisbury in Ireland. His hat lay on the desk, discarded; he glared down at the words he had written, as if displeased by them, and raked a frustrated hand through his hair.

Mother was ensconced in the window embrasure, sewing. None of her ladies were with her.

Ned and I went between them like good squires, offering platters from the kitchen, refreshing their goblets, asking constantly if they required more light, heat, music.

"Stoke the fire, Edmund." Father nodded in my direction. "Make sure it catches well and there is not too much smoke."

I jumped to attention, loading kindling into the brazier. Ned lit several candles that had been extinguished in a draught.

Father glanced at Mother. Her sewing needle fell still. "I have done nought in the governance of this land since we returned from Ireland, other than intervening in skirmishes between Devon and Wiltshire. Something is not right. I feel it in my blood and bones. I must write to the King, Cecily."

Mother swung around to face him. "I fear you might disturb a wasp's nest, Richard."

Father's hand gripped his quill till I thought it might snap. "I…I already feel that Henry is once again displeased with me. I must put my case across so that nought will get out of hand in the way it did before."

"If he believes ill of you, why would a letter change his mind?"

The quill was thrown onto the disk, scattering ink like black blood. "I will get the Bishop of Hereford and the Earl of Shrewsbury to vouch for my probity. Their word must count for something."

Mother's mouth tightened. "Not necessarily. Not if Henry's favourites continue to pour poison in his ears."

"I will offer to swear an oath on the Blessed Sacrament!" Father's colour grew high and his gaze furious. "I will swear that I was ever his loyal servant and shall be until the day I die. I will even swear this oath in the presence of any lords of Henry's own choosing, if the King will accept such proofs."

"If that is what you feel you must do, Richard, then do it you must," said Mother. "I fear, though, your effort to quell these evil rumours will be in vain. The source of the rumours needs to be removed. Permanently."

"And you suggest what?" Father's voice rose a little.

Mother bowed her head, trying to appear meek and demure—but I understood this was a sham. A noble Lady did not tell her husband what to do—well, she *did*, but not blatantly. "I suggest nothing, Richard. What action you take is for you to decide. But I do not believe appeals to the King will do much good." Suddenly she thrust all her sewing items back into their box, and her gaze swivelled to Edward and me, sitting quietly by the crackling fire awaiting our next instructions. "Edmund, bring me another cup of Rhenish, will you? After that, you both may go."

Father jumped in his seat, almost as if he had forgotten we were still present. "Yes, yes," he murmured. "Fill my cup too—and then, off with you! Take my hounds; they need walking." He gestured to his greyhounds, Garlick and Jakke, who lay stretched before the fire's warmth.

I clicked my fingers and murmured "Come on" to the dogs and they sprang up from their comfortable sprawl, shaking their fur, their snouts wearing doggy grins as they snuffled at my legs, hoping for some titbits from the kitchens.

After pouring the wine, Edward and I left the solar with the dogs, and the door was closed firmly and the latch put on. Our presence was clearly no longer required—or wanted.

A lingering shadow seemed to sweep over the halls of Ludlow Castle, even as the ghosts of winter screamed between the crenelations, the snow flying in on their frigid dead breath.

In February, Father wrote to the Earl of Shrewsbury, having received no reply to his letter to King Henry. "You had best know how things stand," he said to me and Ned. "I will have to leave Ludlow soon and know not what the days will hold after I depart. I have named, in public, Somerset as my enemy. I have told all who matter that he labours about the King to bring about my downfall, and aims to see you, my heirs, disinherited without cause, save his own malice and jealousy."

"What does this mean?" I asked in a small voice. "What will you do?"

"I have gathered kin, friends and allies, and will march on Somerset without delay, to see his poisonous influence removed from the King. I did not desire this, but I have dwelt in long sufferance. It cannot continue. Edmund Beaufort cannot rule the King's person and bring England to ruin as he brought the English properties in France to ruin."

Edward's visage was bone-white. "Is…is this not treasonous, Father?"

Vehemently, he shook his head. "Never that. All I do will be within my bonds of allegiance to the King. I do not seek his throne or wish any harm done to his noble person. Do you understand, boys?"

He glanced at us, his eyes keen as lances. We nodded, although with trepidation.

"Good. You will remain here in Ludlow and continue your education. But be warned, if it goes not well, I will do what I can to see you taken to a safety place."

"Where?" I asked, throat dry. My belly flip-flopped.

"I will think upon it. Maybe Ireland. I created you Lord Chancellor of Ireland, remember? Bishop Oldhall was made deputy because of your youth. He would protect you, and I have other friends there besides."

A burst of excitement lifted my heart knowing I might see Tadgh again and meander with him through Dublin's busy streets and have competitions skipping stones out across the Black Pool. But it would not feel the same, not if we were in actual exile, and...

"If you sent me to Ireland, what about Edward?" I glanced at my brother, still as a stone beside me.

"I would have to give further consideration to where Edward might go. It would not be prudent to send the two of you abroad together unless there is no other choice. Separating you would be safer..."

He trailed off.

Safer. I understood what he meant all too well. If Ned and I were found together, we might both die together. If we were sent to different locations, if one was slain, a York heir would still live to inherit Father's legacy.

My throat tightened and I forced myself to swallow over the lump that rose to choke me. I tried to look brave, as was expected from a son of York.

Father's countenance softened. "I know this is hard to hear, my boys, but rest assured, I do it for you...for all my children. If I should die in disgrace, all the calumnies rained upon me would transfer to you. I would not rest easy in my grave if I thought you should lose all that should rightfully be yours one day." His lips tightened, growing white. "Never forget, Edward, Edmund, that the King has, as yet, produced no heir, and mayhap it will remain so. By any man's estimation, the throne should go to me should the Queen remain barren, and if I should fall in battle or otherwise, to Edward. I am greatly fearful that Henry, blind with his love for Edmund Beaufort, might decide to make *him* heir—despite him coming from a bastard line debarred from the throne! This must never happen. Never!"

"What…what will happen to Mother?" I asked. Under heavy guard, she had departed for Fotheringhay several days earlier.

Father toyed with his rings. "Your Mother is made of sterner stuff than one might think…She will cope."

"Will she be safe?" Edward's cheeks were pallid in the candle flames.

"I believe so. She was once on good terms with Queen Margaret and I pray that old friendship would still count for something should all go awry. The King may be weak, but I doubt even his foul advisors would dare counsel him to lay siege to a castle inhabited by a woman with small children who may be bearing another child."

"W-hat?" I cried, my outburst an explosion of surprise. Ears burning, I fell to one knee. "Lord Father, forgive me, I did not mean to…"

He grinned wanly, the first time I had seen him smile all day. "Yes, its true. Although it is early days and may not yet come to pass, your Lady Mother had born so many babes she recognises the changes within her that indicate another chick for the Falcon's nest. This possibility why she wished to depart so swiftly back to Fotheringhay. Yes, if God wills it so and your Lady Mother has read the signs aright, you may have a new brother or sister born sometime in October of this year."

CHAPTER NINE

Heading a force of thousands, bowmen, pikemen, halberdiers, and even skilled gunners, Father departed Ludlow on his black destrier. In the following days, a cloud of unrest hung over the town and the market and streets were quiet and the merchants subdued as they went about their business. Prayers were said in church and priory for Father's safe return.

Ned and I hung around the castle officials as much as possible, so as not to miss any news messengers might bring. Soon we learnt that King Henry had departed London to dwell in Coventry, a town he much favoured and where Lancastrian support was high. Father had proceeded to London as intended but found the gates were barred against him and archers with bent bows lining the city's walls. Knowing he could not breach such well-defended fortifications, he marched onwards to the town of Dartford, where he was joined by the Earl of Devon and Lord Cobham. The Thames was rumoured to be full of his supply ships sailing back and forth.

"The King's scared, he's on the run," I sneered to Edward. We were in the kennels, dandling the pups; I had one little fellow on my knee, snapping with his sharp puppy teeth at a morsel of chicken in my hand.

Edward was more circumspect. "Henry's regrouping, I am certain of it. He won't give up. His toady Somerset will urge him on."

"Ouch!" The pup grabbed my finger in his jaws, missing the scrap of chicken. Specks of blood dotted my skin. I wrenched my hand away and the dog jumped off my knee, tail wagging. It was all good fun for him. "Why did he do that?"

"Because you were teasing him, little Ned. And that, I fear, the King, on Edmund Beaufort's advice, is doing right now. Teasing Father. Henry headed south, then did an about-face and marched north. But soon he will return to London when his minions have decided what course to take. The King's flight will have given him—or rather, his advisors—time to plot. Now, come on, give the puppy back to the kennel master and let's go have your wound cleaned. You don't want to get that bite infected."

A week later a courier brought tidings that the King was leaving Coventry and marching towards London with a force every bit as large as Father's. Agitated by these unwelcome tidings, Edward and I were inattentive in our lessons, both receiving rapped knuckles from our unfeeling Tutors. "You will never be mighty lords if you fret like anxious old women when you hear news not to your liking," said Master Cadnum. "So...*pay attention*, or you will feel the sting of the switch yet again. Do you understand?"

Gloomily, we apologised for our lack of diligence and tried to focus on our lessons. We managed to get by with no further birchings, but at night, when we should have lain sleeping, we were up, staring through the open window shutters, watching the moon sail over the castle, turning walls and turrets an eerie silver-blue. Occasionally we saw nightbirds flying and bats silhouetted against the moon's orb, and once a huge white owl on the hunt, its eyes gleaming gold and its eerie hoots echoing through the empty wards.

The hair on the back of my neck had risen at the sight of the bird, for I here on the Welsh borderlands peasants speak of Blodeuwedd, Flower Face, a maiden wrought of meadowsweet, primrose, and broom, who had been cursed to wear an owl's form and became a harbinger of impending death. Seeing the white owl above the castle was, I felt, an evil omen, made more so as the flower of the Plantagenets is the golden broom from which Blodeuwedd was made, but I said nought to Edward for fear he would laugh. Our temperaments differed in that regard—he paid little heed to legends or premonitions, while they played upon my mind.

Finally, a letter arrived from Edward and me, with Father's own seal upon it. I let Ned break the seal since he was eldest. Father had scrawled a short note. He was well, and hoped we, too, were well, and obeying Anne Caux and our tutors Browne and Cadnum. He told us not to feel afraid, for the King was not bearing down upon him intent on battle. Henry was sending a delegation to treat. Amongst these men were mother's own brother, Richard, Earl of Salisbury, and his son, our Cousin Dick, the Earl of Warwick. Although they were the King's supporters, Uncle Salisbury was friendly with our sire and often listened to his grievances, as he had done when we dwelt in Ireland. And Cousin Dick, aged three-and-twenty years, was the young knight most boys wanted to emulate—wealthy, handsome, intelligent, brave and forthright.

Father went on to write that his only goal was to have Edmund Beaufort face charges for his crimes, and he hoped King Henry would recognise that as the truth. He had already told us his intent before his departure, but the fact that he repeated it made us think he feared that no one believed him. Even us.

Edward put the letter down on the nearby table. "I hope the King comes to terms with Father's," he breathed, "but it seems too good to be true."

My guts contracted; something withered inside me, cold and fearful. "Father knows what he is doing!" I insisted. "If Father can get Uncle Richard to vouch for his motives…"

Ned's hand clamped on my wrist so tightly pain shot up my arm and I squirmed. "Perhaps it would be wise to prepare for the worst and hope for the best, Edmund."

I shook his fingers off. I had no desire to hear gloomy predictions, not from anyone and especially not from my brother. It smacked of betrayal, as if he did not believe our sire could prevail, even though he was in the right about Beaufort. In all the tales of knights and kings, the good ones always won out…didn't they?

Gathering my cloak, I stomped out of the hall and towards the courtyard, slamming the wooden door behind me. The sound of it banging shut made me feel oddly better, although a little embarrassed too. I hurried to the stables and hid in an empty stall, burrowing into a pile of old hay that reeked of horse piss. There, alone, I allowed myself to weep for a bit.

No one came to look for me, not even Ned.

I was glad.

Fear was contagious. I did not want to see the brother I looked up to crumble as I had.

"He's done it…*he's done it*!" Edward burst into our bedchamber, the door flying back so hard it almost tore off its hinges. I was washing my hands in a basin after eating a light repast and surprised by my brother's exuberant entrance, I knocked it over, sending water all over the floor.

Edward slipped and slid through the puddles on the floor. He was grinning like a mooncalf and waving a letter in his hand. "It's from Father! Just now. A messenger came to the gate!"

"Have you read it?" I stared at the crumpled parchment as if it held treasure.

"Yes, forgive me, I could not wait—"

"Give it to me!" Lunging forward, I grabbed it from his hand, slightly hurt that he had not waited so that we could read it together.

Pressing it to the front of my shirt, with racing heart I flung myself amidst the mussed sheets on the bed and raced through the contents of Father's message.

My most beloved sons,

Soon, pray God, I will return to Ludlow. No blows have been struck in my endeavour, but it seems I have won over the King who has recognised my fidelity despite his evil councillors. I told him, once again, that I would bring no hurt upon his royal person, and only wished to remove several evil-doers who oppressed the common folk and left them impoverished—mainly Edmund Beaufort, Duke of Somerset. He sent a message in return and told me that Beaufort had been arrested and sent to the Tower, awaiting charges for his crimes. I am in the process of disbanding my army, and once I have seen his Grace himself, rest assured I will hurry home.

"So, he did succeed!" I cried in joyous wonderment. "They've thrown Edmund Beaufort in the Tower!"

"They have indeed!" crowed Ned, leaping onto the bed and creating a great dent in the feathered mattress. "Can you imagine the look on his haughty face when the guards came for him?"

He jumped up, rammed an old feathered cap upon his head at a ludicrous angle, and began to strut about the chamber, wringing his hands and pretending to be Somerset. "Oh no, oh no, what shall I do now that the King realises that I am a lying poltroon?"

"You'll have to eat peasant soup from now onwards!" I yelled, joining in his game. "Rotten turnips, mouldy oats, and sticks and stones!"

"Alas, alack, forsooth I shall die from such cruel treatment!" Ned theatrically pressed his arm against his brow and effected a faint.

"As you deserve, you scoundrel, Beaufort! I hope you get dog worms!"

"Masters Edward and Edmund!"

An angry roar came from outside the chamber, followed by the sound of a cane battering at the door. It was Cadnum in a fit of anger, as usual. He truly was a disagreeable man like his fellow, Browne. It was hard to say which one was worse. "Your japery can be heard even in the courtyard. I bid you show some decorum or…"

"Or it will be the switch!" I muttered under my breath, as I rolled my eyes.

Ned flung off the ridiculous cap, leaving his fringe sticking up like a Cockerel's comb. Urgently he tried to slick it down should Cadnum barge in to chastise us further. Another surge of laughter roiled within me at the sight of his frantic efforts, but I bit my lips and held it in till my face grew red.

Today was a joyous time for us, and I didn't want it ruined by a beating! Nor did I want Father to hear that we had misbehaved when he returned home to Ludlow.

And after joy came sorrow…

The clang of the gate bell sounded loudly not four days after Ned and I had received news of Father's victory. A hooded rider, his horse lathered, trotted into the bailey and halted. The steward went to greet him. Ned and I had heard the bell's insistent clangs and were watching from our window; dawn had barely broken and mist curled round the towers like smoke. Peeping over the eastern horizon, the dull red sun was a sleepy, baleful eye.

There was a commotion, and other men of the household circled around the courier. Once the steward glanced up at our window, and even at the distance, I noticed the curdled-milk hue of his face.

"Ned, something is wrong. Something bad has happened." I pressed against the frosted panes, trying to get the steward's attention, but he had turned back to the newcomer and was deep in conversation with him.

Glum, only half-awake, Ned and I haphazardly dressed and dashed from our bedchamber, pushing past servants, guards, and laundresses come to change the bed linens.

Down a steep spiral staircase, we fled, and almost crashed into the steward. "I was coming to find you, my Lords," he said, grim-faced, his hair hanging lank across his brow. "Into my office, if you would."

Groggy and clenched up with fear, we followed him to his quarters. A man-servant was cleaning ash from the fireplace when we arrived; he dismissed him with a curt hand wave. "Sit." The steward indicated a bench. In silence we obeyed, eyes fastened on his stiff form. He remained standing, although he looked as if he might retch so pale was he.

"Sir." Edward cleared his throat. "I beg you, do not keep us in suspense, fearing the worst. It is better you tell us your evil tidings without further ado. A swift blow may cause pain, but a wait of long duration causes a different type of pain. Once the truth is out, whatever it might be—we can deal with it."

"You are both so young," said the steward, "but you are also brave, for you have the blood of great and courageous princes running through your veins. Draw upon that illustrious ancestry—and listen closely to what I must tell you..."

"Is our sire dead?" I babbled, blunt in my distress.

"No, Lord Edmund, you can rest your mind on that point," said the steward. "He lives—but he has been taken prisoner by the King."

Edward leapt to his feet, his hands curled into fists. "What madness is this? Mere days ago, he wrote to say the King agreed to listen to his grievances and make Somerset pay for his crimes. Are...are you telling us that King Henry played our father false? That he *lied* to him?"

The steward swallowed hard, his shoulders slumping. "I fear so, Lord Edward. It seems that when the Duke entered the King's tent, he found no welcome. Edmund Beaufort was there, free and under no restraints, grinning as he stood beside King Henry's chair."

"He's a knave!" Edward's eyes ignited with fury. "A bloody knave! He is no fit King!"

"Lord Edward, calm yourself." The man's voice was weary, slow; he mopped his brow with a kerchief. "Such outbursts do no good. There is more I must tell you."

Grumbling, Edward slouched onto his stool. His clasped hands were shaking with pent-up rage. "Go on, then."

The steward sighed deeply. "Three days past, the King rode into London with Duke Richard riding before him as a prisoner, armed guards all around him, making public display of his misery. His Grace was taken to St Paul's, with the oafs gawking and catcalling along the way. Before the high altar, he was forced to kneel and swear an oath. A long oath, transcribed by a clerk, upon which he set his own seal in public, while his enemies gloated."

"But Father was determined to swear an oath anyway," I cried, distressed, imagining the shame my poor sire must have faced, a captive subjected to jeers and ridicule, a man tricked by the sovereign he had foolishly trusted.

"Yes, but the words of his initial oath were changed, twisted. The Duke had to agree never to raise an army of any size again without Henry's express permission."

Ned scrambled to his feet again. "But...but that means he cannot protect his own lands and castles. He cannot even protect *us*, his children! Surely, this isn't right! An oath taken under duress, with such harsh terms, surely cannot be binding."

I glanced with admiration at my brother, impressed by his knowledge. I would not have dared speak so boldly.

"Alas, Lord Edward, the oath was sworn on the Bible, the Holy Cross, and the Sacrament. It is binding. Your father would never break an oath sworn in such a manner and in such a holy place."

Edward's visage darkened. "You are right. My Lord Father would never break an oath. What, sir, is to be done?"

The steward fell silent, considering before saying slowly, "I am sure the Duke's supporters and the good Duchess Cecily will petition the King for clemency. You, my young lords, need do nought. Your safety is assured behind the walls of Ludlow."

"It is not *my* safety that concerns me," snapped Ned. "I cannot believe no lords are rising in his support! If no man will lead an army to free him—then I will."

Mouth agape, the steward stumbled back. "Lord Edward, you have not quite reached your tenth year…"

"Do not laugh at me, sir!" Edward's eyes flashed. "I do not jest. Although I may yet be too young to wield a sword in battle, still may I lead the faithful to free my father."

The steward looked dazed by Ned's statement, but after a moment's silence to regain his wits, he said, "While your enthusiasm is noble, such an undertaking would be unwise and dangerous. You are your father's heir; you must not attempt any acts of bravado that could worsen the Duke's situation—or your own. Why…" he cast Edward a shaky smile, "not even the great Alexander fought in battles at ten years old."

"No, but I am as big as a fourteen-year-old and equally strong. Joan d'Arc went to war at sixteen summers—and she was a *girl.*"

"And you know what happened to her, Master Edward," said the steward grimly.

Ignoring his comment, Ned began to pace the chamber. "I cannot sit here doing nought! If I cannot lead men, I will come up with another way to help. Come, Edmund, we must plot Father's rescue, since no one else has the courage to do so."

He whirled around, grabbing my elbow and propelling me into the corridor. Behind us the steward gaped at our backs, speechless.

Needless to say, Edward did *not* ride out to battle at the age of not-quite-ten, though if there had been no opposition, he would have certainly done so. What the pair of us managed to do, after much cajoling of castle officials and even the chaplain, was write to local landowners who owed allegiance to the Mortimers, reminding them of their oaths and of the unworthy actions of King Henry toward their right good Lord, the Duke of York. Then, with a bit more persuasion (and God's Eyes, my brother could be persuasive, using either great charm or a burning insistence that even unnerved grown men), we were permitted, accompanied by guards in York livery, to ride to those castles and manor houses to deliver the letters in person. At the same time we halted in local towns and villages, showing ourselves and telling Father's tale of woe to knight and dame, burgher and goodwife, barefoot monk and wizened nun.

Such a public performance had the sniff of mummery about it, and we were determined to play the parts of princes to the hilt. Our best doublets, blue velvet slashed with gold for Ned and green trimmed with crimson and tawny for me, were brought out of the Wardrobe, dusted off and worn, along with sumptuous cloaks embroidered with the Falcon and Fetterlock in silver and gold thread. We discussed wearing armour, but since we had only recently begun our training in war-craft, we had not yet been measured for such. Weaponry was the same; our practice weapons were wrought of filmy wood for our own safety and that of any poor soul we might flail uselessly at during training sessions.

However, with pleading eyes, Edward went to the Marshal and the steward and put his case forward that he needed a *real* sword to appear in public as a prince ready to fight for his sire's freedom. After much stroking of chins and worried sighs, it was decided he could wear a blade as long as he did not try to use it on any thick heads. His handsome face beaming, he promised most earnestly that he would not dream of it.

So the Marshal gave him a sheathed sword and Ned proudly buckled it to his belt.

"What do you think, little brother?" he asked as we stood together admiring each other's raiment.

"You look a true prince—but don't forget your bonnet. A gentleman always wears a hat."

"Of course!" Edward gestured for the chamberlain to bring his best velvet hat for inspection. Father had one similar with a jewelled pin. "This will do," said Ned with a grin.

All through the local villages and towns we progressed with our cavalcade—Cleobury Mortimer, Clun, Wistanstow, Halford, and Stokesay. At first the onlookers were small in number but curious; however, as we toured larger towns such as Bridgnorth and Much Wenlock, the crowds swelled in size, and many cried out for justice and Father's hasty release from prison.

Our last stop was Shrewsbury, a place where Father had appealed for aid in the past. Bigger than Ludlow, it was also a wool town, and the wool trade had made it highly prosperous. Riding over Welsh Bridge, we gazed around enthralled at the half-timbered houses, the red sandstone castle near the river, and the wealthy abbey of St Peter and St Paul, home to the relics of St Winifred.

Reaching the wide-paved market square, a sizeable throng had gathered, full of curiosity. It was market day and the square heaved with grimy shepherds herding wild-eyed, baaing flocks; poulterers carrying crates full of live ducks and chickens; pig boys prodding their squealing porcine charges; fishmongers with stalls slippery with guts and scales; and sundry hucksters flogging rope, cloth, candles, pots and more. Nearby, a smelly ducking pool emitted a stagnant reek. Fortunately, the ducking stool for nags and witches was empty and the pond disturbed only by a dozen ducks.

Edward pressed his stout pony on towards the High Cross, towering over the streets near St Mary's church. Here, some fifty years ago, captives from the Battle of Shrewsbury were executed and Henry IV had Harry Hotspur's corpse salted, impaled on a spear, and propped up between two millstones to quell rumours he was still alive. Later, Henry quartered the corpse and sent Hotspur's head for display upon the gates of York…

I shuddered, thinking of such bloody times, and prayed England's fragile peace would hold during Father's predicament. It was clear now that Edmund Beaufort would stop at nothing to see his rival brought low. I doubted imprisonment would be enough.

At the cross, Edward had dismounted. Eager hordes pushed in, and my heartbeat quickened in alarm, pulsing in my ears. Our guards pushed the locals back, keeping them safely from my brother as he mounted the steps of the market cross.

One, two, three steps up, his shoes sturdy on the bowed stonework, carved out by the footfall of generations before him. Reaching the highest step, he turned to face the crowd, which swelled by the minute. In his finery, he looked magnificent, a handsome young prince straight from Arthurian legend—a nascent Lancelot or Percival.

"My good people of Shrewsbury," he cried in a clear, steady voice "I come to you today to tell of an injustice wreaked on my family—on my sire, Richard Duke of York. Through the machinations of his enemies, he has fallen afoul of his Grace the King, although his loyalty has always been to the Crown and he is its greatest servant. Even as we stand here, free men in the town of Shrewsbury, he languishes in the Tower of London, his ultimate fate unknown."

Mutters ran through the marketplace. Some folk had heard the news already, but others appeared shocked and bewildered.

"My sire of York has always been a good lord to the folk of the Marches," Edward continued. "I am sure none here will disagree with my words. Would you trust the lordship of these lands to others who have little care? The Mortimers have dwelt in the Marches long; would you see other men who love you not usurp their long-held place?"

"No, no!" a man yelled. It was only the town drunkard, snaggle-haired and clutching a flagon of ale, but it was a beginning, as it turned out. The crowd surged forward again, their mumbles growing to a dull roar.

"What must we do?" someone shouted, as cries of '*Free him...free him!*' reverberated around the marketplace.

"If it comes to it, I, Edward, Earl of March, Duke Richard's heir, will ride at a head of an army to see my father released!" Edward cried with bravado, thrusting one curled fist towards the heavens. And the heavens smiled on Ned, for a shaft of light, like a lance cast from the Archangel Michael himself, pierced the belly of the clouds, enveloping my brother in a glowing nimbus and lighting up the carving of Christ and the Saints upon the lantern-shaped head of the High Cross.

The townsfolk roared as if witnessing a miracle. Men drew swords and daggers from their sheaths and knelt on the cobblestones to offer them up. The Marshal beckoned to Ned that it was time to leave, for we played a dangerous game and emotions were running high. But at least what we hoped was confirmed—the folk of the Marches would stand for the Duke of York.

In haste, our cavalcade galloped back to Ludlow. Letters were forwarded to various towns, further afield this time, suggesting that Edward would shortly march for London at the head of a vast army. None of these letters were official, neither signed nor sealed, but sent out to confuse our foes and engender rumours that would spread far and wide. Agitators were sent forth from Ludlow too; spies pretending to be journeymen and pilgrims, who told tall tales of the anger in the Marches over the Duke's imprisonment.

Information was carried back to us by these same spies and mischief-makers. News of a possible rising had reached Queen Margaret's ears—and she was afraid! These tidings made Ned and me a little fearful too. What if she convinced the King to ride out against us? He was not a martial man, but with the Queen and Edmund Beaufort egging him on, who knows what course he might take?

"If we heard that King Henry was marching on Ludlow, what would we do, Ned?" I asked. Ned had held a recent meeting with his helpmeets in this subterfuge, and I would lie if I said those men were not concerned by what they had heard.

Edward was paler than usual. His recent nights had been sleepless, as mulling over the implications of what he had begun. "I don't know. If it came to it, I suppose I would have to gather soldiers and march south to meet the King in battle, as I threatened to do."

"Edward!" I cried. "You are not quite ten! This is madness."

"I wouldn't actually fight. I'd be a figurehead—rather like Joan the Maid."

"And as the steward said: 'remember what happened to her'."

"They wouldn't burn me, you goose!" He rolled his eyes.

"What about stab you?" I retorted.

"Well, if you are too young and afraid to join my efforts, I fully understand," he said, deliberately goading.

"Are you calling me a coward? Don't you *ever* call me a coward!" I roared, and leapt for him in a fit of rage.

I had never responded with such fury in all our boyish tiffs, and Ned was caught off guard. He struck the floor with an 'oof' as the air was knocked from his lungs and his head hit the wooden panel at the end of the bed. A fierce red bump emerged at once.

"Jesu…Edmund!" he moaned, pressing his hand over the tumescent swelling.

"Forgive me!" I fell to my knees beside him. "I didn't mean to…"

For a moment I thought he might strike me, but then his furious face relaxed. "This is foolish. We should not be at loggerheads at a time like this. I was wrong to imply you were a coward—truth be told, I am not without fear myself. I want to rescue Father, but perhaps I have set the wheel on the cart rolling, and now it cannot be halted…until it crashes."

"I hope you are wrong," I whispered.

"I hope so too." He clambered to his feet, feeling the sizeable lump on his head with his fingers. "Now, by way of apology, you can fare to the apothecary and get some hyssop to rub on this bruise you've given me."

Whether our ploy had, by some miracle, succeeded, or for other reasons Edward and I were not privy to, Father was released from the Tower a few weeks later. We liked to boast that the Queen was too affrighted by the thought of an invasion led by a boy to keep him imprisoned—but in our hearts, we guessed the truth was that the King felt Father had suffered enough, having been taught a harsh lesson.

Father seemed older and sadder when he reached Ludlow, his hair unshorn and his chin unshaven. He closeted himself in his apartments while a bath was drawn and the barber arrived to make him a lord again rather than a ragged prisoner.

When he felt himself again, he summoned us boys to his apartments. Entering, we knelt before him while he cast an impassive gaze over us. "I heard about what you did, Edward—the rumours you allowed to fly about the country." His grey-blue eyes flicked to my face. "And though I am aware Edward was the instigator, I know well you also played a large part, Edmund."

"Do not punish Little Ned, Lord Father. Edmund tried to stop me," Ned gasped, but Father raised a hand for silence, and Edward bowed his head and obeyed.

"What you did was imprudent. It could have worsened my plight, sealed both your fates, and affected the wellbeing of your mother and siblings. Never do anything so rash again—promise me!"

"I promise…I swear it," mumbled Edward.

"And you, Edmund?"

"I swear too, Father."

"Good." He folded his arms; I noticed he was thinner, his clothes hanging loosely on his frame. "And now that you have been chastised, I will say but one more thing. But do not tell anyone else I said it."

"And what is that, sire?" asked Edward, frowning.

"I say this... God's Nails, you are brave boys, well made in the image of your Plantagenet forebears. I may not be pleased by your dangerous activities, but I can feel nought but pride for your valour."

In September, Father decided to go to visit our heavily pregnant mother at Fotheringhay, taking us with him. For part of the journey, we were allowed to ride out ponies rather than travel in a carriage, which made us feel grown up indeed.

As we crossed the meadows near Fotheringhay, we both at once spied the huge lantern tower of the church rising out of the autumnal mist, a beacon guiding us to our ancestral home.

Soon the humped bridge over the Nene appeared, the waters of the river swelling beneath its arches and curled leaves of gold and red sailing by on its current. Riding over the bridge, we viewed the wharves and docks along the river's edge, with paths leading from them to the foot of the castle walls. Above the crenels reared the keep on its motte, late sunlight turning the pale stone to buttery yellow. From every tower flew Father's banner, fluttering as if the falcon sought to tear free and fly in search of its enemies.

"I can barely remember Fotheringhay," I breathed. "We've been long away. I wonder if George will know us after all this time."

Edward peered up at the covered wooden wall walk, shading his eyes against the brightness. "Ha! Bessie and Meg are up there waving—can you see them, Little Ned? George is there with his nurse!"

Blinking in the glare, I waving frantically back at my sisters. I had missed them—even though they were girls and unable to join in the roughhousing Edward and I enjoyed.

Surrounded by Father's knights, our entourage processed down the main street of Fotheringhay. The House of York was well-loved here and the townsfolk poured from their homes to give welcome, the maidens hurling pressed Michaelmas Day's Eyes and the goodwives calling out blessings. Passing the church, the bells rang out in celebration, their booms echoing off the castle walls.

Once in the castle, Ned and I were whisked to the nursery, where our sisters waited, still pink-cheeked and windblown from standing atop the walls. We bowed and kissed their outstretched hands, aping the noble knights in tales of chivalry. George was with them, a baby no longer, toddling around in his long, ruffled gown, his hair a mass of dusky gold curls. He clutched a small wooden toy horse, which he clearly chewed on, for its ears were missing.

"Do you remember me, George?" I swept him up in my arms. "I am your brother, Edmund!"

"No!" he said in high dudgeon, hitting me on the arm with the toy horse, while Edward guffawed with mirth and Meg and Bessie tittered and nudged each other. "Put George *down*!"

"I'll let you ride pick-a-pack, if you want," I offered, setting him back on his feet. "I'll be exactly like your little horse...only bigger." I reached down to touch his toy with the tip of my fingers.

He paused, considering my offer, then threw the wooden horse down, and said, "Be George's pony."

I knelt on the floor and he climbed on my back. "Put your arms tightly round my neck," I said, before springing up and careering around the chamber while George screeched with unbridled delight.

His yells brought the nursemaids, who stared at us with disapproval. "Don't you lead your little brother astray with your wild ways, young masters," admonished Em, waggling a finger as she took a protesting George from me. "We cannot disturb your Lady Mother at this time."

Murmuring an apology, I hung my head. Mother had not greeted us, for she had gone into confinement to await the birth of our new brother or sister. Locked in her chambers with other ladies and friends, the shutters would be closed, curtains drawn, prayers uttered, and gentle, soothing songs sung. Candles and sweet-smelling incense would burn day and night. Precious stones with magical qualities to ease the pangs of travail would be placed on Mother's belly, and saint's girdles scribed with magickal words would arrive in gilded reliquaries to ensure a safe birth. It was all part of women's mysteries, and hence a forbidden world for me and Edward.

Bessie coughed, breaking the uncomfortable silence that had fallen. "Why don't we all go to the stables? We won't be too loud out there. I have a new pony..."

"Pony!" screamed George, snatching his mangled toy off the floor. "*Yesss*!"

"Visiting the stables would be an excellent idea," said Em. "But remember—keep out of mischief."

Our brother, Richard, was born on the 2nd day of October. Mother's distressing cries had rung throughout the castle despite the stout doors and thick walls. To keep us children from fretting overmuch, Anne Caux marched us out to deliver alms to the poor before praying in the church for Mother's safe delivery.

I could scarcely recall St Mary's from my earliest days, but the church was much-loved by Father, who intended it as a mausoleum for the House of York. His elder brother Edward, who fell at Agincourt, was already buried in the choir.

In the nave, the roof vault soared towards heaven, lit by the church's large windows. A wall-painting of a grinning skeleton capered near the west door, reminding one of how even in life, death always hovered near—which was the intention of the artist. *As I am, so thou shalt be...*

Respectfully, our little band approached the high altar, aware that on the ceiling, the Falcon and Fetterlock stamped the authority of our family in timeless stone.

It was humbling to think that in the far future, my bones might rest beneath that fierce Falcon, alongside those of my kin. I clasped my hands together, staring up.

"What's wrong?" Ned tilted his head and whispered in my ear. "You look half in a trance."

"I-I was thinking…" I muttered.

"About what?"

"You know…The baby…Mother." My gaze drifted to the central crossing and the Lady Chapel where our siblings who did not survive childhood were buried—Henry, William, John and, most recently, Thomas.

Ned understood my meaning; we always had a special bond. He gave my hand a secret squeeze when our sisters were looking in a different direction. "Remember the words of Mother Julian of Norwich, Edmund? Our own Lady Mother taught them to us—*'All shall be well, and all shall be well, and all manner of things shall be well'.*"

At this, I smiled a crooked, wobbly smile, and my heart swelled with gratitude to have such a wise brother. We moved on towards the altar, as my fears lightened a little.

All will be well...

Upon returning to the castle in the falling dusk, I realised something had happened. Servants clattered through the courtyard, lighting torches against the darkness; their voices were raised, although I could not make out the words. I strained to ascertain whether they looked grieved or downcast. It did not seem so, but I had no trust of my ability to read others' emotions. Did I see only what I wanted to see?

A clarion blared from one of the towers, and all within courtyard and bailey fell still. A tabarded herald stepped forward on the wall walk, and cried aloud, "Hear ye all! Upon this day, her Grace the Duchess of York is delivered safely of a son."

"The baby has come!" squealed Bessie, fairly dancing.

"And he is alive," said Ned.

"And our Lady Mother, too!"

Meg grabbed my hand with cold little fingers, bouncing up and down on the balls of her feet. "We have a new little brother, Neddy—let's go see him!"

Earlier fears lifted, the four of us flew for the door of the keep.

It was time to celebrate.

Our baby brother was Christened Richard, after Father and Saint Richard of Chichester. He was baptised in the old Norman tub font in the castle chapel. He was but a little scrap, smaller than the average babe, but screamed lustily when immersed in the holy water—an excellent sign of healthy lungs.

"He resembles you, Edmund," Ned said later, when Father dined with the nobles designated Godparents for the new baby, and we retired to our chamber, having eaten a glorious repast in the babe's honour.

"Who does?"

"Richard. Our brother."

"He looks like a *baby*," I scoffed, although secretly I agreed—or, rather, our sire's look was strong in the new infant as well as in my own features.

"It is nice being here at Fotheringhay." Ned rolled onto his back, lacing his hands behind his head. "All of us together."

"Maybe we'll get to stay for Christmas."

Edward's eyes sparkled. "Maybe. Father is trying to avoid the King. Henry travelled to Ludlow in our absence and had to make do with the steward. I also heard rumours that our sister Anne will be coming."

"With *him*?" I asked, intrigued now.

We had never met Anne's husband, Henry Holland, Duke of Exeter, who was by all accounts a thoroughly unpleasant fellow. Anne was now thirteen now and soon to become his 'true wife' (whatever that meant; I was not privy to such secrets.) She had dwelt in his household since the marriage contract was signed, and we had seldom had her ever since, although she wrote to Mother, her letters full of woeful tales. Exeter as was far from our Father politically as these once, hoped-for allies could be, unfortunately, adding another issue to Anne's marriage.

Edward smirked. "I suspect Exeter will be here if she is, Little Ned. If he let her come on her own, she might refuse to go back to him."

"What a scandal that would cause!" I gasped, slightly appalled by his suggestion. Our marriages were arranged for the weal of our House, and it was our duty to make those marriages work. Mind you, it sounded like attempting to make a decent alliance with the Duke of Exeter was futile, wedding or no.

"Would it cause a greater scandal if I clouted Henry Holland on the nose?" Ned grinned.

I chortled at the thought. "Yes…but if he deserves it, do it anyway!"

The Christmas season arrived and we remained at Fotheringhay. Unfortunately, Browne and Cadnum had journeyed from Ludlow with us, so Ned and I were back at our studies, showing the greatest diligence, as it was now easier for the tutors to complain about our scholarly failures to both our Father *and* Mother.

Mother had received her churching and returned to daily life. She complained to her ladies that the recent birth had hurt her more than any prior; how her lower back ached as if breaking, and how she felt as worn out as a crone of eighty summers. "I am growing too old for childbirth," she said. "Maybe I shall write a letter to the Queen that she may remember our old friendship and feel a little pity for her old companion."

"You mean to write to the Queen?" cried one of the women. "You would write to Margaret after all that has transpired?"

"I was the prime Duchess at her court," said Mother, haughtily. "Some would even call us friends. The Queen had her own woes, as you might imagine, and oftimes confided in me. Whatever one might think of her, I doubt she will have forgotten all friendships. She fears Richard seeks to supplant the King, but if we could speak openly and honestly, perhaps this whole unfortunate situation with Edmund Beaufort can be sorted out."

Another of her ladies—daughter of a countess or such—pursed her lips, looking doubtful. "You might try, your Grace, but she...she is enamoured of Edmund Beaufort. They spend much time alone when Henry is on his knees, praying..."

Mother harrumphed. "I am well aware of those rumours, but I saw no sign of such when at court. Even so, there is surely no harm in trying to rekindle old friendships..." She paused suddenly, the horns on her headdress creating a long shadow as she turned towards the doorway where I stood. "You wanted something, Edmund?" she asked, her tone high and sweet but with a barb beneath.

I went red and sweaty. "Madam...Lady Mother, forgive my intrusion. I merely wanted to ask if I could take George to the Mews. The nurses say he has fretted all morning."

Mother smiled then; she had a soft spot for George despite his rambunctiousness. "Granted. The child is *always* fretting. Oh, and Edmund—close the door behind you. I'd prefer no more *visitors*."

I did, with ever so much care, and then, hot with embarrassment, I fled.

I took George to the Mews as Ned and I had promised him. He was grizzly ever since Richard was born, all too aware that he was no longer the 'baby' and the centre of attention. We strolled among the hawks on their perches, gently chiding him when he made sharp moves that frightened them or stuck his fingers too close to the birds' fierce beaks. George watched, rapt, as the falconer fed the hawks mice, rabbits, and even a flapping bat.

"You will have fine hawks of your own one day, George." Edward patted his curly head as if he were a large puppy.

"Yes! An' a big horse. An' a sword!" George piped, without looking at either Ned or me; he was fixated on Father's goshawk, Arrowflight, who was devouring a small quail with gusto. "Then George be bigger and better than baby!"

"Come now, George. You are baby Richard's big brother." I grinned down at him. "He will be a good playmate for you when he's older. You can teach him how to ride—and how to feed hawks without getting his fingers snapped off." I snatched George's hand away from the beak of Arrowflight, who had finished his meal and was eyeing the room for further tender morsels.

Chubby face determined, George tried to wriggle loose, and Ned and I both struggled to hold him back. His mouth opened in what would be an ear-piercing shriek of Plantagenet rage—but at that moment, there was a commotion outside the Mews. Trumpets were blowing in the distance, and the bailey was full of the sound of frenzied activity.

"Shall we see what's going on?" Edward asked our little brother, trying to make his voice sound enticing—as if the newcomers might have a menagerie like the fabled one at the Tower of London, brimming with lions, porcupines, and elephants. It was probably no more than some mouldy old knight from the shires, come to give his respect to the Duke and Duchess of York and congratulate them on Richard's birth, but George did not have to know that.

The screech of wrath averted, George tore loose and sprinted from the Mews into the castle bailey, the Ned and I in hot pursuit. The last thing we needed for our infant brother to be ridden down by our sire's visitors while we were in charge of him.

Ned caught him after a few paces, swinging him onto his shoulders on one swift motion and we hurried toward the activity near the main gate. A large company with brightly caparisoned horses was entering the castle precincts; I spotted the banner of the Dukes of Exeter—the Arms of England within an azure border, charged with fleur-de-lis for France. Our sister Anne was home!

I strained my eyes, attempting to pick her out amidst the horsemen and wagons, but she was in a chariot with drawn curtains and made no attempt to peer out, even when people began calling her name.

"Come on," said Edward as the cavalcade thundered by and the steward ventured over with his wand of office to greet the newly-arrived Duke and Duchess. "Let us go inside and greet our sister. "I wager she won't recognise us and we won't recognise her. She is probably very much the great lady now!"

George bouncing on his shoulders, Ned began taking long strides towards the apartments. I sprinted along next to him, teasing George with a hawk feather I'd found in the Mews. My heart fairly leapt with joy.

Our whole family together, hale and well, after several years of separation.

It seemed like a Christmas miracle.

The happiness did not last long—did it ever? Later that day, Ned and I were called to the Great Hall to dine with our sister and her husband. The youngest children stayed in the nursery with Mistress Caux and Em; Father deliberated over whether I should have a place, but decided I could attend.

As it was Advent and an Ember Day, following as it did the Feast of the martyr St Lucy, the food laid out on the trestle tables was sparse and plain—fish alongside a mess of vegetables. No spices or sauces or slabs of butter were permitted, making the fare bland and dull. Honey beer and wine also fell under the prohibition, with only the weakest drink served. After days of such dining, on and off, many in the castle were already growing tetchy and short-tempered.

Anne sat at the high table next to Mother, as she was not only the eldest of our siblings but a Duchess. I tucked into my trencher, eyeing her with interest. As yet, we had not been re-introduced as the Duke and Duchess of Exter went straight to my parents for a private welcome.

Observing Anne, she seemed shy, her eyes demurely downcast at all times. She wore a bourrelet headdress but had not yet adopted the fashion of older ladies in plucking off the eyebrows. Her gown was of dark green silk that appeared almost black in the candlelight till she moved; then the colour would leap out in rolling verdant waves. Unfortunately, its darkness further bleached her pallid countenance; she resembled a small white doll propped up on cushions.

Henry Holland sat on the other side of her, sporting an irritated expression, his glance darting hither and thither as if he wished he were anywhere but Fotheringhay. His face was comely enough, as much as I could judge such things, but spoilt by a tight mouth like a cat's arse and a crop of florid pimples. I guessed him to be in his early twenties.

Father was trying to hold congenial discourse with him, but Holland was answering in grunted monosyllables while jabbing fiercely at the plain fare on his trencher with his eating-knife. Every few minutes he was calling for more watered-down ale or a new napkin or complaining that the fish was cold and not nearly as fine as that served on his table in his Devonshire holdings, some of which were near the sea. "We have fresh fish all the time, straight from the boat," he bragged. "Don't we, Anne?"

Anne jumped as if startled. Her fingers nearly lost hold of the stem of her goblet; she set it down with a clatter. "Y-yes, Henry," she said in a thin, uncertain voice.

Mother's eyes narrowed dangerously. Father was still trying to be conciliatory and even jovial. Averting anything political or any of his troubles in the past year, he attempted to talk with Henry Holland about pleasant, ordinary subjects such as hounds and horses.

His efforts seemed to bore Henry. "I suppose I must get a horse for Anne soon," he sighed, "if she will learn to ride properly."

Mother cleared her throat. "Anne rode well enough as a child."

"On a pony," said Henry, his tone condescending. "I would teach her to ride a fitting rouncey, but she says she is afraid. She *will* learn, though and soon; a Duke's wife would be a laughing stock riding about on an ambling child's pony. You wouldn't want that, would you, Anne? Townsfolk pointing and laughing?"

"No," Anne stared down into her lap.

"Perhaps I could purchase one suitable for her," said Father.

Henry grinned. "No…no, I will not hear of it, my lord Duke. I can look well enough after my wife's needs. I would not dream of you having to open your purse to bestow such a gift; not when it is known that you…well…" He held out his hands. "I do not mean to insult, but it is common knowledge of your money woes." He let his words fall away, like hot turds down a privy chute.

I glanced at Edward, sword-straight, his eyes glassy with rage. "What an obnoxious oaf!" he spluttered. Every bit as bad as people claimed."

Father was still holding his temper in check, no doubt for Anne's sake. "I see. I assure you my situation is not quite as dire as that."

"Oh, that news pleases me," said Henry, smarmily. "Hopefully soon you will return to the King's good graces."

Holland's voice was loud and many in the hall fell silent in embarrassment. Never had I eaten a meal where there was so little amiable chatter amongst those partaking. Mother turned icy; Father's attempts at conversation, failing, became an extended silence as he ate with a murderous expression on his face. Anne's drained cheeks became splotchy; I thought she might cry. Henry Holland flung back another goblet of watered-down ale, let out a belch, and said, smugly, "Ah, as I feared, the fish was off. Or maybe it was this sour drink. Thank you anyway, for the fare, Duke Richard…."

I thought Father might swing for him then, but he managed to keep his anger in check. "As it is still Advent, I think we should forgo any more food and retire early," he said stiffly, rising from his seat. "My Lady?" He offered his arm to Mother, and they both swept from the hall, leaving the rest of the household stunned and confused. The servers flooded in, silent and glum, scraping the remains of the trenchers into the voiders.

Holland looked a little stunned himself but still smug. "Your Father has spoken, wife," he said to Anne. "Time to go." He extended his arm to her as our sire had done to Mother, but when she linked her arm through his, he leapt up abruptly. The unexpected jolt pulled Anne forward, almost toppling her from her seat. She grasped the table to steady herself, knocking over Henry's half-filled goblet.

"How clumsy," said Exeter.

"He did that deliberately!" Ned half rose, fist clenched.

I yanked on his sleeve. "Ned, no. It's what he wants!"

"What he wants is a good thrashing!" growled Edward.

"Yes—but it is not for you to give it to him. He is a Duke, and a man grown. He...he could kill you!"

"I hate him," Ned muttered darkly, wearing an expression I had never seen before on a lad his age. I was his brother, and it even frightened me.

Over the rest of Christmas, Henry Holland remained boorish but not as obnoxious as on that first horrible night. He loved to hunt and would go out almost every day to Park Spinney, the deer park near Fotheringhay. As his host, Father accompanied him, but while Henry remained at the lodge in the park, surrounded by men from his own entourage, he trudged wearily back to Fotheringhay.

"I often regret that we married Anne to that brute," I overheard him say to Mother. "He loves her not, and his delight in showing us this truth makes my heart rage. I would gladly keep her here when he decides to leave—which I pray will be soon."

Mother sighed, slamming the breviary she held shut. "She is his wedded wife, Richard. To keep her from him would cause a scandal. We would have to come up with a reason for an annulment."

"Consanguinity usually works," said Father grimly. "It has for many others."

"Yes, but you forget, Henry Holland is already, to all intents and purposes, of dubious loyalty to this family. If you should separate him from Anne, he will use it as yet another excuse to come against you—perhaps with arms. Do not worry about Anne; she knows her duty, for I taught it to her. Henry may well come to appreciate her as she matures and looks comelier to his eyes."

"He goads me whenever he can and smiles even as he gives offence," glowered Father.

"He is testing the boundaries as young men often do."

"He is well in with my enemies already." Father tossed a crust of bread into the brazier, where it burst into flames. The dogs lying near the fire's warmth looked mournful at being denied the titbit. "We have always treated him well, but he is a selfish fool."

"I cannot disagree with you there," Mother nodded. "Proud, arrogant…and rather stupid. If he does not grow out of these mannerisms—Well, men of his temperament often end up in an early grave. However, if he should get a child on Anne before the inevitable happens, all we had hoped from their marriage might still come true. An alliance between two noble Houses and a grandchild of York to inherit Exeter's lands."

"What do you think, young Edmund?" asked Father. "Have you spoken to your sister's husband at all?"

"I have not." I attempted to be tactful. "I have hardly spoken to Anne, either, alas. He has her trailing behind him as if she were on a leash."

Father made a choking noise and his mouth worked in rage. I flushed before realising he was not angry at my honest words but with Henry Holland. "See, even the boy notices!" he cried. "He sees his own sister maltreated by that caitiff!"

"Richard, calm yourself," said Mother. "This…drama does no one any good. Let time take care of things one way or the other."

"If he should harm her…"

"If he should cause her any physical hurt, Richard…" Mother grabbed a long pin that fastened her hennin and thrust it into the cushion she rested upon. "You need not bestir yourself. For *I* shall hunt him down myself and relieve him of his…"

"Cecily!" Father cried, astounded. Red-faced, he flapped his hands in my direction. "Edmund, your services as squire this evening are no longer required. A good night to you."

Bowing, I hurried away through the dim hallways, eager to tell Ned, who was in bed nursing a winter cold, what our parents had said about horrible Henry Holland.

Twelfth Night rolled around, the final day of the Christmas festivities. A lavish feast was held—and our less-than-pleasant brother-by-marriage was present. Now that the time of fasting was over, the trenchers were heaped high with boar, venison, goose, crane, salmon, crayfish, and eels—although I could scarcely bear looking at the latter, let alone eat them. Their heads were left on and their spiky maws resembled the Hell Mouth depicted in church Doom scenes.

Some years ago, the Pope had abolished an earlier celebration called the Feast of Fools (a pity—it sounded like a riotous time was had by all save the sourest priests) but some of its ancient traditions had grafted themselves onto Twelfth Night.

In true festive style, mummers cavorted around the hall in wooden masks and shaggy hides, becoming beasts and figures from mythology, sharp-toothed bears, lewd satyrs, a hobby horse wearing a real horse's skull, a cow-horned man wrapped in patchwork skins, and a holly king all wreathed in prickles and mistletoe.

The castle chaplain was also in the hall, gathering a crowd as he intoned his predictions for the coming year. This was not considered sorcerous blasphemy, as one might imagine, but was based on methods of divination in the Bible, which foretold events from observing the natural world.

"On the day of our Lord's birth, I witnessed a rainbow over the battlements," said the priest. "This betides hope and promise as it is the symbol of Christ. However, I noted the winds blew fierce from the north, which foretells a year of hardship for men of station and power."

"I shall weather any such storm," boasted Henry Holland, nursing a large goblet of wine—about his sixth that eve. "However, I am sure weaker souls may be blown away like leaves on the wind."

Henry reached over and snatched a large piece of marchpane cake from a platter brought to the celebrants' tables and inelegantly thrust it into his mouth, leaving a haze of crumbs on his lips. Suddenly he stopped, his eyes growing wide.

"Maybe he's choking on it," Edward whispered to me, hopeful.

But Henry rose from his seat, fishing in his mouth with a finger. "I—I have it!" he cried. "I have it!"

"What now? Has one of his teeth fallen out?" I mused.

Henry was waving around an object held between his thumb and forefinger. "I have it! The bean!"

He had found a bean hidden in his cake, and that was not any old bean. It was the one that gave its finder a title for the night—the Lord of Misrule. I nearly groaned at the thought, for the Lord of Misrule was permitted, for one evening only, to order the other Twelfth Night celebrants to do whatever he commanded.

Henry snaked out into the centre of the hall, his little eyes raking over the feasters. His gaze skimmed over Mother and Father then slid to the benches—even he would not dare command my parents, tradition be damned.

For a moment, he glanced at me and I felt Ned grow tense, but for whatever reason, Holland whirled around and turned his attentions upon my poor sister Anne instead.

"Anne, my dear," he said, "as the Lord of Misrule, I demand that you come to my side."

Miserably she shuffled over to Henry, her head hanging. "Smile for me, Anne!" he ordered. "It is Twelfth Night, after all! A night for laughter and merriment. But you are never merry, are you? Well, tonight, as the Lord of Misrule, I command you to be!"

He beckoned to the mummers who had earlier entertained us. "You!" He gestured to the man dressed in the hideous wooden mask mounted with ribbon-decked cow's horns. "Let me have your mask."

The mummer hesitated but dared not say no. Uncertain, he took a step towards Holland. "My Lord Duke?"

"You heard me! Give it to me! I haven't got all night." Exeter reached out and snatched the mask from its owner's face even as the man began to remove it.

"Stand still, wife!" Henry said, thrusting the mask over Anne's shocked countenance. "Now we will dance! Come, musicians, play a lively air!"

A piper and a drummer stepped forward; they were not Father's personal musicians but part of a small troupe that travelled with Henry and Anne, to alleviate boredom as they fared between various manors and castles. They began to play a jaunty, somewhat comical air; no stately dance but music one might expect in a rowdy tavern. A singer emerged, dressed as a woodwose, and with him Henry's personal Fool, an old dwarf who served Exeter's sire for decades. The Fool was wrinkled and gnarled like a little monkey; he had a sinister visage with bristling brows and a huge curved nose and chin. He wore the full parti-colour outfit of his profession and the crescent-shaped hat with its ring of bells. He capered around in circles, his evil beady gaze fixed on his master.

Henry took Anne's arm and swung her round as if to begin a roundel or some other sprightly dance. Unable to see through the ill-fitting mask made for a grown man, she stumbled blindly. Behind Holland, the singer began to bellow the words of a ridiculous old ditty—

The Man in the Moon came down too soon,
and asked the way to Norridge.
The man in the South he burnt his mouth
while eating cold pease-porridge!

The Fool mimed eating, then gurned and stretched his mouth with clawed fingers as if his lips were burnt. Sniggers abounded in Holland's entourage; the rest of the feasters looked flabbergasted.

Suddenly the Fool tumbled to the ground, chin on the rushes and buttocks raised—a staged fall, for he winked and grinned. The music grew even louder, and Henry lifted Anne in her horned mask and whirled her right over the body of the Fool, while the woodwose bawled,

High diddle-diddle, the cat and the fiddle…
the cow jumped o'er the Moon!

The insult was now obvious. And horrible. An audible gasp rippled through the onlookers. Mother and Father sat as if frozen on the dais, unbelieving.

Anne ripped the mask from her face and flung it to the floor with a clatter. She gazed down at the Fool, still with his rump in the air, and at the hairy Woodwose. "How dare you!" she spat at both of them, her voice childish and tearful at first, but strengthening as pure anger set in. "And most of all…" she railed at Henry, "how dare *you*, Henry Holland! *Husband.* Why don't you repudiate me, if you find me so repulsive that you must humiliate me before your friends, my kin …and even my Lord Father and Lady Mother, who have made you a guest in their house!"

"Oh, Anne, I am the Lord of Misrule!" he whined, sounding more childish than the angry young girl facing him. "It was meant as a jest. Surely everyone in this hall knows that."

There was silence. Even Holland's own companions looked abashed.

"Stay with your Fool," said Anne, "if you enjoy 'jests' so much. Now leave me be!"

Shoving past him, she swept from the Great Hall, head held high but still clearly upset, her footsteps growing louder as she broke into a run.

Henry stood there, gormless, finally realising through his wine-soaked haze that he had gone too far.

Next to me, Edward muttered a curse and sprang from his bench. I thought he might lunge for Henry, but instead he rushed out of the hall after Anne. I decided to leave Holland to the mercy of my parents, and charged after Ned, while the Twelfth Night feasters gaped at my retreating back.

"Where do you think she went? I cannot see her anywhere!" I almost careered into Ned's broad back as I exited the castle into the pitch-dark gardens.

My brother was staring this way and that in frustration. The winter's night had long drawn in, and moon and stars were obscured by a mass of thick, ragged-edged clouds. The air was freezing and held a scent I could only describe as 'snowy."

"I don't know, Ned," I said. "Maybe she's hiding. I could hardly blame her."

"I hope she hasn't gone to the Great Pond...." His breath fogged in the air and he began to stride toward the sluice gate.

"Why would she go there?" I rushing after him, as with dawning horror, I realised he thought she might leap into the icy water rather than return to her piggish husband.

But suddenly Ned halted, pressing a hand to his brow. "No, no...What am I thinking? She would have to cross the outer bailey and for sure the watch would have seen her. She must be, as you said, hiding in the gardens." He swung back towards the empty flower and herb bed, the bleak trellises, the bushes dripping red berries. Frost rimmed the edges of leaves like icing on a subtlety. All was still—but there were plenty of places where a small, slim girl might hide and remain unseen.

Ned and I wandered on into the garden. We thought about calling for Anne, but if anyone else was about—like Holland—our voices would alert them, making her even more likely to bolt or do something foolish through fear.

As we swerved between bushes and naked trees, the frosty grass crunching under our feet, I realised the night had begun to lighten. A rising wind was clawing the clouds apart, and a rind of moon appeared like a fingernail paring, casting a bluish glow across the garden. Absolute darkness lifted...and I saw her. Anne.

She was poised on the edge of a little fishpond, its surface covered by a sheet of ice. Her expression was mournful; she bit her lower lip as if straining to keep back tears.

Nudging Ned, I pointed, and we strode in her direction. Anne leapt back in fright as we burst from the tangle of bushes and dead vines. Once she realised who it was, a fiery expression filled her eyes, reminding me of our mother when she was angry. "Did our sire send you? Or our Lady Mother? I shan't go back inside just to please them. I am weary of being teased and humiliated by the man who is supposed to be my 'loving husband'!"

"We won't make you do anything, Anne." Ned reached out to put a comforting hand on her arm. "Edmund and I merely wanted to make sure you were all right here on your own."

Her brow creased and she shook off his hand. "Why wouldn't I be all right? I am in a garden...not a dungeon."

"We thought you might have tried to escape the castle," I said. "It's slippery and dangerous, especially at the Great Pool. You were so upset, we feared you might…might…" I faltered.

"Might what?" She let out a bitter laugh of realisation. "You thought I might cast myself in the water to drown like some lump-headed maiden in an old tale! Come, I may seem foolish and weak to you—but to commit such a sin over *him*? Never!"

"No one thinks you are foolish and weak," said Ned. "We…we do not like him, either. We're your brothers; we want to protect you, as is our duty."

"Protect me from my own lawfully wedded husband." Her lips drew tight, making her look far older than her years. "You…you are both still children too young to understand. I am bound to him, no matter what. Duty—I must do my duty. Ask our mother; she impressed me upon this every day before my wedding."

"So why are you out here if you are so dutiful to Holland?" Edward folded his arms, a bit sulkily.

"Duty or not, I refuse to suffer such humiliation. Henry has imbibed too much drink and is showing off—well, he can crawl into his bed and sober up. I won't be his object of ridicule, a tool that he uses to needle Father. He has nailed his colours to the King's faction, and he certainly wants to show it."

"You cannot remain out here," I said reasonably. "You'll freeze. It's the dead of winter and your garments are made for indoors."

"I know," she said. "It was never my intention to stay all night. I hoped that Henry would grow bored of his sport and stumble off to his chamber."

"You thought wrong, my dear Lady Wife." We jumped as the slurred voice of Henry Holland cut through the gloom. Turning, I watched him stagger through the garden, his top lip raised in an unpleasant sneer. He was weaving in and out, his breath steaming in the air—the scent of drink stretched into my nostrils even before he reached us.

Henry bowed mockingly to Anne, almost falling over in his drunkenness. "I would not lie abed when my sweet bride was missing! What might you do without me? What might you say? Now, *come*!" His wheedling, falsely sweet voice grew hard, commanding—as if he spoke to a misbehaving dog. He pointed to his side; again, as if our sister was an animal who needed to come to heel.

Sick nerves mingled with red-hot anger. I was intensely aware, and it was not a pleasant feeling, how powerless I was before this man, this Duke. How all three of us were.

Cold sweat creeping at the nape of my neck, I glanced at Edward. Fury was obvious in his narrowed eyes, the set of his jaw. I quailed with fright, for he appeared like a wolf about to spring, all taut muscles—but he was not a wolf, he was a ten-year-old boy, and his opponent was a man trained in the arts of war.

"Ned…" Instinctively I reached for his wrist, ready to restrain him.

He yanked away without a glance in my direction, his gaze focussed, unwavering, on Henry Holland's face. "*You…*" he spat. "You caitiff! You are afraid Anne will spill tales of your cruel ways to our Father…yet all the while you spread tales of *him* to your faction at court. He gave you much when you were his ward, and yet you have cast in your lot with his enemies."

Henry swayed, a gasping laugh exiting his mouth. "A child such as you knows nought of such matters, Edward of York. One learns swift enough that in this world one must seek out those amongst the powerful whose stars shine brightly—and not lumber oneself with noble and worthy dullards who are out of favour and whose influence and power wanes…"

"You *dare* to insult my father!" hissed Edward, his hands clenching and unclenching. "I should strike you, and would if it were not for the presence of my sister Anne."

A bellow of mirth erupted from Henry Holland. "Oh, Jesu, should I shake in my boots at that threat? A pompous little boy threatens to smite me? Oh, what terror the thought brings! How shall the infant do his deed of valour? Will this insolent babe strike me with his rattle?"

"Henry, please…" Anne tried to take her husband's elbow and guide him away from the confrontation. "This will not end well for anyone. Calm yourself."

Angrily he threw his arm back, hitting her shoulder, and she stumbled with a pained cry.

It was the last straw for Ned. With an enraged cry, he launched himself at Henry, pummelling him with his fists. Henry swung at him in return, but he was so intoxicated that he missed and lurched to one side. Yelling in frustration, he swung at Edward again, but Ned was ready for him—though not with his hands. Lowering his head as if he were an angry ram, he charged straight into Henry Holland, his skull ploughing into Henry's belly and knocking the air out of him. Gasping, Henry staggered backwards, teetering on the edge of the fishpond.

"Have a bath, Henry!" shouted Ned. "Maybe it will sober you up." He leapt forward, giving his foe another sharp shove.

Henry howled in rage and surprise and toppled over backwards, striking the thin ice of the pond. It shattered around him, sticking up like blades in the cold blue moonlight. Luckily for him, the pool was not terribly deep and clogged with leaves, so there was no fear he would sink and drown. However, his sotted state rendered him unable to rise; he flopped and twisted like a hooked fish, roaring a string of profanities.

It was, in truth, hilarious, and I found it hard to contain my mirth, the sound of which would have inflamed Holland's black heart even more.

Anne stood frozen like a statue of ice, too fearful of her husband to approach and help. Ned was still dancing with rage, clearly eager to have another go.

"Wife, assist me!" bellowed the Duke of Exeter, stretching out a hand dripping gobbets of mud.

Anne stared emotionlessly at the hand, as if it belonged to an animated lich or some other monster, and didn't move an inch, though her cheeks grew even whiter under the harsh moonlight.

Her reluctance made Henry grow even wilder. "You will pay for this—the lot of you! Jumped up little bastards from a House aligned with nought but ruin. When I get hold of you…"

"You'll do *what*?" Father's voice sounded from the shadows. A wavering light bobbed into view. Father was marching through the gardens, his Chamberlain bearing a burning lantern before him and several soldiers unsheathed swords at his back. "What by God's Teeth is going on out here?"

Holland began thrashing again, sending up a spray of mud. "Your feral brat…the great lout…he pushed me in!"

Father's lips twitched. "I dare say you deserved it!"

"I want him punished—no, I *demand* it!" Henry fairly screamed.

"You'll demand nought in my house, Exeter," said Father. "Especially as you are leaving."

"Leaving? But I thought to stay on as we agreed! The roads to Devon are flooded and covered in fallen trees. You wouldn't send your daughter out to face such peril, would you?"

"Anne may stay here at Fotheringhay," said Father, with a falsely benign smile. "Once you ascertain the way is safe enough for her to travel, the Duchess of York and I shall send her on after you. Now get out of that pool. You look ridiculous."

Holland, whose teeth had begun to chatter from the cold (or maybe he was grinding them with rage!) stuck his hand out in Father's direction. He glanced down at the dripping, slimy fingers and grimaced, before gesturing to his men to pull Henry free of the pond.

"Anne, Edward, Edmund, let us go inside," he said, and then to the Chamberlain, "See that his Grace the Duke of Exeter is warmed up and that his things are packed for travel. He will be leaving Fotheringhay at first light on the morrow."

Edward leaned over the table while Master Cadnum, under Father's watchful eye, applied a switch to his posterior for pushing Holland into the fishpond. One blow, two, three. Ned barely winced. Father watched, and then as Cadnum lifted his switch for another blow, he caught the tutor's wrist. "Enough. You may depart."

The tutor bowed and hastened from the chamber.

"You did wrong, Ned," said Father as Edward stood up and adjusted his raiment. "I fully understand your anger, for Holland has turned out to be a sore disappointment—but he *is* wedded to your sister, which makes him your brother-by-marriage. He is also a Duke, and you are but a son of a Duke. He outranks you, and although you acted in defence of Anne, your behaviour to a superior was not acceptable. Is that understood, Edward?"

Ned nodded. "Yes, my Lord Father, and I regret shaming you with my rash actions. But I do not regret pushing him into the pond. He deserved it! But I will never act so thoughtlessly again."

"Good."

"As for you, Edmund…" Father faced me, as implacable as a stony mountainside. "I am sure you played some part in this too, hence you were made to watch your brother's punishment. Learn that you do not have to be Edward's shadow. He is not right all the time, and he is not your lord. I am…and God above all else."

I hung my head. "Yes, Lord Father."

"You are both free to go, without further censure, but remember this day. And remember, try not to make too many enemies." His smile was wry. "I certainly have done so, though not necessarily of my making. I have only tried to do what I deem right, but so much I have done has been taken amiss." He folded his arms, worry imprinted on his features, then he shook his head, tossing away the gloom as he did so.

"All will be well," he said. "Winter is nearly over. The sun shall soon shine brightly again upon us all."

At the sign of the first thaw, shortly after the Feast of Candlemas, Big Ned and I said our farewells and set out on the long road to Ludlow.

Upon our return to the Marches, we were thrown into our studies, our Tutors pressing us ever harder to study, write, recite. Our training in arms changed in intensity too; our light 'waster' swords were replaced by blunted metal ones, or thick wooden cudgels the same length, weight, and shape as a real sword. We were encouraged to build up our strength by running around the bailey, riding, and competitively throwing stones of increasing heaviness. Guided by the arms master, we aimed to follow the *Epitoma Rei Militaris*, a tome on battle-training written ages hence by the Roman Flavius Vegetius. Running, jumping, and swimming were foremost for building strength and endurance. Riding too; our small ponies were now replaced by larger Welsh ones. When we were not riding real animals, we used a wooden horse kept in the stables to practice various ways to mount and dismount with speed. Archery practice went on for an hour in the morning, while our other martial pursuits lasted for two hours before Prime. At night, after attending Mass, we tumbled exhausted into bed, with little time for any sort of games or other pleasures.

Gradually we became accustomed to this heightened activity. Our limbs ceased aching from strain; our bodies and faces became leaner. Ned grew several more inches in height. I grew, too, although I recognised that I would never catch him up. I learned not to be envious, though, for I was quicker on my feet and oftimes bested him in our swordplay. Each of us had our strengths and weaknesses.

Not much in the way of news came from Father, who remained at Fotheringhay, but Ludlow was never dull, the town at the castle's foot always bustling with traders and journeymen from afar. From such passers-by we frequently heard tell of foreign affairs—how the Old Talbot, John the Earl of Shrewsbury, had gone to France in a final attempt to reclaim Gascony for England. The natives were unhappy with French rule because of the harsh taxation they suffered. There was also much rejoicing across England when word came that after years of barrenness, Queen Margaret was with child. At last, King Henry would have an heir. This must have been a blow to Father, whose claim to the throne was good, but equally to Edmund Beaufort, who most likely hoped that Henry would nullify the ruling that the Beauforts could not ascend the throne and name him his successor.

In some ways Edward and I were glad that Margaret was pregnant. An obvious legitimate heir might lessen the tensions between the various noble factions. Our family's security might improve, with no more repetitions of our sire's incarceration in the Tower.

However, our childish hopes soon died into darkness. Parliament was called, and Father's enemies deviously brought up the Jack Cade rebellion. "He called himself 'Mortimer,'" they sneered, as they declared that although Cade was long dead, he was a tyrant whose 'name was to be eradicated from Christian lips forever' and whose wicked deeds would be 'be quashed, annulled, and destroyed.'

With this new condemnation of Cade, the cloud of suspicion descended on Father again, and many of his positions and offices were removed—including lifetime grants.

Ned and I raged to hear such things, but there was nothing we could do. The folk of the Marches remained loyal to York, praise be to God. And they remained at peace. Elsewhere, the Percys and Nevilles were feuding, and Lord Egremont had gone as far as attacking our cousin Thomas Neville's wedding party on the road from Lincolnshire to Sheriff Hutton. It was mooted that Egremont and Percy were being egged on by a certain Henry Holland...

Abruptly, Father turned up at Ludlow, giving no warning of his imminent arrival. He was at the gate mere seconds before hurrying to his apartments. I fretted, wondering if some disaster had befallen. After what felt like eternity, we were permitted to enter his presence. Rushing into the solar, we closed in, full of questions shot out as swiftly as arrows from a bow: "Are you well, Lord Father? Is our Lady Mother hale? And our sisters? And George? And baby Richard?"

"Fear not, boys, they are well," he assured us. "I cannot say the same for much else, though. I have come to Ludlow to prepare for possible unwelcome events. I shall have the walls of town and castle strengthened."

Ned paled. "The King is not wanting to imprison you again, is he? We have heard how your foes try to pin Cade's treasonous folly on you and Sir William Oldhall, who has ever been a loyal ally."

Father sighed deeply. "In many ways it is worse than that. Remember the Old Talbot—no friend, but undoubtedly a brave man of honour? He is dead, and the English forces routed at a place called Castillon. Gascony is lost to England for a second time. I fear that it is now lost forever."

Neither Ned nor I spoke. At our ages, battles fought far away meant little to us. At least, I thought, Father cannot take the blame for Gascony's loss or Talbot's failure.

"John Talbot's death is not the worst of it, though." Father poured himself a goblet of claret; I was surprised to see his hand tremble. Almost imperceptibly, but the tremor was definitely there, making the deep red liquid in the cup form waves like a bloody sea. "The problem is with the King."

"Is he ill?" asked Ned.

"In a way. He...he..." Father faltered, then blurted in a rush: "He was never strong of mind, but he has gone mad, like his grandsire

Charles before him, he who believed he was made of glass. When he heard of Talbot's death and defeat, he collapsed in a trance. He has remained so ever since. He cannot walk, nor even lift up his head. Many cures have been tried—shaving his head, bathing him in cold water. But he will not awaken to the living world."

He strode across the chamber, staring out of the window to where masons and workers had already begun to strengthen the stonework of the gatehouse. "As of now, my sons—England has no king."

CHAPTER TEN

"He wouldn't even look at it."
Edward and I were in the stables, currying our Welsh ponies. Stableboys darted here and there, hauling tack; the Master of Horse leaned in a doorjamb talking to a courier who had reached Ludlow the prior day to deliver news to the castle's Constable. The newcomer was having a good gossip about the sick King, Queen Margaret—and the new baby, Edward of Lancaster. "Old Buckingham brought the child to Henry to be acknowledged, as must be done according to custom, but the King remained in a stupor, drooling like an imbecile."

The Master of Horse made a revolted noise. "A dire situation, Jesu help us all."

"Men wonder..." The messenger licked his lips as if the gossip he imparted had a delicious taste. "They wonder if the new babe is the King's—or the byblow of someone in his court. After all, we know Harry was more interested in praying than procreating."

"Indeed. At one banquet did he not see dancers wearing gowns that bared their paps, and he flew into a frenzy, crying, 'Fie on you! For shame!'? Can you imagine that?"

"In Henry's case, I can. 'Tis said he had to be coached to have carnal relations with the Queen, and that his confessor was as prudish as he and advised he practice abstinence."

The Master of Horse snorted, caught between laughter and outrage. "That priest was as mad as Henry. All Kings must do their duty and produce an heir—even Holy Harry."

"I hear tell that Edmund Beaufort often consoled the Queen when she was lonely," said the messenger slyly. "Can't say if it's true or not, but it was known he also 'consoled' dowager Queen Catherine after Harry Five expired. That's why she was sent from court. Mind you, she picked up with that Owen Tudor quick enough! Fancy a dowager Queen secretly marrying a Welsh servant!"

"Aye, shocking, but the King is enamoured of his half-brothers Edmund and Jasper Tudor, so it seems her unseemly behaviour was forgiven."

"Edmund Tudor," smirked the man. "Ever thought why the dowager Queen named him 'Edmund', rather than a French or Welsh name?"

"Ah well." The Master of Horse seemed to notice Ned and I for the first time. "Perhaps we should not ruminate about such subjects. At least there is a prince in the royal cradle; perhaps his arrival will bring peace."

"It won't if Henry never acknowledges him," said the courier. "But as you wish; it is time I set off back to London anyway."

The two men exited the stables, leaving us still brushing our mounts amidst the smell of hay, dung, and leather. "Can you imagine, Ned?" I whispered. "A prince born and his own father will not recognise him!"

"Even if the King *does* recognise him, rumours will always follow him," said Ned. "There will always be those who say he is no true prince and that he has no right to the throne."

"And if that should happen, and the Three Estates decided against his rule, who would next be heir?"

Ned's eyebrows lifted. "Edmund—I think you already know."

CHAPTER ELEVEN

King Henry remained in a stupor. The Queen attempted to pass a bill which made her regent until he recovered, but the council greeted this idea with horror. The notion that a foreign woman should rule over the country appalled them. Margaret had never been popular; too haughty and aloof...and all too French.

Instead, our father was made the Lord Protector. When Henry's health declined, our sire's popularity increased despite all the troubles that had gone before. Such are the vagaries of Dame Fortuna, who brings a man to riches and power. and in the next moment hurls him down into penury or the grave!

One of those who had ridden high on Fortune's Wheel but landed with a resounding thump was Edmund Beaufort. Ned and I did a little celebration dance in our bedchamber when we learnt Beaufort was locked up in the Tower of London. "Where he most assuredly belongs," said Ned, smug with satisfaction.

With this change in fortune, our lives at Ludlow became more content. Fears that Father might end up imprisoned or worse diminished; every newcomer at the gate was not seen as a potential threat. My brother and I lived as young princes and were accorded the greatest respect as sons of the Lord Protector.

"I pray one day he'll be more than just our protector, our blessed Duke o' York!" screeched an old woman selling apples in the marketplace as she grabbed my hand in her palsied claw, almost as if my touch was saintly because of my York blood. "He's the true king to many o' us, you know...."

I smiled but said nothing, withdrawing my hand. It would not do well for rumours about Father becoming king to spread. The little Prince Edward was still heir, even if the traditional acknowledgement of his birth had not taken place. This tradition was set aside for the time being, with councillors arguing that the rules must be bent, for never before had a senseless king sat upon England's throne. Eager to appear entirely disinterested in claiming the throne himself, Father agreed with the postponement, and the baby was made Prince of Wales and

Earl of Chester, with a golden circlet set on his brow, a ring placed on his finger, and a golden rod laid in his cradle.

The year drew on. More revolts shook the north, with the revolting Exeter joining in. I laughed gleefully to hear of the letter Father had sent him, calling him a string of slurs—heinous, ungodly, demeaning, outrageous, and seditious. "And spotty," I offered. "He should have also called Holland spotty."

Even better, our most unbeloved brother-in-law was soon captured and sentenced to prison in the castle of Pontefract, one of the most fearsome castles in the north of England and a place of great infamy. King Richard, second of that name, had been murdered there, some say by starvation so that no injury could be seen upon his flesh. I hoped Henry Holland would think of that long-ago death as he sat mouldering in his cell. I supposed he would be treated well enough, due to his high ancestry, but I enjoyed the thought of rats leaping on his pallet in the night and foetid water dripping on him from the ceiling.

In the weeks that followed, though, I began to wonder if God was punishing me and Edward for our uncharitable japes about Holland. Newcomers had come to stay at Ludlow Castle—the two Croft brothers, Richard and Thomas. The Croft family was well known in the region of the Marches; they had often served the Mortimers, acting as stewards for various Mortimer castles. These two Crofts were of a younger generation and had been sent to Ludlow for training in becoming gentlemen, perhaps to assume the duties of their forebears in due course. They were some years older than Ned and I, and from the moment we met, I scented trouble like a hound scents a rabbit.

The Croft brothers took against us immediately—and that was an understatement. They were appalled to have to share duties with younger boys and clearly let us know this on the very first day.

Dick Croft was big, with a raw-boned face and bushy brows on a large, jutting forehead. His dark hair was shorn in a blocky style above the ears, which made his lumpen features even more prominent and unappealing. His brother, Thomas, was slighter and fairer-haired, his visage more refined if rather foxy and sly, but he deferred to Richard in everything, and the two of them showed their disdain at every turn.

Ned was less shy amongst strangers than I, so he was the first to approach the brothers, who we had thought to make welcome, for it was always hard to be the new boy, no matter your wealth, stature, or parentage. Upon their arrival at their lodgings, Ned sought them out, while I trailed at his heels.

The Crofts were sharing a room with various squires and pages and looked put out as Ned approached them. Dick Croft's arms were folded and his brow lowering so much he reminded me of a troll in an old legend.

"Greetings and welcome to the castle," Ned said pleasantly, extending a hand. "We are pleased to meet you."

The brothers glanced at Ned's outstretched hand as if it were a leper's rotted arm. "Who are you?" asked Dick. "What kind of place is this that sends little children from the nursery to greet guests?"

Edward flushed, his shoulders tensing. "I am Edward," he said, and paused, expecting them to realise who he was without any grandiose introductions. This was, in transpired, a grave error.

The Crofts glared down their noses. "Do you not have a sire-name, boy?" asked Thomas, hands on his hips. "Or are you one of the stableboys? If so, I must complain—when I dismounted, I stepped into a pile of horse shite. It ruined my new shoes!" He raised one foot, shod with an incredibly long-toed poulaine, which was indeed smeared with ordure. "Why was this not swept away by the castle *gong-fermour*? Or do you not have one? It's an outrage. I should make you kneel down and clean it off, stableboy."

Dick Croft sniggered. "I think you should make him, Tom. We need to establish a pecking order here at Ludlow. We, it would seem, are the eldest of the youths here, so their natural masters...or should I say 'leaders'?"

"Oldest, perhaps, but not the noblest and certainly not the brightest," Edward shot back.

The Croft brothers gaped at him as if he had grown a second head upon his shoulders. "You have an over-eager tongue, for one with no name, stableboy Edward," growled Dick.

"Oh, but I *do* have a name, Dick Croft. It is one you might have heard of."

"Maybe. I've known a few Cocks and Dunderheads in my time." Dick elbowed his brother in the ribs, amused by his own weak jest.

"I am sure you have," said Edward, face so angelic that his tormentors did not seem to realise he had turned the 'joke' back on them.

"Come on, stableboy—what's this laudable last name of yours?" asked Thomas, blundering on.

Ned looked him straight in the eye. "It is Plantagenet."

A stunned silence fell, but only for a second—then the Crofts burst into gales of raucous laughter. "Oh, and I'm King Henry's secret byblow!" crowed Dick.

I walked to Ned's side. "He tells the truth. He is Edward, Earl of March, and I am his brother, Edmund, Earl of Rutland."

The brothers fell silent again, this time glancing nervously at each other. Dick Croft swiftly recovered his unpleasant demeanour, and lumbered forward, pointing into our faces. "You lie. Both of you. You are trying to make fools of us! I won't have it, I tell you!"

He thrust himself into Ned's face; spittle struck my brother's cheek and trickled down.

Ned stepped back, wiping off the spray with his sleeve, his expression one of disbelief. The next moment he seemed to have grown wings and was flying through the air—straight towards his burly tormentor. A flurry of fists ensued and Croft hit the ground with a thud, Edward on top of him. Ned caught Dick's collar and twisted, eliciting a gagging noise from his opponent.

"You're in my father's home, you oaf!" cried Edward. "We extended the hand of friendship to you and you spit in my face?"

"Get off me!" howled Dick Croft, but I noticed he was no longer attempting to hit Ned, so perhaps reality was dawning on him—that we had told the truth about who we were. "Or I'll…I'll…"

"You'll what? I have thrown Dukes into ponds," said Ned. "I'm not afraid of the likes of you!"

Thomas Croft began to look panicked. "Help…stop him!" he cried, his voice comically high, waving an arm in Edward's direction as he half-throttled his brother.

One of the pages had already run for assistance, and the Constable was striding into the room wearing a thunderous expression. Edward released Dick Croft and jumped to his feet.

The Constable leaned over and dragged Croft to his feet none too gently. He then hauled on Thomas' arm, giving both youths a hard shake that reminded me of terriers shaking rats they had caught. "Your first day here, and you do *this*! Come with me. Make haste!"

He stormed from the chamber, the brothers scowling and round-shouldered with shame as they hurried behind him; I caught the elder Croft giving me an evil glare as they went. The pages and squires were suppressing giggles.

I sighed. I had a bad feeling that we had not experienced the last of the Croft brothers' mischief.

The Crofts quickly learnt that we were indeed the sons of Richard of York and earls to boot. (I was also Lord Chancellor of Ireland, by my sire's decree, but owing to my young age and the fact I was in England, meant my duties were assumed by the Bishop of Meath.) However, this did not make them like us any more than when they thought we were humble stableboys.

The issue with the Crofts in some ways was worse than Ned's spat with Henry Holland. Henry had immediately left Fotheringhay afterwards, but we were stuck with Dick and Thomas. Father had invited them here, remembering the good service of their family in the past. If we acted against them, *we* were acting against Father's wishes and making ourselves appear small-minded bullies. We were expected to lead by example, even in the face of loathsome behaviour from others.

But it was hard. The Crofts, especially Dick, were determined to make life difficult, but in a far more subtle manner than before. The brothers grew sly and wily, slipping in insults whenever they could, but always insults that could be taken in many different ways. When we were at arms practice, they liked to deliver buffets much more fervently than they had been advised to, enjoying seeing us wince and limp away. Mostly we did not spar with them, because of the age difference, but on occasion the Master of Arms wanted Ned, in particular, to take on an older boy because of his increasing height and strength. "It will do you good to stretch your abilities," he was told. He went for it with gusto—a true warrior was my brother—but sometimes he bore the purple bruises of such roughhousing on his flesh.

There were other issues too. Precious books we had borrowed from Father's library went missing. One ended up in the river, and I took the blame for not 'taking care of others' goods." Ink was spilt all over the chamber where we took our lessons; Thomas Croft, his face guileless, had told Master Cadnum he had found it there after Ned and I had been at lessons. "One of their lordships must have accidentally knocked it over," he said. "Accidents do happen."

Oh, yes, they did indeed. A hawk was released from its perch just after Ned and I had visited the Mews. Horse harness was found strewn haphazardly on the floor when we knew that we had put it away. Ned found a mouse in his dinner, hidden amidst parts of a roast chicken. Cook took the blame, poor man, but we had both seen Thomas scuttling around the kitchens, sweet-talking serving wenches in order to find out which meals were ours. Chess pieces went missing, and some of our garments had been pilfered from the washerwomen's baskets—and ruined. We took the blame, of course, being told we were 'such careless lads' while the Crofts strutted by, wearing knowing smirks.

Before long, it began to feel like they tainted everything around us. No more physical altercations or name-calling took place, but there was a grinding air of adversity that made Ned and me increasingly uncomfortable. Going riding, the Crofts would follow, thick as thieves, trying to spook our ponies by suddenly shouting or laughing—then they would apologise with false sincerity. Swimming—they would come barrelling in, splashing water in our faces—accidentally, of course. It seemed the Crofts were *everywhere*; even at Mass a long-toed shoe would surreptitiously emerge to trip you, followed by a stream of insincere apologies and much exaggerated bowing.

What made it even worse was that the other boys training as pages and squires began to notice their antics—and would often laugh at them. Of course, it was amusing to an eight-year-old to see his lord's son fall flat on his backside in front of the chaplain or tumble off his horse in the mud. But amusement over 'mishaps' was rapidly turning to disrespect.

"I do not want to go out there," I said to Edward one day, as I peered from the window into the courtyard. "Dick and Thomas are there, purposely waiting for us. The sun might be high and no rain in sight, but I don't care. I am tired of dealing with them. Tired of having to watch my back. Tired of sniggers and japes." I sat on the edge of the bed, mournful and horrified as tears started to prick my eyelids. I prayed Ned would not notice.

Edward put aside the flute he was playing (my brother was surprisingly musical) and sat beside me, arm around my shoulders. "It isn't right, Edmund. And really this bullying must come to an end. We must do something before the Crofts' behaviour grows even worse."

"But what? We'll sound like priggish weaklings if we complain to the Constable or the other officials."

"We won't complain to them," said Ned grimly. "There is only one man who can help us now. Father."

"But he is busy ruling the country in the King's absence. That is why he sent us Sir Walter Devereux from Wigmore and some of his personal servants. He won't be able to come and sort out our petty troubles."

"No, I understand that. We shall write to him. He will listen. He knows we would not pester him with mere childish complaints."

So we penned Father a letter, written in Ned's own hand since we wanted to let him know how desperate the situation was. We began our missive with fulsome praise, as was expected, and thanked him for sending his servants to Ludlow for our comfort and also for some green velvet garments he had gifted us at Candlemas.

And then we came to the crux of the matter—the Crofts. We fussed and argued over some of the wording, but soon the message was done, signed, sealed, and handed over to a trusted courier called William Smyth, who had worked long for Father. We also confided to Smyth a list of all the wicked torments that the Crofts put us through and asked him to recount them to our sire should he ask.

The finished letter read well, and I hoped Father would take it seriously:

Right high and mighty Prince, our noble Lord and father, we recommend us to your noble grace, humbly beseeching your blessing: through which we trust much to grow in virtue in all matters. We thank our blessed Lord not only of your honourable conduct in all your business, and your prevailing against the malice of evil-willers, but also of the knowledge that it pleased you to send us Sir Walter Devereaux, knight, John Milewater squire, and John Nokes, yeoman of your chamber.

Also we thank you for our green gowns, sent for our comfort; and beseech you that we might have some fine bonnets sent to us by the next secure message, for necessity requires it. Above this, right noble Lord Father, please it your highness that we have charged your servant William Smyth to declare unto you certain things on our behalf, namely concerning the odious rule and demeaning of Richard Croft and his brother. Wherefore we beseech you to hear him in exposition of the same, given in full faith and credence.

Right high and mighty Prince, we beseech almighty Jesu to give you a good life and long, with as much prosperity as your princely heart desires.

Written at your Castle of Ludlow on Saturday in the Easter Week. Your humble sons

E. March and E. Rutland

Eagerly, we watched from the bailey as William Smyth departed the castle and disappeared into the teeming streets.

"What do we do now, Ned?" I glanced around nervously in case a Croft brother was in the vicinity, waiting to trip me or 'accidentally' barge into me in hope that I would fall into the mud in that fine green gown Father had sent.

"Only one thing we can do, brother." Edward turned back towards the castle. "We wait for a reply."

We endured several more weeks of insults and minor aggressions from the Crofts, but our hearts were lighter having written to our sire. If only he were not so busy! I bit my fingernails to the bone with nerves even when walking the periphery of the castle; Thomas Croft had managed to feign a stumble and fell against my shoulder, sending me crashing into the brambly bushes there. I wanted no apology as it would be feigned anyway; I wanted to plant my fist on his nose, although I recognised my own violence would only make the situation worse. After all, he was twice my age, even if he did not act it.

And then William Smyth returned to Ludlow. Ned and I wanted to run out and find out how Father had responded, but our Latin lessons were scheduled at the next ring of the church bells, and we did not want rapped knuckles from Master Browne or worse. We both stared longingly at Smyth's back as he strode to Sir William Devereux's chamber to deliver whatever his master had given him.

All a-jangle, we fared to our lesson and quickly fell afoul of our stern tutor. He began to chastise us, the switch appeared in his grip…but he halted as something crashed to the floor deep within the castle. The noise was followed by a number of raised voices, and Ned glanced at me, suddenly smug.

It was them—the Croft brothers. Some kind of an altercation was taking place on the level below us. And we were missing it.

Master Browne was furious, his eyes bulging from his liverish skin as he toyed with his ridiculous moustache. "How am I expected to teach with such a ruckus? It makes my head ache, and you…you two retrogrades squat there grinning like apes. For shame. Consider our lesson finished for today as we will get nothing accomplished." He flapped his black-clad arm towards the door. "Get out. Hurry, before I change my mind!"

Ned and I arrived in the hall the moment Richard and Thomas were exiting the door leading outside. Both had bowed heads and their faces were puffy, mottled red and white. Sir Walter strode before them; several household men walked purposely behind. They looked like…*prisoners*. I was certain Dick Croft, at least, would turn his head and glare threateningly as he usually did—but no, he acted as if I were invisible.

Walter Devereux noticed us, however, and giving a signal for his party to go on into the courtyard, he approached, countenance stern and serious. "Richard and Thomas Croft's behaviour is being addressed," he said. "I doubt they will bother you again, but if they do, suffer not in silence but speak of your woes to me in the absence of your sire, the Duke. Do not let such aggression get out of hand again."

"Yes, Sir Walter," we chorused, and he inclined his head in approval and went to join his men. Shortly after we heard the thunder of hooves as he left Ludlow with the Crofts in tow.

The brothers were back a week later. We never heard exactly what happened to them, but whispers abounded amongst the other boys, some likely containing a grain of truth and others outright fantasy—that they had spent the time in a rat-infested dungeon in Usk, that Sir Walter chased them through the wood on horseback like the mythical huntsman Wild Edric, even that they were subjected to a version of the humiliation rites of decadent European universities, where students were cleansed of their 'beastly' nature before acceptance into university life. These youths were made to wear goat's horns, given muddy water to drink, called smelly, foul, and a devil's son, threatened with hanging in the privy, rubbed in dung, and forced to recant a litany of crimes real or imagined—and, as a final insult, they would be 'persuaded' to pay for a feast for their tormentors.

Whatever the case, the Crofts returned changed. They avoided us as if we had the plague and got on with their own training and duties, as they should have done from the start. Soon they found their own companions within the household and we no longer mattered to them. We could even pass each other without scornful glances. We even spoke occasionally, a brief 'good day' or 'good night.'

As winter drew in, Ned and I had almost forgotten their odious behaviour. We hoped Father or Mother might come to Ludlow before Advent, or that we might travel to them, but Father wrote to say he was tied up with the business of government. He wished us good cheer, hoped our gowns were still warm enough and that the bonnets he sent were suitable, and that he was pleased to learn the Crofts were no longer being vexatious. He promised that 'soon' we would meet and assured us that Ludlow was well-stocked for the Christmas Feast—although it sadly must take place without him.

Christmas Day came and went, a banquet filled by local knights and wealthy merchants who had dealings with Father. It began to snow, and the towers of the castle were frosted white like those of the subtlety served at the feast. The Teme was half-frozen, though not enough to skate upon, for in the centre was still a grey current of fast-moving water. Beyond the town's edge, the trees were naked, their spiky limbs grappling with the lowering sky. Viewed from the wall walk, the season felt bleak, and I longed for Fotheringhay, even if it meant we'd have to hear Bessie and Meg prattle about their poppets…

Just before Twelfth Night, Ned and I sought our bed early, for the day was so dark and overcast that night had crept in even more swiftly than usual. The snow had stopped but the cold had settled in, bringing frost that made patterns on the greenish glass windows that Father had purchased from Staffordshire glassmakers. I tried to settle but couldn't. Ned was asleep, breath soft in the gloom, and I did not wish to disturb him with my tossing, so I threw on an over-gown, and crept to the window, candle in hand. I stuck the candleholder on the stone sill, watching as the icy frost-patterns melted. Outside, the sky was still clouded, no moon, no stars, but the shadows were broken by the braziers lit atop the wall walk, giving light and warmth to the men of the night watch. Suddenly the sentries began to move, a rush of darkcloaked men hastening to the far side of the curtain wall. I pressed against the glass, straining to see what had caused such a commotion. Out in the town, beyond the strong external wall, the cathedral-sized tower of St Lawrence's was lit by torchlight—or was it a beacon? Even as I watched, its bells began to peel, deep and sonorous, breaking the silence of the night.

Immediately lanterns and brands flickered into life in the snowbound streets of Ludlow. People ran between overhanging buildings towards the church.

Now Ned was awake and sitting up, hair mussed and matted from lying against the bolster. "What is it, Edmund?" he asked groggily.

"I don't know, but they are ringing the bells in the church."

"Something of import must have happened." Flinging on a robe, Ned hurried to join me at the window. "Usually, the ringing of bells at such an hour betokens a death. An important death. Or an invasion, or some other calamity."

"Don't say that, Ned," I said weakly. "We just don't know."

"Now, look, they are opening the castle gates and it is long gone curfew!" said Edward. "I wish I could see more clearly…see a banner or badge." He wiped furiously at the damp window with his sleeve. "Ah…" he paused, stunned. "Riders—bearing the Royal Arms."

"Maybe Old Mad Harry has died." I tried not to sound hopeful—as that would be treasonous, even for a child. "No one can lie abed senseless for years and live a long life."

Lanterns blossomed across the bailey, turning the snow to gold. The bell-ringing began in the castle chapel too, the sound reverberating from wall to wall. Now, in the distance, came the clangour of other bells in village churches, the sound carrying through the still, windless night.

A rap sounded on our chamber door. Sir Walter entered, snow caked on his boots, his long cloak smelling of winter. "My young lords, news has come from Windsor," he said, and paused.

"Yes?" asked Ned, impatient.

"King Henry has recovered from his stupor. Men are calling it a miracle, for he opened his eyes and began to talk on Christmas Day. He remembers nought of what took place after falling ill, nor does he remember that the Queen was with child. He went so far as to say the babe must have been brought by the Holy Ghost! But that aside, he has accepted Prince Edward as his son."

"So that is why the bells are ringing," said Edward, "in gratitude for the King's recovery."

"Yes," said Sir Walter, and he stared down at his feet, which were now in a puddle of melted snow. "Gratitude."

He did not sound overly joyous, and as a leal servant of our sire, that was not surprising.

I was not joyous either and could tell by Ned's expression that his thoughts were on par with mine. Father had run the country for a year, proving himself a competent, just administrator. What would happen now that Henry was awake? With absolute certainty, Edmund Beaufort would be released from the Tower and the problems of the past would return.

After Devereux had departed, Ned and I sat on the bed, slumped over and morose.

"Father should have killed Beaufort," Edward muttered, as if reading my unhappy thoughts. "Henry might have been angry at first—but what could he do? His favourite would remain just as dead, and there were men other than Father who hated Beaufort and thought he was guilty of treason and other crimes."

"Father has tried hard to keep the peace. He has always sworn to serve the King."

"Father needs to stop playing peacemaker," snapped Ned, which startled me, for seldom did he criticise any of our sire's actions. "If I were in his place, I'd have had Edmund Beaufort beheaded!"

I went silent, crawling under the covers and drawing them up. I did not want to discuss Beaufort; the prospect of his freedom was too daunting. Ned lay down too; I guessed he felt much the same.

Once sleep finally descended, in the early hours of the morn, I had loathsome dreams of battle and beheadings. And it was not Edmund Beaufort's head I saw impaled above a city gate…

Father fled north with Uncle Salisbury, shutting himself inside Sandal Castle, while Salisbury fared on to the stronghold of Middleham. Queen Margaret had moved swiftly upon the King's recovery—out went the physician called from Bethlem Hospital to treat Henry, out went Father's faction as his protectorship was declared null and void. Father's position as Captain of Calais was stripped from him and the title of Lord Lieutenant of Ireland removed, both cruel blows to a man who had tried to heal the country's ills in a time of crisis.

Even crueller was the knowledge that Edmund Beaufort was free from incarceration, and we looked to the gates in consternation every time messengers arrived. We were no longer safe, and not so far from the centre of England, where the King and Queen had mustered their forces. Fully restored to high position, Beaufort had returned to Henry's side, fawning and obsequious, pressing him to look harshly upon his cousin of York. Rumours spread that the King planned to attack Ludlow itself, while Father was marching from Sandal Castle to London. We saw the gloomy faces of our men-at-arms and saw swords and axes being honed, bows stacked, and arrows fletched. Huge tree trunks were dragged from the forest to give added support to the town and castle gates if our opponents should arrive with battering rams. Scouts galloped from the castle daily, checking for approaching armies. Riders galloped in and out. carrying tidings of what had been witnessed throughout the land.

It was a warm May Day, with trees in bloom, flowers out, and a sky of robin's egg blue, when a messenger finally brought the news we dreaded but knew was going to come sooner or later.

Father and his army were camped outside a southern town, trying to negotiate with King Henry.

The name of that town was…St Albans.

CHAPTER TWELVE

"He's dead! Dead and gone!"

Big Ned was flushed with excitement, dancing around the chamber.

He ran to me, pulling on the arm of my doublet, as if to shake me into joining his excitement.

"Edmund Beaufort, gone at last! God was smiling on Father, Little Ned. Oh, how I wish I could have seen it! Beaufort hiding like a rat at an inn, then bursting out to meet a hedge of swords! Cousin Warwick creeping through the back gardens of houses to attack the market square! And poor old Uncle Buckingham, hit in the face with an arrow. Cousin Humphrey Stafford was also badly wounded in the fighting. They chose the wrong side to support—but I will still pray for their quick recovery."

"Was not the King hurt too?" I asked. My belly hurt and my head was spinning. I was not ill, at least not in body, but my mind was overwhelmed by the enormity of what had happened at St Albans.

"Yes, an arrow scraped his neck. He'll live," said Edward, carelessly. "Percy is dead, though, and Clifford, and the Earl of Devon. Beaufort's son Henry was injured and carried off in a cart...." He suddenly halted, gazing at me quizzically. "You do not seem very excited, Edmund. Looking at your face, you'd think the tidings from St Albans were bad."

"But, Ned—the King was injured. It was Father's allies that injured him. Isn't that *treason*? And the price of treason is death..." I swallowed, unable to continue.

He gave me a glare like never before, almost making me quail. "If any come at Father, he will take them down too. Jesu, Edmund, I never thought you, of all people, would show so little faith. So little loyalty."

I grew angry myself. "I am every inch as loyal as you, but I know reckless acts can have consequences!"

"You know *nought*, brother." Edward turned his back on me. "You are but a child still."

I stood stunned by his cruel mockery. Edward was thirteen now and would be fourteen next April. I was only a year younger, but it seemed the gulf between twelve and thirteen was huge—and ever widening.

Why was Edward behaving like this? Despite everything that had befallen, he was like Saint Peter—my rock. I did not wish to become unfriends.

Wordlessly, I slipped from the chamber, fighting back the urge to slam the door and show my displeasure, and went to the chapel, where I strove to forget my quarrels with Ned and prayed for the continued safety of my father.

"Look, I was right!" Ned held out a letter. A missive had reached Ludlow from our sire.

With trembling fingers, I took it, read it with amazement.

It seemed King Henry had accepted that Father's actions were spurred on by the evil intent of Edmund Beaufort, who had refused to pass on letters sent through Father's herald before the battle at St Albans. Henry now realised Father and his allies were loyal liegemen and decreed that they were not to be harmed or molested for their actions upon the twenty-second of May. Pardons were offered to all who had taken part in the battle.

I let out a deep breath I had not realised I'd been holding.

"Read on!" Ned pointed to the parchment dangling from my fingers. "They have decided to give Father back the Protectorship. The Queen is at Hertford Castle and Henry will be joining her there."

I frowned. "Why is Henry going to Hertford? I thought his wound was trivial."

"There are rumours of a relapse of his moon-madness—maybe caused by the scrape he took at Sint Albans. It is hard to say; his closest servants have kept mum. But soon he will be at Hertford, and long may he stay there. Better he stays, dandling his babe, if it *is* his babe, than he returns to Westminster to resume the role of a helpless sheep decked with a crown. Far better to leave the governing of England to Father, with Uncle Salisbury and our cousin Warwick at his side to give aid."

I nodded my agreement but offered no opinion on the matter. In recent months, differences between Ned and I had grown. It was not merely the solitary year between us...it was our temperaments. Edward was fierier than I, more decisive, more likely to surge forth boldly no matter the consequences. Confidence radiated from him, burning like the sun; losing was not an idea he endured. On the other hand, I was quieter and more likely to brood or worry. I doubted myself daily, particularly in Edward's shadow, which grew ever larger as he gained even more height and muscle. On top of that, he had a new interest, one I did not as yet share—girls. Right and left, he charmed them, pretty maids in the household down to snaggled-toothed crones selling apples in Ludlow market. When he spoke to the prettiest ones, his voice gentle and melodious, something else glowed in his eyes at the same time. Something that made me turn my face away, embarrassed.

In late February, it turned out that my fears were justified. King Henry had grown bored at Hertford and was eager to return to ruling, doubtless prompted by that harridan, the Queen. After dismissing Parliament, he set off with Margaret on progress and ended up inside the solid red walls of Coventry, a town packed full of Lancastrian loyalists.

Father rode to Coventry seeking to speak with Henry on important business regarding the advance of Scots over the borders, their raids fully authorised by King James of Scotland—but he found that although Henry was vaguely sympathetic, Margaret was openly hostile towards him. To make matters worse, he was attacked on the road shortly after leaving the town and was saved only by Uncle Buckingham, who had ridden alongside him with a contingent of soldiers, trying to play peace-maker and offer advice.

Edward and I knew this, for after the altercation, Father returned to Ludlow and told us with his own lips. "I have ever tried to be the conciliator," he said, bitterly. He had lost weight; more grey streaked his hair than I remembered. "For all the good it did me. Margaret distrusts me...Nay, worse, I would say she hates me after her favourite's death. When the Scots raided over the border, I moved to halt their plundering, and she was most displeased. She's French, and the French have often allied themselves with our Scottish enemies. She whipped King James into a fury, for Beaufort was his brother-by-marriage, and, I deem, all blame for his demise was put on my shoulders and none on Beaufort for his actions."

"I thought the King had agreed that none of those who fought at St Albans were to blame," said Ned. "Everyone was pardoned."

"Yes." Father nodded. "However, some Kings are fickle and some are ruled by evil councillors…and sometimes even by their own queens."

"And some are simple!" snapped Edward. "That's King Henry."

Father put his finger to his lips. "Hush, or I will not say another word."

Eager to hear more, Edward shut his mouth with a snap.

"When I wrote to King James, I told him my true thoughts—that raids where he struck then fled into the hills were cowardly and unworthy of a great prince. Henry had permitted me to send a prior letter, reminding James that Henry was his overlord. But my second letter, for reasons unknown, Henry rejected. He wrote a note upon it, claiming that it was sent without his approval, and he was concerned about the harshness of my 'tone." Father's voice was rising a little; his suppressed anger boiling over. "But worst of all was the slur he laid upon me at the end of his note. He told the bloody Scots that I had caused unrest in England ever since Jack Cade's rebellion! So all his words assuring that no past events would be held against me were lies. Or, as I suspect, the Queen told her husband to write these words, egged on by Henry Beaufort, who has taken his sire's place at court."

"And thus the troubles begin again," said Edward softly. "One Beaufort goes, another has arisen."

Father nodded. "It would seem so. Margaret Beaufort, the little heiress, has given birth to Edmund Tudor's child. Only thirteen and already a widow."

"We heard the older Tudor was dead. What happened to him?"

"Earl Herbert imprisoned him at Carmarthen where he died of plague. Many speak of poison but I doubt that is true. At any rate, I had no hand in it, although some will likely point the finger." He gave a shrug. "Jasper is with Margaret and her infant at Pembroke, an almost impregnable fortress. He will have plenty of castles to set up a home for her and the child, though—the King has taken three of mine,

Carmarthen, Caerkeny and Aberystwyth, and presented them to Jasper."

"That is...*dishonourable*," breathed Ned, eyes wide.

Father shrugged again. "I presume I will receive some form of payment. I will not start any hostilities over the transfer to Tudor."

"They are doing this deliberately!" Edward seemed genuinely upset, gesticulating wildly with his hands. "I *know* they are. They are trying to provoke you into attacking the King or his favourites so that they can accuse you of troublemaking—or treason."

Father's lips curled. "I shall not give them the satisfaction. Let the castles go. They matter not at all. For now. Later—who can say?"

"I am just glad you are safe," I said. "It has been so long since we saw you."

"I know." He smiled at me, crinkles fanning from the edge of his eyes. "I am glad to be here with my two eldest boys. Tomorrow we will go on a hunt, and pretend, if only for a short time, that all is right in this wicked world."

1457 faded away, and Father remained at Ludlow. Money was tight—Henry never paid him for those lost castles—but we managed to have a good Yuletide nonetheless. The Christmas feast was scaled down—Mother did not attend, for she did not wish to travel with so much lawlessness in the land—but we supped on pottage flavoured with almond milk and a meaty *brewet* rich in spices, and although there was no boar of swan, the goose we had was tender. Fish was always abundant, as we had our own pond, and Cook made sure it was flavoured with the finest sauce he could devise. No lavish and ostentatious subtleties ended our meal, but stewed apples in honey sauce and cream custard tarts kept our bellies full.

Ned and I were happy, enjoying Father's presence as we rode through the countryside, checking on his many holdings and listening to the requests and grievances of the locals.

Such normality did not last long. At the end of February, as ice melted from the river and the first buds sprouted on the trees, Father was summoned to a Great Council along with Uncle Salisbury and Cousin Warwick.

"I do not like it, Father," said Ned, when we learnt of the Council.

"I do not like it much, either, but go I must." Father said. "Or perhaps you, my wise counsellor, have devised some clever stratagem to get me out of this meeting."

"I haven't..." began Edward, and then, in a rush, "but you should permit us to accompany you."

Aghast, Father fell back in his chair. "You—you would enter that maelstrom? No. I forbid it. Far too dangerous."

"We face danger here, too, without you. What if the Queen made moves on Ludlow, as she did on your other castles!"

He harrumphed. "She would not dare. This castle is mine through blood and right."

"That termagant cares nought about your rights!" Ned tossed his head, nostrils flaring in his passion like a wild stallion's. "Come, Father, it is time to admit Margaret is your sworn enemy. The King may not be, but he is easily influenced. She is the danger."

"And what would *you* do to protect me?"

"Remember, Margaret feared that I would raise an army to free you from the Tower, and I was only ten. Now I am near to fifteen summers, older and stronger. Our kinsman, Edward, Prince of Wales, God assoil him, fought at Crecy and was knighted at sixteen."

"That was honest battle. Here...there may be treachery."

"Let the Queen and her minions see me and Edmund," Ned said fiercely. "Let her know that if ought should happen to the Duke of York, his sons will take revenge."

Father was silent, stroking his chin. I thought of the sons of the Lancastrian nobles who fell at St Alban's. Did they feel the same way as Ned? No doubt they did. Shivers slid up my spine and not because of the draught from the window.

"I am likely a fool, but some truth is in your words, Edward. You are not entirely safe at Ludlow when I am far away, not in these times. When in London, I shall reside at my castle of Baynard, a stout fortress on the riverbank. If I allowed you to accompany me, you shall be both safe and within my reach at Baynard's. I am still undecided if this is truly wise, though. What trouble breaks out along the way, even though the King has given me safe conduct?"

"If you permit us to travel to London, I swear we will obey your every command," said Ned. "Whether that means to fight by your side or hide in the castle cellars amidst the tuns of malmsey. Please...*please* let us come!"

"Edmund, is it your wish too?" Father nodded in my direction. "You've remained silent throughout this discussion."

Like any curious lad, I wanted to see London, even if only from the back of a horse or from the wall of Baynard's Castle. I had heard the city was so large a man could not see it all in a a week, and that all life afforded was available there, from the sinful and debased to holy houses with shrines and relics to worship. Then there was the impregnable White Tower, and London Bridge bristling with traitor's heads, and Smithfield where jousts took place—and many executions too, such as that of the wild Scot, William Wallace, the rebel leader Wat Tyler, and not so many years ago, the Witch of Eye who used black arts to try to give the Duchess of Gloucester a child that would have a claim to the throne should Henry VI expire childless.

"Yes, Father," I murmured. "I'd dearly like to visit London. Ned and I can serve as your squires, and when you do not require our services, we will be quiet as mice and you'll hardly know we are there. I swear this by the Holy Trinity!"

"You are not a lad who would make such an oath lightly." Father suppressed a laugh. "So, yes, you both may come. But you must obey my wishes at all times, and if I need to dress you as maidens and bundle you out of the city, you must go without complaint."

"We will, we will!" we shouted ecstatic...and, to be truthful, in my case at least, a little fearful.

Children no longer but still tender in age, the sons of York were faring to London Town, which seethed with treachery, violence, and old hatreds ready to boil over like a cooking pot left too long over the fire.

Ready to scald and burn the unwary.

CHAPTER THIRTEEN

Our Lord Father entered London Town accompanied by four hundred retainers. Ned and I, dressed in princely garb, rode with him on sure-footed horses. City folk peered down from the jetties of the tall townhouses, most waving with enthusiasm but a few glowering and making crude gestures. Young girls were drawn to Ned like bees to honey—and many of their mothers were too. They blew kisses and cast him coy looks. "I swear," said Ned, startled and laughing, "that one old beldam on the upper floor of that silversmith's shop flashed her...ah...her bosom!"

"No, I don't believe you!" I retorted, while hastily scanning the outcrops above for the brazen woman.

"It's true, I swear it." Ned cried, still laughing; several of the foot soldiers cast him strange glances.

We fell silent as the company filed down a street filled with Cordwainers' shops. A little further and the St Paul's spire emerged from a clutter of buildings, its height dwarfing every church we had ever visited. Bells were ringing from its bell-tower and from the nearby Blackfriars, Whitefriars and Greyfriars. The streets were knee-deep in people, mostly commonfolk about their business, but also nuns, monks, and priests—and, disconcertingly, many fighting aged men wearing the livery of their lords. I tried to note whom these men served, watching for any who might bear us ill will. Luckily, many wore badges of our Uncle Salisbury and Cousin Warwick. The ones we feared most, Beaufort and Clifford, were conspicuous by their absence.

Passing the preaching cross, where a Dominican friar bawled about hell and damnation, the retinue progressed toward Queenshithe, called so from the days of our Norman forebears, when Queen Matilda was granted duty payments from ships that docked there. Although still an important dock, its use had declined in recent times, save for the fishermen bringing in a fresh catch. Father had promised us fresh fish—a nice treat after the barrels of salted ones we received at Ludlow when our small fishpond proved insufficient for supplies.

As we moved on, the pungent smell of the Thames rose to greet us; I was reminded of the Black Pool of Dublin. Soon we spied the river itself, serpentine, wide and brown, the pallid sunlight glinting on its surface. Boats of all sizes bobbed on the swell; barges glided serenely by, filled with lords and ladies seated under canopies; cogs lumbered along, shadows black on the dingy water.

Another turn and Baynard's castle stole into view—four wings ringing a courtyard and a flat wall topped by projecting towers facing out over the water. Drawing near, a cobbled path led to the gatehouse; further down, a jetty thrust out into the sullen waves of the Thames. Supply ships were moored there, and men were carrying in items needed for Father's stay.

As the company entered the gatehouse, Ned gazed up to inspect the archers lining the parapets. Sunlight caught on lighter strands in his brown hair, making the top gleam like a brazen helmet—or a crown. With his height and bearing, he seemed majestic, and I watched him in awe. Deep in my heart, I had a presentiment of great things to come for my brother—he had worn that aura from earliest childhood—but for myself, I could not even guess. My future as a Duke's younger son was unknowable; when I mused upon it, it felt as if I stared into the heart of a storm where figures moved like shadows, their intentions unknown.

Ned and I were soon settled in Baynard's apartments, with the fires stoked up and a mouth-watering repast to quell the grumblings of our bellies. Before long Father had us brought to meet Uncle Salisbury and Cousin Warwick, who had ridden in from our uncle's London mansion, L'Erber, to greet their kinsmen.

We were deeply honoured to meet these great magnates, their exploits the stuff of legend. Uncle Salisbury, Richard Neville, was our mother's brother, one of Ralph Neville, Earl of Westmorland's huge brood. He was tall and broad, his hair a gleaming deep brown bowl. He had likely been handsome once, but age had blunted his features, and a life of riding in the cold north had caused his skin to wrinkle and toughen.

Hands on hips, in his dark green doublet, his chaperon a slash of midnight blue, he roared as we entered the room, "So these are your eldest two lads! A fine pair, Richard. The tall one has our Cis's eyes and cast of face, while the younger resembles you—and perhaps, to some degree, his maternal grandmother, my mother Joan."

Cousin Warwick strode over, his eyes probing as if we were young colts he might be interested in buying at the market. Lithe and slender, he had curling dark hair and pale eyes tinted with green that could be, I imagined, quite icy and menacing if he became enraged. His emblem was the Bear and Ragged Staff, and he wore a large brooch of that bear on his hat, pecked out in rubies and infilled with crystals.

"I am your cousin of Warwick," he said. "You may call me Dick, for there are too many Richards in this room. It grows confusing."

Ned and I both laughed politely, for we felt that was what he was expecting. We were a little over-awed by our guests and afraid to make the wrong move lest they think us gauche ninnies from the Marches.

If Cousin Dick thought our laughter insincere, he did not show it. "Come..." He made a sweeping gesture with his hand that encompassed us all. "Let us gather round the fire and talk of what is happening in London. I have many things to tell you, Richard."

"Can we stay too, sir?" asked Ned, rather boldly.

Dick grinned. "I assumed that's why you were summoned. To learn in preparation for the future. Far more valuable than endlessly reciting Latin—though I dare say such book-learning is important for you young gentlemen too." He cast Father a look with his eyebrow cocked impishly.

I had no idea if our sire intended us to join the conversation of these worldly-wise men, or merely to greet important family members and then depart, but stay we did. I was grateful, for banishment to our chamber would have made me feel like an errant child sent to bed while the grownups talked.

Instead, we all drew chairs nearer to the fire, while servants brought in frittours, savoury tarts, and various cheeses, followed by hippocras, wafers, and wine. Ned and I sat in silence, though we nodded sagely at the others' conversation and murmured at spots where we thought it appropriate.

"So..." Father stretched his legs before the merry blaze. "How many men have you brought to this council?"

"Five hundred," answered Uncle Salisbury. "Dick has brought six hundred from Calais. I fear, though, that it will not be enough, even including your soldiers, Richard."

"Why? What have you seen?" Father's knuckles whitened as he gripped his wine goblet.

"The new Duke of Somerset, Henry Beaufort, is in London with eight hundred men—and your son-in-law, Exeter, too, still cursing the world for the months he was imprisoned in Pontefract. The whole mess of them have taken over Temple Bar, and already there has been brawling and lawlessness. Percy, Lord Egremont, and Lord Clifford are at Holborn, and between them," he paused, then spat out like gall, "between them, those bastards have mustered 1500 men."

"1500!" Father's eyes widened. "Unwelcome tidings indeed. We are well outnumbered by the supporters of those young hotheads. None of us came here clamouring for a battle. We are here for a council meeting and, if God wills it, to make peace."

"They lost their fathers," said Salisbury mildly. "They want vengeance. Isn't that what young hot-blooded men do?"

"I hardly think this a matter for jest, my friend."

"I am not jesting. If we were their age and circumstances were the same, what would we have done?"

Father paled, setting set his cup down. His father had met the headsman's axe in Southampton for joining a plot against Henry V. There was no question of 'revenge' for Richard of Conisborough's death; as a traitor's son, Father could make no real complaint, especially as his sire was not attainted, meaning that he could inherit his titles and estates.

"However," Uncle Salisbury continued, "they have made themselves extremely unpopular, which is why Percy, Egremont, and Clifford are at Holborn, on the outskirts of any activity. The Mayor refused permission for them to lodge closer, for it was clear they came in anger, desiring war, and baying for the destruction of the three of us."

Father refilled his cup without summoning a squire. Red liquid dripped from the brim, leaving crimson droplets on his tawny velvet doublet. "Why does the King love these violent, fractious young men so?"

"At least the city's guards are at the ready and willing to rise against their malice if they should make a move," said Dick. "There are 5000 citizens in harness prowling around the city to quell any troubles. At dusk, 3000 more take the night watch and prowl the alleys and lanes of London to make sure no mischief is brewing."

"And the King and Queen—what news? Are they in London yet? I have heard nought from the palace."

"Tomorrow they arrive, according to my spies. A pity the Queen is there, but we both know who truly runs the country…and it is not Henry."

"Do you believe we will be attacked, despite the safe passage Henry granted?" asked Father. He twisted his ring, his usual nervous habit.

Cousin Dick had got up and was peering through the unshuttered window at the river and the city. Night boats passed by, lanterns hanging from their prows; houses on the far bank were filled with firelight, and the streets writhed with smoke and fog curling off the water. He thought for a few moments on Father's query then turned around.

"Yes," he said. "They will attack. But those young fools will not best us."

"Can we ride with you?" Ned begged after Mass the next morning.

Father was dressed in his most luxuriant gown and bonnet, ready to ride to Westminster with Salisbury and Warwick.

"Absolutely not!" he said. "You heard the truth of the situation. The danger is too great. You are both to stay here and…" he fixed us with a stern glare, "make no attempt to follow me. The gates will shut once I have left, and a watch will be set upon you. Now, enough of this tomfoolery. I am in a hurry. I expect to return ere midnight at the latest."

He swept from the room and we watched from one of the projecting towers as he left Baynard's safety and met with our uncle and cousin's forces on the road beyond. We could see many banners flapping in the wind—the Neville Saltire, Salisbury's Green Eagle, Warwick's Bear and Ragged Staff. The dominant colours of the livery of both uncle and cousin were red and black, blood and shadow, and the whole host appeared very warlike, especially when joined by Father, flying his Falcon and Fetterlock and the White Rose of York.

"What are we to do then?" Ned heaved a weary sigh. "Maybe we could persuade Fustilugs over there to let us out—just for a little while."

Fustilugs was what we mockingly called the guard chosen by Father to watch over us while he was gone. He was exceptionally tall, exceptionally fat, and exceptionally ugly, with a bristly bald head and a nose deformed by an old knife cut. He was also bad-tempered, tough, and immovable as a rock.

"He'll never let us out," I said miserably. "It's not even worth trying to persuade him. We will have to make our own entertainment while Father is at Westminster."

Plans thwarted, we wandered through the castle gardens, still miserable and muddy, although a few shoots showed green in the damp soil. There was a neglected pond, and we noted stones along the base of the walls that held a red tinge—a fire had destroyed the castle earlier in the century, leading to a major rebuilding by Humphrey Duke of Gloucester. Roman bricks had randomly been reused, their shape and size distinct from the other building material. We stalked around, looking for loose stones or signs of buried foundations, hoping against hope to find some secret underground Roman chamber, preferably filled with treasure.

Needless to say, no such find occurred, and our enthusiasm began to wane. The sky clouded over and a sheet of drizzle descended, causing our hair to cling to our brows and sending shivers down our spines.

Ned glanced up at the frowning heavens. "The clouds thicken. Time to go inside, I fear, lest we catch our deaths out here."

We raced each other back through the garden and into the courtyard. The drizzle had now turned to heavy rain, lashing down and bouncing off the cobblestones. Though the cobbles were slippery and dangerous underfoot, we laughed at any peril and careered toward the stairs to the apartments.

"I am going to win this race, brother!" Ned yelled over his shoulder. He was grinning, his hair slapping into his eyes. "Last man in has to clean my shoes."

"You're winning only because you have huge, long giant's legs like Fustilugs!" I shouted after him, my own vision obscured by raindrops.

"Cheeky git!" Ned flung back over his shoulder, and then...

"Ned! Stop! Look out!"

Wildly I waved my arms, but it was too late. He had crashed into one of the castle servants who was hurrying across the courtyard with a huge basket of laundry.

Ned gave a shocked roar of pain as he thudded down on the drenched cobbles. The basket went flying, showering linens. One of the laundresses lay face down on the ground, winded, after being thrown through the air like a rag doll by my brother's headlong charge.

I hurried over, avoiding Edward and going to the fallen laundress. Ned was a big fellow and strong—what if she'd struck her head and died? "Mistress..." I bent over and lightly shook her shoulder.

The woman moaned, and relief rushed through me as she hauled herself into a sitting position. Now I saw that she was only a girl, maybe three or four years my elder. A bruise was already showing on her cheek where it had struck the cobbles. She had blue eyes, and as she sat up, her white linen coif fell off to reveal long, wheat-coloured hair, fine as silk. She was, I had to admit, extremely pretty, even when wincing in pain. Gauche and tongue-tied, I stared, struck mute despite my brain frantically seeking the appropriate words to say.

Suddenly I was pushed aside. Ned was off the ground and was drawing the girl to her feet, almost lifting her bodily. "Jesu, forgive me, demoiselle," he said, his gaze fixed on her face—which was, as I saw it more clearly, small and heart-shaped. "What an oaf I am! I did not even see you there."

"My washing!" the maid cried, ignoring his apology. "Look...*look*...it's all ruined! There's dirt all over it. I shall receive a beating from the head washerwoman, Ma Agnes!" Tears spilt from her eyes, mingling with the rain.

"No, you shan't," said Ned, confidently, and he reached out, bold as brass, and wiped the tears and the rain from her face. "I shall make sure this Agnes knows the accident was solely my fault."

The girl flinched a little at his touch and then seemed to realise who he was. Fully in awe of the golden god that was my brother, her delectable rosebud lips parted in shock.

Apparently forgotten, I began to pick up the sodden washing and throw it back into the fallen basket. Rain trickled down my collar and my motions became angrier and angrier, hurling the wet sheets and garments into the basket with a satisfying slapping noise. I hated my own petulance, so unbecoming in a well-bred youth—but why was I running about like a servant while Ned found time to flirt with a maid? And why did that flirtation bother me so much, filling me with an almost incomprehensible rage?

Was—was I jealous of my brother?

Ned was still talking to the girl. "My name is Ivette," I heard her say.

"A lovely name." Ned loomed over her, one hand lightly on her upper arm, intently gazing into her eyes.

I had finished loading the basket with its heap of muddy linens. "Here you go!" I loudly announced, thrusting the laundry toward Ivette.

Edward intercepted and took the basket. "I will carry it in for you and explain my guilt to Agnes."

"Oh, thank you, my lord Earl," breathed Ivette, looking less frightened and awestruck. Now, it appeared, she was beginning to enjoy my brother's company, perhaps too much. Her cheeks had gone rosy.

I trudged ahead through the torrential rain, ignoring them both, and went to my chamber without glancing back.

Edward took a long time explaining Ivette's spoilt washing to the head laundress. A *very* long time. I stalked around the bedchamber, feeling stupid for acting petulant and yet unable to ease the irritation that niggled me. Sourness squeezed my heart, unpredictable, unwanted, and unasked for. What, by Christ, was wrong with me?

The door ring turned with a metallic clunk. Ned sidled in—and in his hands he held a platter with several tarts and pies upon it. A peace offering, I wagered.

"I got these in the kitchen," he said, "after I explained to Agnes that I was to blame for the ruined washing, not Ivette."

"And did you tell her it would still be lying spread about the courtyard if Edmund Earl of Rutland had not picked it up?" I said, dripping sarcasm.

"Ah, Little Ned, don't be like that." He sighed, placing the pies down.

I grabbed one, shoving it into my mouth like a savage, crumbs flying everywhere. "Like what?" I snapped. "And don't call me 'Little' Ned anymore. It's a child's nursery name and I like it not."

"Then do not act like…"

"Edward!" I leapt to my feet, face burning, hands clenched. Do not say it. *DO NOT*!"

He didn't, and again, guilt at my own behaviour washed over me.

Ned tried to make amends then. "Shall we play chess?" he said. "It is a good way to while away the time until Father returns from Westminster."

I grunted my assent, and Edward set up the chessboard. We both played badly but, in the end, I defeated him. "Ha!" I cried triumphantly, glad of this small victory over my brother. "Checkmate. I win."

"So you did," said Ned, much less bothered than I had hoped he would be. 'Jesu, look how late it's getting—it is pitch-dark outside."

"I wish Father would return. What can be the delay? I do not trust the younger Beaufort—and I do not trust the King, not with Margaret present. They must have arrived in London by now. What if they sent orders to their creatures to…"

"If aught was seriously amiss, we would be the first to be informed," said Ned solemnly and a little patronisingly. "Father has his spies in London too, you know. Now, come, the hour's late and I am weary." He yawned widely, stretching in an exaggerated manner.

"We should get some sleep. Father will return later tonight or send a message if he stays elsewhere, perhaps with Uncle Salisbury. I am sure they have much to discuss."

In silence, I got into my sleeping robe and crawled into bed. The fire had gone out earlier in the day, and although a few embers still burnt in the fireplace, the bedsheets felt damp, clammy. Groaning, I pulled the coverlet over my head and leaned my head against the bolster. A few minutes later, the bed dipped as Ned got in. I rolled over, my back to him. Soon I heard his slow, regular breathing, and then I too fell asleep.

I woke in darkness. The candle on its shelf had burnt completely down, leaving a waxy scent in the air. The bed next to me was empty and cold. Edward was gone.

"Must have gone to the privy," I murmured and rolled over, adjusting the covers, seeking a return to slumber. But after much time passed, I sat upright, irritable and sticky. My brother had not yet returned. What was he playing at?

Getting up, I flung a mantle over my nightrobe, and crept out into the corridor. I was surprised to see none of the castle servants lying on their sleeping pallets. Usually there were several on duty if we should require assistance in the night. Maybe they were all in the Great Hall, awaiting Father's return.

My bare feet making only the slightest noise on the floor, I hurried towards the castle privies, situated in an end tower with long stone chutes going down to the river. There were two of them, the chutes covered by a wooden lid. Pinching my nose against unpleasant odours, I peered into one privy then the other.

Ned was not there.

Uneasy, I continued my perambulations through the dim castle halls, passing from one floor to the next. Suddenly I heard a familiar noise; Edward's muted laughter, followed by a girl's high giggle. I trudged on, noticing a curtained window embrasure on my right.

Sneaking up to it, I peered through a small gap in the curtains—and got a fright as I saw my brother's bare buttocks almost level with my eyes. At once I realised that he had the pretty laundress he'd bowled over (in more ways than one, clearly) in there, and that they were...*fornicating*. I was not of a monkish bent and was well aware of how it went between men and women, one could not escape it while living in a castle, but if Ned had congress with women before, he had never mentioned it. Perhaps I was naive. Embarrassment flooded me for seeing such a lurid spectacle; shame for viewing such a private act, and a little anger too. Again, I questioned my own heart—was this jealousy? My gut knotted, and with a mumbled profanity, I gripped the curtain and pulled it down. With a rush, it fell heavily on Ned and his leman. The girl shrieked in dismay; Ned let out a surprised shout. I fled the scene, feeling stupider and angrier than ever, as my brother rolled on the floor, his pleasures forgotten as he struggled to kick the weighty curtain away, while Ivette lay sobbing, realising her harlot behaviour had been witnessed.

In the bedchamber I flung myself under the covers, pretending to sleep. A few minutes later, the chamber door banged open, almost dragged from its hinges. Ned was at the foot of the bed, raging like a mad bull. "Was that you, Edmund? Did you pull down that curtain?"

At first, I intended to deny what I'd done, but to lie seemed craven. "Yes, I did. You dishonour our sire by tupping some slattern right in his house while he is away, risking his very life…"

"How dare you! You little prig." Edward's face was crimson; he shook with rage. "You understand nothing, Edmund. You're still a boy…a foolish little boy. Or maybe you have callings as a priest? If you are aiming to be some pure Galahad, a perfect knight who bears no sin—well, brother, that is merely a story. It's not *real*…"

"What is real is what might result from you…you *humping* a servant. At least I won't bring shame…"

Edward's mouth hung open at my impudence, and I truly imagined his big fist striking my nose, but a bell began to ring at the gate and I heard shouts from outside and the sound of the portcullis creaking up. Neighing horses and a multitude of hoofbeats cut through the night.

"Father's back!" I sprinted to the window and flung open the shutters. In the courtyard below, men were running hither and thither with burning brands. There were shouts and commotion at the gate, and Father cantered in on his destrier, flanked by Salisbury and Warwick. Reaching the inner courtyard, he climbed carefully from the saddle. It was only when his personal physician flew out of the nearby door that I realised Father was holding his arm. His right sleeve glistened darkly in the torchlight; it was soaked through with blood.

"Jesu, Ned...he's hurt!" I cried, all animosity towards my brother forgotten.

I glanced at Edward; no longer enraged, his face had grown taut with concern. "We must go to him! Now|!" He rounded on his heel and flew down the corridor, while I thudded along behind, my heart hammering in my chest.

Father and our Neville kinsmen were in the solar with the physician in attendance. As Ned and I stormed in, panting, Father, sitting in a seat with his sleeve rolled up to the elbow, gestured for the servants to depart, leaving only the steward and the physic.

"Lord Father, how have you come to have this hurt?" cried Ned, skidding to a halt beside his chair.

"How do you think, cousin?" said Warwick. "Percy, Egremont and Clifford were lying in wait. Luckily, they were fools, hot-headed and disorganised, and we were soon able to beat them off."

"So it is war between us." Ned's eyes flashed. "Father, let me ride with you against them."

"No!" Father's brow lowered. "No heroics. It is what the Queen wants, for me and mine to seem the aggressors. I see her hand in this failed ambush, although I cannot prove it."

"But your arm..." I gasped.

"Nought but a scratch. I have had far worse in the past." Father winced as the doctor washed the wound with a vinegar-soaked swab, then packed it with honey and wrapped it in a linen bandage.

"The King promised you a safe conduct." Taut as a bowstring, Ned stood with folded arms. "This is...evil."

"Men are evil; an important lesson to learn, my son. And sometimes evil men will prevail, and we cannot deal with them as we would like."

Father glanced at his brother-in-law and nephew. "I thank you for standing with strength at my shoulder today."

"It should not be otherwise," said Uncle Salisbury. "At one time, I was steadfast for Henry, but as the years passed, the scales tumbled from my eyes."

"Do you and Dick want to stay at Baynard's for the night?"

Cousin Warwick grinned. "Well, I'd rather not worry about a knife finding my back in the dark of a London street."

"Then you both shall stay."

Later, Ned and I returned to our quarters. Embarrassment and remorse made me silent and sulky; Edward was unusually quiet, too. As we reached our chamber, I finally spoke, "Earlier...I was wrong. I behaved like a tantrummy child. I would not be surprised if you never wanted anything more to do with me."

Ned stared. "What? I am not so fickle-brained I'd lose my brother's love over a girl. And a girl like that. Jesu, I'll never see her again once we leave London. She was just a brief...*diversion*. Be that as it may, I accept your apology. Just keep your nose out of my doings in the future."

"I promise that I will turn my face away."

"No doubt, before long, you too will find the comforts of the female sex to your taste," he grinned impishly. "Just wait and see."

Father was back and forth from Westminster Palace as the Great Council commenced in earnest. His enemies made no further moves against him with force of arms, and towards the end of March, King Henry had the heralds announce across London that a settlement had been reached among his warring nobles. Henry was overjoyed, believing that he was forcibly healing old feuds, but there was no joy from the perspective of Father and our Neville kin.

"It is outrageous!" Uncle Salisbury pounded his fist on the table where he sat. "The King has put the blame all upon us and nothing on those upstarts who tried to attack us mere days ago!"

Father rubbed his hand wearily over his tired visage. "5000 marks to Edmund Beaufort's widow Eleanor and her family. This payment would have utterly broken me, Salisbury, had not the King agreed that compensation would be drawn from years of my unpaid wages. I am certain it would have been worse if Margaret had her say."

Salisbury grunted and downed a mazer of ale. Froth gathered on his lip, making him resemble a rabid dog. I'd have laughed had the situation not been so dire. "I got off the lightest, having only to cancel fines owed me by Percy and Egremont—but even that is galling.

Those upstart bastards are laughing...laughing at us." He glowered, brow black as a thundercloud.

"It is, as you say, an outrage," said Dick. On his feet, ever active, he strode around the solar in the manner of a caged beast seeking freedom. "I am ordered to pay Lord Clifford a thousand marks as recompense for his father's death. I loathe the man as I loathed his sire."

"And then there is the final insult," said Father. "Sending copious amounts of money to St Albans Abbey for prayers to be said for the souls of our slain foes. No mention of any of *our* losses. No prayers for *our* dead."

"Which were thankfully few," said Dick smugly, arms folded. "The King's minions were over-confident and paid the price."

"No, now *we* pay the price." Father shook his head. "Not one man from the other faction was sanctioned at all, except Lord Egremont. At least you will have no trouble with him for ten years, according to the terms of the agreement he made with the King."

"He will break the agreement." Uncle Salisbury scowled into his mug. "He is not a man of his word. He will never hold to such terms."

"What will happen now? Are we going home?" I piped up.

The three men glanced in my direction as if they had forgotten I was there.

"No, cousin," said Dick Neville. "His Grace the King was in a marvellously cheerful mood when last we saw him—and he says he has an announcement to make on the morrow. An important announcement that involves all the nobility of England."

They called it Loveday. A time of healing old wounds. A time for peace to reign.

It was nothing but a sham.

Edward and I walked at the rear of the Loveday procession, along with minor nobles, knights and their offspring. At the front shuffled the King, his crown slipping, his robes bulky and hanging on his flaccid frame. Behind him strode Father, his hand entwined with the gloved hand of Queen Margaret. He looked stony, she looked murderous. Next was Uncle Salisbury, clasping hands with Henry of

Somerset, both ignoring each other. Finally came Cousin Warwick with, of all people, our hateful brother-by-marriage, Henry, Duke of Exeter. Still pimply and petulant, he scowled and winced as Dick clamped his fingers in a vice-like and no doubt deliberately painful grip. As he passed into St Paul's to hear a special mass, Warwick swivelled his head in our direction and winked, all the while crushing Exeter's sweaty hand.

Ned and I loved him that day; he was like a god of war, fearing nothing and no one.

After Mass, Edward and I returned to Baynard's. Father joined us, on his own, some hours later. "It is time to leave London, my sons," he said. "Sleep well tonight, and we shall take the road to Ludlow at sun-up. Once we are safely there, I will send for your mother and the rest of the family."

"You are bringing them to Ludlow?" I was surprised. "I can only assume you do not think the King's new peace will last."

"It won't last," he said bluntly. "I have seen the hatred in my adversaries' eyes. In the Queen's eyes. Henry is bursting with pride over his 'cure' for our ills—but it is like placing a flimsy cloth over wounds that need stitching. Those wounds will bleed and bleed until the injured die...unless they receive *proper* treatment to make them heal."

The following day began cold, the wind strong from the northeast and the sky dappled with scudding clouds. We left Baynard's Castle the moment night's curfew was lifted and the gates of London flung open. As our company made its way down the winding streets, I heard a man singing in a tavern, his voice surprisingly strong and clear over the din of the city—

Sorrow and shame have fled to France,
As a criminal that has forsworn his land,
Love has tamed false governance
In every town, both free and bound.
In York, in Somerset, I understand,
In Warwick also is love and charity,
In Salisbury too, and Northumberland,
That all men may rejoice the concord and unity.

At St Paul's in London, of great renown,
On Lady Day true peace was wrought,
The King, the Queen, with lords many a one,
To worship the Virgin as they ought.
They went in procession and spared nought,
In view of all the commonality,
A token that love ruled heart and thought—
Rejoice England the concord and unity.

Father heard the song too, and the expression on his face was one I had never before seen. Grief, sorrow, anger—I thought he might even weep, which would have shocked me to the core, for he was not given to wild emotions.

I glanced at Edward to see if he had noticed, uneasier than when Father had spoken to us the previous night. Ned was concentrating on other things, however—waving to pretty maidens on the roadside, the burghers' plump daughters, the quick-fingered seamstresses in shop windows, the higher-born ladies with their shaved brows and outrageous headdresses.

As Father's entourage marched through the gate and out onto the road where carters, peddlers, pilgrims, and all manner of humanity milled in disarray, I glanced back once—and immediately regretted doing so.

High above the gate's portcullis, a human head teetered upon a spike, black with tar and eyes pecked out, the mouth gaping in soundless scream to show a row of gleaming teeth. Behind it, purple clouds boiled up, casting shadows over London's churches, castles, manors, shops, and brothels. Shadowy tendrils swept over the sky like reaching fingers, and in the far distance, thunder boomed like cannons fired in some great heavenly battle.

A storm was coming, ready to engulf us all.

CHAPTER FOURTEEN

Richard and George, my little brothers, were running through the halls of Ludlow Castle, thrilled by what they believed, in their innocence, was an exciting adventure. I could scarcely believe how much they had grown. George was approaching ten summers and Richard almost seven. George had kept his forceful personality and his shaggy head of dusky gold curls—he towed Richard everywhere, explaining this and that as if he were his younger brother's tutor. Richard was quieter and more thoughtful, and his fair baby hair was growing in brown at the roots, much as mine had done at his age. He was shy with me and Ned at first, but that shyness soon vanished—within a week Ned was sparring with him using a wooden sword, and I took him and George fishing in the Teme. Richard caught the biggest fish and brought it home to present as a gift to Mother, who was missing the comforts of the more homely Fotheringhay. George managed to extricate the fish's head, goggle-eyed and thick-lipped, from amongst the scraps the cook left after preparing the fish for table, and mysteriously it had found its way into my sister Margaret's bed.

"You are a beast, George!" Meg chased him down a corridor, braids flying in the wind of her speed, the offending fish head clutched in her hand. George was too quick and eluded her grabs, so she flung the fish head at him with surprising accuracy for a maiden unused to practising throwing skills in ballgames. It flopped onto the top of his head and George screamed. Richard collapsed into gales of laughter, as did Edward.

"Well aimed, Meg!" Edward wiped tears of mirth from his eyes.

In the corner, George was grumbling, and Richard began helping him pick fish scales from his hair.

Meg put her hands on her hips, expression cross. She was thirteen now and was tall, far taller than most grown women. She had inherited her height from our ancestor Lionel of Clarence, even as Edward had, but it was more unusual to see in a maiden. You wouldn't want to tangle with Margaret, as she preferred to be called these days.

"I do not know how I will survive this winter in this nest of boys," she said, stamping one foot. "Pranks every day—spiders, toads, worms, and mouldered old fish heads. Noise and squabbling. How I wish Bessie was here to give me some relief! I will write to her and tell her all about your misbehaviour…"

Elizabeth had married John de la Pole the previous year. His father was William, Duke of Suffolk—he who had ended up dead on the sands of Dover, his head cut off after a mock trial. His son John was allowed to inherit but kept a very low profile in his eastern estates. Father had been no friend of William while he lived, but he had seen the value in extending an olive branch to his son by means of marriage to our sister.

"Elizabeth won't be interested in your tittle-tattle, Meg…I mean *Lady Margaret*," teased George, mimicking her hands on hips stance. "Soon she will be thinking of nought but producing babies, I'd wager. Ugh!" He flicked a fish scale in Meg's direction.

The fracas over, Margaret stalked off to lave her hands, while George and Richard's tutor (poor little creatures were stuck with Browne) came to hustle them away to the schoolroom.

Ned and I had no training slated till later in the day, so we decided to take a foray into Ludlow town, since it was market day and treats of all sorts would be on display. Wind was screeching over the battlements, and fallen leaves golden as a king's crown danced and twirled as if they were living beings. Soon, down below the ramparts, the weir would be clogged with them, and the woods around the castle denuded. In another month, I could take my younger brothers out into the forest to look for colourful toadstools and antlers shed by the fleet roe deer.

As we crossed the bailey and entered the cobbled market square, filled with scores of peasants, merchants and tradesmen, Edward pointed to a gaggle of people clustered around a ragged figure on the steps of the imposing Market Cross. He waved his arms wildly and shouted, but I could not make out his words.

"Shall we see what is going on there?" Ned asked. "Whoever he is, he has quite a crowd."

"Oh, probably a preacher of sorts ranting about sinfulness and Hell," I said, "but we can have a look."

We headed to a stall where Ned brought us sticky sweet pastries filled with dried currents and slathered with honey. No one recognised us in the drab garments we wore in anticipation of our later training session; both were clad in dull, off-white arming jackets, dark woollen hose, and warm cloaks more practical than lavish.

Sticky-fingered, we trundled towards the Market Cross. The man bellowing and gesticulating was, on closer inspection, a mendicant friar, his feet in shabby sandals caked with dirt and his cassock so ragged it looked as if a strong gust of wind would have it off, which would certainly give the townsfolk more entertainment than they had expected. The friar was scrawny, his bristly red tonsure overgrown, making him resemble a badly thatched cottage. His face was splotched with grime, his eyes staring and perhaps a little mad...

"I tell you, repent, for war is coming!" he cried, shaking a fist. "Terrible war. You know 'tis writ: *Nation will rise against nation, and kingdom against kingdom. There will be famines and earthquakes.*"

"No famine here," chortled a large-bellied merchant, slapping his stomach and pushing a pie into his mouth, to a chorus of laughter.

"Nor earthquakes either," quipped another wit, "though when Hal here falls down drunk—" He patted the burly merchant on the shoulder. "He makes the earth shudder!"

The mendicant friar scowled furiously. "Mock all you like, sinners—but the signs are there, clear as day. In Bedfordshire, bloody rain fell from the sky, soaking a goodwife's sheets as she hung them out..."

"Was that not from her virgin daughter taking a lover her parents knew nought of?" cawed an old toothless woman wrapped in a dingy mantle.

"Pray that your evil tongue be stopped and you learn womanly modesty, crone!" cried the monk. "There are other signs too. And rumours from the wicked court of King Henry."

"Wicked court?" a man yelled, rolling his eyes. "You're havin' a laugh, shave-pate! Mad Harry's half a saint. He don't even remember how his son was begotten."

The priest's eyes flashed. "Yes, and that has been noted far and wide. The Queen has, like the strumpet Jezebel, taken on a role too high for a mere woman. While the King is unmanned, unable to truly govern as a king, she steps forth, brazen, and rules the country in his name, gathering her own favourites around her and inciting them to war. The King only thinks of taxation and lets her do as she pleases. He that is named 'Prince of Wales' is in doubt as the legal heir to the throne—no one knows who his true sire is, but it is whispered that the King was incapable of begetting a child! So, who...was it Edmund Beaufort or one of her other favourites who held her in adultery?"

Edward nudged me. "A bold claim to speak in such a public place."

"It is..." I nodded toward two bailiffs who were pushing through the crowd, alerted that the fire and brimstone preacher had spoken near treason. Noticing their arrival, the mendicant friar scooped up his robes and ran for it. There was a brief chase, but he was as swift as a stoat and vanished into the tangle of little lanes leading from the market square.

The crowd dispersed and Edward and I returned to the castle bailey. We began to prepare for our training session in the yard when one of Father's squires ran up to us breathlessly. "My lords. I have long searched for you. His Grace the Duke says today's training must be postponed. He wishes you to attend upon him on a matter of some urgency."

"What have we done now?" I muttered. Father's temper had been short of late as he surveyed events across England, and he took some of his ire out on Ned and me. In uncustomary fashion, he had criticised our dress, our hair, our manners, and even our proficiency with weapons. He had come to watch us train in combat and stood with a pained scowl as the Master of Arms put us through the paces. "They aren't quick enough!" he had called out. "Edward, by Christ, you are a huge target for any enemy. Get moving, boy. Look behind you. And Edmund, you are quicker; I have seen you turn cartwheels in your armour, but today—today you are dancing around like...like a girl!"

I remember blushing red to the roots of my hair, ashamed of my own seeming incompetence. On the sidelines, young henxmen, sons of worthy families in the area, had sniggered at my chastisement. The Crofts did not dare—but I knew what they were thinking.

Edward put a comforting hand on my shoulder. "We had best find out what he wants. Do not worry, brother; his tongue may have sharpened but the fault is not ours. It is because of the heavy burden he carries as Henry's false peace begins to fail."

We went to Father's solar and greeted him as respectful sons should. He gazed at us with a strange expression I had not noticed before…maybe sadness? "Sit." He gestured to a bench.

We sat.

"I am sure you are not ignorant of the troubles in the world beyond Ludlow," he said. "The Earl of Wiltshire, without any experience to justify his position, had been made Lord Treasurer and bleeds the poor dry to enrich himself."

"He's the one with the 'pretty face,' is he not?" sneered Ned.

"Yes, the one known for running away because he fears battle might spoil his handsome looks. But there is worse, far worse than Wiltshire's mismanagement. The actions of Queen Margaret."

"There was a friar in the marketplace who told all and sundry that she sought unlawful power beyond the station of a consort," I said.

"This friar was not far wrong. I have it on good authority that Margaret seeks to compel, with sweet words and other blandishments, her husband the King to resign his throne and engage in a monkish sort of life. Prince Edward would then assume the throne, and his mother rule through him for the duration of his minority."

"She has great presumption!" sputtered Edward.

"Yes, and all of my enemies are her friends—if such faithless men can truly be called 'friends' by anyone. Their loyalties change like the weather. But she woos them by taking the child with her wherever she goes, making him hand out badges with *his* device of a swan upon them. That says, without so many words, exactly what her intentions are. Some may argue that her gestures are harmless, but I am convinced this is untrue."

He stood up, drawing in a deep, raspy breath. "I will not be caught unawares. I have written to Salisbury to have him bring his forces to Ludlow. Dick is still in Calais, keeping the trade routes clear of pirates, but I have asked him for the strength of his right arm in this struggle. He will come."

"Why did you call for us, Lord Father?" I asked. "Are you going to send us away to safety?"

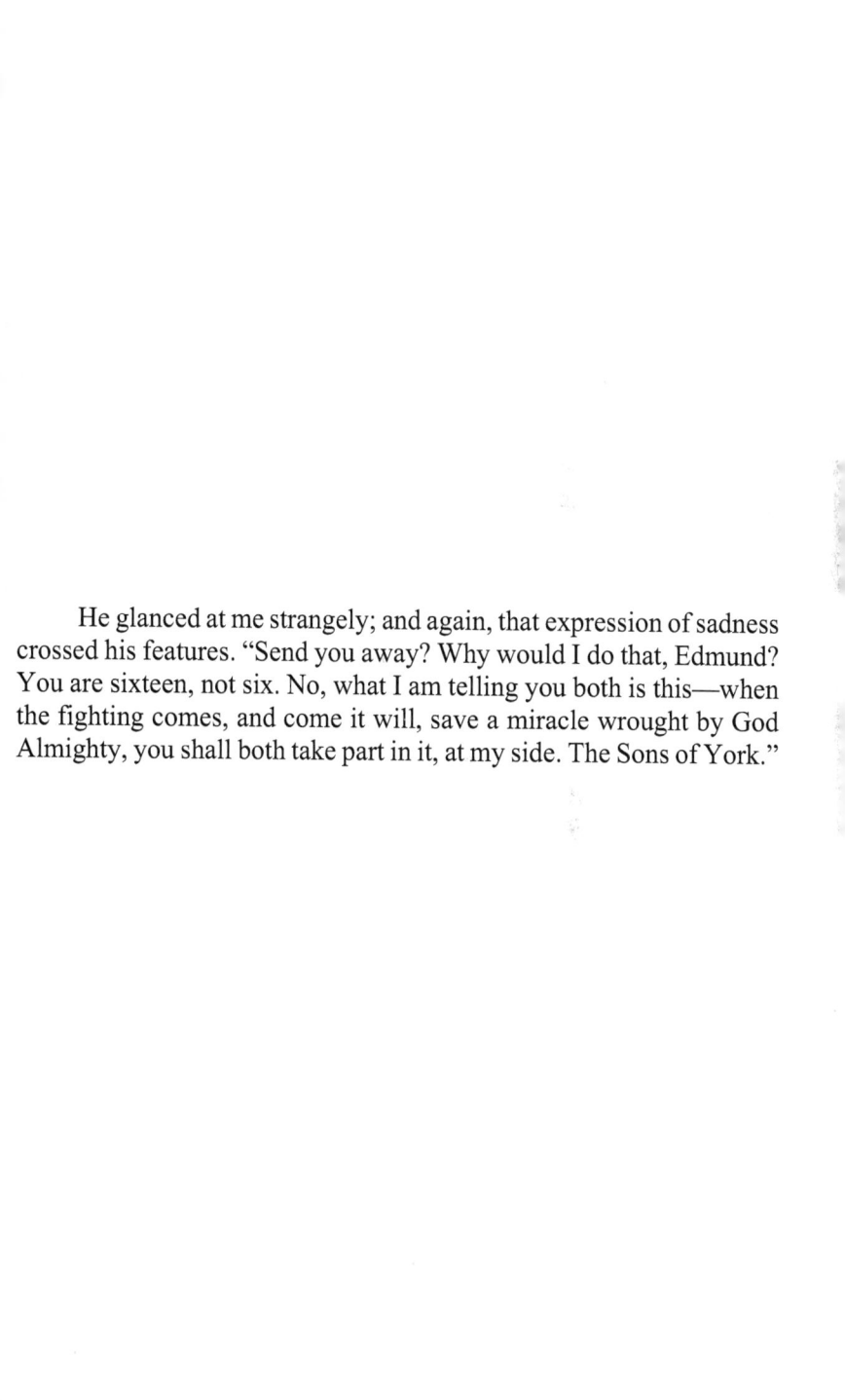

He glanced at me strangely; and again, that expression of sadness crossed his features. "Send you away? Why would I do that, Edmund? You are sixteen, not six. No, what I am telling you both is this—when the fighting comes, and come it will, save a miracle wrought by God Almighty, you shall both take part in it, at my side. The Sons of York."

CHAPTER FIFTEEN

Battles were beginning; peace had fractured like unstable ice on a lake. Uncle Salisbury, while heading to Ludlow from his northern lands, had skirmished with the Queen's men at a place called Blore Heath. Despite the royal army being far greater in number than his soldiers, Salisbury had prevailed on the field of battle, and Lord Audley, fighting for Margaret, was slain.

Our uncle sat in Ludlow's Great Hall conversing with Father about the confrontation. "I caught sight of the enemy banners above a tall hedge," he said, "so I was alerted to the peril. God was with me upon that day!"

"And where exactly did this happen?" Father asked. He had a parchment map stretched upon a table and was placing marks upon spots where the Queen's men had been spotted so that he could track their movements and prepare for any assault.

"On the border of Staffordshire and Shropshire. Near a place called Loggerheads—a fitting name." Salisbury's smile was wry. "I could have withdrawn and fled away as the Lancastrian host had not yet seen me, but I did not wish to have them come nipping at my heels, perhaps right up to the gates of Ludlow itself. I ordered the wains to close in to form a partial circle, with my soldiers arranged before them. Many of the men knelt and kissed the ground, for they thought this would be the place where they died..."

"What did you do next, uncle?" Ned was as rapt as any child listening to tales of high deeds.

"At first, I called upon my archers to loose. The enemy, under Lord Audley, did likewise, but neither of us bested the other—the distance was too far. A brook lay between us, wide and of unknown depths..."

"You did not ride over it?" I asked. "If it was only a brook and not a wide river..."

"Listen to me, Edmund." Salisbury leaned close. "It is always a temptation to 'have at' one's enemies and act in great haste. On rare occasions, such an attack might work. But if it fails—death is almost certain. You have never seen men crossing water in armour, their horses' hooves churning up the mud. It slows the advance, makes you vulnerable—and if a man should slip and fall, he quickly dies, trodden into the mud or face down in the water with dozens of soldiers and their mounts passing over him."

I grimaced, images of drowning foot soldiers and thrashing, fallen horses of knights in my head. Rushing water, running red...I had so much to learn—and not much time to learn it. Of course, the only way to truly learn about war was to participate in it—and come out alive when the day was won by your side.

Uncle Salisbury continued his story between mouthfuls of Rhenish wine and *Erbolat*, a confection of goose eggs and herbs mixed with diced sausage. He waved a slice of meat in my direction on the tip of his eating dagger. "I decided to try and trick my opponents. I ordered the middle to back off and pretend they were about to take flight. Audley and his captains fell for the ruse and charged towards us on their horses. They were galloping through the brook when I gave the command for my troops to turn...and hew them down while they were in a vulnerable position."

"How did Audley meet his end?" Father left his map and sat down beside us.

"Sir Roger Kynaston took him down; the fighting was fierce."

"Ah." Father nodded. Kynaston had been the Constable of Denbigh Castle, which had opened its gates to us after we returned from Ireland and found Beaumaris closed against us.

"Lord Dudley took over the command when Audley was slain, but he was inexperienced and it went badly for him. He had only foot soldiers, and many of them turned their coats and joined our side." Uncle Salisbury laughed and slapped his calloused, be-ringed hand against his knee. "There were still many of the Queen's supporters wandering around after the battle, so I devised a way to cover my journey toward Ludlow. I sent to a local monastery and got one of the monks to stay all night on the heath, firing a cannon. Dudley thought I was still there, hidden in the darkness, but I was on the way to Ludlow!"

We all crowed with mirth at the thought of the Lancastrians stumbling around the night fog, terrorised by the cannon's booms when it was only a solitary monk in flimsy sandals manning the gun.

Salisbury finished his repast. A page brought water and a towel for him to cleanse butter from his fingers. Another wine goblet filled to the brim, he stared towards the window, red with sunset. "Now…where is that son of mine, Dick? I pray he has not been delayed by mischief while on the road!" He tried to sound jovial, but I sensed an undercurrent of fear in his voice. Cousin Warwick had a long trip from the port to Ludlow with enemies swarming around him.

"Maybe we should pray for his safe journey," I murmured.

The others looked at me, surprised, then Father nodded. "Yes. Pray. We should. We need God on our side and not on 'Holy' Harry's."

No one in the room disagreed.

Warwick reached Ludlow near midnight. Grand and dramatic, he arrived at the castle like a clap of thunder, riding a dappled-grey courser, and with the Bear and Ragged Staff fluttering overhead. Trumpets signalled his approach.

"That's my Dick!" laughed Uncle Salisbury, relief clear on his face. "No dullard he, and no sluggard either!"

Cousin Dick was escorted to the solar, where he swept in like a storm, his hair wet and tossed upon his brow, his long, maroon cloak smelling of fresh rain mingled with the faint tang of salt. "Forgive my lateness. The sea was not friendly and neither were many of the ports. I had to choose wisely."

"You are here now, dearest nephew." Father gathered him in a warm embrace. "My thanks for supporting my cause."

"We heard that you recently attacked the ships of Genoans and Spaniards who were edging into English waters!" I said, with enthusiasm. Ned and I almost worshipped our heroic kinsman and wanted to emulate him; every time word reached us of his deeds, he had accomplished some act of daring or valour, just like a knight errant in an ancient tale. "Is it true that you relieved them of their money—

thousands of pounds—and imprisoned so many the gaols of Calais could not hold them?"

"All true, little cousin," said Warwick, as the squires took his cloak to dry and the pages brought him wine and food. "Later I will recount my exploits on the high seas, but at the moment I must know all the details of why my good Uncle York summoned me."

"The Queen moves against me, her actions growing stronger and more violent," said Father. "A battle has taken place at Blore Heath..." His gaze slid to Salisbury's broad, wind-beaten face.

"Yes," our uncle nodded. "I fought the Queen's minions there—and Lord Audley was slain on the field."

Cousin Warwick paused, momentarily stunned, his high mood instantly changing to solemnity. "Jesu," he murmured, "so it has come to actual blows at last." He spun on his heel to face Father. "I had not expected such a swift move from the Queen. I fear there will be equally swift retaliation. What is your plan, Uncle? You cannot mean to winter here...so many men, so many hungry mouths. Ludlow is a wealthy town, but I fear it would not remain so full of soldiers."

"We will march...march on London," said Father, and with a violent motion, he leaned over the map pinned to the table and thrust a dagger over the image of England's greatest city. "Whoever holds London, holds England."

"When you say 'hold', what mean you?" said Warwick, voice sharp. "Say it now, Uncle."

Father faltered a little, conflicting emotions streaming over his face. "Nought evil. I do not dream of usurpation if that is your fear. I am loyal to Henry—but not to the she-wolf Margaret. England flourished whilst the King was ill and I was left to govern. All I wish is for it to be known that I will not be sidelined, that I will not brook slights and lies...and that I only desire to assist the King in his governance of the realm, because it is clear to all men that Henry cannot do it. And the Frenchwoman with her band of favourites certainly cannot..."

"You have attempted such before," said Warwick, dubious. "With near disaster."

"It will not be as it was at Dartford. I will not be deceived like that ever again," Father shot back, and there was a fury in him unlike anything I had seen before, a fire lit that could be quenched in only one way. He felt betrayed, he wished for justice. For himself and for the people of England.

He should have been King... The thought burst into my head, as vivid and violent as lightning. I knew our family history, the Mortimer claim to the throne—knew that we had to suppress any such thoughts of rising to that dignity, as they would lead to death and disaster as had happened in the past.

I began to wonder then if Father *did* mean to do more than merely guide and counsel the King. The look on his face, frustration, longing—a hint of desperation.

A man at the end of his tether.

The moment was broken as Cousin Warwick flung back his head and laughed, then downed his wine to the dregs and hurled the goblet upon the table, spraying droplets of red across the parchment.

Red like a spray of blood...

"Excellent news!" boomed our cousin. "We ride for London!"

Hordes of men marched into Ludlow—Father's supporters from the Marches. The town was full to bursting. Encampments circled the walls, their campfires glowing after dark along the riverbanks and the smoke from those fires thick as morning mist. Tradesmen in Ludlow revelled in having so many prospective new customers—until the usual thievery and fighting began. Taverners rejoiced too, upping the price of ale and lodgings until brawls broke out and heads were broken. A murder happened too, a shopkeeper robbed and stabbed to death at his own front door, and several of the town's women were abducted and despoiled by drunken soldiers. Father sent the bailiff and sergeants to seek the miscreants, and when found they were hanged on common land outside the walls and buried in unconsecrated ground, save for the murderer, whose corpse dangled in a gibbet—a grisly warning that any man caught robbing, looting or raping would find no mercy.

During that time of muster for war, my brother Richard had his seventh birthday. Earlier in the year, I had promised to take him riding on that day, but now with the march to London imminent, it could not be. I came across him in the stables gazing longingly at the horses. "I am sorry we cannot go outside the town walls," I told him, "but it is truly not safe."

"I understand," he said. He did not look at me but stroked the white blaze on a large bay mare.

"I swear the moment I return to Ludlow after this is all settled, I will take you on the best ride ever. We'll go to Wigmore Castle—some of our ancestors lie buried in the priory there."

Richard shivered a little, his thin shoulders tensed. "What if you *don't* come back? What if nothing is ever settled?"

"Don't be so gloomy, Dickon." I went to his side, wanting to give him a hearty hug, but he shied away from me as if fearful of my touch. "We'll be back."

"You cannot say that for certain!" he said bitterly. "You might die. You, Ned, Father. I know what death means. I may be but seven, but I am not stupid. I knew when our sister baby Ursula died that I would never see her again, and I was even younger than I am now."

I sighed. "I am not saying you are stupid, Dickon, just that what you imagine won't happen. You'll see. Anyway, as we cannot go riding, I bought you a gift instead."

"Oh? What is it?" Richard began to thaw, his voice a fraction more cheerful. He stopped stroking the horse's nose and gazed at me inquisitively.

Reaching to my belt pouch, I withdrew a small item wrapped in a scrap of cloth and pressed it into his hand. "Have a look."

He opened the present. It was a wood carving of a wild boar with sharp tusks. Silver paint gave it a luminous sheen.

"I'd like to say I carved it myself," I said, "but I am afraid I would be lying. It came from the workshop of a town carpenter. I chose a boar because...there are lots of wild boars in the woods hereabouts. You see them sometimes rooting amidst the trees... When Ned and I return, perhaps we can all look for some boar. Not to hunt, though, as we have neither mastiffs nor boar spears. Just to watch—and admire."

Richard made the carved boar run across his palm. "Boars are not the biggest animals, like elephants, but they are among the fiercest, aren't they? As fierce as lions or wolves."

"Yes, every bit as fierce, maybe more so. I think you are like a boar, Dickon."

"What do you mean, Edmund?"

"You are only little, but I trow that you are fierce, and no one should underestimate you!"

Richard stepped forward, shyly, and gave me a quick hug. "My thanks for the gift, Edmund."

"Keep it hidden. You don't want George getting jealous."

"It's his birthday soon. I am sure he will receive many fine gifts."

"No doubt, but you know our brother. He would want them *now*, otherwise he would feel he was somehow missing out."

Richard gave a little laugh. "Yes, that is George."

He fell silent again, staring at the little silver boar, rubbing his thumb across its flank. Then he asked, very quietly and softly, "When are you leaving, Edmund?"

I knelt in the soft, smelly hay and put my hands on his shoulders. "Tomorrow. Before dawn breaks, we will begin our March south. You will be sound asleep."

"I will wake up George and watch you and Edward go," he said firmly, sounding years older than his age. "Then we will make George go to the chapel, and we will pray for your safe return."

Worcester, the first halt on the journey to London. Its cathedral overhung the River Severn, swollen by recent rains, a welcome sight from the far side of the many-arched bridge that spanned the flow.

Father, Ned, and I headed to the guest house of the cathedral priory, which was run by the Benedictines. While our sire conducted business with Prior Musard and dealt with the logistics of moving vast quantities of men through the city peacefully, we were permitted to visit the cathedral, which stood conveniently close to our lodgings. The Worcester Benedictines were known for their learning, and their library held rare books on mathematics, law, history, astronomy, and more. Father had arranged with Prior Musard that we might view some of these manuscripts. "We may ride to war, but you still need an education," he had said dryly, a mirthful glint in his eyes.

A lay brother emerged from the north transept, introducing himself as Brother Martin. Guiding us to the library, he proudly showed off work by the Venerable Bede, one of the cathedral's greatest treasures...and even a scandalous Wycliffe Bible. 'It is not inherently heretical," Martin informed us. "It is the translation that is the issue, and the use of the text to incite violence and uprisings." Most beautiful was a book of Psalms, its pictures painted with gold leaf and its cover glittering with gemstones; but the most intriguing appeared to be a large animal skin devoid of hair, which was rolled up and thrust under a table. There were holes in it as if it had been nailed to a wall.

"What is that?" Edward pointed to it. "What a strange thing to keep here with these treasures!"

Martin's snub nose wrinkled in disgust. "*That*...they say it is a man's skin, a Norseman who entered Worcester to pillage and burn centuries ago. No one knows for certain, even the prior, but for centuries it was nailed to one of the outside doors. Eventually, it was removed—we are civilised men now—and it rolled up and placed here in the library."

"Why...why don't you just bury it?" I was puzzled by the gory talisman, although intrigued too. It was not every day one saw the empty skin of a Norse raider!

Brother Martin's expression was one of shock. "Bury it? Goodness, no! Where would we entomb it? It's the skin of a heathen if the legends are true, and as such it cannot lie in hallowed ground."

"You could burn it instead," suggested Edward.

"No, we truly could not do that either, my lord of March," said Martin, "because, as I mentioned, it is only a *legend* that it came from the back of a ravaging Northman. The truth cannot be ascertained. It could just as easily be the hide of a *Christian* criminal who repented of his wickedness in his final moments. To burn a Christian's remains would be sinful of the part of the Brethren."

We left the library after viewing the will of King John, our ill-starred forebear, who was buried before the high altar. Passing his handsome tomb, he saw his effigy stretched out in a ring of candlelight, candles at his feet and incense smoke coiling around his head like a vanished crown. He was a despised King, devious and cruel, yet here he was buried in a monk's habit, if the records were to be believed.

"The barons tried to replace him with French Louis because John was so hated even a French ruler seemed preferrable," I murmured as we paused, staring at the stony likeness of our ancestor. "'Tis said he was a wicked man whose death made hell even fouler by his presence."

"Wicked and inept," said Edward, "if the chroniclers can be believed."

"Would the barons of today, you think, remove a King who is not wicked, who some even considered holy—but who is inept and detrimental to the realm?" Words slid from my tongue seemingly of their own volition. Words of treason, but maybe also words of destiny.

Edward glanced at me, the light raking through the windows hitting the planes of his face, making him resemble one of the beautiful carved stone angels that soared in the nave. "Perhaps, Edmund. Goodness of intent, without ability, will not feed the overtaxed poor, protect towns from ruffians, or keep corrupt men of high standing from unlawfully furthering their own causes."

Saying farewell to John's tomb, we exited the cathedral into the twilit streets of Worcester. Torches swam through the murk, and the town was noisy with men, horses and the clatter of armour and horse harness. Townsfolk rushed by, fearful of this martial display, and eager to reach their homes and bar the doors.

"My Lord March, my Lord Rutland!" One of Father's servants, an older man called Ralph, appeared, running through smoke-rings and the banks of fog rolling off the Severn. Puffing and gasping, he slid to a halt.

"What is it, Ralph?" Ned stepped forward, extending a steadying hand.

"Duke Richard has received important tidings from his scouts. You must come without a second's delay. Indeed, be fleet…run if you would. Do not wait for me…I can no more, till I recover my breath. Just go, as your Lord Father bids."

I felt guilty at leaving him there, clutching the cramp in his side and panting, but one look at Ralph's expression told me not to linger. Ned and I began to run, pushing aside passers-by, their identities cloaked by the thickening fog. Fortunately, the guest house was immediately behind the cathedral, and soon the porter's lodge, a squat room built over a strong gateway, stuck up like a giant's thumb through the mist, candlelight pouring from its solitary window.

I hammered on the wooden door and yanked the bell, nervous and impatient, and soon a burly monk puffed down the steps from his room, slammed back a panel in the door and glared blearily out.

"Who goes?" he cried, cheeks rosaceous in the glow of the lantern he held. I suspected, by his dazed look, that he had been tippling from a jug of ale secreted in the lodge.

"March and Rutland!" Ned said forcefully. "Here at the Duke of York's request."

The monk's bloodshot eyes widened. "Ooh…Yes, my lords…Come in, come in…" A wooden latch thudded and the door swung wide with a squeal. Pushing past the porter, who teetered and almost dropped his light, Ned and I rushed headlong toward the guest house. All around, Father's men were on the move, saddling horses and lifting goods onto wains. We bounded up the stone stairs into the Guest House, taking two or three steps at a time. With his long legs, Ned reached the top first, and reaching backwards, grabbed my doublet and hauled me after him.

Father and his captains were gathered in the prior's quarters. He glanced up as we burst into the room, his countenance peaked with strain. "My scouts returned not an hour ago," he said, "and the news they brought was the worst I could imagine."

"Margaret's forces are on the road?" Edward's desire to fight his first battle burnt within, making his words unwise. "Surely we can crush them as Salisbury did at Blore Heath!"

"Silence!" Father's voice was harsh. "Be still, Edward, and by God, listen to me!"

Ned whitened with shock at this chastisement and took a step backwards. I shook my head at him, praying inwardly that he would hold his tongue. With a real battle perhaps looming, we could not start to fight amongst ourselves.

He kept quiet, bowing his head in acknowledgement that he had acted improperly.

I breathed out, relieved.

Father leaned on the prior's desk, hands splayed. "A huge army marches from the east, many times our number. They move at great speed, and men swell their ranks at every turn. We cannot overcome such a force—to win would take a miracle. And..." he wiped his sleeve across his brow, sweaty despite the chill of the evening, "Miracles are in short supply, it would seem."

"Could we not hold Worcester against them?" I asked. "It has walls."

"Aye, but they are poor quality compared to York, Chester, or Coventry. I am certain they would hold out under any bombardment. We are also unprepared for siege warfare. Our supplies would be gone within a week or two. I could not bring such suffering to the people of Worcester. However, there is another reason why we cannot meet our foes head-on..."

He looked grey in the face, as if an illness had taken sudden hold. Hands clammy, I swallowed; I had heard of men his age—he was not many years from his fiftieth name day—dying suddenly when faced with terrible news.

"Father? What is the reason?" I asked quietly. "I beg you tell us."

"It's the King. A rumour has reached my ears; it seems impossible, but I feel in my bones that it is true. Men say that Henry fronts his host, arrayed in full armour and with banners raised."

"With his banners raised!" murmured Edward. "Jesu, if this tale is true, and we commence battle..."

"High treason."

"So...so...are we to surrender?" My voice emerged as a high-pitched croak, making me cringe in embarrassment.

"No," said Father. "Not in these circumstances. Henry I would trust with my life, even now; the Queen I do not, since she is the ruler of that little nest of vipers, Beaufort, Clifford, and their ilk. We must retreat. Go back to Ludlow and devise our next move."

"We must leave by midnight and march through the night," said Edward, and then, realising he had spoken out of turn once again, he flushed. "If it is your wish, Lord Father."

"It is," said our sire, "but ere we depart, we will go to the Cathedral and hear mass. We must not forget our duties to God, and perhaps He may show us a clear vision of what must be done."

The Teme roared, its waters grey and swollen from heavy rainfall. The old bridge was to the back of the camp set up when the army returned to Ludlow from our failed expedition. Father's soldiers had marched relentlessly through the dark hours, managing to evade the King's larger, more ponderous forces. However, rather than stopping at Worcester when told of Father's retreat, Henry was pushing onwards into the Marches. Peering at the solemn, sullen faces of the men in the camp, it was clear this news weighed heavy upon them. They had sworn oaths to Henry, even if dissatisfied with his reign. If they fought against him with the Royal Standard raised, they were traitors and liable to suffer a traitor's fate if the Yorkist forces were overwhelmed. Hanging. Drawing. Quartering.

Above the sky wept, a steady stream of rain that pattered on the marshy soil of the meadow and stippled the river currents. Leaves swirled along its swell, beside broken tree branches clawing upwards like bony hands. I recalled Uncle Salisbury's tales of rivers running red with the blood of the battle dead, and of how men and horses would pound over the living men fallen in the mud, where they would gasp out their life's breath, their mouths clogged with water and soil.

"Don't look so glum, little brother." Edward joined me where I sat on a bench made of an old log. "The King may not come all the way here. He might change his mind."

"Do you truly think so, Ned?" I raised an eyebrow, dubious.

"No," he admitted, "but it does not mean he will come for war. He must have been enraged and even afraid when he first heard of Father's army, hence he raised his banner. Even a King with such weak sensibilities as Henry understands what effect that would have on an opponent's morale. Father, Dick, and Uncle Salisbury have written to him, in hopes that calming words may soothe his ire."

"And what's Father going to say!" Testily I picked up a flat stone and sent it skimming over the river's surface. "'Sorry, your Grace, I was only out for an afternoon's jaunt with several thousand archers and pikemen?'"

Edward blinked, surprised at my cynical tone. "They reminded him of the indenture they had signed, which Prior Musard and Father

Lynwood from Worcester Cathedral sent to Henry. Father stressed his loyalty, assuring the King he only wanted to see hotheads such as Henry Beaufort removed from his council, for they would never sue for peace. He played upon Henry's piety, knowing that he is loath to see the blood of Christian men spilt."

I harrumphed and cast another stone into the swell of the Teme. "How is Father going to explain that we are sitting in a muddy field with an army, armed to the teeth, hiding behind earthen and timber barricades!"

"He will say it's for his own protection...and it is. Remember who rides with King Henry these days and how the Queen spurs her malicious favourites to violence. Father will ask for safe passage for himself, Dick and Uncle Salisbury, and once that is given..."

Another stone plopped into the river. Turning my head, I glanced at the castle louring behind the town walls, the low rain clouds streaming over its conical turrets. I thought of my mother, sister, and two younger brothers trapped inside, no doubt terrified by the unexpected turn of events. Maybe not Mother so much, for, when she needed to be, she was strong and cold as steel...but the younger children would. And Jesu, how I longed to be with them in the castle's warmth instead of a muddy, sodden field.

"If safe passage is given," I said slowly, without glancing at Ned, "do you suppose it will be respected? It wasn't at Dartford—why by Christ's Toes, do you think it fucking would be this time?"

I seldom used profanities, but curses exploded from my mouth as rage, fear, and despair built like a storm in my breast.

Edward stared at me in surprise. "I have never seen you so distraught, Edmund."

"No, I well believe you never noticed how I feel." My tongue continued to run on, burning with fire. "I was always the smaller brother, the plain brother, the studious brother. Of late, I sat at my books, learning, while you were off swiving serving maids. Oh aye, I swore not to take you to task over that, and in truth I care not where you take your pleasures. But I have my own desires, and no one ever asks. I am tired of being a shadow! *Your* shadow. A spare."

I expected Ned to react angrily, but he became suddenly thoughtful. "You know, do you not, that you are Father's favourite?"

I let out a harsh laugh. "Don't be so stupid. Of course I am not."

"You *are*, whether you believe it or not. *I* can feel it. Sometimes when he looks at me—it is not the way he looks at you. You are like him, in so many ways. My height, my features—I resemble him not at all."

"You take after Mother's family. Nevilles. Only with the height of our royal ancestor, Lionel."

"Ah," said Edward, "that is undoubtedly true, but men expect, rightly or wrongly, that a son should resemble his sire in some wise. Otherwise they talk, gossiping like old beldams in the marketplace…"

"What do you mean 'talk'?"

"You know… what many say about Henry's son has also been said about me. That the cuckoo is in the nest."

"If they speak such slander, they should be whipped!" My fists clenched. "That is vile and preposterous. Mother would never…*ever*…"

"Lower your voice, brother," warned Ned, as heads turned in our direction. "Let us not give the gossips cause to flap their tongues and cause more aggravation." He made to say more, but the sound of a trumpet on the far side of the river made him whirl about. "Hark! —a rider at the bridge-head. A herald wearing the Arms of England on his tabard. Quick, we must learn what he has to say."

I stumbled from my perch, mud sucking at my boots, and we hastened over to the tent where Father was receiving the King's herald. We stood outside the flaps, afraid we were intruding, but Cousin Warwick gestured to us to join him inside.

The herald was a small man, perhaps a year or two younger than father, with glossy bobbed hair the hue of copper. His visage was emotionless for the most part; when it was not that, it was full of disdain.

"The King has received your missive, your Grace," he said to Father in a clipped voice, every word spoken precisely. "He has offered to give pardons to you, the Earl of Warwick, and all your followers. But he cannot pardon the Earl of Salisbury who took arms against royal forces at Blore Field. If you surrender now and hand over Salisbury, all will be well between you and His Majesty."

"This is unacceptable," spat Warwick, standing beside his sire, who spoke not, but wore an enraged expression. His arms were folded belligerently as he glared at the pompous herald.

"And if we do not?" asked Father.

"If you do not, Lord Duke, the King will ride forth to Ludlow and battle will commence."

Father said nothing. Heart racing, I held my breath. Salisbury was his brother by marriage, and because of his sense of loyalty and honour, he would not abandon him to his fate. However, how would his soldiers feel when they heard that he had refused Henry's pardons for his men?

As the uncomfortable silence continued, the King's herald, uneasy himself, stirred. "Your answer, your Grace. I must have it now." His flinty little greenish eyes fixed on Salisbury, who still stood unmoving, Warwick at his shoulder with the appearance of a wolf about to spring for a lamb's tender throat.

"I cannot do as the King asks." Father's voice grated from beneath clenched teeth.

The herald appeared faintly pleased by his decision. "I shall depart and inform his Grace the King of your decision." He turned smartly on his heel and strode from the tent into the endless rain.

October 12, year of Our Lord 1459. The heavens still were open, emitting an almost Biblical deluge. The Teme was spilling over its banks, sucking at tufts of grass and drowning the path on the far side of the bridge. Ludlow town was eerily quiet, the entrances to streets barricaded with piles of wood and any other object that could impede the progress of a hostile army. The gates were all shut, their main inner faces bolted and barred, although there were safe words and secret ways to enable those in the know to pass. The monks in the little hospital of St John, close to the river, had packed up their goods and fled with the hospital's aged inhabitants. The little stone building stood empty, its door open so that invaders would not smash their way in, believing there were riches inside.

As dusk fell, fires bloomed on the castle walls. Shadows of archers moved like wraiths through the dimness. In the camp by

Ludford Bridge, what bonfires remained alight hissed and sizzled, the wood damp from the rain. Clouds of cloying smoke rose into the air, causing men to have fits of coughing.

King Henry had come with his army, true to his word. His soldiers camped in a large field within sight of our encampment. Henry's banner, unfurled, hung down like a sodden rag—but when the breeze moved its wet fold, the lions and lilies shone out—a warning, a threat to those who would move against an anointed king.

I sat in the tent I shared with Ned, near Father's pavilion. My armour lay ready for use; a young squire crouched beside it, mindlessly polishing a non-existent spot. Outside, a soldier was whistling cheerlessly as he went about his tasks.

Edward was toying with his dagger, testing the edge, then spearing a withered apple in a bowl on the table. He inspected the cut, grunted, and stabbed at the apple twice more.

The sound irritated, making me even more tetchy and nervous than I already was. "Edward…" I murmured, as the rain, at long last, began to let up. The clouds parted, and the moon floated over Ludlow Castle, turning its stones silver blue. I deliberately avoided the other direction, beyond our hastily thrown-up earthen defences, where thousands of night-fires burned amidst the uncounted tents of our enemies. Tents full of young men like Beaufort, Clifford, and Percy, all eager for bloody revenge.

"Yes?" Edward was twirling the apple on his blade; it suddenly fell in two, and the pieces tumbled to the floor.

"Are—are we going to die?"

Ned stared. "No, we are not going to die. Edmund, where are all these troubled thoughts coming from again? The King may never engage; he may change his mind; he may grant pardons for everyone."

"No, he won't. This time is different. If he had softened his stance, he'd have asked to parlay."

"He might do so yet—but we are *not* going to die, Edmund. Well, I certainly do not intend to! The world is full of beautiful wenches and high adventures, and I intend sampling them all."

As much as I tried, I could not smile back; melancholy descended over me like a cloud. "Oh, Edmund, Christ's Nails, get some sleep!" Edward tossed a sheepskin, smelling like a wet sheep, in my direction. "You'll be of no use to anyone if you work yourself into a lather. Nothing will happen before dawn anyway."

I took the sheepskin, wrapped it around my body, and hurried to my portable couch. I thought sleep might be impossible, but after a while, nervous exhaustion took its toll and my eyes drifted shut.

Around midnight, I was woken by a commotion in the camp. Eyelids flying open, I stumbled for the tent door. "You—your armour, my lord Earl?" My squire was on his feet, waiting for a command.

"Wait! *Wait!*" I waved my hand for him to shut up, and mercifully he did so.

I poked my head outside the tent. Ned stood a few feet away, unarmoured as I was, but with his sword in his hand. Ahead, blobs in the gloom, men were scrambling over the defensive earthen walls.

"W-what is going on?" I could make no sense of what I was seeing. I had thought the Yorkist camp was under attack, but these men were scurrying *towards* the King's forces, not towards our army.

Edward spat out an oath. "Damn them! They are deserters, Edmund. They are going over to Henry!"

Together we charged towards the centre of our encampment. Everyone was in an uproar, men storming after the departing traitors, pockets of fighting, shouting, and cursing. First, we happened upon Cousin Warwick, blade unsheathed, his expression murderous. "Anthony Trollope has betrayed us and taken most of the Calais garrison with him. The filthy turncoat! I would kill him with my bare hands if I got hold of him…"

Father emerged through the woodsy smoke, moving as slowly and stiffly as an old man. "We are undone. Trollope is a skilled soldier and privy to all our plans. He will reveal all to Henry to line his purse. Our cause is lost."

Falling silent, he glanced from Edward and then to me. Despair twisted his features. Then, swift as lightning, his expression changed. He was angry now, a fire burning in his eyes.

"Quickly!" he said. "Get dressed and get your weapons. Do not tarry. Time is short."

"What? Where are we going?" I asked.

"Council of war," he said loudly. "Up in the castle. You, my sons, along with Warwick and Salisbury." He gestured to the two

Earls, and they went to him while he spoke with quiet urgency. They nodded, grim and grave, though the glances they gave each other were uneasy.

"What about the rest of the captains?" Frowning, Edward stared out over the encampment. "Are they not to join this council?"

Father licked his lips; his eyes were glittering almost feverishly. "No, they will stay to keep the peace in the wake of Trollope's defection. Do not question me, Ned—every moment wasted brings us close to doom."

The five of us, one Duke and four Earls left the encampment, striding over Ludford Bridge to the town. Heading to the main gates on the hill behind St John's Hospital, Father rapped on the bolted side door three times, followed by two large knocks. A lantern glowed above and the sound of footsteps on stone was audible. A small slit opened in the door but neither face nor eyes was visible. It was disconcerting, almost as if a ghost stood watching us, a revenant of an ancient sentry who lived there when Ludlow's walls were first built by the de Lacey's.

"Who goes?" A hoarse, almost sepulchral voice drifted out of the darkness behind the door.

"Mortimer," Father whispered, giving the surname of his mother, Anne, from whom he had inherited the Mortimer lands and castles—and his claim to the throne from Anne's forebear, Lionel of Clarence.

There was a grunt as a heavy object was moved inside the unknown space beyond; then the metallic grind of an old metal lock turning. The door floated open a slim crack, revealing a man cowled right up to the eyes, and even those were hidden by the brim of a low-slung hat. It was a shock to realise that he was dressed thus so that neither friend nor foe would recognise him. If he failed to hold the gate safely, Father could not bring blame upon him, and if the King's men forced their way in, they could not accuse him of trying to keep them out of the town.

We slipped through the gap and the gateman shut the door, locking it behind us. At the same time, the lantern went out. Crammed together like cattle, our party stumbled through unbroken darkness.

As my eyes adjusted, I was able to make out a narrow, winding stair that led to the upper floor and cobblestones beneath our feet. I had travelled this path running at the side of the gatehouse dozens of times, yet in the blackness, it seemed unfamiliar, even threatening.

The gateman shoved his way through the midst of our little band, all proprieties forgotten in his haste. At the other end of the cramped corridor was the opposing door which led straight up into the town. It was locked securely in that direction too, making the folk of Ludlow prisoners within their own walls. I swallowed, imagining what might happen if Henry's men swarmed in, angry and eager to loot and destroy.

The disguised gateman shoved aside a heavy, braced timber with a grunt and jangled his keys again. The townward door slid open; light from a lantern hung on the exterior danced across the wet cobblestones. "Out you go," grated the gateman, pulling his hat down further to ensure his concealment, "my Lords. And may God go with you."

Out into the night we went, scuttling like rats in the rain-slick streets and alleys, keeping out of sight as best we could. Even though this was friendly territory, the less people who saw our passage, the better.

Soon the Market Square appeared, deserted except for a few scavenging cats, and near it the castle walls and the gatehouse, both bristling with guards. Striding up to the outer door, Father revealed himself to the watch. The portcullis cranked up and we were hastily ushered inside. The doors fell shut again with a bang, and the portcullis slammed home once more.

In Father's apartments, he called for meat and drink and had the candelabrum and the brazier lit too. "What is this mysterious night flight all about, Richard?" asked Uncle Salisbury, throwing off his wet hat. "What do you propose? I see no way out other than you surrender, and I give myself up to the King."

"No!" Father and Warwick shouted almost in unison.

"Do not play the hero, my Lord Father!" said Cousin Dick to Salisbury, eyes flashing. "Remember they have refused to pardon John and Thomas too, since they were also at Blore Heath. Would you have them go to the block with you—or worse, see them hanged, drawn, and quartered before your eyes?"

Salisbury slumped into his chair, glowering. He may have cared little for his own life, but he did care for the lives of his sons.

"I have a plan." Father strode back and forth in front of the fireplace like a caged animal. "You won't like it, I expect—but I wish you to consider it and think with your head rather than your heart."

"What is this plan?" asked Dick. "If you think to surrender in my sire's place and claim it was on *your* orders that he attacked the Queen's men at Blore Heath, that is not acceptable either, even if the King should believe you. Not that he ever would, not with Margaret and her favourites baying for the blood of the Nevilles. She'd have all of us killed; we have learned that 'safe-passages' and 'pardons'' mean nought to her, and Henry is too weak to uphold them.

"No, Dick, that was not my plan. I have another idea."

"Spill it out, then!" Sailsbury banged his hand on the arm of his chair, his rings gouging the wood. "Do not keep me in the dark!"

"We must leave."

"Leave? What do you mean 'leave?'" bellowed Salisbury, the strain of the past few weeks taking their toll. "We can't bloody well 'leave' with a massive army waiting outside."

"We need to do it now. Tonight. In secret. Dark clothes, fast horses. You and Dick go to Calais, where Dick has many loyal to him. Take Edward with you. I shall head to Ireland and take Edmund with me."

Silence fell. The fire gave a loud crack like a snapping bone, making me jump.

Father's strides became more agitated. "Speak! Are you with me or not?"

"You are asking us to desert our own men?" asked Salisbury, his shaggy brows raised, his hands now gripping his chair, the knuckles stark white. "To leave them to the mercies of an angry King and his bitch-wife?"

"It may save them," said Father. "It places more guilt on us, and gives them chance to surrender on their own terms. Henry may be a fool, but he is seldom eager to shed blood if there is another way."

Silence descended again. Warwick stroked his chin, thoughtful. "It feels craven to leave like thieves, but perhaps—perhaps you are right. With Trollope's defection, there is no hope of prevailing if battle is engaged at dawn."

"It is a hard decision for me as much as anyone." A bead of sweat broke on Father's brow, ran down his cheek. "For I shall have to leave my wife, daughter, and youngest sons here in Ludlow and pray that our enemies will not be so base as to assault—or kill—a woman and children."

"You are not taking Cecily?" Uncle Salisbury's jaw dropped; he seemed flabbergasted.

"No. If she fled, the danger to her would be greater, and bringing small children would slow us down and prove a weakness."

"Jesu, how has it come to this?" groaned Salisbury, bowing over and holding his head in his hands. After a moment or two, he glanced up with one burning eye. "What of my sons, John and Thomas? They are in danger."

"I will send word to the camp and have them meet you and Dick outside the town's precincts. I will make sure they have a written summons if the captains should question them—a summons to join our 'council'."

Uncle Salisbury lifted his head. "What say you, Dick?" He glanced over at the Earl of Warwick.

"It is a mad, rash plan, but in truth I cannot see any other action to take. Richard is right—our departure may save the lives of our men by putting all the responsibility on ourselves. Ignoble flight might seem, but at least we will live to fight another day."

"So, we are all agreed?" Father stood before the fire, silhouetted against the blaze. It was a disconcerting image, a trick of light and of perspective; he looked as if he flamed, a falcon rather than a phoenix, soaring up from the ruins with new hope.

Edward cleared his throat. "I would stay at your side as a good son. To defend your honour and your noble person. To die in your defence."

"I thought you might say that, Ned...but no. You are my heir. It would not do well for the three senior men of the House of York to travel together. If we were caught..." He made a slashing motion with his hand, implying beheading. "No, you shall travel to Calais with Salisbury and Warwick. You will learn much from the experience, I am sure of it."

I feared Ned might protest further but he kept his peace. In fact, I detected a small flicker of excitement in his face.

On the other hand, I was conflicted. I had never journeyed afar without my brother; even when we fought over foolish things like girls, the anger never lasted between us. So close in age, we were almost like twins—not in appearance and not in our mannerisms, but yet we shared a deep, strange bond. I was afraid that bond would be broken forever. But I knew, too, that it was unsafe for all of us to travel together. Dispersing to different places would also confuse our enemies.

"So...it is decided," said Father, stepping out of the ring of firelight, fresh determination in his face. "Salisbury and Warwick, go you to the Corve Gate and exit through there. I will write safe passes to ensure the gateman lets you through unhindered. I shall also see that Thomas and John join you. As for you, Edmund, Edward, collect what you need and put it in chests to follow on should we be successful in our escape. Dress warmly and in dark colours to blend with woodlands and shadows. We must move fast and travel lightly. Now I must speak to your mother, the Duchess, and then we must go. Be swift. Edmund, meet me near the postern gate. Edward, go with your kinsmen to Corve gate."

I hurtled down the corridors to the apartments, Ned racing at my side. Once inside our chamber, I flung on travelling clothes, dark green and featureless. Edward likewise donned concealing raiment—although his height was a giveaway of his identity. Other personal items, for later collection, were thrust into chests and coffers.

As we readied to depart, Edward put his hand on my shoulder. "Brother...Little Ned."

This time, I did not revolt against that childish nursery name. A lump growing in my throat, I threw my arms around him and we clung together in a fierce embrace.

"We'll meet again, I promise you," he said, with such fierceness that I believed it must be true. "Keep yourself safe, and Godspeed, Edmund."

"Yes...yes...We are in winter now, but the spring shall surely come again. Be well, my brother—my dearest friend."

We stepped apart, and I made to go down the corridor to the left. Edward headed right, toward the door leading to the bailey.

At the end of the passage, he paused, looking back. The light from the burning flambeaux fastened to the walls made a nimbus around his head as if the sun rose behind him. "I told you that you were Father's favourite, didn't I? Protect him, won't you? The road you take is a perilous one."

Before I could answer, he strode away and was gone.

Fighting emotion, I hurried toward the postern gate where I would meet Father. Ned and I were sundered and the paths we took, diverged for the first time, and I had no way of knowing if we should ever meet again in this mortal world.

The journey into exile was fraught and unpleasant. Father and I, accompanied by a small quota of servants, galloped like madmen through the darkness, our cloaks streaming in the wind of our speed, our steeds' breath fogging in the air. The rain and wind returned, pounding us, blowing icy droplets straight into our faces, which soon became red and raw. I wore gloves but my hands were close to numb; my toes, too, had no feeling.

To avoid detection, our company skirted hamlets and towns, but it meant the journey ay was longer and harder—clambering over muddy hillocks and through gnarled, leafless woods where skeletal tree branches stabbed at us, as if they, too, had suddenly become our enemies. Many times, I wanted to ask Father for a stop to ease the dull, nagging aching in my back and thighs, but I ignored the pain and carried on. Pursuit was a distinct possibility, and we had to put distance between the King's army and our small band.

Eventually, we halted at some remote place, where a man with a lantern met us beside a roadside stone pillar sticking up through the murk like a bony grey finger. He gave us drink from a wineskin he carried and exchanged our weary mounts for fresh ones tethered in the field beyond the stone. Then we pushed onwards, ever onwards, hastening towards Denbigh where a ship waited to bear us to Ireland. It was still ten leagues away, and we were not safe yet. Father's scouts still might return to tell us the town was barred against us in the King's name, or that the ship's master had refused to take fugitives.

Dawn came, grey and windy, before we reached Denbigh. The company decided to lay low in nearby woodland to give the horses a respite and ourselves too. As I sat in the gloom—no fires or even strike-a-lights permitted on Father's order, I wondered where Ned was, and if he had managed to safely leave Ludlow with Warwick and Salisbury.

"I would rather not make ourselves known in the day," said Father, hunkering down on a twisted tree root. "The town cannot be regarded as friendly to our cause just because it aided us in the past. We will wait here till dusk—it comes early this time of year. Now eat, Edmund; you look almost ready to fall over."

Gratefully I took a slab of hot meat that a servant cooked over the fire and a mazer of watered-down ale. Then, with the horses cropping grass, and the rain still pattering on the leaves above I took a saddlebag, laid my head upon it, and slept, uneasily but for long enough to ease my fatigue a little.

Just after sunset, our company packed up and set off again. Night swept in, enfolding us in a starless cloak. Ere long, the tang of salt struck my nostrils; we were nearing the sea. I caught a glimpse of fire and lantern light in the distance—the town of Denbigh ringing the mighty feet of the castle. But we turned aside from the town and travelled on lesser-known paths to a secluded cove where a small cog lay anchored, bobbing on the tides.

A rowing boat came across from the ship as we clustered on the shoreline, staring out over the water. Father and I dismounted and handed our mounts to those servants who were to remain in England. It would prove too arduous to get the horses onboard; Father would look to Sir Christopher for help when the ship reached Howth.

Once we were ensconced in the rowboat and sliding through the choppy waves, I sat stiffly with my hand on my dagger hilt beneath my cloak. Well I remembered the tale of the unfortunate William de la Pole, seized aboard ship while heading into exile and summarily executed by six blows from a rusty blade...

Fortunately, my fears of a similar attack amounted to nought, and soon Father and I were on the cog's deck speaking with the ship's master. There would be no delay in departure, he told us; the wind was favourable, and the sea, if not calm, at least was not stormy.

For once, Father's plans had gone the right way.

Without more ado, the cog's anchor was drawn up, dripping water and weed. The cog glided out of the cove and, turning its prow, sped into open waters like a speeding arrow. I remained on deck, the night wind in my hair, sea salt burning chapped lips. The shadowy coastline, a series of vague featureless humps and bumps, faded away into the distance. The wind began to rush through the riggings, an eerie, mournful sound.

I wrenched my gaze from the diminishing shores of Wales and turned my face towards the west.

Soon, soon, I would be in Ireland.

CHAPTER SIXTEEN

Trim Castle, familiar and yet strange without Edward's presence. Bleak, too, as winter descended with a roar and early snow fell. Mother was missed too; memories like ghosts haunted Trim's austere halls. She was a prisoner now, along with Meg and my younger brothers. A comfortable enough confinement, faring between Maxstoke and Tonbridge Castle in the keeping of my Aunt Anne, wife of the Duke of Buckingham, but prisoners nonetheless.

I remember Father's relief when he received news of Mother's safety; leaving her at Ludlow had weighed heavily upon his mind and conscience. As it turned out, the King's army *had* pillaged Ludlow, drunk and out of control, burning and sacking and stealing. Mother, brave as a lion but foolhardy considering she was a noblewoman, had left the castle's safety to appeal for mercy while standing high on the Buttercross with her children holding her hands. Prowling men ripped the jewels from her clothes, and worse may have happened save for the arrival of Humphrey Stafford, Uncle Buckingham, who had beaten off the attacking thugs and taken her into his protection—although also his prisoner.

However, by November, Father had received more tidings to darken his heart. Parliament had convened in Coventry, and it was clear it had only one thing on the agenda—to destroy the House of York and all its supporters.

"I name it the Parliament of Devils." His hands shook as he held the parchment sent from England by one of his loyal followers. "Not one man was there who would raise his voice to defend me. All were either King's men or Queen's—Exeter was there, of course, gloating, the slimy toad. My poor Anne."

"I would do more than throw him in a pond if we should ever meet again," I said, remembering his arrogance and cruelty, his smug, spotty face. "So do not hold back, Father. I want all the details of this Parliament."

"As usual, it was claimed that my only desire is to wrest the crown from Henry's head," Father said wearily. "They called me 'diabolical' and full of 'wretched envy'."

"We have heard such claims since Jack Cade began his rebellion," I said. "These are just words, foolish words from foolish men."

"It gets much worse." Father's smile was bitter. "They claim I was planning to assassinate Henry when summoned to meet him at Kenilworth. Of course, the oh so noble Beaufort, Exeter, and Clifford selflessly warned him of my 'evil plot.' The plot that never, by God, existed, as well they know, the lying bastards!"

"Sit, Father." He was so agitated that I guided him to a chair. It felt strange to do so; he had always been so strong in the face of adversity. To my surprise, I realised as I stood next to him that we were now of equal height. So the youth becomes a man, and his sire an old man—my sire was not a greybeard by any means, but there were new lines around his eyes and more silver sprinkled in his hair, and the one-time firm, strong jaw sagged a little.

"It is not the only lie," he continued, chucking the parchment on the fire with disgust. "They also said I proclaimed Henry dead and had a Mass said for his soul."

"What?" I frowned, deeply shocked. "No Christian man would do such a thing, especially not one of your piety."

He shrugged. "Henry's creatures seem to believe it, or more like hope to convince the King of it. Can you believe they even say I fired cannons at Henry? They may as well say I have grown a devil's horns and tail and fly through the night with a pack of demons!"

Suddenly he grew sombre, his wrath fading. He looked morose, beaten. "But here is the part that hurts, my son, as it affects you. Many attainders have been passed by Parliament. Dozens of good men, including not only your Uncle Salisbury and Warwick, but Harrington, Conyers, Lord Clinton, the Bourchiers, have all been attainted. Your Aunt Alice too…"

"Alice! How could she be blamed? She has stayed at Middleham throughout..."

"Where, according to her accusers, she was nefariously plotting against the King and Queen. All nonsense, of course. As your uncle held his lands through the right of his wife, accusing Alice of treachery was the only way to destroy his power utterly."

"Bastards," I muttered.

"But here is the worst part. You, Ned, and I have all been attainted too."

"I expected as much, once you began to speak of those Parliament has condemned." My chest tightened as my anger left, and a cold knot of fear and loss replaced it. An attainder meant the loss of everything—titles, castles, lands. Once we were of the blood of kings, but that mattered not a jot anymore. We had been thrown down, struck into the dust by our enemies, with little hope of rising. We were no better than outlaws if we stepped on English soil.

But here in Ireland, it swiftly became obvious things were different. Father did not long dwell on the cruel vagaries of fate; he immediately began to re-establish his position as a good lord to the Irish people, and they warmed to him, as before. Threats came from the Crown that any Irishman who supported Father would lose their lands for sheltering a rebel outlaw. The Irish nobles hooted in derision at such orders and burnt the messages as they arrived. Indeed, they seemed to enjoy flouting the wishes of their foreign overlords.

When Parliament opened in Ireland, Father was confirmed as Lord Lieutenant, despite his outlawed status in England. Declarations were made across Ireland, telling the populace that Richard of York, Earl of Ulster, was to be honoured and obeyed, and that if any man should attempt to slay or injure him or deliver him to his foes, they would stand accused of High Treason in the Irish Parliament.

His powers were so great in Ireland, he was close enough to a king...

The Irish were no sluggards once the wheel of change began to turn. Mints sprang up in Trim and Dublin and quickly began producing new coinage—the Ireland, the Patrick, and a groat. A Great Seal of Ireland was fashioned, and the nobles agreed they would not accept orders given under any other seal. They still acknowledged King Henry as their liege lord, but it was a light allegiance indeed, and their contempt for his weak rule was obvious. No more would the lords of Ireland be dragged overseas to face charges in an unfamiliar, unfriendly territory. Instead, they would answer to Father; a lord who was aware of their issues and dealt with their grievances fairly and in person, rather than from afar.

One day Father came to me, as I sat in the solar reading a manuscript sent to me by my old tutor, Tadgh. I was disappointed he was no longer resident at Trim, as he had gone hence to tutor another noble youth, but his hand-scribed translation of *The Voyage of Máel Dúin* went some way to alleviating my sorrow. "You are content here, Edmund? Settling in well?"

I was not certain how to answer. Daily I thought of my Lady Mother and of Edward and wished I could, at the very least, hear from them, although I understood this was likely impossible. However, despite this, I was far from unhappy. I was old enough to realise that my fortunes in Ireland might rise in a way they could never do in my homeland unless by some miracle the attainder laid upon me was lifted.

"I know you miss Edward's company," said Father, guessing in which direction my thoughts lay. "I pray one day Ned might come here. At some point, the rest of the family must be released; they cannot remain prisoners forever, as they are guilty of no crime."

"The Mortimer boys, the heirs presumptive of Richard II, were kept imprisoned in various castles for *years* by the usurper Bolingbroke," I reminded him. It was rather refreshing to speak of Mad Harry's grandsire in such terms now that I was far from England. "They were there so long one lad died. The other was released, but it seemed the desire to fight for his birthright had gone out of him."

"It was a different time, Edmund. Henry is weak, and Margaret, although she loathes me, was at one time close to your mother. With time, the past can take on a different complexion."

"Not soon enough for me!" I huffed, and felt immediately sorry.

"I understand your impatience. I am impatient too, but have learned over the years that caution can be the wisest action one can take. However, would it sweeten your exile if your appointment as Lord Chancellor of Ireland, given to you when you were only eight and held by others in your infancy, is now assumed by you? You are old enough, I deem, although with someone to guide you. It is time you started to assume the responsibilities suited to your birth."

"My...my Lord, I am not worthy." I dropped to one knee before him, filled with gratitude.

"No one is more worthy, my son. I did not give you the position in childhood for mere show. Of my two eldest sons, you, Edmund, are the most similar to me. I will aim to teach you all that I know and have the utmost trust in your abilities. Ned is my heir, but I hold a special fondness for you. I'm also aware that my Norman holdings, once intended as part of your birthright, are lost forever. Perhaps, if you assume a high position in Ireland, you will regain some of what was lost to you. Although this is not a rich country, Edmund, it is a good country, and if bridges could be built between us and the common people, who knows where that might lead? If not for me...maybe for you."

So I became Lord Chancellor in reality rather than through proclamation only, and without Edward at my side. For the first time, I became *noticeable*, his smaller shadow no longer. I began to dally with fair maidens, of which there were plenty in Trim and Dublin, although not so blatantly as Edward, and with more care for my position and theirs. I had no wish to add a crop of bastards to my worries.

Other worries did come, however. Aunt Alice arrived unexpectedly on a ship from the north of England. She was in a state of agitation but still had the wherewithal to bring her jewels and gowns when she fled.

"Alice..." Father was almost speechless as she entered Dublin Castle's Great Hall, weary from her journey but with a grimly determined expression. "Had I known, I would have readied chambers for you..."

"I had to leave Middleham quickly, under the cover of darkness," she said. "I could not bear to stay a moment longer watching the King's lackeys root through my castle and filching whatever they liked. They threatened to extricate me from Middleham, so I decided that if I had to depart, it would be on my own terms, not theirs. So I chose safety in Ireland, even as you, Richard."

Father went to her, took her hand, and kissed her cheek. "You are always welcome in my house, Alice. I cannot swear all will be well, but as long as you remain here, you are under my protection."

"My son will come for me, I have no doubt about that," she said firmly. "I have written to him in Calais."

Alice had many sons, but it was Cousin Warwick she spoke of. Brave, dashing Richard Neville, the terror of the seas. "Have you heard from him?" I asked, eager to know if any word had come of Ned.

She glanced at me, shaking her head. "Not as yet, nephew. My messenger's path was perilous but he appears to have left England without issue. I presume Dick has my letter by now and is aware that I sailed for Ireland. How long it might take him to get here, who can say?" She let out a long, mournful sigh.

"I am sure he will come for you as soon as it is possible," I said. "He is never sleepy in his actions."

"No, that is true." Aunt Alice smiled weakly. "Goodness, I am so weary after my journey. The sea does not agree with me."

"Edmund, see to it that Countess Alice is served a light repast while I have apartments readied for her." Father began walking towards the chamber door.

"I have brought all that I could thrust into travelling chests," Alice added. "And there are young squires and soldiers outside. Oh, and my maids, too. I hope you do not mind so many extra mouths to feed, Richard."

"Not at all," he said, although the smile on his face was insincere. He was still short of money and the Countess was used to a lavish lifestyle. "You will excuse me while I work out their lodgings and your own."

He vanished, a posse of servants in tow, and Alice turned her attention to me. "Last time I saw you, you were at your wetnurse's pap. You have grown into a fine young fellow. Hm, has your father spoken of any marriage plans as yet?"

Reddening, I stammered, "No—no, my Lady Aunt."

"I suppose he has too many other things upon his mind, like poor Cecily and the little ones, locked away in Humphrey Stafford's castles under the strict rule of Anne, who is so unlike her other siblings in temperament. Hm, it's a pity your cousin Katherine is no longer free, but she has recently wed William Bonville. However, Margaret, my youngest daughter, is still unmarried—I must see about introducing you when this unpleasantness is over. Dispensations would need to be obtained for the closeness of your blood, but that should not cause a great issue..."

I was struck dumb at this proposal, unable to think of a polite retort. Margaret was likely a fine girl, but this was all too sudden! Luckily, Father returned to the hall with the steward in tow. "Countess, your chamber is ready. If you would follow Master O'Flaherty, he will take you to your room. Another servant is fetching your attendants, and your chests shall be carried up to you soon."

Aunt Alice reached out and gripped his hand. "Thank you, Richard. I have always liked you." She gestured imperiously to the steward. "Lead on, sir! I am tired and must lie down for my health." She flounced out of the chamber, following O'Flaherty.

"What were you talking about with your aunt?" Father inquired. "Your face is the colour of flame. What has unnerved you so?"

"Marriage!" I gasped. "She talked of marriage! To one of her daughters!"

Perplexed, he stared at me and then began to laugh. "Although the Nevilles are our supporters and our kin, I hope to find a better match for you, Edmund, once all is settled. Maybe a maiden from Burgundy, or even a French princess." He laid his hand on my arm, squeezed. "I have high hopes for your future, my son."

The burgeoning popularity of the House of York in Ireland was soon put to the test. An official trotted up to the gates of Trim and demanded admittance in a loud, arrogant voice. "I come from England," he shouted when the guard challenged him. "I am William Overey, squire, sent here on an important matter by his lordship, James, Earl of Ormond and Wiltshire, who is, as all Irishmen know, your *true* Lord Deputy and Lord Lieutenant, and who now serves as Lord High Treasurer to his Grace Henry VI, King of England, France, and Lord of Ireland. I come on his lordship's behalf and demand immediate entry to the presence of Richard of York."

Overy's disrespectful omission of my sire's title told everyone within hearing that this was no friendly visit. A crowd began to gather by the gate and within the castle bailey, curious and not terribly friendly towards the newcomer.

A squire who overheard the conversation with Overey scuttled through the bailey to bring word of this unwelcome newcomer. Father was in a meeting with many Irish lords and looked both peeved and strangely excited as the boy informed him of Overey's risible demands. The nobles around him glanced furtively at each other, grinning. Tadgh had once told me that the Irish loved nought better than an almighty brawl with their foes and enjoyed baiting them, almost as if it were a sport rather than a matter of life and death. I had begun to believe him.

Father gestured to the soldiers manning the doors of the Great Hall. "Go and fetch this William Overey. Indeed, drag him from his mount and carry him in, if it is a swift meeting he desires."

The guards clanked away, and before long angry shouts rang through the castle's corridors. "Let go of me, you bearded ape! Are you a mooncalf? I have told you who I am—Earl Butler's man! I am also on the King's business…"

He was thrust into the hall by a smirking soldier. He stumbled, not expecting to be so jettisoned, and landed on his knees with a thud before Father's high seat. The Irish nobles hooted with mirth, full of derision.

Overey was a small, round man with the face of a butcher in the marketplace. His sandy hair was cut in dishevelled wedges around flat, indeterminate features, red and ruddy as a slab of raw meat. He wore a rumpled tunic bearing the Arms of his master, three covered cups of gold. Huffing, he staggered to his feet, assuming an aggressive stance, his legs far apart and his fleshy chin thrust out "The Earl will hear of this vile treatment!" he snarled, glancing around, his eyes wild. "And so will King Henry, mark my words."

"No one here is afraid of the Earl of Ormond," called out one of the Irish, a big fellow with a flaming beard. "He's not like his father, God assoil him. Spends all his time in England,with his Beaufort wife, forgetting his people back home, and we've heard he values his pretty face so much he wins all his battles by running…"

"By running away as fast as he can…" interrupted the Earl of Kildare, "as if the divil himself was after him."

Overey sputtered in stunned outrage. "Are you going to let these ruffians insult me and my master the Earl?" he spat at Father.

"Your own behaviour is an insult to me, fellow." Father sprang from his seat, a dark energy I'd never noticed before flowing from him. I would not have wished to stand in William Overey's shoes…"What right do you have to come into this country and behave in the manner you have?"

"Right? I have every right!" Overey lunged forward and flung several rolled parchments onto the table before one of Father's guards pulled him roughly back. "You, your sons, and your followers are all attainted traitors as decided by Parliament at Coventry. These documents that lie before you are the warrants for your arrest! Not just for you, York, but your whelps and all your main supporters."

"Jesu," said Desmond, another Irish Earl, rolling his eyes, "you came all this way to arrest him, and you not having an army, just a few sorry men-at-arms who are out in the courtyard getting drunk. That's a bit mad, don't you think?"

"I am on King's business, as I have already told you, you Irish dullard. I am the law!"

"Oh, are ye now?" One of the O'Neills flicked a bone from the chicken he'd devoured towards Ormond's minion. It struck Overey's crumpled tunic before tinkling to the ground. "You're a jumped-up fellow, considering you are only a squire. Did your master, young Butler—God forgive me, but that vain sot is *nothing* like his old father—did he promise you riches or lands?"

William Overy spluttered, but his outrage began to have the taint of fear. What had the man expected? That these proud lords would fall at his feet, acting like obedient dogs to gain favour with the King of England and a mostly-absent Earl? "Look—look at the Seals!" he cried, voice shrill. "The documents all bear the royal Seal of King Henry. To ignore them will bring you doom!"

The Irish laughed. The Earl of Desmond shook his head. "Oh, sure, you are not well informed, Master Overey. We've held our own parliament here in Ireland not so long ago—did you not hear of it in your fancy palace of Westminster? Ireland has its own Great Seal now, and we refuse to accept as official any seals not directly from an Irish source when the matter pertains to those residing within Ireland."

"You jest, surely!" Overey roared, spittle flying from his mouth. "How am I to deal with you? It seems I gaze upon a gathering of children, playing at governing and making up the rules as they see fit. You dogs will bark for my Lord King should he send…"

"What did you call us, squire?" Desmond again, his eyes narrowed, dangerous.

The laughter fell silent; smiles died and faces grew rigid, angry, threatening. No one was permitted to carry a dagger or sword in the Great Hall, but I was certain any one of the Irish nobles could finish Overy with his bare hands.

The squire backed up a step, sensing the increased tension in the hall, perhaps finally realising that no one here respected his mission or his master.

"Leave," said Father, "while you still can. As for these…" He held up the arrest warrants with two fingers, as if they were rotten meat, and flung them into the fire brazier.

Overey glared at him and made as if to exit the chamber, his shoulders hunched in defeat—but suddenly, he whipped around and with a demented yell, launched himself towards Father's seat. Reaching into a fold of his garments, he drew a wicked-looking dagger, its blade gleaming in the firelight. He crashed down on the table, sending wine goblets and platters flying, his weapon stabbing madly at the air.

Father was quicker than he, despite being years older. He sprang up, kicking his chair across the room, and caught Overey's wrist in his left hand, twisting it hard. The crack of bone rang throughout the Great Hall. Overey screamed but managed to fling himself away, falling heavily on the floor. The knife shot out of his grip and fell into the rushes.

"Get him, boy!" Desmond shouted to the huge, shaggy grey wolfhound that had lain, snoring, across his boots. The hound heaved itself up, lips rolling back in a snarl as it leapt on Overey, its fangs slicing into the meat of his thigh. Overey screamed again and snatched at the fallen dagger with his uninjured hand.

I reeled towards Father's assailant, the shock of his unexpected assault fading and anger rising in its place. "Let it be, you bastard!" I cried, and I stomped on his fingers, crushing them.

He howled and the wolfhound went wild, biting him a second and a third time. By now, the guards had poured into the Great Hall.

Desmond pulled his hound away, red-muzzled as soldiers grabbed William Overey off the ground, roaring in pain and fighting them with his fists. I snatched up the dagger he had intended to commit murder with, and as I stared at its honed edge, the rage inside me flared white-hot, clouding my judgement. The dog's growling faded; the shouts of guardsmen and soldiers slipped into nothingness. My gaze fixed on Overey's shapeless, slab of meat, butcher's face—he would have been a butcher indeed, if the Fate's Wheel had spun him high instead of throwing him down.

He had tried to assassinate my father.

I wanted to kill him. I wanted to see the light fade from those hostile piggy eyes. "You swine!" I spat at him and thrust the dagger towards his chest.

I was grabbed from behind and pulled away from my quarry. The knife dropped from my fingers and was kicked across the room. "Get off me! Get off me, damn you!" I shouted—and then I realised it was Father gripping me so tightly, hauling me back from his assailant. One of the guards had William Overy in a headlock; the squire was wrestled out into the corridor and dragged towards the dungeons.

"You—you should have let me kill him!" I gasped, feeling suddenly breathless and dizzy. "He tried to murder you."

"I came to no harm." Father's face swam before my bleary eyes. "It would not be appropriate to slay him outright once he was overwhelmed. We are not assassins and cutthroats like him. The man must have a trial. Do you understand?"

I nodded. A servant was thrusting a mazer of wine into my hand. My grip was weak, trembling; I saw my own drawn visage reflected in the red depths.

"Drink up," ordered Father, guiding me to a bench near the fire, for I was shaking as if I had gone swimming in an icy river—the aftershock of Overy's treachery and nearly making my first kill. I collapsed in a heap and flung the warming contents of the mazer down my gullet. At my feet, Desmond's wolfhound had calmed and was licking the blood from his lips. As I watched him, he raised his head and gave me a wide doggy grin.

Reaching out, I fondled one of his shaggy ears. "Good boy," I murmured. "I'll see you have some mutton for your supper."

William Overey was tried two days later in front of my sire. Overey snarled and spat, still convinced that he would be spared for fear of repercussions. "If you harm me, an emissary, you shall reap the whirlwind!" he bellowed. "It goes against all decency and protocol! King Henry will come down upon you like a hammer on the anvil."

The noblemen seated around Father listened to the tirade, sniggered and shook their heads.

"You do not seem to understand," said Father, calm but stern, his eyes like keen grey lances. "You tread upon the liberties and privileges of Ireland as was agreed in the Parliament of this land. Those writs and letters you brought are worthless here. You have, with your presence and your actions towards me, the Lord Lieutenant of Ireland, attempted to incite bloodshed and rebellion. He glanced at the men seated around him. "My Lords of Ireland, I am a scion of the Mortimers and hence the de Burghs—but I was not born on Irish soil. What do *you* say should be the penalty upon this Englishman, William Overey, messenger from the Earl of Ormond and Wiltshire."

"Death," growled O'Brien.

Death echoed the other nobles, one by one. *DEATH*.

Father rose; he wore a robe of black velvet trimmed with gold, falling to his ankles, and a black chaperon with a brooch filled with white crystals. His countenance was pale and strangely serene against all the blackness, his features angular and stark. He wore black gloves that came up past his wrists then flared out, and the ruby eye of the golden Falcon depended from his chain of office, glistened as if it were alive.

It was like gazing upon the Angel of Death himself, only without the scythe.

"William Overey, squire, servant of James Butler, Earl of Ormond and Wiltshire, you have been judged guilty of diverse crimes against my person and against Ireland and its people. The penalty for such an abomination is death. Many gathered here thought you should suffer the punishment of hanging, drawing, and quartering for your actions, but I will show mercy. At cock's crow tomorrow, you will be taken from the dungeon and beheaded in the town square. Your head shall be returned to your master in England. God have mercy on your soul!"

The deed was done in the hours of the morn between darkness and light. Shivering in my cloak, I stood in the marketplace of Trim. William Overey was half-swooning as he was brought from his prison to the block, but he did not cry for mercy and submitted to the axe.

The headsman was skilled and swift. The blade flashed in the first crimson rays of dawn and redness splattered the cobbles of the town square. Many people watched, up early, ready for their daily tasks; their faces, lit by that cold dawn sun, were scarlet as if they too bled.

I turned away as the severed head was raised by its gory hair, its lips seeming to still move.

I had no sympathy for this man who had tried to kill a Duke within his own castle but I wondered how Overey's execution would be taken by King Henry and Queen Margaret. Poorly, I imagined.

I had begun to think it would prove impossible for Father to ever return to England—unless he arrived with a different attitude that was *not* one of reconciliation. One that would bring his enemies to their knees and make him untouchable.

I shuddered, although I knew not whether it was from the chill of the morning or from the sudden realisation that a blood-spatter from William Overey's bodiless head reddened my cold white knuckles.

Cousin Dick sailed to Ireland, setting down anchor in the town of Waterford, the second most important town in Ireland and the one where Henry II, long ago, first set foot on Irish soil and claimed it for his own.... Father and I greeted him in the comfort of the nearby castle while Countess Alice flung herself upon her son, embracing him and weeping. "Oh, Dick, I am so glad to see you hale and well. I had to abandon Middleham to those rogues of the King; I pray your sire will forgive me. But there was so much mischief afoot, and so many wishing to unseat us... I dared not stay. The wolves were closing in—that's what it felt like, Dick. Wolves waiting to devour me."

"Do not weep, Mother," Dick gently disentangled himself from her embrace. "You are safe and unharmed, and that is all that matters. I am here to take you to Calais to join Father."

"How is he managing? How are my other two sons?"

He grinned. "Well. Father says the dryer climes help his aching joints. My brothers? They champ at the bit to return to England and make things right—as do we all."

Dick's gaze flicked to my father, who stood, arms folded, watching the reunion. His smile faded and then reappeared as he turned his attention back to Alice. "Go have the servants make your chests ready and I will see they are transported to my ship. We shall set sail for Calais soon. I am sure you have no wish to tarry here longer than necessary."

"How right you are, Dick." She grasped his hand and kissed it. "Bless you, my son, for your courage and fortitude. I will go and ready for departure."

Countess Alice bustled from the chamber, leaving Dick with Father and me. "We must talk," said Warwick. "It is time to speak of an invasion of England to reclaim our lands and titles."

Father was silent, toying with his rings.

"Richard, what is wrong?" Dick frowned.

"I have thought of late—maybe my destiny is here. In Ireland. The people warm to me, and I can do much for them, they who have long been ignored by Henry."

"Set yourself up as King of Ireland" Cousin Dick threw back his head and laughed. "Oh, surely you jest. Even if the Irish voted you their High King, they are well used to setting up new rulers then tearing them down. You cannot be serious."

"I am serious, Dick. Never more so."

"What of my Lady Aunt Cecily and the rest of your children? They are treated well enough at present, but would they remain so if you set yourself up as a rival king, advocating for Irish independence? What you suggest is absurd."

Father tensed with anger but his words were calm. "What would you have me do, Dick?"

"Join us! We supported you at Ludford Bridge, Richard, and now you waver, thinking to become some kind of petty king? I never imagined you would follow such a path."

As he was getting little response from my sire, Warwick strode over to me. "What do you think, Edmund? You have been silent throughout our conversation. You are not a child any longer—your opinion should count for something. Come, speak up."

My heart told me to be loyal, to cleave to my father's will, but another part of me, wilder and stronger, rebelled. I liked Ireland well enough and enjoyed playing an active role in its governance now that I was older, but it was still a place of exile, where we were sundered from our family like criminals. "Before any decision is made as to where the House of York should abide, I would see my Lady Mother and the rest of the family safe."

Warwick strode up, friendly, congenial...but, in his deep eyes, a question, an enticement. "Edward longs to see you again, Edmund. He speaks of you often. How sad it would be if he were left languishing in Calais, while you established yourself here."

"Edward could join us," I said.

Warwick shook his head. "You are Lord Chancellor here. The Irish appointments were made in lieu of the Norman lands you would have inherited had they not been lost. As it stands, Edward has nought, no lands, no title—nothing. The same holds true for your uncle of Salisbury and for me. My wife and daughters waste away in Calais, dwelling in unfit lodgings. Look, all of us are blood kin. Many loathe the Queen and feel the King is suited to the cloister rather than the crown. If we band together, Plantagenet and Neville, the shambolic reign of this mad old fool and his termagant wife can be ended."

"I swore to Henry that I would not seek his crown." Agitated, Father approached us. "I would not prove myself a usurper like Bolingbroke."

"There are other ways to give you what many consider your rightful place," said Warwick. "One must be creative. Listen, Uncle, as long as we have your backing, my father and brothers are willing to make the first move into England. But I must know if you will side with us. If we wait overlong and Henry gets wind of our actions, he will, beyond a doubt, send men to blockade all the coastal ports."

"What do you require?" asked Father. His face was etched with pain; he was conflicted and yet...I knew he thought of Mother, of his lands in England, of his rightful inheritance.

"Write again to the King, as a loving and concerned cousin, and remind him of the wrongs done us, and how we are, in truth, his loyal servants. Remind him how we were forced into poverty and exile by the will of his favourites...or rather, *Margaret's* favourites. Remind him that we are not alone with our grievances; even the commons groan under harsh taxation imposed by his grasping minions."

Listening to Warwick, Father looked uncertain, even peeved at first, but as Dick went on, silver-tongued, his own confidence and enthusiasm contagious, I could sense a change in him—a longing. He had tried to put the wrongs done him behind, to forge a new life, but the want, the *need* for justice burned brightly for good or ill. He *must* return, even in peril of his life.

One. More. Try.

"Yes...yes," he said, sounding surer of himself. "Have you heard of the French-style band of guards Henry has hired by the counsel of his favourites? A great expense, unneeded. Only Ireland and Calais still financially serve the crown—but what do they get in return? Threats and spies, agitators trying to stir certain factions against us."

Warwick nodded. "I swear by God's Name that the toads croaking around the King's throne would rather Calais was taken by the French than remained governed by me."

Father began to pace as he often did when troubled. "It is because of my royal blood. They did it to Humphrey, Duke of Gloucester, too, and he was cruelly murdered. You are included in their hatred because you are kin and stand at my side."

Cousin Dick reached out and grasped Father's hand, his grip firm, a binding clasp. "So, you *will* write this letter to Henry. Soon."

Father took a deep breath, hesitated, then gave a curt nod. "I will, nephew. You have my word."

"I knew you would not fail me and my sire of Salisbury," said Dick, obviously pleased. "And your heir Edward, who is eagerly waits to engage in his first battle, upholding the honour of York."

Warwick turned to me, rummaging in his belt purse. "I almost forgot, Edmund, I have a letter here from Ned." He handed me a crumpled parchment. "I fear it is a little worse for wear."

I took the letter carefully, almost as if it were a holy relic and opened it, my back to the others. *"My Beloved Brother. I wish you health and good fortune. Calais is an exciting town and having Cousin Warwick as my mentor here has been a great boon. How do you fare in Ireland? I pray you are well. Soon, Dick and Uncle Salisbury say, we will sail for England to reclaim what is ours. This fills me with great passion and great hope. We will not fail, and we will take back our lands. I pray you can join us soon, Edmund, back in England and back in our rightful position.*

Your loving brother, Edward March.

Send my affections to Father, I bid you.

Having finished reading it, I thrust the note into my tunic breast. "Cousin Dick," I said. "Can you take a short message to Edward?"

"Of course."

"Just tell him—yes, soon we will meet again, God willing."

In July it rained. It seemed as if the sky itself wept endless tears. The Boyne at Trim overflowed, and men and beasts trudged miserably through mounds of mud. The castle smelt dank, the tapestries hung stained and curling. Dampness leached between stones and little leaks sprang in the tower roofs.

The sky wept in England too; incessant, a stream of water that made rivers and streams flood.

It was at this time that Warwick, Salisbury, and Edward sailed from Calais to confront our enemies, accompanied by the papal legate, Bishop Coppini. Father's letter to the King had been utterly ignored, so my kinsmen took this as a declaration of war.

Cousin Dick's popularity drew men to his cause, and when his army reached London, the gates were flung open, though the Tower remained unbreeched, its walls impregnable. With great gusto, Uncle Salisbury laid siege to it, rolling up engines and wooden towers filled with men bearing grappling irons, while Dick and Edward rode upcountry to meet the royal forces massed in the Midlands.

The combatants met at Northampton, near an old headless cross dedicated to an ancient Queen, nearly in the orchards of a convent full of terrified nuns, and in the midst of an almost biblical deluge. The rain blew into Dick and Edward's faces, half-blinding them but the downpour caused the Lancastrian cannons to misfire, so the inclement weather aided the Yorkist cause in the end. The day was Warwick's when Lord Grey of Ruthin turned his coat, neatly stepping aside to allow the Neville soldiers to storm the royal camp. The King's pavilion, draped in his banner and adorned with painted scenes of the Virgin's life, was an obvious target. It was defended by Shrewsbury, Beaumont, Egremont—and by Uncle Buckingham, the chief commander of Henry's forces.

All four men died in the onslaught, falling in the mud and the blood and the rain outside the tent. A humble archer called Mountfort broke into Henry's pavilion and captured the King.

The news of the victory reached Father swiftly, brought by a fast courier sent by Cousin Warwick.

Father slumped into a chair when the news came, overwhelmed. "So...it is done. Alas for poor Humphrey Stafford. He could be a stubborn old bull, but he did not deserve to die face down on a muddy field. Well, everything has changed now, Edmund. Everything."

"We will definitely return to England?" My heart raced, sounding loud in my own ears.

"Yes, but first I must settle all my business in Ireland and ensure the country is left in able hands. This may take a few months, even if I work ceaselessly. However, it seems Warwick and Salisbury have everything in hand. And Edward." He gave a proud little chuckle. "I heard he acquitted himself well on the field of battle, Edmund. He came at his foes like a knight out of old legend, and all wondered about the identity of this tall warrior who drove his enemies before him like leaves before the storm."

A swell of pride toward Ned enveloped me, too—but unworthy though it was, the vaguest sense of resentment tainted it. I always foresaw my brother's potential greatness, but I wanted to share in it.

"Your mother is free," Father continued. "She officially left her sister's custody after the battle, although it appears Anne allowed her to travel unfettered months ago. She resides with your brothers and Margaret at Fastolf Place, which the Bishop of Winchester has let out to her."

"I am eager to see her…and of course the younger ones. Are we to sail to London?"

"No, I am afraid not, although it is in my heart too. I have decided to put ashore in Cheshire. Salisbury and Warwick have procured commissions for me, enabling me to punish lawbreakers on the journey south. I will visit Ludlow, Shrewsbury, Hereford, Leicester, among other towns, and gather men to my host as I go. You may think this a tedious procedure, but I assure you, it is necessary. The commons must see me and believe that I will work for their benefit."

I stared at my feet. He was correct, but had we not taken this tack before? What could make a change across England? Nothing… unless Henry abdicated the throne and Father…I pushed that dangerous thought away.

Instead, I thought of mighty Trim and busy Dublin, the Black Pool stretched behind the castle; Waterford with its mint, soaring tower and impressive walls; Drogheda, where Father had called Parliament in the castle on the hill called Millmount, where the Irish said a god of song and poetry lay buried in a vast stone chamber. Tadgh had told the tale to me and Ned one wintry eve, his face grown old and fey and strange, as if he were an unearthly being born in the dawn of the world. We had knelt beneath sheepskins as our tutor, oddly animated, shadows from the candles dancing on his face, his eyes glittering diamond-hard, spoke a long tract in the intelligible language of the Irish, fast and furious, like a tongue from the very Tower of Babel itself. Halting, he spoke the words again, this time in soft, dull English, for our benefit—

I am the Wind stroking the sea
I am the Ocean's glistering wave
I am the mighty Stag of seven proud tines
I am the Hawk of May upon the grave.
I am a tear-drop fallen from the sun
I am a wild boar burning with ire

I am the swift salmon of knowledge,
I am a God in whose head burns sacred Fire.

I am the Queen of every beehive
I am the bone-fire bright on every hill
I am the shield over every man's head
I am the sword that drinks the blood-kill...
I know the secrets of the dolmen on the slope.
I am the tomb of all vain hope.

All Vain Hope... those haunting and somehow prophetic words reverberated through my mind, mingled with memories of smoke and shadow.

And what had the vain hope been? That my father would settle in Ireland and we'd live in peace for the rest of our lives? A fool's dream, if one truly thought about it. Even if the Irish ceased to fight amongst themselves and rose united to support the House of York, still war would come hence with heavy tread urged on by vengeful Percy, Clifford, Beaufort...and Plantagenet kin from Lancaster's House.

Vain hope indeed.

September was a gentler month, the seas surprisingly calm as the ship on which Father and I travelled glided down the River Dee into the harbour of Chester. The city's red walls and towers stood out sharp against the cerulean sky, an imposing sight with the rectangular castle keep rising over all. Once, Father told me, the Romans had built a fortress at Chester which they named Deva, and its stonework underpinned the foundations of the extant walls.

As we alighted onto the quay, the locals came out in vast crowds to welcome us. I breathed easier, for on the journey my head had whirled with dire thoughts about a hostile reception. Father knelt on the cobbles near the quayside, his hands splayed out and his head bowed as if in prayer. His lips moved but did not form the words of any prayer I knew. It was as if he swore an oath—a silent, personal oath. I could only surmise what it might be. The townsfolk whispered amongst themselves and then began to chant, "*A York, A York.*"

My sire rose from the ground with benevolent countenance, and he gestured to one of his squires, who brought over a money purse. Father opened it and began distributing coins to those crammed on the quay.

The crowd roared in joy, surging forward. A greybeard with a fishing pole fell off the pier, to much laughter. "First bath you've had in years, grandad!" some wag shouted. A girl wriggled through the line of the soldiers protecting us and planted a damp kiss half on my mouth and half on my chin. She smelt of candied violets, and big white Michaelmas daisies were threaded through her hair. I wondered what Ned would have done in a similar situation. No, I *knew* what my brother would have done, but I was not him, even if not so innocent as once I had been.

After stopping for the night in Chester Castle, Father and I continued down country, halting at various towns where he would administer law and order. I remained alert to any attacks on the road, but if there was opposition to our coming, I saw few signs of it. At Ludlow, men rejoiced at our return and the bells of St Laurence's rang in thanksgiving. Even Coventry, known for supporting the King and Queen's faction, was friendly enough, opening the town gates and sending the mayor to invite us to dine in the guildhall.

As we were on the way from there to Hereford, Father received a dispatch that brought joy to both our hearts. Mother had departed London and planned to meet us on our journey. Meg, George, and Richard were still at Fastolf's, but Edward had promised to visit them daily.

In Hereford marketplace, Father and I watched for the arrival of Mother's entourage through the south gate. As she entered the town precincts, we were both stunned to see the opulence in which she had travelled. Mother passed into Hereford like a Queen on a progress, seated on an elaborate chair unholstered with royal blue velvet, which was drawn by four pairs of caparisoned white horses.

Father handed her down from the chair, clad in blue and white satin with embroidery of golden fetterlocks as symbols of his heritage. Mother, too, was dressed as a most highborn lady in red and silver brocade; grey and white vair lined her long sleeves, and a bejewelled bourrelet headdress drew gasps of envy from the goodwives and maidens milling in the street.

Trumpeters hailing our passage, the shouts of well-wishers all around, our party passed in splendour towards the cathedral and the Bishop's Palace, where we would lodge for the night. No welcome from Bishop Stanberry, however—a former confessor of King Henry and unpopular with the commons, Warwick had taken him prisoner at Northampton. He now graced a dungeon at Warwick Castle.

With Stanberry gone, it felt as if the palace was ours. The servants were a little nervous, but bowing and gracious. It was almost as if they welcomed their true King and Queen into the ancient timber-framed hall with its carved pillars, once painted but now dark and glossy from smoke and the touch of hundreds of hands.

On that day, in that town, I truly felt the weight of destiny. Something had changed. I guessed it from the glances my parents gave each other, and the conversations they had which no others were privy to.

"You are right, Cecily," I overheard Father say, taking Mother's slender hand in his. "It must be. Peace will never come otherwise."

Peace. What we all desired. So why did my heart miss a beat and a cold sensation chill me to the core?

Old greybeards and goodwives, filled with superstitious dread, would have surely told me a hare had leapt over my grave.

South we travelled, and town after town greeted us with joy. Trouble had been anticipated by Father's intelligence, but if any opposed us, they faded away like mist before the sun when they saw the grand receptions we were given and our ever-swelling band of fighting men. I had never eaten from so many rich tables—gentry, knights, abbots, town mayors—in such a short time, dining on pigeon pie, heron, roast venison, bream, eel, and every manner of culinary delight. Nor had I ever drunk so much wine, French, Spanish, and Burgundian, evening after splendid evening. Some mornings, when I took horse and rode next to Mother's fabulous blue velvet chariot, my head was swimming and my belly bloated and painful, but I kept my head high and a smile on my face as I waved to well-wishers.

By the time we reached the town of Abingdon with its vast abbey, our journey had indeed become a facsimile of a royal progress. Father flew banners bearing the Arms of England—a bold statement indeed—and on his livery the Falcon soared, claws dancing above the open Fetterlock, amidst cascades of White Roses, the emblems of his Mortimer ancestors.

Another feast took place at the sprawling Benedictine Abbey of St Mary's, where we were welcomed by the aged abbot, William Ashendon. Malmsey flowed, Mother feasted on lark's tongue and honey cakes; Father sat in state beneath the royal banner. Then it was a visit to the abbey church, with its holy relics—the bones of St Edmund the Martyr and a Nail taken from the True Cross. Abbot Ashendon kindly showed us Edmund's shirt as well, blood-stained and crusty but still mostly intact.

Then it was on to London, our final destination. Fears nagged at me about what might transpire there. How would the King react to Father's appearance and his use of the Royal Arms? Yes, Henry's army had been soundly defeated at Northampton but Warwick, Salisbury, and Edward had all knelt before him and affirmed that he was still their Sovereign and would meet no harm. Cousin Dick, bearing the Sword of State, had even guided him to the Bishop's Palace in London in regal procession. Henry was still there, not quite a prisoner, but not at liberty either. As for Queen Margaret, she had fled from Coventry to Wales, taking her son Edward with her. She would cause us grief if she could, of that I had little doubt.

The streets of London were as I remembered them from my brief earlier visit—grimy yet somehow vibrant and exciting at the same time. Smells of piss and dung and old blood mingled with cooking smells from bakeries and the stalls of street sellers dealing in pasties and fritters. Merchants heaved by, intent on business, and nuns and monks in grey, brown and black robes swirled by. A vielle whined, the sound plaintive; a bagpipe wheezed, its tone infuriating. A one-legged man slouched on a street corner, making a monkey dance for thrown pennies. Dozens of ragged urchins clustered around, staring and poking at the poor beast.

I pitied the unfortunate animal because I, too, began to feel I was the subject of similar scrutiny as we passed deeper into the press of tall houses and shops. Not all faces were friendly here; one old man in a grey hooded cloak hawked phlegm in front of our horses. "You have no right to parade in here like goddamn kings!" he yelled in a voice harsh with rage. "Henry is our King, you York bastards." Emboldened, another man grabbed a cudgel and stormed towards Mother's carriage. I reached for my sword, fully intent on using it for the first time.

But at that moment, a clarion sounded in a side street, and the Bear and Ragged Staff banner lurched into view. Men in Warwick's black and red livery marched purposefully towards us, and the pugnacious would-be assassin melted into the crowd.

"Well met!" Riding on a roan charger, Cousin Dick emerged from the mass of soldiers. He removed his helmet. "I am glad you have made it to London. Forgive me for not getting to you before that uncouth oaf had time to start his mischief...I pray you were not too frightened, Lady Aunt."

"I was not afraid at all, Dick," Mother retorted, leaning from the carriage window. She held a handkerchief across her nose—London had grown exceedingly muggy that September afternoon, making all its jumbled scents the more overwhelming. The river alone stank worse than a leper's armpit.

"I am glad to hear it," said Warwick, "and I was foolish to doubt your courage for even a moment. Now, I will escort you all to Fastolf's Place. My men and Uncle York's together should easily hold off any of Henry's supporters, should they try any antics."

"W-where is Edward?" I asked, trying to pick him from out amongst Warwick's men and failing. "I had hoped..."

"That he would be with me? No, Edward had a more important job today."

I lifted a quizzical eyebrow. What could be more important than greeting his Lord Father—and his devoted brother—returning from exile?

"He is at Fastolf's Place visiting your sister and younger brothers, as he does each day, and preparing them to meet you after so long apart."

I laughed, my heart lifting. I could hardly be angry with Edward for that.

Ned was in the garden of Fastolf's Place. The rich scents of the flowers permeated the air, overwhelming the less pleasant odours from outside the house's walls. Damask roses bloomed on arches, next to Rosa Alba, the White Rose. Marygolds nodded yellow heads—a good flower, useful for treating agues and even plague, while next to them flowered Purple Skullcap, Seal-Heal, and Sea Holly with its spiky stems that could cure poison arrow wounds or make a lover more potent in the bedchamber.

I heard the sounds of children shouting and I hurried on a paved path in that direction. As the path petered out, I paused to take in a happy, exuberant scene. George and Richard were running madly at a wooden quintain set up in the centre of the lawn, bashing at it with wooden swords. Even as I watched, the arm on the quintain swung, and Richard, small and slight, ducked underneath and ran triumphantly away. George, however, was not quite so lucky—the arm struck him on the back of the head and sent him lurching head-first into a flowerbed. He started to holler then suddenly went quiet.

"George! *George!*" Richard flung down his wooden sword and dived onto the ground beside George's inert form. He shook George's shoulder. No response.

Richard looked panicked. "Ned…Ned, where are you? George…he's hurt!"

I lunged forward, even as Edward burst out from behind dense shrubbery—along with a maid who was quickly adjusting her garments and tucking strands of hair into her linen cap.

He hadn't changed.

Eyes fixed on our fallen brother, he did not notice me. He flung himself onto the flowerbed where George sprawled, pushing Richard out of the way. "George, can you hear me? Tell me what hurts…"

A snigger erupted from George's mouth. His eyelids fluttered. "I *can't* get up. I'm dead, can't you tell?"

"George!" Richard punched him on the arm, as a grinning George hauled himself into a sitting position.

"Fooled you, Dickon!" he teased, plucking a flower and throwing the head at our youngest brother.

"I imagine you'll still have an almighty bruise," I said. "But you are definitely very much alive!"

"Edmund!" Richard and George squealed in unison, and then both were on their feet and leaping on me like over-excited pups.

Edward joined them moments later, clapping me on the shoulder before enfolding me in a rib-crushing embrace. He had grown even bigger in the short time we were separated, and an air of maturity clung to him that had not been there before. My brother was no longer the eighteen-year-old son of a Duke, green but eager; he had fought in his first battle, acquitted himself well, and become a man. Exile in Calais and the bloodshed of Northampton Field had changed him forever.

"How was your journey here?" he asked, releasing me.

"It was…marvellous," I said, remembering Hereford and the other towns where the House of York was feted and adored. "I admit I miss Ireland, though. I had become quite comfortable."

"No time for comfort!" Ned slapped me on the back. "There is much business to be done in the days to come. The opening of Parliament, where we can, God willing, reclaim our titles, lands and whatever else we lost."

"Yes, my first English Parliament," I murmured.

"It is mine too," Edward reminded me. "I pray I won't appear callow and foolish."

"Never that! Ned, the people love you. As we rode down from Cheshire, they called out, 'Where is Edward Plantagenet, hero of Northampton Field. Where is the golden giant?'"

"Did they truly say that?" he asked, clearly pleased.

"Would I lie to you, Ned?" I laughed. "Especially in front of our little brothers."

"George would lie," said Richard innocently, giving George a gentle nudge in the back.

"No, I wouldn't!" exclaimed George, his cheeks flushed.

"But you just did," said Richard, completely guileless. "You told everyone you were dead!"

"But…but I did not mean…" George was becoming agitated; short-tempered, he found only his own japes amusing.

"Enough, both of you," I said. "I'm weary from my travels. Come with me, and let's go inside the house. I believe Mother has ordered the cook to make almond cakes—the nicest kind, with the brittle sugar coating."

Hearing this, their minds were on their bellies, as young boys' often were, and their grievances forgotten. As we walked back through the garden, our shadows stretched long before us over the grass.

"The four sons of York," I said, pointing. "Made giants by the sun at our backs."

"Ned is nearly a giant anyway," said George. "One day, I deem, I will be the same." Pridefully, he puffed himself up; I dared not tell him he resembled a pigeon more than a prince, but I held my tongue. No use causing a scene, even if only jesting.

Overhead, a cloud tumbled over the sun, partly obliterating its light.

"Edmund, your shadow's gone," said Richard in a hushed voice, gesturing to the ground. Where my shape had been was only a formless mass of shade. My three brothers, walking several feet to the left, were still stroked by the waning October sunbeams; their shadows marched on, stretching, enduring.

"Nought to worry about," I said in a jolly manner, though my unexpected erasure sent a shudder through me, ridiculous though it seemed. "The sun will return again, once the wind has pushed the cloud away—and my shadow will be back! Let's find Meg, I have not yet greeted her—and then we can find those tasty *emeles*, fresh from the oven."

A human being is only breath and shadow. The words of Sophocles, that ancient author of tragedies, tumbled through my mind like the clouds in the sky.

Westminster Palace.

Its magnificence dazzled my eyes. The Hall, constructed in the reign of William Rufus, the scene of many coronation feasts, squatted like a giant at the heart of the other buildings, its walls resting on older Norman foundations. St Stephen's chapel, all pinnacles, glass, and golden stone, glowed like a rich gem. Flourishing gardens around the Queen's Apartments ran down to the river's edge in a riot of colour.

Father seemed nervous and agitated as we walked across the vast courtyard, its cobbles swept clean before the arrival of the nobility summoned to Parliament. Once again, he wore the Yorkist emblems, and one of his knights bore his banner, the Leopards and Lilies of the Royal Arms on full display, their hues vivid against the grey stonework of the surrounding buildings.

Flying the banner seemed provocative, here of all places, but I was inexperienced yet to question my sire's wisdom. I wondered what Edward's opinion might be but after our brief reunion at Fastolf's Place, he returned to Warwick's London home, L'Erber, where he was residing. I had not seen him this morning, though I had spotted a banner with the White Lion of March and the Bear and Ragged Staff, so I presumed my brother was already inside with Dick and Uncle Salisbury.

Parliament had convened several days before we reached London, so Father and I were newcomers and perhaps not expected by the less informed. As we strode toward the Painted Chamber, where Parliament convened, I noticed many servants and household staff were staring and whispering amongst themselves. Some appeared shocked, others openly hostile. This was not the reception we had received on our journey hence, though perhaps it should have been expected; many of those servants were still loyal to Henry, confined to the Bishop's Palace as a virtual prisoner, or to Margaret, who fared through the wilds of Wales with her son even as Parliament sat.

"Here we are, Edmund." Father nodded as the doors of the Painted Chamber opened before us, inviting us to enter. Or perhaps there was no invitation, but rather a passage into a dragon's maw. Nervously, I glanced at Father and noticed a bead of sweat on his brow, although the day was not warm.

The hall was magnificent, breathtaking. Paintings covered the walls—Virtues strove against Vices, Edward the Confessor was crowned, seraphs sailed above the heads of prophets, Antiochus ruled in splendour, Judas Maccabeus fought Timotheus. At the end of the room was a bed covered by a starry canopy; England's kings had slept there while Parliament was in session since the reign of Henry III—not at other times. Apparently, the royal bed was too draughty.

A throne stood in a niche, where the monarch would preside over Parliament.

It was, as expected, empty.

Near the throne, various lords milled about preparing for the upcoming session. I spotted Edward immediately, a head above most of the other men. Salisbury and Warwick stood near him wearing robes of velvet, their livery collars burning like fire in the light from a dozen candelabra. John Green, the Speaker, walked stiffly amongst them; he was a lawyer trained at Gray's Inn who had recently embraced Father's cause. I also saw a Bishop and various high-ranking clergy, and many unfamiliar lords and barons, some with haughty, pinched expressions—I presumed they were Henry's loyalists, wishing to be anywhere but here.

I glanced at Father, who had stopped in his tracks. He stood as if frozen, the prophets Isaiah, Jeremiah, and Jonah staring down at him from the painted ceiling, as if in holy judgement.

Frowning, I moved closer to him—and at that moment, noticed the sword girt at his side, mostly hidden by his cloak. I swallowed; it was unlawful to carry weapons into Parliament, although on several occasions this had not deterred combative members from using fists, shoes, cups, or hidden cudgels. But my sire would not break the rules knowingly. He must have merely forgotten, his mind full of other things...

I reached out, tapping him on the arm while trying to stay unobtrusive. "Lord Father...the sword. *The sword.*"

He started at my touch. "Edmund..." He pressed me into a corner away from other members of Parliament entering the Painted Chamber. His back was towards them, folds of his cloak hiding the blade; there was a kind of desperate madness in his eyes. He drew the sword, holding it low so none could see it—and then he thrust the hilt into my hand. The cold metal jabbed into my palm, the carving of a rose pressing into my flesh as if it were a brand.

"Take it," he whispered in my ear, urgent. "Take the sword and walk before me holding it upright."

"W-hat?" Flummoxed, I shook my head. "I cannot do that! That is how a king enters a room, with the Sword of State held upright before him."

"Do you think I do not know that? Edmund! Do not fail me now!"

Dread knotted my gut, but he was my sire, my lord to whom I owed all. I dared not refuse his request, but I was sick with fear, not knowing what he had planned.

Taking a shuddering breath, I adjusted the sword, holding it up before me. I fixed my gaze on the shiny blade so that the faces in the Painted Chamber were indistinct blobs. I feared to see the expressions—curiosity, hostility, mockery.

Slowly, I began to walk forward. Father's footsteps at my back seemed loud as thunder on the floor. I could hear his breathing, fast, harsh.

Silence descended upon the Painted Chamber, the buzz of men's voices falling away to nothingness. I approached the empty throne, not sure what was required once I reached it. My shirt below my doublet was damp with sweat as were my hands; I struggled to keep the blade in its proper position.

"Step aside, Edmund." Father drew up next to me, speaking in a murmur. "Lower the sword…slowly…and move aside."

Relieved, I did as I was told. The room and the candles lighting it swam blearily in my sight. I noticed Dick, Uncle Salisbury, and Edward standing in a line, their faces taut with puzzlement. So they knew no more than I …

Father walked over to the empty throne, staring down at it. The air in the chamber grew tense, heavy. I held my breath, unaware at first that I was doing it.

Father turned, facing the members of Parliament. Then he reached out and laid his hand upon the throne—a gesture of ownership.

Gasps of shock rippled through the Painted Chamber. Men recoiled, horrified. Salisbury turned puce while Edward's mouth opened as if he might speak, but no words emerged.

Father glanced around, appearing surprised. Had he imagined the lords of the realm would proclaim him King? Bolingbroke had claimed the crown in such a dramatic way, but that was long ago, and the world had changed.

The silence that now fell was broken by a feigned cough from the Archbishop of Canterbury, Thomas Bourchier. "Your Grace, would you, er, would you like to speak to the King?"

Father bridled. "I know of no other man within this kingdom who should have the right to have him attend upon him."

Another gasp went through the assembly, followed by enraged muttering. Father's visage had gone bone-white; he snatched his hand from the throne and backed away. He glanced once towards our kinsmen, standing silent and sombre amidst the crowd, while rage and embarrassment warred in his eyes.

They all ignored him. Even Ned.

The rest of that day's session was mercifully short. Father refused to speak, and the gathered nobles avoided his gaze. Edward could be seen in frantic discussion with Dick, whose arms were folded and his eyes glaring. Salisbury was almost apoplectic, smearing a kerchief over his face between gulps from a wine goblet brought by his page.

I sat alone with no one, not my humiliated sire, and not with Edward, who remained at Warwick's side. I was an earl—but felt more like a Fool. All I needed were bells attached to my cap and a pig's bladder with which to beat myself.

The shouting was deafening. I was in the grand solar of Warwick's house, L'Erber, along with Father, Ned, Salisbury, and Dick. Away from the Painted Chamber, out of the sight of the other nobles, the Nevilles let their frayed tempers spill forth like lava from a volcano.

"God's teeth, Richard!" roared Salisbury, hurling his chaperon across the room and frightening two hounds that lay dreaming before the fireplace. "What were you thinking? Have you gone mad? For years, we have repeatedly sworn that we were loyal to Henry, that you did not seek his throne! You've made us look like liars and frauds…like traitors!" The last word exploded from his mouth like shot from a bombard.

Father, silent ever since that mortifying moment he laid his hand upon the throne, erupted also. "I thought long and hard about my position!" he cried. "Perhaps I should have stayed in Ireland, but why should I lose all my lands and rights here?"

"They were going to be given back anyway, Father," Edward interjected, trying to inject some commonsense. "That was one of the main issues in this session of Parliament, the reversal of our attainders. I pray that matter is not now jeopardised…"

"Oh, do you? Christ, my own son turns on me!" Father strode towards Ned. Horrified, I thought he might strike him and dreaded the outcome of such rashness, but instead he whirled around and charged towards Cousin Dick. "In Ireland, you hinted that I should attempt to take the throne if you successfully invaded England. Northampton Field was won, Henry lost. So why do you reject me now?"

"It's the way you went about it, Father," said Ned, pushing in. "You never discussed it with any of us…except maybe Edmund." He gestured in my direction. "Brother, tell me true, did our father indicate to you at any time that he was preparing to claim the throne?"

My cheeks burned hot as fire. I felt all eyes upon me. "No." I stared at the floor, unable to look at either Ned or my sire. "When I rode through England with Father, I did, in my heart of hearts, question the wisdom of raising a banner with the Royal Arms…but it was not for me to question."

Father purpled; he clearly wanted to chastise or argue, but he kept his temper and instead glowered into the fireplace.

"And what about the sword…the sword you bore in as if it were the Sword of State." Warwick came up to me, standing closer than was comfortable. I felt like a felon on trial. "Did your sire tell you of that plan ere you entered Westminster?"

"He did not," I said miserably. I swivelled away from my cousin and flopped heavily on a bench, head in my hands. My temples were pounding. "I cannot tell a lie…I was shocked by what he asked of me, and even more shocked by what he did."

Father continued to stare into the fire's flames. They danced on the surfaces of his eyes, red and angry. His hands gnarled into fists at his side. "So, my younger son makes of me an enemy, too…"

"You know it is not so." I lifted my throbbing head.

"What are we to do now?" asked Edward. I noticed he did not look at our father but at Warwick and Salisbury.

"There is still hope," said Dick. "My younger brother, George, the Bishop of Exeter, is also Lord Chancellor. He was educated at Oxford and is clever in his dealings with friends and foes alike. I will see if he can produce a document showing York's entitlement to the throne that will win waverers to our cause. And if they do not agree, other ways may get us what we desire—and what the Kingdom needs."

"You mean you would see me perform a king's duties while only acting as Lord Protector, just like before?" Father folded his arms in a defensive motion. I have grown weary of that role. No matter how I tried to do good, I met resistance at every turn."

"No, that is *not* what I meant, Uncle. Not at all. I will take counsel with my brother on the morrow. He will come up with an idea, of that I am certain."

George Neville was a man of high intellect, as Dick had told us. Hastily but thoroughly, he conceived a document setting out Father's claim to the throne, emphasizing his descent from Lionel, second son of our esteemed ancestor, Edward III. As Henry only descended from the third son, John of Gaunt, his claim was inferior, made doubly so by the usurpation of the present King's grandsire, Henry IV. As there was no Salic law in England forbidding inheritance through the female line, Father's claim was not only valid but preferable under law.

"I will deliver it to the Lords at once," Cousin George told Father, the document rolled up and held tightly in his fist. "They must deliberate on it before any decision is made, as you are surely aware."

"Do you believe my chances are high?" asked Father.

"I have done what I can. I believe your chances are strong, but that is in God's hands."

"Ah, brother George..." Seated at a table playing chess with John Neville, Warwick raised his head and looked at the Bishop. "Pray give us less churchly talk. This matter will be decided by MEN, not the Almighty, and it will depend on who benefits, or does not from a weak king's reign, and who is, or is not, brave enough to accept necessary change."

"Men guided by God then, I hope." Bishop George paused by the door. "We will see. I will keep you informed of what happens when this scroll is presented."

The majority of the Lords were like frightened sheep, not knowing which way to turn. Arguments broke out, some ending in fisticuffs. Eventually, it was decided several appointed nobles would go to Henry himself, show him the Bishop of Exeter's findings, and find out his thoughts on the matter.

It was a very strange idea.

Cousin George was most perplexed by what happened next. "The Lords thought Henry would become irate when faced with documentation that weakens his own claim. He did not. He lay slumped in his bed and meekly asked them for help in coming up with new proof of his right to the throne."

"Has he sickened again?" asked Father. "It sounds as if he is weary and failing once more. A few months ago, when he attainted us all, we saw a different Henry, one angry and vengeful."

"I do not believe so," replied the Bishop. "He seems merely *downcast*. The nobles are stunned that he has not risen to fight for his throne, instead of leaving others to search for a means to keep him as King."

"Maybe, deep in his heart, he never truly desired to rule," I said.

"I agree," said Dick. "The man always had the demeanour of a monk. No interest in ruling, no interest in his wife…One can scarce believe he is the son of the victor of Agincourt."

"His mother's family was tainted by madness," said Father. "Do you not know the story? Charles VII went mad in the forest of Le Mans while leading an army against Brittany, charging at his own knights, including his brother. He recovered but nearly burnt to death at the 'Ball of the Wild men,' where he had donned a mask and costume and was dancing with nobles similarly clad…until the dancers' costumes came into contact with a torch held by his sotted brother, the Duke of Orleans. Four of the performers died and it was only the Duchess of

Berry's quickness of mind that saved Charles' life—she hurled her skirt over him and smothered the flames. After that, he fell into madness again and a regency proclaimed."

"Ah, yes, the famous Ball," said Edward. "An awful 'accident'. Doubtless Orleans felt much the same about Charles as we do about Henry. A king who could not rule, a king who brought misfortune to his country."

Father cast Ned a stern glance. "No harm will come to King Henry," he said, "no matter what arguments for and against my assumption of the throne are given over the next few days."

"Of course, Lord Father," said Edward, "but remember, Henry will always have supporters who could rise against you at any time. Beaufort may be dead; his children are not. Clifford hates you…"

"I will cross that bridge if and when the time comes," said Father. "The fight may go out of those young hotheads when they realise their actions might be tantamount to treason."

"I pray you are right, Father," I murmured, too quietly for him to hear above the snaps and crackles from the fireplace. "For if I were in their shoes, and you were slain, I would seek vengeance as long as there was breath in my body."

The controversy dragged on, the Lords thrusting the matter onto the shoulders of the Justices, and in turn, to the sergeants-at-law and the King's own attorney. All slunk away from deciding who was the rightful king, while muttering, "Such a thing as this has never taken place in England" and, "Alas, we are not learned enough to give an answer on such a weighty proposition."

Cousin George decided to attempt a different tactic with the Lords…"Go hence and think about Duke Richard's claim," he insisted. "Devise some questions he might answer, which may lead you to say Yea or Nay to his claim."

The Lords warmed to this idea, so Father was summoned before them for questioning. Nervously I took my place on a bench to watch; next to me, Edward looked tense as a taut bowstring.

One of the assembled dignitaries rose, clearing his throat. "If none object, I will begin the questioning of his Grace, the Duke of

York. Parliament cannot proceed with regular business until all here is considered and decided."

"Aye, aye," muttered the gathered Lords, stiff, dour figures in their parliamentary robes.

"The first question is this, your Grace: What about the oaths of loyalty sworn to King Henry in Coventry? It makes many men uneasy to forgo such oaths."

Father gazed steadily at the questioner. "God's law makes me King. The duty to God rises above the allegiances of men."

"What about the Acts of Parliament that confirmed the kingship of the King and his ancestors?"

Father seemed almost gleeful. Ned tensed and cast me a small, surreptitious grin. I understood then that our sire had an excellent retort planned for this very question.

"What 'acts', sir?" he replied to the questioner. "There was but *one*, passed long ago in the year of Our Lord 1406, and the very fact that such an Act had to be passed implies that there was a question about the legitimacy of the claims made by the House of Lancaster. If Henry of Bolingbroke was England's true ruler, why did Parliament have to approve his claim at all? Answer me this, all of you within this chamber!"

Much muttering and murmuring filled the air as the Lords discussed Father's answer in low tones. I strained to hear what they said, but the buzz of their voices resembled that of a beehive, and no clear words were audible.

Another of the Lords stood up to take the stand, a tall, and burly man, exuding arrogance. "If you seek to claim the throne through ancestry, Lord Duke, why is it known you favoured the arms of Edmund of Langley, rather than those of Lionel of Antwerp?"

The mutterings of the assembly rose in volume; dozens of heads nodded furiously. "He will have trouble explaining that away," I heard someone whisper.

Father lifted his chin and spoke calmly and clearly. "I could have worn the Arms and livery of my ancestor Lionel had I chosen to do so. However, I did not seek to assert my right because of the circumstances. You all know what those reasons were. I desired peace, but there came a time I could no longer abide the injustices done, not only to me and mine, but to the kingdom of England and the good people within this realm. A claim may lie in abeyance for a time, still it does not decay, and it never perishes."

More murmuring ensued, but I thought I detected a lighter note. A few old men stroked their beards, deliberating; some of the younger ones nodded. Only a few, the usual suspects, sat glaring with stony faces and folded arms.

George Neville stood up, the amethyst set in his pectoral cross flashing purple fire. "The Duke of York had presented his case. Now we must deliberate upon what is to be done with the knowledge of his claim."

Father exited the chamber, Ned and I following him. In a side room, we sat and waited. Father, so calm before the Lords, was now prowling around like a caged beast in a state of agitation. "Did I say enough?" he asked. "Did I acquit myself well?"

"There was nought more you could have said, Lord Father," I assured him.

"But will the Lords accept my words? Henry has reigned since he was a babe in arms, and some have fared well enough under his rule. Others pity him and feel tender-hearted toward such a saintly, unworldly soul while still others hold out hope for his son, Edward of Lancaster, whether the boy is Henry's get or no."

"All men of good heart shall surely heed your words," I said heartily, affecting a show of confidence. Confidence I did not entirely feel. Men liked their comforts, familiarity...and there were still Edmund Beaufort's sons living and Jasper Tudor, the King's half-brother to worry about. Their factions were large—and hostile.

Edward was staring at his knuckles. "If this attempt to make the Lords see reason fails...I would counsel you move to seize the crown."

White with rage, Father rounded on him. "The other day I set my hand upon the throne, and you chastised me as if I were a callow youth with no sense!"

"It was not the correct way to go about it," said Edward, keeping his temper in check. "May I speak plainly?"

"Go on." Father folded his arms.

"When you laid claim to the throne in the Painted Chamber, you told none of your supporters of your plan in advance. What if one of the King's loyalists had struck you down in your moment of folly? It felt to many as if you had ignored and endangered those who helped you most, such as Salisbury and Warwick—the very heart of the Yorkist faction would have been torn out had soldiers been summoned to make arrests. Luckily, restraint was shown by all…including those who oppose you."

Father's expression was furious, but then he began to laugh, low bursts of tired laughter. He flopped onto a chair and rubbed the heel of his hand against his eyes. I suspected he had not slept much, if at all, the previous night.

"Jesu," he said, "all my life I have tried to act cautiously, taking action only when others directly acted against me. The one time I act in haste, and all I plan goes to ruin, and I jeopardise the safety of my family and kinsmen."

Footsteps sounded in the corridor beyond the room where we waited. All three of us froze, then sprang to our feet. George Neville burst into the chamber, his purple cassock flying. "They have decided…"

"You do not smile. Have my efforts failed?" asked my sire. "Out with it quickly, Bishop."

"We have had partial success," replied George.

"Partial. How so?"

"The Lords were not happy at the idea of thrusting Henry from the throne he has occupied for so long. However, they decided you indeed had the superior claim. So their idea on how to deal with this matter is as follows—Henry will continue as King unto death, but then you, Richard, will ascend the throne instead of Edward of Lancaster, and the heirs of your body shall inherit the royal dignity after your death."

Father was silent awhile, digesting the Bishop's news. The world felt as if it had tilted under my feet and I had to sit down. Ned alone seemed unaffected—my dearest brother who, under this new Act, would one day wear a crown.

"Has Henry been told?" asked Father.

"He has indeed."

"And how has he taken this disinheritance of his heir?"

"Well enough," said George. "His reaction surprised us all. He agreed to the proposal."

Father blinked, stunned by this news. "Just like that!"

"Aye, Richard, just like that.!"

"I can scarcely believe it. After so long and so many trials…"

Edward moved to our sire's side. "It is a great victory for the House of York, but we must still remember to take care and be not overbold or incautious."

"What troubles you, Edward?" asked George Neville.

"The Queen," Ned said. "Her pup has been disinherited. The She-Wolf, I fear, will show her teeth before long."

CHAPTER SEVENTEEN

"Your Grace…Queen Margaret has given Berwick-on-Tweed to the Scots!" A messenger, wayworn and weary, knelt before Father, bearing grim tidings from the far north of England.

"Damn her!" My sire's lips drew into a bloodless white line. "Such overweening arrogance, to give away that which she is not entitled to give, with the people of Berwick treated as less than cattle, traded to a foreign power."

"That is not all, sire." The messenger clambered to his feet as Father motioned him to rise.

"What else?"

"She plans an alliance of blood with the Dowager Queen of Scotland, Mary of Guelders. Her son shall marry one of the Dowager's daughters."

"So the Scots are involved. I should not be surprised if that viper Margaret makes a permanent nest there," Father sighed. "But, Jesu, Berwick and its people…" Rage gripped him, and he smote the edge of his chair with his fist. "What she's done is unlawful and cannot be tolerated!"

The messenger cleared his throat. "The Queen's forces are slowly moving south, my Lord Duke. She has granted them full leave to burn and ravage any village or town they see. She has swelled her own numbers with Scottish soldiers eager to get their hands on English wealth."

"French bitch," spat Father. "She seeks to give the throne to her whelp, but despises England and would wreak harm upon the innocent. Well, there is no doubt in my mind what must happen next…"

He paused and glanced from me to Edward. "Father," I said shakily, "what do you intend? If it is exile again…this time, I am loath to go."

"Exile?" His brows shot up. "Did I say a single word about exile? I must take a force into the north to curb Margaret's rebels. And far from sending you away, I plan to take you with me." He turned to Edward, placing his hands on my brother's broad shoulders, "Ned, I have a different mission for you. I want you to ride to Ludlow and start gathering men in the Marches. Bring them to me at Sandal Castle when you are done. Later, you can forge into Wales to deal with Jasper Tudor—and you might even find Exeter haunting the place. He needs to be dealt with, one way or another. You'll be on your own, this time, in this endeavour. I plan on leaving Warwick here to protect London."

"It is my honour to serve you in such a manner." Edward inclined his head. "I am grateful for your trust in me."

"You will be King one day," said Father. "Do your noble ancestors proud." He dismissed the messenger and threw himself down at his desk, toying with a quill while a scribe was found. "I have much work to do in preparation for leaving—summonses and the like. I bid you hurry, my sons, and make ready for departure."

In silence, Edward and I rode from Westminster to the gates of Fastolf's Place and were admitted by the Porter. We had said little as we navigated our way through London's streets, but now, behind safe walls, the reality of this new enterprise struck deep.

"I had hoped it would not come so soon—another rebellion, another leave-taking."

"That was also my hope," Ned sighed, "but the Queen is a fierce and determined woman. I wish I were going north with you, Edmund."

"I wish the same," I said. "So much has happened since Ludford Bridge and our flights to safety—me to Ireland, you to Calais with Cousin Dick. We have hardly had time to talk of it all."

"I am sure you do not want to hear my tales of exploits with the fair ladies of Calais!" jested Ned.

"I may have some tales of my own about fair ladies in Ireland!" I shot back.

"Oh?" His brows rose with interest, his eyes twinkling mischievously. "Do tell!"

"No," I laughed. "I, unlike you, brother, am too much of a gentleman!"

"If we had more time together, I'd get it out of you," he teased. "I'd take you across the river to the stews."

I pulled a face. Harlots held no interest for me; I'd seen them touting their wares both here and in Ireland. Mostly raddled, often diseased, their shaved heads covered by lurid red wigs and the distinctive striped hood of the strumpet.

"No need to make a face, brother! I was not referring to some old toothless wretch on a street corner, but pretty and talented young wenches, who are looked after well by their bawds…"

"Hush now, Edward!" I was eager to change the conversation. "Our younger brothers are coming towards us. We must be good examples of morality and decency as our parents would wish!"

"As *you* wish, Sir Galahad," mocked Ned.

"Ned, Edmund!" Richard's voice drifted across the frosty garden. "Have you come to play with us?"

He came running up, frost crackling beneath his shoes, his cheeks flushed and his breath fogging before his lips. George followed on his heels, equally flush and dishevelled. "Richard and I have been wrestling…I won."

"Yes, I can see that, George," I said. "Your cloak is covered in mud and so's your hose. If Mother sees you, she will be furious."

George sniffed. "Richard is just as bad…he has a *tear* in his hose. And he lost the fight."

"But I won playing Hoodman's Blind!" countered my youngest brother. "You looked so funny wandering about like a mooncalf trying to find me. Up and down you wandered, and missed me in my hiding spot every time."

"Good for you…both of you," I said, "but alas, we are not here for horseplay. George, Dickon, Father has received news of trouble in the north."

"Is it the wicked queen?" asked Richard in a hushed voice, his eyes wide.

"Yes. Englishmen spurred on by her malice…joined by many Scots."

"Scots!" cried George. "They are sotted sheep-biter!"

Ignoring George's outburst, for which I am certain Mother would have him chastised, I continued, "We are going to have to leave. Fight if necessary. I am going north with Father, to Sandal Castle. Ned is going to the Marches to raise troops there. We have come to say farewell to you and to Meg and Mother."

Both boys stared, their air of boisterous jollity vanished. "You—you will miss Christmas," said Richard.

"I am afraid so," I said. "I swear that I will come visit you as soon as the troubles are ended."

"When…"

"I cannot say." I pushed a stray lock of his wavy hair from his eyes. "Later."

Leaning over, I gathered each of my young brothers close for a last embrace, as did Edward, his expression growing sombre. The winds buffeted us, cold, freezing, blowing down from the distant north.

The cold, rebel-haunted north where I was fated to go.

CHAPTER EIGHTEEN

Black and white and grey—the colours of the winter of the world. Father's retinue followed the line of the Great North Road, a column of steel, the banners of the House of York the only brightness in a frozen landscape. Snow flurried now and then, blowing into our faces on a capricious wind; in the fields, the trees were bleak skeletons, boughs stretched toward a louring sky and cackling rooks perched in the crooks. Every few miles villages appeared, smoke curling from huts, spires of churches spearing the cloudbanks, but the march went on without respite. We could not risk getting snowed in, and at least the Great Road, once trodden by the Roman legions, was still passable. Occasionally a traveller lurched out of the whirl of snow, red-faced, eyelashes laden with flakes, beard as white as that of Old Man Winter, but there were no greetings made. Father's army tramped grimly onwards, knights, halberdiers, archers—and the strangers on the road scurried past, afraid.

Father called for a halt in Stamford, a welcome relief but of short duration. Before sun-up, the army resumed its march, the heavy wains full of weapons and supplies bouncing down the rutted road. Father fretted over the baggage train as it skidded and lurched on ice hidden under a glaze of snow. "If we lose any supplies, there could be dire problems. Victuals and weapons are both in short supply. As ever, my coffers could not extend to paying soldier's wages and feeding them too."

The supply train survived but, alas, the artillery train, under the command of a Kentishman called Lovelace, was not so fortunate. Under its weight, the wagons sank into the mud, one overturning.

"The cannons are too dangerous and will slow us down to bring it." Father gave a heavy sigh as he observed the wreckage. "Master Lovelace, I bid you return to London. I will proceed to Sandal without the bombards. I know not if they would have availed us much anyway."

A few miles outside of Worksop, a town lying on the northern fringe of fabled Sherwood Forest, the army halted again—and it was there we first skirmished with our Lancastrian enemies. Father's fore-riders, scouting ahead to determine if the way was safe, unexpectedly encountered a group of soldiers from Henry Beaufort, Duke of Somerset's contingent. Our men were taken unawares and several killed, but it was, in the scheme of things, a fairly minor encounter, with Beaufort's men hastily departing from the scene of the fray and travelling on into the north as night drew in.

Father and I arrived in Worksop after darkness had fallen. The townsfolk had gone into hiding; from houses around the marketplace, women and children sobbed in fear behind barricaded doors. On the cobblestones lay our dead, twisted and hewn, their blood turned thick and black beneath their splayed bodies. Snowflakes fluttered down to land on the surfaces of lifeless eyes, to freeze on parted, bloodied lips made dumb forever by death.

"These were good men." Father's voice was thick with emotion. "Let us take them to the priory where I will speak with the prior about their burial."

With care, the stiffening bodies were lifted and carried in solemn procession to Worksop priory with its large facing towers and ruddy stonework. Father went inside to meet the prior, returning a short while later. Monks emerged carrying biers, on which they placed the slain before taking the bodies to be washed, shrouded, and buried in a pit.

"We should join the prior in prayer for the souls of those who supported us and lost their lives doing so," said Father. "My heart is heavy tonight, and I fear this is only one encounter of many."

After the requiem for the dead was over, Father donated coin to the priory and he and I sought our lodgings. It was a short, uneasy respite from the rigours of the road; soon we pressed onwards again, as the weather became even more inclement, hurling its strength against us like a battering ram. Fields near the rivers we passed were flooded, drifts began to line the sides of the road, and fresh snow clung to the horses' fetlocks. Wind pummelled our faces and whined in the boughs of Sherwood Forest's oaks, now coated with jagged icicles as sharp as daggers.

I dozed as I rode, the tall saddle holding my weary frame in place. My nose ran, its wetness freezing upon my lip. Father plodded on, grimly, his eyes ringed by darkness yet full of determination. Scouts came and went, leaping out of the snowy murk, hair stiff and white, clothes stiff and glittering, like Jack Frost taken on a living form. They brought dispatches and intelligence about the movements of our enemies.

"Queen Margaret is at Pontefract," Father informed me when the last messenger had departed once more into the swirling white snow. "She has a large force with her."

"Larger than ours?" I asked through cracked lips.

"Yes. Much larger." His voice was flat. "But Edward will come, and all will be well. The walls of Sandal are stout and its hill high."

A winter siege. The thought of such an assault made me shiver more than the frigid weather. Trapped inside, eking out provisions, running low on wood for the fires, fearing poisoned wells or having no water at all…

Please come soon, Ned….

At last, the snow began to subside, leaving the land sprawled beneath a frozen white blanket. Wan and weary, the sun peeked through scurrying clouds before disappearing again. On the western horizon, an ominous band of cloud boiled like the contents of a witch's cauldron—another snowstorm was brewing.

But the northern sky held a hint of hazy blue—and peering forward, eyes shaded from the snow-glare by my gloved hand, I spied a castle on a hill, black against the brighter backdrop of the heavens. Threatening barbican, towers capped by red-peaked roofs, a motte dusted white with a shell-keep proud on the summit. A river ran near it, glimmering dully as it wended its way toward Wakefield.

I spurred my mount on to draw level with Father. "Is that Sandal I see before me?"

He nodded. "Aye, praise be to God."

The sun started trying to break out again as we galloped towards the fortress, and for the first time in days my spirits rose as I dashed through the drifts with the wind in my hair and the faint warmth falling on my back.

For the moment, we had outrun the storm.

Sandal Castle was damp and perhaps not as well-tended as it should have been. Nonetheless, I had warm chambers with a fire, and servants hauled in a huge wooden bathtub and filled it with buckets of boiling water. A discreet screen of linen was mounted over the top, and I climbed in, calling for a squire to scrub my aching back with a brush. Food was brought and placed on a rail set across the bathtub. In accordance with the rules of Advent, it was simple, meatless fare, pottage and salted fish with a mazer of watered-down ale. Nonetheless, it settled well in my belly as I luxuriated in the water, my toes and fingers burning as they thawed out after my long ride.

Once my ablutions were done, I had thought to retire early, but a summons came from Father to attend a meeting with his councillors. Changing into fresh garments with the aid of a squire, I hurried through the dim corridors to Father's apartments.

I found myself in the presence of Uncle Salisbury; Thomas Neville; William, Lord Harrington; William Bonville; Sir John Parr; John and Thomas Harrington; distant relatives Hugh and John Mortimer, and others whose names were not so familiar. "It is best you join us, Edmund." Father gestured to a bench. "I have received a letter from the Queen."

"Would I be foolish to hope it might detail her surrender?" said Uncle Salisbury with cynicism.

"There is a greater chance of pigs sprouting wings," said Father. "Margaret will never give up. She tries to provoke me into action, I fear. Listen to what she wrote." He unfolded a rumpled parchment. *"To the would-be usurper of my son's right, I give you not greetings but only my scorn. At Pontefract I sit with an army thrice that of yours, and I shall hold my Christmas court as ever. My supplies are many; I have knowledge that yours are not. If you disband your army and surrender yourself and the treacherous Nevilles that support you, I will willingly offer pardons to your other followers. My kindly offer lasts unto the Day of Our Lord's Birth and no longer."*

"The woman is mad," sputtered Salisbury. "God's Teeth, why would any decent Englishman follow this French harlot, who is doubtless trying to pass off a cuckoo in the nest as a rightful heir?"

Father flung Margaret's message into the fire; it went up in a blaze. "What worries me most is that she is aware we are poorly supplied. She knows she need only wait. I have no doubt she has cut off any other possible supply routes."

"It is bluster, no more," said Bonville. "Margaret may have no more supplies than we do, in truth. She is French; both lies and insults come easily to her lips."

Father cleared his throat. "We must ration what we have, both food and fuel, I fear, against unforeseen possibilities. It goes ill not to celebrate the birth of Christ in proper fashion, but there will be no lavish feasting here on Christmas Day and the days of Christmas thereafter. God will understand, and our sacrifices will not, I pray, go unnoticed by our heavenly Father."

Men muttered, expressions bleak but full of resignation. This was war. They knew what was expected of them.

Downhearted, I sought my little chamber once the council had been adjourned. I glanced out the window; pitch-black, the only lights those in the castle windows and the fires of the watch. Snowflakes swirled down again, hissing as they struck the horn pane.

Watching, I recalled that today was December 21st, the old heathen Solstice, the year's shortest day, followed by the longest night. After tonight, the days would gradually lengthen and the shadows of winter and death recede.

Spring would begin a slow march toward the end of Winter, bringing fresh renewal of our wicked world. As I dragged the heavy shutters closed, I thought of the Antiphon, sung in churches on this day before the reading of a canticle or psalm--

O Oriens,
O Morning Star
Splendour of light Eternal
and Sun of Righteousness.
Come and enlighten those who dwell in Darkness
and the Shadow of Death....

Despite the rationing of foodstuffs, the castle servants tried their best to add a festive feel to Sandal Castle by decorating the Hall with holly, ivy, and mistletoe plucked from the highest branches of oak trees. The green, woodland smell of this foliage brought a freshness into the smoky hall and obscured the unpleasant scent of sweat, dogs, and soggy unchanged rushes.

One of the castle laundresses, a woman called Bel, had crafted a rondel of greenery threaded with blood-red haws and winter berries. She stood on a stool, hanging it above the main hall fireplace with scarlet and green ribbons. I complimented her on her work, and she blushed. "I make 'em every Christmas, my Lord Earl. Brightens the dull days."

"It does that," I agreed. "Maybe you should make a few more."

Her smile faded. "Well, I would, my lord, but I do not feel comfortable going into the woods these days."

"And why is that?" I asked. "Wolves?"

"I wish it *were* wolves, my Lord—they are often more scared of you than you of them! No, I saw another kind of wolf prowling about."

"What do you mean?" My heart skipped a beat.

She looked uneasy, licking her lips. "I was out there, using shears to cut the holly when I heard rustling. Glancing over my shoulder, I saw a man's shape passing through the trees. He did not look back and I did not follow him. He felt *wrong*, if you know what I mean, sir. I didn't recognise him as one of the locals; his cloak was good quality wool of a pale greyish hue as if meant to blend with a wintery wood."

"But he could have just been a passer-by…"

She shrugged. "Maybe, my Lord—but I doubt a random traveller would trudge around a snowy wood instead of taking the road to Wakefield over the bridge."

"Have you informed my father of this stranger?" I asked.

She shook her head. "I wouldn't dare speak to so mighty a lord as Duke Richard… I'm not in trouble, am I? You don't think it's one of the Queen's…?"

"You're in no trouble, but I must tell the Duke what you witnessed. He may want to speak to you, he may not, but we cannot take any chances with our enemies so near at hand. Do you understand, Bel?"

She paled but nodded. "Of course, the Duke will want to investigate. For everyone's safety…"

I hurried to Father's closet and found him there with maps and books on war tactics spread on his desk and a sweet tallowy candle burning low. He pushed them to one side as I entered. "Edmund, what do you here?"

"A laundress spotted a man in the woods. A stranger, who gave no greeting but hurried away."

"Hardly that unusual," said Father, perhaps a little peeved at my interruption of his studies.

"She said he felt *wrong*. And that he wore raiment clearly intended to blend in with the greenery."

Father chewed his lip at hearing that, thoughtful. "Hmm, *that* is more worrying. I suppose this sighting is worth investigating. I will send a party out to the wood while it's still light."

A band of chosen men set out from the castle, walking knee deep in the snow. I watched from atop the keep as they entered the dark line of the woodland—then watched again as they trudged back towards the castle, churning the soggy slush beneath their boots as they entered the bailey.

"Nought there, your Grace," said the leader of the expedition when he reported back to Father. "No sign of anyone and no footprints or traces of horses. Saw some rabbits, though—if we get desperate for meat, we could trap them."

"Good to know," said Father, dismissing the men to return to their other duties in the guardhouse or armoury. He swivelled in his chair to face me. "Is your mind at ease now, Edmund? It was as I suspected—the overactive imagination of a serving woman."

"Yes, I am content now." Forcing a smile, I bowed and left the room. Alone, in the corridor, I leaned against the cold stone wall, breathing heavily. The scouting party had come up with nothing—why did I continue to feel such unease?

After my supper of yet more salt fish and shrivelled vegetables, I clambered into bed and dreamed.

Dreamed of a dark wood full of unspeakable things, where the roots of trees writhed like serpents and drank the blood of slain men who lay all around, faces green and gaping, rooks pecking their eyes, the trampled snow crimson beneath their bodies…

Christmas Day arrived. Mass in the little chapel at daybreak was heartfelt, presided over by Father John Aspel, who was also my part-time tutor at Sandal. Even in time of war, my sire wanted my education to continue unabated.

Later, there was a paltry meal in the Great Hall, nothing like the feast Father would have held in normal circumstances. The usual salt fish was on the platters, alongside a spicy *brewett* with chunks of beef, some frumenty, and a few small birds, woodcock or pigeon. I thought of Edward who, hopefully, was marching toward us from the Marches. He would have it worse, marching in the inclement weather. Mother, Meg and my younger brothers I hoped were indulging in the usual manner, enjoying many courses, spiced sauces and jelly and custard tarts. As I drank my watered-down wine (our stores of drink were ominously low) I began to dream of past banquets—peacocks with feathers on, gilded pies, the Christmas Boar's head, codlings, geese, pastry *entremets*…

My reverie was broken when a youth ambled into the centre of the hall, strummed on a lyre, and began to sing. No tumblers or mummers were at this sorry, snowbound supper, but it seemed one of Father's allies had a minstrel travelling with his retinue, and he had been prompted into performing for the troops on Christmas Day.

The singer was a tall, thin fellow, maybe two years older than myself with stringy shoulder-length hair so fair it was near enough white, and a long, sad, pallid visage, the eyes deep set and hooded. In fact, everything about the fellow seemed sad and cheerless, much like our situation, and the raiment he wore was plain and dark, making him look all the ghastlier.

It was almost like gazing upon a living ghost, but the voice that emerged from his thin, colourless lips was easy on the ear, and the lyrics he sang haunting, causing a hush to fall over the Great Hall.

As I lay in a winter's night,
In uneasy slumber ere the day,
I thought I saw a marvellous sight,
A body, upon a cold bier lay,
That had once been a comely knight,
Who little served Lord God to pay.

Lost he had this life's frail light;
The ghost was out and would away.
And when the ghost from him should go,
It turned again, and beside him stood,
Beheld the flesh where it once dwelt,
So sorrowfully with sombre mood,
And said, 'Alas, I wail in woe!
Your fickle flesh, false and cold,
Why do you lie, now stinking so,
Who was once so wild and bold?

When he was done a few minutes of silence fell, followed by a round of clapping.

"A grim enough song when shortly we will join in battle with the Queen's army," said Father, "but I believe the words mean more than they might seem. The song tells of the fight between soul and body, of which one is eternal and the other transitory. Is that not so, Father Aspel?"

The priest, sitting near to Father, nodded. "I know this rhyme well. It imparts that the soul is far more important than the earthly body and must be cared for in greater measures than the flesh. A further line in the poem reads—*I am neither first nor last that shall drink of that cup. All men shall die*...But the faithful, with a care for their immortal souls," he crossed himself, "shall live forever in Christ."

The sombre moment was broken when one of the knights swaggered out before the dais, clearly deep in his cups. "I'd wager we need some cheering up after that unhappy dirge!" he cried, and fell into a loud, offkey, drinking song known by all:

Bring us in no bacon, for that is passing fat,
Bring us in good ale, and give us enough of that;
And bring us in good ale, good ale, and bring us in good ale,
For our Blessed Lady's sake, bring us in good ale!

Bring us in no butter, for therein lie many hairs,
Nor bring us in a pig's flesh for that will make us bears;

*But bring us in good ale, good ale, and bring us in good ale,
For our Blessed Lady's sake, bring us in good ale!*

The mood in the chamber lightened and many men joined in the song, roaring with mirth at the line about bears, which reminded us of Cousin Warwick whose badge was the Bear and Ragged Staff.

Despite the paucity of the banqueting food, I found myself trudging to bed long after midnight, a little sotted. Head spinning, I yanked back one of heavy wooden shutters to take a breath of the chill night air before retiring.

...And saw, out in the woods, a bobbing green light. It flared three times, like a signal, before darkness fell again. Growing stone-cold sober, I strained my gaze into the darkness, trying to see if I could catch any movement beneath the trees. Nought moved, and the light did not return, although I waited long while coldness crept into my bones and made me shiver. I debated telling Father, but what could he do? A foray in the darkness would not be advisable. At any rate, the light might only have been no more than the lantern of a villager seeking kindling or even Fool's Fire leaping around a mossy, mushroom-laden tree trunk.

In the sky, the moon emerged, rising through a band of clouds wrapping its middle like a girdle. The snow beyond the castle was pristine, the trees of the grove more defined now, their branches bejewelled with ice and the stars.

There was nothing there. Nothing.

As the moon sank into the clouds again, I fastened the shutters and climbed into bed. A squire had left heated stones in a cloth bag beneath the coverlet to keep my feet warm; it felt nice.

I slept.

For two days little happened of note in the cramped and crowded castle. Father, Salisbury, and their captains drew up plans of various possibilities for offence and defence against Margaret's host. They argued, grew angry, cursed, and swore, before regaining their composure and devising other potential plans of action. The Queen, being so close at Pontefract, sent several letters in this time, delivered by strutting heralds in their unmissable, bright tabards. All the letters were full of ridiculous jibes and insults—'*Why have you not ridden to Pontefract, Duke Richard—are you afraid of a woman? Oh yes, you most certainly are—I know this for I knew your wife well.*' "*You speak of my son as a cuckoo, but have you looked at yours? Not one drop of your blood.*'

"The French slut is still trying to goad you into making a rash decision," grumbled Salisbury.

"A foolish tactic which won't work," said Father. "Words do not hurt. A sword…now that *would* hurt." He laughed and flung the Queen's messages to the floor, treading upon them to show his disgust.

All those gathered in the chamber laughed, and I laughed along with them.

Three days later, groups of our soldiers billeted in surrounding villages came tramping through the snow. They hammered on the castle gates, crying for admission.

The sentries allowed them into the bailey while their leaders were escorted to Father's quarters.

"The Queen's forces are here," said a grey-bearded old veteran, a bandage over the socket where an eye had been lost in some long-ago battle. "From what I can tell, they stretch in a rough circle around the castle, taking in many a nearby village and hamlet. Wakefield appears to be clear, however, with a path still free over the old stone bridge where stands St Mary's chapel."

"So you saw them, turned tail and fled here," huffed Uncle Salisbury, rather uncharitably, his arms folded and his glance like daggers.

"No helping it, my Lord Earl." The greybeard's jaw tightened. "We'd have been cut to ribbons if we took 'em on. We were vastly outnumbered. They let us go, at least…I think they were waiting for more reinforcements."

Father forced a smile. "I suspected this might happen. My thanks for your assessment, soldier. Rest; we will find beds for all of you in the bailey. Tents shall be erected if necessary."

The man nodded and limped away. Uncle Salisbury still glowered. "More mouths to feed, Richard. More hungry mouths."

A flash of anger lit Father's eyes. "Better than having deserters. We need every man who can hold a sword or bow."

"But if he cannot eat, will he be able to do his duty? He might decide he no longer wants to fight. A revolt might ensue. The situation is dire."

"As we knew it might be—but Ned is marching from Ludlow. If the roads remain clear of snow, he cannot be so many days away."

Uncle Salisbury harumphed and glanced up at the empty minstrel's gallery above the hall, clearly not wanting to continue the conversation for he would never agree.

Heart heavy, I went to arms practice in the bailey. Thrust, slash, parry...Slush and mud slid beneath my feet, and I fell, cursing. "You'd be dead, boy, if you were in the field!" screamed the Master of Arms, pressing a blade to my throat. "Get back up and do better!"

Dripping mud, I wrenched myself up and flung myself at the Master, my sword clattering against his, our bodies pressed together, striving to make the other lose his footing or show some other weakness. Over and over, we repeated the same moves—until at the end, I saw the Arms Master, not young, begin to tire, his face reddening and his breath ragged. One flash of an arm to mop his brow and I was on him, throwing him backwards with great force. He thudded to the ground, and now it was *my* blade at *his* throat. "I win this time," I said. "And you're food for crows, sir..."

I withdrew my weapon, and he sat up, rubbing the back of his head beneath his arming cap. "Just remember to assail your enemy like that when you engage in a real battle. Do you understand, my Lord?"

I returned to my chambers as the daylight dimmed. A scrap of fish was dinner again. The saltiness dried my mouth; watery ale did little to alleviate the dryness. My eyes burned from both the cold air outside and the candles within the castle. The best quality candles had all been used, and what was left were made of coarse fat, which hissed, spat, and smelt greasy and foul. I took a quill and began writing a letter to Edward. Father said that on the morrow he was sending a courier abroad to find Ned on the road and tell him to make all speed for Sandal Castle.

Well-beloved Brother, I recommend me heartily to you... I began formally. I paused, not knowing what next to write—pages of cheerful bravado, laughing about the weather, the unsatisfactory food, the smelly fat candles…or less pleasant news about the enemies outside our gates, still in hiding but undoubtedly behind every tree, every rise?

Desperation washed over me, and I scribbled on the page in a passion, ink splattering, "*Jesu, Ned, I pray you get here soon. The castle walls be strong, but hunger is stronger. The Queen's army lies close around; its next move unknown. My heart is heavy with it all, for I know good men will die no matter the outcome. The melancholy of winter is upon me, my dearest brother and friend, and oftimes I feel it shall never pass to spring, that I shall never feel the warmth of sun on my face again.*

May God go with you and lend speed to your horses on your journey hither from the Marches.

Your most-loving brother, Edmund (Rutland.)

I folded the letter and sealed it with trembling hand, the red wax dripping hot on my fingertips. There…ready. I would present it to Father on the morrow when he sent the messenger on his dangerous quest.

A hand shaking my shoulder woke me around cock's crow. A peaky squire loomed over me, his white face aged by sleeplessness and nerves. "My Lord Earl, his Grace requests your presence."

I slid from under the covers, the shock of the cold air and freezing floor taking my breath away, and summoned my own lads to help me dress. When I was presentable, I picked up the letter for Ned and thrust it inside my doublet as I hurried down the passageway to Father's solar.

He was grey and unshaven, appearing his full nine and forty years and maybe older. "Edmund," he said. "I have news."

"And it is not good…" I murmured.

"It is not good. I sent out a scout. Westward roads are blocked. I cannot contact Edward. Oh, he will come, of that I have no doubt—but when? Will it be too late? The men are starving; there was a fight earlier over a breadcrust. A man was stabbed. There are whispers of desertion…"

"That is stupid and short-sighted!" I cried. "If these faithless fools suddenly emerge from the castle gate, they could easily be cut down by Margaret's army, if they are indeed all around us."

He nodded. "Aye, but desperate men do desperate acts, Edmund. If their demands for sustenance are not met, rebellion will brew. There is a good chance they might switch allegiance, turn on *us* and kill us all, before opening the gates to the Queen's soldiers and begging for mercy."

"But—but you argued with Uncle Salisbury about allowing them in! So, he was right—he said they would turn on us when their bellies grew hungry."

"Yes, he was right," Father said heavily. "I was overconfident, I fear, believing that loyalty would win out. I should have listened to Salisbury, but even so, if we had not allowed those men in, they would be thirty leagues hence by now, likely swelling Margaret's host."

"Jesu," I said. "What are we to do?"

"I will have to send out a foraging party."

"But where?"

"The nearest village. Wakefield itself. It is rumoured there is still a way through to the town."

"But it would be watched, even so. I am sure of it."

"You are likely right. But we must try." He placed his hand on my shoulder, perhaps trying to bring comfort. I flinched away, wanting no false comfort. I wanted plans, a solution.

"And what if our foraging party is attacked? Do we just watch them cut down before our eyes?"

"No. If the worst happens, I shall sally out with my soldiers to meet the attackers. So, Edmund, my dearest son—I bid you be ready to ride."

He left me with my troubled thoughts, and I, snatching the letter to my brother from my doublet, hurled it with shaking hand onto the brazier. Flames leapt; the edges of the parchment curled, writhing like snakes before they disintegrated into ashes that blew through the grate in a draught.

Ash. My mouth tasted of it. Ash and ruin. *Ashes to ashes, dust to dust...*

Edward would never receive it. And aid was not coming.

Father and I stood on a parapet, watching a band of volunteer foragers march stoically across the field towards Wakefield. Slush splashed beneath their feet; the bitter cold had lifted and the snow was melting fast. In the distance, beyond the sullen, serpentine coils of the river, the chimneys of the town puffed blueish woodsmoke, a beacon for our men, bringing the promise of food and fuel.

To one side of the party stretched the wood, snow gone from the tree branches, leaving clawing skeletons that clashed like dry bones in the wind. My gaze left the column of men and trained on the woodland, recalling that bobbing light I had seen after dark a few days before, the Fool's Fire I had dismissed as nothing.

And, with a sick feeling, I detected movement, a flurry of indistinct figures like ghosts moving amidst the oak, ash, and holly. My head reeled dizzily; it was as if the hoary, winter-bitten world was coming to life, the wretched, blasted trees transformed as if by a sorcerer's spell into…*armoured men*.

The Lancastrian forces of Margaret of Anjou surged forward, leaving the cover of the trees. Soggy snow-clods flew up and dissolved before their feet; men roared battle cries, and then, as a cacophony of trumpets sounded, cutting through the still morn, the enemy cavalry crested the nearest rise. At first, in the hazy morning, they appeared like ghosts, or perhaps the Horsemen of the Apocalypse—the foremost was indeed a Rider on a Pale Horse, but his face was not a bleached skull, but a hard-faced warrior, and above him bloomed the standard of Henry Beaufort, Duke of Somerset, here for his revenge. *Souvente me Souviens,- I always Remember*—flared across the heavens, beside the portcullis emblem, its spikes like a row of teeth, and a wyvern holding a sinister hand coupé.

The wind carried the metallic clang of horse armour as the riders moved forward. They halted suddenly, surveying the land and its surrounds—and then they surged forward in a headlong charge, galloping madly towards our hapless men. The foraging party broke apart, men flying this way and that in terror. One was ridden down instantly, his body smashed in the snow, turning it vibrant crimson. Others drew their blades, but they were met by a hail of arrows. More bodies tumbled, bleeding, onto the churned slush. And yet more Lancastrians appeared, pikemen, spearmen, archers, and horsemen. Other banners boomed as the wind caught their heavy folds and lifted them on high—Northumberland, Clifford, Roos, Devon...

Our men began a hasty retreat as best they could, but almost instantly it ended in a mad panic, with some running to the left and the trees, others towards Wakefield, and a number back towards the castle.

"Father..." I cried, but he was already in motion, sprinting toward the stairs down from the parapet. "Edmund, come, hurry!" he shouted. "We may save some of them yet."

"But Father, did you not see the numbers of the foe? It was no lie; they must outnumber us at least two to one."

"I am not craven!" he flung over his shoulder. "I would not gladly let any supporter of mine be slaughtered without a fight!" He almost fell as he rushed the rest of the way down the spiral stairs shouting, "To arms! *To arms!* We must defend our comrades and the castle!"

Father was ready to take the field. His expensive German armour gleamed; on his surcoat he wore the Arms of England, the Lions and Lilies. I wondered if such ornament was wise, as it made him a clear target for our enemies, but my sire would never deny the truth that he was King by Right, and, as of Parliament's last sitting, the designated heir to Henry's throne.

I watched as he mounted a huge black destrier, covered in its own armour, complete with spikes on the *chanfron* that protected its face. Taught to bite and kick, the beast was an extra warrior for York in its own fashion.

Once Father was carefully seated, firmly wedged between the pommel and the back-support of the cantrel, he yanked down his visor. With his visage hidden, he looked immense and alien, an unstoppable man of metal. He truly looked like a King, eager to win his kingdom on the field of battle.

I watched him closely as my own squires rushed about, arming me in similar fashion. Over my doublet of fustian lined with silk went the breastplate, and over the hose of worsted wool the greaves and cuisses, and the pointed sabatons were tied tightly to my shoes. Vambraces were slid onto my arms and gauntlets onto my cold hands. A small, sharp dagger was hung at my right hip, and my sword upon the left. My heart pounded and I felt strangely detached, as if I watched someone else, a stranger, prepare for battle.

I am not afraid, I am not afraid! my mind screamed, but, with withering shame, I had to admit how frightened I was. *Christ, I wish Ned was here,* I thought, hoping against hope that he would arrive with his recruits at any moment, like a valiant knight in a tale of yore, slamming into the rear of the Lancastrian army and causing them to scatter.

But real life was not a heroic story. Edward was on the road but miles from Sandal. The Yorkist army was vastly outnumbered, and we had played straight into our enemy's hands by sending out the foraging party. God rest the souls of those not quick enough to escape the initial charge of Beaufort and his companions since He did not see fit to spare their bodies.

"My Lord Earl?"

I shook my head, clearing it, attempting to focus on the here and now, the importance of what I was about to do. A squire, pale and solemn, came to my side, holding my most important piece of equipment—an armet helmet, a new style of helm that would completely enclose my head but was lighter and more comfortable than the Great Helm favoured in the past. I took it carefully in my gauntleted hands, placing it with the squire's assistance over the padded coif I wore. It was the final piece of armour to go on, and once firmly in place, the chin strap fastened, it would remain on for the duration of the battle. My vision and, indeed, my ability to speak clearly, would be hampered, but I had been warned not to remove it under any circumstance—many a man, wrenching off his helm to see better, had lost his eye, or his life, to a stray arrow.

My mount was brought in by a groom. A charger, grey as mist, with a mane of metal, a petrel to protect its heart and a tailpiece fashioned into the head of a basilisk. In a surreal daze, I swung into the saddle.

The squire gazed up at me, blinking in the torchlight. Were those tears in the lad's eyes? "God go with you, Lord Edmund."

I set my spurs to the horse's flanks, and the beast surged forward, towards the south gate. Father was a short way ahead of me, his tabard the brightest thing in the grey day. With my restricted vision, I caught sight of the chaplain, John Aspel, mounted on a horse. "Father Aspel," I cried, my voice muffled and metallic. "Why do you ride out? It is not safe. You are not a man of war."

He trotted his horse up in line with mine. "I am a priest, my Lord Edmund, and it is my duty to minister to the souls of those dying on the battlefield. While my safety is not assured, few would deliberately kill a man of the cloth. I am not afraid; God will lend my strength." He licked his lips, nervous despite his brave words. "Also, Duke Richard asked me to…to look out for you, owing to your tender age."

"Look out for me? What do you mean?"

"I promised your Lord Father that I would do all within my power to escort you safely from the field if all went awry."

"Run away?" I cried. "I would never leave my sire. I would stay and fight until the breath left my body…"

"Sometimes it is best to live so one may fight their battles another day."

"I have sworn an oath to stand beside him through thick and thin!"

"What if he commanded you leave, Edmund? What then?"

I struggled to make answer and to my great surprise, a strange malaise flooded through me. With a jolt, I realised it was resignation. I was silent. *It won't happen*, I told myself. *He'll prevail…at the very worst return to the safety of the castle."*

I was ready, if one could ever be ready to face his own mortality a hundred times, to fight against men filled with so much hate that chivalry or anything like it was forgotten. *God help us this day*, I prayed, silently. *Give us victory over our enemies…*

Our contingent exited from the southern side of the castle, skirting the massive walls, though keeping close enough that we could retreat quickly if need be. By now, the tattered remnants of the earlier foraging party were in complete disarray. Some men, Dame Fortune favouring them on that fateful day, had managed to reach Sandal, the archers positioned on the battlements protecting their flight as they drew within range. They stumbled past me to safety, many wounded and bleeding—a youth screaming with one eye put out, a man with an arrow embedded in his shoulder, another whose arm dangled from a thread fainting as he was jolted between two comrades.

Ahead of us, I saw those already dead lying in the crimson slush while enemy horsemen wheeled about, trying to corral the remaining Yorkist soldiers so that they could cut them down. Mostly the enemy's backs were to us, giving a faint, momentary glimmer of hope.

"We must break through their ranks!" Father shouted, his voice muffled by his helmet. "Archers—cover us!"

Longbows were drawn, nocked. Our mounted knights thundered into action, hoofs churning the snow and the earth beneath as they began a charge straight at the enemy flank.

Beneath my thighs, my mount tensed, its powerful muscles sending it careering forward. A man rose up, snarling, a poleaxe in his hand, and swung at my thigh. Almost as if by magic, my sword appeared in my hand, crashing down on my assailant's head with all the strength of my right arm, cleaving his kettle helm in two. Metal crumpled, as did the hateful visage below it. Teeth, blood, and bone—the gory ruins of what once had been someone's son, lover or brother.

But any sympathy for the first man I'd ever slain was short-lived. Another soldier and then another rushed at me, and I cut them down. They would treat me no better if they had managed to drag me from the saddle.

Ahead, Father was wreaking destruction amidst the Queen's forces, his arms reddened to the elbow. I stayed as close to him as I dared. Together, we scythed through the heart of our assailants, striving to reach the Yorkists trapped on the other side of the Lancastrians. Next to me, I heard a man scream, gurgling in his own blood. He had reached for my stirrup and an arrow had sprouted from his throat, killing him instantly.

Over and over my blade rose and fell, cleaving steel and flesh. Within my helmet, my teeth were gritted in concentration, and sweat streamed beneath my coif. I was numb; no longer battling against fellow men but cyphers, ghosts, inhuman creatures. I bore them no hatred or malice, but neither was there pity or mercy. I had to kill them if I wished to see another dawn.

Father surged ahead, spurring his raven-black destrier to greater speed while his standard-bearer galloped frantically at his heels in an attempt to keep up. The Queen's soldiers parted before the deadly hooves and teeth of my sire's well-trained mount and he crashed into the midst of Beaufort's contingent, now armed with a fierce, black iron war-hammer. Wildly he swung the hammer from side to side, driving his foes before him with brutal strength, shattering helms, breaking skulls. He hit one mounted knight, and the man's visor buckled, spouting gore. The man crashed to the ground with a metallic clang and his riderless steed raced past me, reins dangling, blood smeared on its neck, its eyes rolling in terror.

Suddenly I heard, faintly, a shout from the back of the Yorkist forces. I attempted to crane my head around, but could not because of the restrictions of my helmet. "What is it, man? What's happening?" I shouted to a foot soldier wearing a sallet that left his face free, as he tried to rush by.

Gasping for breath, he skidded to a halt. "More Queen's men hiding in the willow clumps near the river! They are attacking the flank and trying to get behind us to crush us!"

Acid burnt from my gullet to my bone-dry mouth. *No, Jesu, no, not more enemies! We can only withstand so much. No matter how valiant…it is too much…*

Before my horrified gaze, the lines of the Yorkist rescuers wavered and then dissolved into disarray. Knights in enemy colours and snarling foot soldiers rushed in from all directions. Father's wild charge toward their centre was halted abruptly and a wild melee began, men flailing against other men, stabbing, hacking, slashing. Bodies tumbled to the ground, limp as ragdolls, and were trampled underfoot by both men and panicked horses; the ground was a hideous soup of blood, mud, entrails, and hewn limbs.

Father was now even further away, far beyond my reach. He was still striking out powerfully as pikemen circled, forming a wall of sharpened blades, while several mounted knights pushed into the crush with dripping swords ready to strike. With a jolt of horror, I realised Father was ensnared, unable to move either forward or back.

The trap was sprung. He was like a spider's prey, caught in a tangled web he could not cut through.

A pike thrust forward, testing, seeking. It found a gap in the peytrel worn by Father's destrier and slid into the flesh beneath. The horse gave a hideous whinnying scream and reared on its hinds, front hooves striking out at its attacker, but the enemy soldier forced the tip of his weapon in as far as it could go, visage grimacing with effort beneath his dented sallet. The destrier's heart was fatally pierced and it crashed down into the mud, throwing Father from the saddle with the impact of its fall.

I yanked on my reins, not believing the disaster unfolding before my horrified eyes. I tried to concentrate on my own predicament, hewing and chopping at the hands that reached to grab me, the swords that sought to find chinks in my armour, the halberds slashing toward the unarmoured parts of my mount. But ever my gaze was drawn towards my father, unhorsed, ringed by a baying mob of soldiers wearing the livery of Somerset and Clifford.

Two soldiers caught hold of Father's swinging right arm, ripping the war-hammer from his hand while other men assailed him from behind—an act of cowards. Kicking and struggling, he was pulled over backwards, ending up on his knees in the morass. A dagger flashed, cutting his helmet strap. The helm was thrown into the scrum, where men screeched like feral animals, fighting each other for possession of the 'trophy.' Father was left panting on the ground, blood streaming from a nick where the knife had torn his cheek.

Roughly his enemies dragged him along the ground and hurled him on a mound of earth that stuck up through the melting snow—the remains of an old anthill. The Lancastrians lashed out at him with armoured feet and mailed fists, blows meant not to hurt so much as humiliate. "Hail King, without rule!" they shouted, their laughter harsh as the cawing of crows in the nearby trees. "Hail false King, who has neither subjects nor crown! Hail, King of Traitors and miscreants! Hail to the King's Fool, who will this day burn in Hell!"

Father struggled to regain his feet. He was a ragged and terrifying sight, his hair clotted with mud and blood, the wound on his cheek streaming redness. He reached for his rondel dagger, but his hand would not work. He stared at it as if willing it to obey him, but it was curled like a crushed spider and covered in blood. I realised, nausea gripping me, that his adversaries had stamped on it and broken all his fingers when they beat him upon the anthill.

"A King without a crown—now a King without a weapon!" one of them chortled, swaggering over to relieve father of his dagger.

Frozen, I watched this terrible scene play out. I seemed unable to move, as if my limbs had turned to stone, a tomb effigy that yet lived. My heart screamed at me to charge madly at my father's assailants, uncaring that I would be instantly slain. My mind, however, warred with my heart—*You cannot save him. Why die for nought....*

Father suddenly lifted his head. His tormented gaze met mine, locked, even at a distance. Over the clashing and tumult of the battlefield, I heard him cry out, voice pained and desperate—but not for himself. I saw in his hopeless eyes that he had no thought of escape. He cried aloud for me, his second son.

"Ride, ride, you fool! For God's sake, fly while you can! The day is lost! *Lost!*"

I strove to speak, to call out, but my tongue clove to the roof of my mouth and no sound came forth. Father raised his eyes, as if seeking some sign, or forgiveness from the Almighty, and then a honed sword whistled down and the wintry sky was hazed with red spray.

That awful sight, the terrible finality of death, unleashed my frozen limbs from their paralysis. Glancing from left to right, I beheld complete carnage as our forces, now leaderless and confused, were herded into groups like cattle and butchered without mercy.

Several survivors streaked across the battlefield, flinging away their weapons as they ran. The mounted knights thundered after them, and I heard one of the Lancastrian captains bellow, "Hunt the dogs down. Give them no quarter. Take no captives!"

"My Lord, my Lord, come this way!" A reedy, panic-stricken voice cut through the din of battle and the screams of the dying. Forcing my mount around, I saw a huddled, hooded figure on a horse beckoning frantically at me.

John Aspel, the castle chaplain and my sometime tutor.

I cantered towards the priest, drawing up next to his horse. "This morning you held up the Cross to give our men courage," I babbled, close to incoherent in my grief. "Now, for most, you can only say the rites for the dead...Oh, Jesu, help me, help me, my father is slain...."

"My Lord Earl!" Aspel shouted again, his eyes desperate in the hollow skull of his face. "Listen to me! I can help you escape. Come away now, follow me; it is your only chance!"

I wavered. "But...but, Father...I must get his body for burial..."

Aspel's bony hand shot out, clutching my armoured wrist. "His spirit is gone to the Lord, Edmund. You must not go to him. They'll kill you. You. Will. Die. The Duke wanted his son to live, remember that!"

Tears began to slide down my cheeks, but I cared nothing for that. I would leave. It was my father's last wish. "Show me the way, priest."

"Quick," he pointed towards the river, "there's a gap between two groups of fighting men—do you see? Then there's a stand of willows, which may provide some cover. If we can gain the bridge and get into Wakefield, there are hidden underground cellars where I can hide you till the threat is passed."

"I do not know if I can permit you to do this, Father," I said. "If they catch us together, I do not think they will show mercy, even to you. The bloodlust has fallen upon them and they are as pitiless as wolves."

He shook his head. "My life means nought. I have always loyally served the Duke of York and his heirs and will continue to do so. If I am slain, I go to a heavenly reward. Now *come*, Lord Edmund, before the chance is lost forever!"

The chaplain and I raced between groups of embattled soldiers, ploughing through heaps of hewn, hacked corpses. An arrow whistled above my head, missing by mere inches.

"Look out!" Aspel gave a sharp cry as three Lancastrian soldiers sprang away from the bodies they were looting and stabbed at my mount's legs, seeking to bring it down. I struck one on the pate with my sword, making him fall down senseless, and charged straight at the other two, riding the nearest one down. He rolled about, shrieking, in the snow while his fellow fled, uttering curses.

I galloped onwards with the priest.

Soon the willow clumps appeared, sad and mournful. Several men were fighting amidst the gloomy, drooping trees, and bodies lay piled up against the boles, feeding the roots with shed blood. I forced myself to avert my gaze from split skulls and contorted faces and continued riding between the swaying boughs.

On the far side of the willow grove, the River Calder came into view, wide and slate grey, its current fast flowing, tossing dead branches and chunks of melting snow. A nine-arched bridge crossed the torrent, its stones warped by the lick of the waters, and upon the central span stood the chantry chapel of Mary the Virgin, a haven for passing travellers day or night. Cautiously John Aspel and I guided our horses onto the riverside path. Thankfully it was empty, although there were footprints of iron-shod feet in the mud.

"Listen." Aspel's visage grew even paler if that was possible. I paused, removing my helmet at last and ripping off the sodden coif, shaking my sweaty hair loose. In the distance, I could hear thrumming hoofs, horses galloping, men shouting. They were coming towards us at a great speed.

"They know," the priest moaned. "I think they saw us leave…"

I swore under my breath. No doubt I had been recognised by my tabard, the Arms of England differentiated by torteux gules for York and lions purpure for my great-grandmother, Isabella of Castile. I wished I could have hurled it away, but there was no way to remove it while engaged in combat.

"We're still far ahead of them," I gasped, throwing the unwieldy helmet onto the ground. I was not in the midst of battle now and wanted to breathe freely and view my surroundings. "Let's ride on, Father Aspel. Let's ride with all speed into Wakefield!"

I struck my spurs to my horse's flank. Sparks flew from the worn flagstones, as the horse mounted the bridge approach. In the distance, Wakefield town hovered in the haze like some mythical, desired fantasy, its gaggle of topsy-turvy houses and inns beckoning with the promise of safety. Of life. A place where, hiding in some cellar, I could plan revenge against those who had slain my father. Ned would come and together we would ride forth in splendour, and he would subdue Queen Margaret's malice and execute her favourites—and then Edward would go to Westminster to be crowned King.

A row of armed figures blocked the far end of the bridge on the town side. I saw their stark white livery and a pennant bearing the motto *Desormais*—Henceforth—and the blood turned to ice in my veins. Clifford's men. The soldiers of a man who had sworn revenge on the House of York for the battle of St Albans.

Grinning, the white-clad men converged into a triangular formation, the points of their bills directed straight towards us. I slowed and glanced at Aspel. "W-what should I do?"

"I-I have no answer," the priest said with brutal honesty. He sounded as if he were about to weep. "I-I think there is only one course to take. We cannot go back…so we must go forward." He bowed his head and began to pray, using an ancient prayer written by the holy St Anselm, "*We bring before Thee, O Lord, the troubles and perils of people and nations, the sighing of prisoners and captives, the sorrows of the bereaved, the helplessness of the weak, the despondency of the weary. O Lord, draw near to us; for the sake of Jesus Christ our Lord. Amen.*"

The sound of his impassioned prayer ringing in my ears, I drove my steed forward, trying to ride through the midst of my assailants, to cast them aside with the force of his speed. One man fell, his leg bone snapping like a twig, another toppled backwards, knocked over by a flying hoof. But the last soldier, crouching low, his leer foul as a demon's, stabbed up with his pike at my horse's unarmoured belly.

And then it was over for me as it had been for Father. My mount fell onto the span of the bridge, kicking the air with his hoofs before collapsing in a shuddering, heaving pile.

Rough hands grabbed me, pulling me to my feet. I struggled against their cruel hold, but there were too many of them for my efforts to succeed. "What have we here? A deserter?" one of my captors bellowed.

"Something much better than that," grinned his companion. "Look at the quality of his armour—and look what's on that tabard."

The first man, hatched-faced and flinty-eyed, goggled. "Jesu, is that really his? Did he steal that?"

"I am no thief!" I spat. The spittle from my vehement denial struck the ruffian's stubbled cheek.

"You little bastard!" the man roared, putting me in a headlock.

"Stop, *stop!*" John Aspel began in desperation. "Think of what you do, I beg you! You stand before the very doors of a chapel dedicated to the Blessed Virgin; such violence is anathema to Our Lady. Besides that, he is a prince and scarcely more than a boy; have mercy on him!"

The man dropped his arm from my neck, but the other soldiers laid hold of me even more firmly, although they raised no hand or dagger to strike any blows.

"Get his weapons," growled the first assailant, who appeared to be a leader of sorts. Quickly, my enemies divested me of my sword and dagger, drooling like dogs over the quality and arguing about who got what to keep.

"So you're a prince, eh?" continued the man, eyeing me up. "A likely tale! You're more likely some little squirt of a squire wearing your master's goods 'cos he's dead. Just as I said. A thief."

"Nah, Mauger, I think the priest speaks true," said another soldier with a straggling red beard. "By Christ, forget the tabard—just look at his *face*. He looks just like old York, who is now nought but worm-fodder! It's York's spawn, I'd bet my life on it!"

"My Lord Clifford will be most pleased." Mauger grinned with wolfish broken teeth as he gestured to his companion to bind my hands together with a length of rope. "I'll send James to take a message to him and let him know what we have for him. I am sure he will be pleased...*very* pleased indeed."

The day darkened, cooled again; light snow began to fall as I awaited my fate on the bridge. I did not look towards my smirking captors or John Aspel, who stood wringing his hands, but towards the façade of the bridge chapel, with its soaring arches, saints, and delicate pinnacles. The sad, carved face of the Virgin gazed out at me; tears wrought of snowflakes wetting her stone cheeks. *Now and at the hour of our death, Amen...*

I sensed a change in the mood of the men surrounding me—growing excitement. Tearing my eyes from the image of Our Lady, I glanced toward the end of the bridge. A hulking, purposeful man in blood-splashed black armour had ridden from the direction of the castle. Dismounting, he flung the reins to a henchman and clanked aggressively in my direction.

Pushing up his visor, he fixed me with a flat, emotionless stare. His eyes were a strange hue, slate grey speckled with yellow. Luminous, wolfish, pitiless. He was younger than I thought, maybe seven or eight years my senior, but the harsh cast of his features made him appear far older.

"You are Edmund, called Earl of Rutland, son of the traitor, Richard Duke of York?" His voice was gruff, uncompromising.

"I am he," I said. Now that I was truly caught, there was no sense in denying it. "And my father was no traitor but the rightful King of England, as all men of worth know."

John Clifford gave a dull, grunting laugh. "Well, traitor's son, do you know who *I* am? I am John Clifford. My sire, Thomas Clifford, was slain at St Alban's thanks to the dog that begot you! Mad dogs and their whelps should be put down, one and all."

Father Aspel hobbled over, stretching out a quivering hand. A sweat of fear beaded on his furrowed brow. "My Lord Clifford, have mercy! Do not harm him! He is young; his tongue is sharp from youthful folly and his own sorrow. I assure you his family will pay well for his safe return."

"I care not for any of that," Clifford snarled, and his wolfish eyes lit up, yellow as lanterns. "As his father killed my father at St Albans, so shall he too be slain!"

A rondel dagger appeared in Clifford's gauntleted hand as he hurled himself at me. I shied away from his blow, but my hands were tied together as were my ankles. The first dagger-strike hit harmlessly against my cuirass, but then he grabbed hold of my hair, dragged me close, and with brutal, practised skill forced the dagger-point into the unarmoured flesh beneath my arm, driving the weapon up to the hilt.

John Clifford released me, making a satisfied grunt. He was smiling. I fell to my knees on the bridge, my legs suddenly unable to hold me. I felt little pain, which surprised me, for I was aware that the wound I took was mortal. The heavens whirled above my head; the snow came down even heavier, or perhaps it was not snow but a problem with my eyes. Everything wavered, distorted, grew white and frayed at the edges. A terrible coldness, worse than any of winter's blasts, gripped me; my extremities were numb, useless.

Glancing up, Clifford's triumphant face loomed above. Strangely, he did not seem so frightening now. Beside him, Father Aspel stood with his hands thrown up in fright and his lips moving frantically in what? Chastisement? Prayers? Screams?

I could no longer hear—a buzzing filled my ears, the sound of a thousand bees.

Vainly I struggled to take in more air; my chest hurt and I felt as if I was being smothered. The whirling of the sky ceased, and it became very bright, and I thought I could see Edward, come beyond all hope, his head crowned by shooting sun rays, his banners snapping around him. Father was standing at his shoulder, an indistinct shadow—but I knew it could not truly be him, for he was dead.

My strength receded, diminishing with the blood that cascaded from my body. I strained weakly towards that final comforting vision of father and brother, but it faded like mist, and through its departing glamour, I saw instead the panels depicting the Annunciation, the Nativity, the Resurrection, and the Coronation of the Virgin on the front of the chantry chapel.

The stone Virgin looked at me, her eyes, no longer stone, filled with pity—I imagined she held out her hand.

It was time to go.

"Edward..." My head struck the freezing stone, and as my sight faded, sunbursts lit that eternal darkness, and white roses were falling, falling through the winter sky, their petals stained with crimson tears.

AUTHOR'S NOTE:

This was not an easy story to write, for many reasons, not least of which was the computer issues that caused one whole edited chapter to vanish!

Very little is known of Edmund of Rutland, so I have 're-created' a story about him based on that little knowledge and on the timeline of his family, particularly his father, Richard Duke of York. I am not certain all the family went to Ireland, but presume they did due to the youth of the children—Cecily did travel there with her husband and George of Clarence was definitely born in Dublin Castle.

Anne of York's husband, Henry Holland, Duke of Exeter was an obnoxious and violent man as portrayed. In fact, he was likely far worse. Edward may have never pushed him in a pond…but he should have!

The Croft brothers were problematic. They are mentioned in an existing letter to Duke Richard from Edmund and Edward, but what they wrote has been interpreted in different ways. Most think the boys complained about the Croft's odious behaviour towards *them*, but it has been suggested they were standing up FOR the Crofts against another oppressor. The first makes for a much better, dramatic story, though, so I have gone with that. Interestingly, one historian believes the 'wrong Crofts' are mentioned in the letter—not, as usually thought, the lord of Croft Castle, who later served Edward as King and who seems too old to have been receiving training at Ludlow, but another cadet branch of the local Croft family.

All poems and rhymes are authentic, my translations, although some are considered 'traditional' and may not necessarily fit exactly to the mid-15th century.

J.P. Reedman, December 2024

IF YOU HAVE ENJOYED THIS BOOK, PLEASE CHECK OUT MY OTHER WORKS OF RICHARD III, THE WARS OF THE ROSES, STONEHENGE, ROBIN HOOD, AND BRITISH AND IRISH MYTH AND LEGEND

UK AMAZON LINK TO AUTHOR PAGE:

https://www.amazon.co.uk/J-P-Reedman/e/B009UTHBUE

USA AMAZON LINK TO AUTHOR PAGE:

https://www.amazon.com/stores/J.P.Reedman/author/B009UTHBUE

'

Printed in Great Britain
by Amazon